THE CALVANNI

By

Chris McMahon

The Calvanni

Chris McMahon

Published 2013 by Lanedd Press, an imprint of Pop & Top Publishers.
www.popandtop.com.au
Please direct all enquiries to the publisher at:
publisher@popandtop.com.au

ISBN: 9780992299408

PRINTING HISTORY
Sid Harta edition published 2006

Cover Artist: Daryl Lindquist
Edited by: Tracy Seybold

National Library of Australia Cataloguing-in-Publication enty:

Author: McMahon, Chris, 1965-
Title: The Calvanni / Chris McMahon
Edition: 2nd edition
ISBN: 9780992299408 (paperback)
Series: McMahon, Chris, 1965- Jakirian Cycle ; bk. 1.
Dewey Number: A823.4

Chris McMahon's website: www.chrismcmahon.net

This novel is dedicated to my wife Sandra, for her love, support and unfailing faith in me.

Acknowledgements

Thanks to all the people who contributed over the years to the final work that the Jakirian Cycle became. Getting anything into print really is a team sport. Special thanks to my editor Tracy Seybold, cover artist Daryl Lindquist and critique partner Gary Kemble. Thanks to all the very patient readers of the first *Calvanni* edition in 2006, who have waited some time to see what happens in *Scytheman* and *Sorcerer*.

A Note on the World of Yos

Yos is a world where all metal is magical, and cannot be forged, appearing as *glowmetal*. The weapons and armour are either constructed of natural materials or a special class of composite ceramics developed for hardness or the ability to hold an edge while maintaining strength and flexibility.

Glossary

Bakta - A clear alcoholic spirit distilled from the baal cereal crop.

Calv - A long knife made of lanedd.

Druid - Magic user who relies on the Essence of Heaven, which varies according to movement of the suns and moons. Ability common.

Druidin - Class of Druid that gives no allegiance to the Temple of the Sisters.

Eathal - Natives of the vast cavern complexes of Kelas and evolutionary cousins to humans. Male and female known as thal and thel. Thickset and hairless, with sensitive eyesight.

Glowmetals – A naturally occurring blend of light, energy and metal. Arising in all sizes, shapes and combinations, they can neither be created nor destroyed, but can be manipulated to store and release their native energy.

Greatscythe - Staff-like weapon with twin concealed lanedd blades, one at either end, operated by a mechanism central to the haft.

Heat - Biological mechanism triggered by the extreme cold of Storm Season. Gives life-giving warmth, but releases inhibitions and makes self-control almost impossible.

Kelas – Continent formerly ruled by the Bulvuran Empire.

Lanedd - Specialised ceramic that can be cast into a blade, which holds a razor-sharp edge that can be sharpened.

Mought - Heavy cast ceramic used in armour, blunt weapons and fortifications.

Priestess - Wielder of Earth Essence, which flows only in certain locations. Ability to access Earth Essence rare in men (Priests).

Sarlord - Ruler of a Sardom by right of royal birth.

Scythe - A short pole weapon with a single lanedd blade.

Sisters - Yos' two suns, Larus and Uros, also worshipped as goddesses by the people of Yos. Larus, the Yellow Sister, and Uros, the Red Sister. Larus is the larger of the two.

Sorcerer - Wielder of magical Fire. Ability derived from hereditary and extremely rare. Practice currently outlawed by the Temple of the Sisters.

Storm Season - Sudden drop in surface temperature and subsequent violent storms that arise twice a year when Yos' two suns, Larus and Uros, eclipse.

Sundar - Supreme ruler of the Eathal of Yos.

Suul – Class of ruling nobility in Yos. Also Suulvey, senior peers and Suulqua, nobles of minor rank.

Temple of the Sisters – Dominant religious force in Kelas.

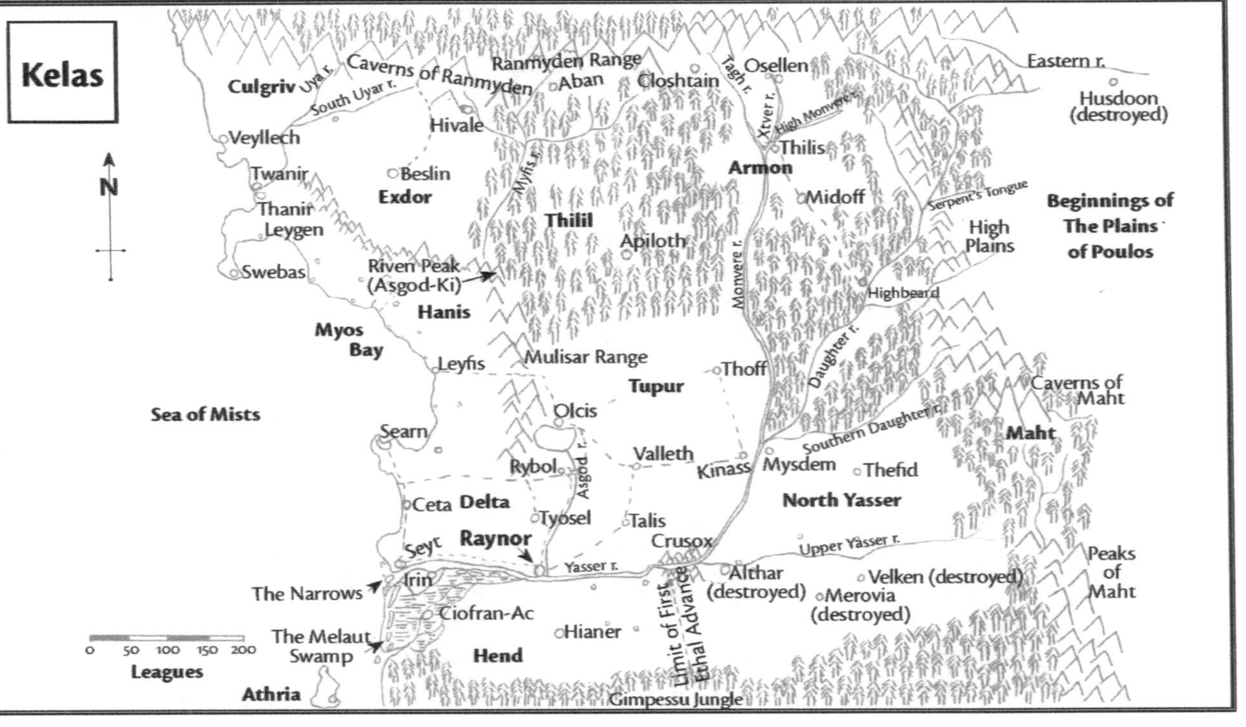

Kelas
N
Culgriv
Uya r.
Caverns of Ranmyden
South Uyar r.
Ranmyden Range
Aban
Closhtain
Tagh r.
Osellen
Eastern r.
Husdoon
(destroyed)
Veyllech
Hivale
Xtver r.
High Monvere r.
Thilis
Armon
Twanir
Beslin
Exdor
Midoff
Serpent's Tongue
Beginnings of
The Plains
of Poulos
Thanir
Leygen
Thilil
Apiloth
Monvere r.
High
Plains
Swebas
Riven Peak
(Asgod-Ki)
Highbeard
Hanis
Myos
Bay
Leyfis
Mulisar Range
Thoff
Daughter r.
Caverns of
Maht
Tupur
Maht
Sea of Mists
Olcis
Southern Daughter r.
Searn
Valleth
Asgod r.
Rybol
Kinass
Mysdem
Thefid
Ceta Delta
Tyosel
Talis
North Yasser
Raynor
Crusox
Upper Yasser r.
Seyt
Yasser r.
Althar
(destroyed)
Velken (destroyed)
Peaks
of
Maht
The Narrows
Irin
Limit of First
Ethal Advance
Merovia
(destroyed)
Ciofran-Ac
The Melaut
Swamp
Hianer
Hend
0 50 100 150 200
Leagues
Athria
Gimpessu Jungle

Chapter One

Sarlord Myan Cintros lay on the dais below his overturned throne.

'Father!' Ellen cried as she pushed through the ranks of scythemen. She sought him across the Bridge of Minds, but there was nothing, not even the formless colours of his sleeping mind. Fear sent her heart racing, and the vast chamber contracted to a roaring tunnel.

Ellen rushed forward; she could not lose him – not now. At the thought of her life without him, a frightening emptiness filled her. She would be left alone with the secrets of the Cintros, forbidden to share her knowledge with anyone.

Five Druids of the Temple surrounded her father's body, shielding him from further harm.

She longed to go to him, to embrace him, but her limbs were suddenly weak, as though reluctant to bring her any further.

He cannot just die like this, Ellen thought, as two physician-Druids in dull brown robes worked a potion into his mouth. Her father was one of the most powerful defenders of the old Empire, the man who had turned back the Sorcerer-Lords of the Eathal. Who remained to stem the tide of chaos and war that was engulfing them? Two black-robed Moon-Druids, their necks adorned with gem-studded effigies of the twin moons Asic and Rea, knelt together in open supplication and prayer, determination creasing their brows.

Crephis, a big Moon-Druid with straight, dark hair watched gravely, softly directing their combined efforts in a calm, even tone. He was Athria's most talented healer. Renewed hope spurred Ellen forward. She pushed through the Druids and sank to the floor beside her father.

'Is he dead?' asked Ellen.

The pungent smell of the potion made her dizzy, burned the back of her throat. He looked so pale and grey. She took his calloused hand. It felt as cold as the marble beneath her, his skin clammy with approaching death. Tears fell. Ellen struggled with her royal composure. Lifeless, she thought, reaching once more across the Bridge to be again confronted with formless grey.

'Close,' said Crephis. 'He is just clinging to life.'

The throne room, usually so noisy with debate and conversation, was strangely silent. The ranks of robed courtiers and Suulqua messengers were absent, replaced by scythemen and palace guards. The sound of a squad of soldiers marching on the gravel of the courtyard below came up through the wide open windows, the coarse commands of the Razor seemingly loud as he disciplined a soldier, oblivious to events above.

'Crephis, tell me he will live,' pleaded Ellen, looking up to the Druid's bright golden eyes. 'Please tell me you can bring him back.'

Bowing his head, Crephis said nothing.

The ranks of scythemen guarding the chamber parted, their long white cloaks, emblazoned with the grey Cintros raptor, swishing across the floor. She turned to see the Regent Kerril, robed in a fine grey cloak edged with white fur, approaching, with the tall, skeletal Warlord, Aris Cinev, hard and unemotional, at his side. Always austere, Aris disdained the use of cloaks, preferring instead to wear plain trousers and a shirt of white, a small Cinev crest of the Yos' twin suns, Larus and Uros, emblazoned in yellow and red over his heart – a mark of his family's ancient allegiance to the Temple of the Sisters.

As one, the gathered assembly bowed to the Suulvey lords.

'Where is my brother?' Ellen's voice shook. 'Torren should be here.' Torren was the eldest of her two older brothers. Her brother Estle was in Raynor, days away even by war-galley.

Aris appraised her coolly, adjusting the patch of dark leather that covered his left eye; it was a mark of courage, which he wore as a symbol of his power. 'I have ordered him to remain with his troops,' he said, dismissing her question. 'The Captain of the Wall must never leave his post.' His long, lined face, framed with short-cropped silver-grey hair had never looked more severe.

Ellen let out a ragged breath. Torren would be relieved. No doubt he would be waiting for news of his succession as Sarlord. Her bond with her father was one Torren had never shared, and she had always felt his resentment, his jealousy, like a knife. She loved her two brothers and had wanted all three of them to be like a family around Myan. Now . . . it would never happen. Her heart twisted as she looked into the future, seeing them split apart even further as the fractures between them finally cracked open; Myan, the centre of their lives together, gone.

'Can we save him?' asked Kerril.

'No, my lord,' said Crephis. 'The poison has all but destroyed his nervous system. The assassin chose his time well, striking in twilight when the Sun-Essence fades and the Moon-Essence is yet to rise.' The Druid paused. 'What meagre Essence we have gathered has merely delayed his death.'

Uros the Destroyer, the red Sun-Goddess, had turned her terrible face towards Ellen's father. Not content to wait for Storm Season, her time of power when she eclipsed her yellow sister Larus the Protector, she had given Myan her dark blessing.

Ellen buried her face against her father's cold chest. 'No, no ...'

Then twenty-three years of court life asserted itself. She straightened, smoothing back her braided, honey-blonde hair; refusing to appear weak in front of the Suulvey lords. She may only be a Suulqua – the lowest rank of nobility – but she was the Sarlord's daughter. Myan had been a traditionalist, insisting his sons and daughter earn their rank as full Suul lords of the court like any other Athrian noble. Most nobility remained Suulqua throughout their lives. Only those with senior positions at court were rewarded with the title of full Suul lord. The Suulvey, members of the Council, ranked above all.

Her knees began to ache with the cold, but she did not move from his side. A gust of wind came in through the window, sweeping away the fumes of the potion and carrying the scent of the sweet incense burning near the throne towards her. It seemed inconceivable that it should continue to burn as her father lay dying.

'So there is no hope for him?' asked Kerril.

Crephis shook his head gravely.

'Uros' blood!' Kerril shouted, for the first time showing emotion. He turned away from Myan's body, looking out the wide windows of the throne room. His brown eyes glistened with moisture. His brown hair, shot with grey for as long as Ellen could remember, now seemed more grey than brown.

Kerril was one of her father's closest friends and advisors. Ellen wanted to say something to ease his grief, but she was barely containing her own.

Outside, the twilight was fading. The sky was full of dark shapes, thousands of bats flying silently to their nightly feast. The children of Kallor, the Lord of Death, rising from his realm of Llors. Ellen's hands tightened into fists.

Kerril turned to Crephis. 'Can you rouse him long enough to confirm the succession?'

The big Moon-Druid raised a chubby hand to his chin, his eyes flashing with intelligence. 'It is possible. I can reverse the paralysis and restore his powers of speech, but only for a short time.'

'How long will he remain alert?' Kerril looked anxious.

Crephis sighed, the symbols of office clattering against each other as his massive chest rose and fell. 'Only the briefest of moments, my friend. Llors will have him within the hour.'

Ellen's heart skipped a beat. She could save him. She could use the power of Sorcery – the Matrix of Form – and save him. And in doing so damn herself. Sorcery was forbidden by the Temple.

She stood.

'There must be a way.' Ellen looked directly at Crephis. Only Crephis, in all of Athria, knew of the hereditary powers of Sorcery she shared with her father.

Crephis' eyes widened. He shook his head. 'No, Ellen.'

'I must,' she said, reaching for the Fire.

Crephis gripped her shoulder, stopping her. 'No. His veins are filled with poison. His nerves destroyed. No magic can save him. Even if the Moons were full and we could heal his tissues, the poison would destroy them again, and again. It would only condemn him to more agony.'

'You must accept this, Ellen. Myan is beyond their arts,' said Aris, unaware of the subtext of their conversation.

Ellen's knees went weak. She leant into Crephis for support, and he grabbed her arm to steady her.

Father.

'Rouse the Sarlord,' said Kerril, walking across the room to where another body lay.

'Is that ...' said Ellen.

'Yes. *The assassin.* Kerril himself killed him. The Regent was talking to your father when the assassin struck,' said Crephis.

The assassin's body lay at the base of the Sister's Dance – a vast statue of cast ceramic depicting the two Sun Goddesses, Larus and Uros, locked in their endless cosmic struggle. Coagulated blood soaked the assassin's rich clothes, and his dead fingers still clutched the blowpipe. The deep and ruddy colour of last twilight, the light of blood-red Uros, bathed the statue.

The handle of Kerril's throwing knife still protruded from the body.

Kerril ripped open the soft silk of the assassin's shirt, scanning the tattoos on the torso.

'Here! The mark of the teremb, the night-hunter.'

Ellen shivered. *Assanni.*

'Uros spawn,' said Aris in disgust.

Kerril viciously pulled his knife from the corpse and straightened. He waved at a palace guard who stood stiffly at attention against one of the columns.

'Have this body removed,' commanded Kerril.

'Yes, Lord!' said the warrior, bowing.

Kerril watched the guard and his two comrades carry the body out, his jaw clenching and unclenching. The guards avoided his gaze.

Ellen looked on numbly as the two Druid-physicians packed

away their potions and stood, looking to Crephis for instructions. He nodded gravely and waved them away.

Crephis knelt with the two other Moon-Druids; sweat sheened his smooth brow as he sought to harness and direct the weak Moon-Essence. The chant of the Moon-Druids rose steadily to a final crescendo then ceased.

The weight of expectation grew heavy in the silence.

Myan's eyes flickered open.

'Thank the Goddess!' said Ellen, smiling as she wiped away her tears. She knelt at his side, next to Crephis, and took her father's hand. 'How long does he have?'

'Only minutes,' replied Crephis.

She gripped his hand tighter. She could not believe her father would be gone so quickly. She sniffed, trying to stifle another wave of tears. Once her father was gone, a new, empty world would begin. It was only moments away, and nothing she could do would delay its arrival.

'My Lord. The poison has left you paralysed,' said Crephis. 'We have driven back its effects for a time and given you a potion for the pain.'

Ellen took a cloth from her robes and gently wiped away a trail of the green potion, which trickled from the corner of his mouth. She clenched the cloth in her hand to keep it from shaking.

Myan closed his eyes for a long moment. When he opened them, he seemed resigned.

Kerril came forward and knelt. They held each other's gaze for a long moment, a silent exchange passing between them. They had been friends since their childhood.

'The heir, Myan. We must know,' said Kerril finally. 'Can you confirm that as eldest son, Torren will succeed you?'

Myan's eyes swept from side to side.

No.

'Then who? You must choose one of your two sons. Do you want to recall Estle from his duties in Raynor to be Sarlord?'

'No. Ellen,' whispered Myan.

'Ellen?' said Kerril. 'Are you saying you want Ellen to be Sarla?'

'Yes,' said Myan, his eyes clouding with pain.

'Impossible!' exploded Aris. 'He is confused. This must be a mistake.'

Crephis placed his hand on Myan's brow then looked levelly at Aris. 'No, Warlord. He is quite lucid.'

Myan looked at Aris, his face set with determination. 'Ellen.'

'No. Torren is the only one fit to rule!' snapped Aris.

Kerril's eyes flashed dangerously. 'It is Myan's will, Aris.'

Ellen was stunned.

I am to be the next ruler of Athria.

Her world collapsed. All the things she regarded as important – her liaison with Palsus, her ambition to be an ambassador, the endless indulgence of the young Suulqua – all seemed trivial and shallow. How could she sit on the throne of Athria? She was a scholar, not a ruler. The only thing Myan had ever put her in charge of was the administration of court records and legal documents. Her *empire of bookish scribes*, as Torren called it.

Myan looked to each of his old friends one last time and indicated with his eyes they should leave. They bowed low and withdrew, along with the Moon-Druids.

Myan turned his head towards Ellen, staring into her soul with dark green eyes, the twin of her own. They glowed with the unwelcome shine of coming death.

'Father,' she said, her voice choked with grief.

'Listen,' he said, drawing her gaze. 'Belin was here.'

She struggled to clear her mind.

'But, Father, Belin is long dead ...' she said, convinced the delirium of the poison had begun to destroy his mind. Belin was one of the generals of the old Empire. Even if he had survived the destruction of the Cinanac dynasty, old age would have taken him long ago.

Myan's gaze grew in intensity. 'Listen!' he repeated. The cool clarity of his voice caused Ellen's heart to miss a beat. 'Cedrin must be found. He bears Belin's signet ring. You must find him and protect him.' Weakness suddenly overcame him and his eyes rolled. He was fighting for consciousness. 'I had hoped to ... prepare you.'

'Father. Father!'

She took his face in her hands, looking down into his eyes. He was fighting and losing a desperate battle. She felt the Fire surge within him, his mind seeking hers.

The Bridge of Minds was formed.

Her father's desperation flooded over her in a wave, amid a thousand images of his past; people, names, places, laughter, war-cries, love and battlefields. Far below the torrent pulsed a spinning gem, barely perceived as it followed the flow; spinning, coherent, it pulsed with its own energy, rapidly slipping from her vision.

Then, at last, his mind found hers, and the torrent ceased. *Ellen. There is no time ... left. Remember, the Scion must stand in the Temple of the Iris.*

For a brief moment their minds lay silent, touching like breath above their mingling seas of emotion. Her father's love flowed through her, lifted her, and then abruptly he was gone.

Ellen screamed, her hands clutching at his shirt.

The throne room was silent as she closed her father's eyes, forced herself upright to stand looking down on him. Her father's cryptic pleas meant nothing to her at that moment. All she could understand was that her beloved father was dead; taken from her by an assassin.

She felt Kerril's touch on her arm and let him lead her through the throne room to her father's ante-chamber. It was full night now and guttering torches filled the room with the familiar, acrid smell of oil and pitch.

Ellen was numb. Around her people moved, quiet words of grief were spoken, but she heard nothing. Gradually the room emptied, leaving her alone with the Regent.

Kerril poured her a goblet of strong bakta, a clear spirit distilled from the baal cereal crop. She drank deeply, letting the liquid's warmth spread through her, easing the empty numbness that had replaced her father's love. Vaguely she became aware of the Regent and stared at him.

'Ellen?'

She focussed on his face. The sharp lines were drawn tightly with the burden he now carried. His brown eyes seemed darker, duller with grief, as though he had receded within. He had always been a distant figure, part of her father's life of power.

When she spoke, it was like another person, self-assured, stern. 'What do you require, Regent?'

Kerril looked at her, searching her face, waiting for something. A moment passed before he stood and poured himself a goblet of bakta.

'I need to know of Myan's last words. It is my official duty.'

'He talked of Belin. Said he had been here.'

'Belin?' Kerril sounded surprised, concerned.

'He told me to find Cedrin and protect him. That he would have Belin's signet ring. Then he talked of the Scion.'

'The Scion,' said Kerril, nodding grimly.

Downing his small cup of bakta, Kerril moved to the window to look out over the lights of the great port-city of Athria.

'It's hard to believe this is where it ends,' said Kerril.

The Regent turned, looking deep into his now empty cup. 'We left Athria together, you know. Two young Athrian Suul at the Emperor's court, invincible – at least we thought we were.' He looked up at her; a softness she'd never seen before touched his eyes. 'Your father and I fought together on the Plains of Poulos, walked side-by-side through the streets of Raynor with the world at our feet.'

Kerril walked over and sat opposite Ellen. 'And together we watched as the Empire fell, the provinces squabbled while petty warlords and pirates thrived in the carnage; the Eathal nation waiting like a carrion bird to consume what remained.'

Ellen nodded, at last understanding. After the fall of the Empire and the death of Emperor Riin Cinanac and the slaughter of his family, her father and Kerril had dreamed of nothing but the rebirth of the Empire. Riin's Empress, Evylin, had given birth scant days before her death. The legends claimed the child was saved, delivered from the Eathal shapechanger by the mysterious Hero of the Last Days. Myan and Kerril had devoted their life to finding the Scion. Yet, after decades, they had found nothing.

For Ellen and her two older brothers, Torren and Estle, it was a vanished time. A shining dream for old men. Everyone knew the Eathal were finished as a power. The Yasser States had smashed them at Raynor thirty years ago. The strange, cavern-dwelling humanoids had not attacked since, and their forces remained south of the Yasser river.

'What has Belin got to do with this, and who is Cedrin?' asked Ellen, touching the Regent's hand.

Kerril shook his head.

'Cedrin was Belin's bastard. He was brought to Athria after the Last Days by a faithful lieutenant of Belin's after his death. Myan had become obsessed with finding him. He was convinced he possessed some key to finding the Scion. Perhaps it's this signet ring he spoke of.'

'Then what? Was Myan going to present the Scion at the Warlord's court in Raynor?'

Kerril looked back at Ellen, his jaw set. 'I know what you think, Ellen. Restoring the Empire is a quest for fools. For someone like you it is difficult to see what has happened to Kelas since the fall of order. We were looking to the future. Not the past. How long is it before the pirates, given shelter by the northern ports, grow too powerful even for us to control? How long before Athria is in flames and we lose it all? Ruled by an upstart Warlord like the cities of Swebas or Lyfis? Men who care nothing for their own people? For justice?' Kerril's eyes lost the brief softness and were again hard with anger and determination.

Ellen was only too aware of how important sea-borne trade was to the island-Sardom of Athria. So far they had been insulated from the devastating wars that had crippled the mainland, Kelas, since the fall of the Bulvuran Empire.

But surely more co-operation between the Sardoms was the answer. Trying to restore the Cinanac line in Raynor seemed unrealistic. The former provinces – now Sardoms in their own right – would never accept rule again.

Kerril stood abruptly, his demeanour becoming official. Kerril would have his own private grief to deal with.

'Did Myan say anything else? Who would want him killed?' Kerril straightened his robes, squared his shoulders to take on what he knew would come from Myan's death.

Ellen shook her head.

'Then that's the end of it. For now at least.' Kerril put down his cup. 'You should get some rest.'

She could see part of the burden of the last hours lifting from him, leaving only heavy weariness.

'May Myan walk the caverns of Llors in peace,' said Kerril.

Ellen lowered her head, but said nothing.

'If you will excuse me, Sarqua, I have other duties.'

'Yes of course, Regent. When will my father's choice be made public?'

'I will address the Council tonight, but have no fear of it being kept a secret, most of the Athrian Suul will already be aware of it, I am sure. Even so, a public announcement is impossible this close to Storm Season with most of the population indoors.'

As Regent, Kerril would technically rule Athria until she formally took the throne. Even so, with her father's choice clear, the power was already hers.

'I understand.'

Kerril bowed and withdrew.

Sarqua. Heir to the throne.

Ellen's sense of unreality was lifting. The grief returned in a savage wave, but she withheld it. She must be strong, she told herself. Sarqua. Yes, she must be very strong.

She rose.

She could still hear her father's voice in her head and see the cool clarity of his gaze.

The Scion must stand within the Temple of the Iris.

The world shifted, her vision spun. She cried out, throwing out a hand and grabbing at the small table beside her to stop herself from falling to the floor.

'Uros!'

Ellen put down the cup. The bakta must be too strong for her at the moment. She needed rest.

Despite her own views, she was bound to follow her father's last will. The force of those words had taken on a compelling quality in her mind. The Temple of the Iris was hidden somewhere beneath the Cintros mansion, but her father had taken its secret location to the grave.

The Scion?

It seemed she would have to join this insane quest for the lost heir. For the thousands of dispossessed refugees and starving peasants on the mainland, it had become an easy banner to hold. In her view, it was nothing more than a destabilizing political force with no hope of achieving anything positive. Even so, there were plenty of people who stood to benefit from controlling and manipulating the mob, especially in Raynor itself, the old capital of the Bulvuran Empire. Idealists like Myan and Kerril were rare.

Wearily, she raised herself to her feet. Time to brave the court.

Ellen walked over to a mirror and looked at herself critically. She gathered her braided hair and let it fall over her left shoulder, pushing stray wisps back from the golden Suul mark on her forehead. The small bird totem on her left cheek looked livid and dark. She smoothed her cheeks, wiping away the ghosts of tears and tried to get some colour back into her soft oval face. She looked nothing more than a distraught Suulqua.

'Better start acting like a Suulvey,' she told her reflection.

Taking a deep breath, she moved from the ante-chamber into the throne room. The two spearmen guarding the entrance took up position behind her as she walked across the great room.

Her eyes were drawn to the dais, the cold marble where her father had breathed his last. A hard knot of pain made her catch her breath, and she blinked back tears. With Father gone, she was alone. Alone with her power – and her secrets.

'My lady.'

Ellen turned to see Galsian, the Overseer of Records, who worked directly beneath her, helping her manage the hundreds of court scribes.

'You have my sympathy, my lady. Myan was a great man.' Galsian was solidly built, a balding former officer who lost his left hand at the siege of Raynor. He was efficient, but prone to intimidation by the highborn.

'Apologies for bringing this to you now, but the Leygen ambassador is demanding an answer on his proposed changes to the trading agreement.'

She silenced him with a look. 'He can wait, Galsian. I will come to see you tomorrow.'

Galsian bowed and withdrew.

At the ornate archway of the entrance, ten scythemen stood in precise ranks. They came to attention and lifted their scythes as she passed, also falling in behind her. *I see Kerril is taking no chances with me.*

The hallway was packed. The crowd turned to her and surged forward, filling the air with excited chatter.

'My lady,' said one woman, touching her hand. 'We are with you in your time of grief.' More people spoke. Too many to make any sense from the words.

Ellen looked down at her hand, surprised at the touch, then up to the woman. It was Yasthel, plump now with her second child. They had been childhood friends, but like so many of them, she had married long ago, taking the full Suul rank of her husband. Yasthel had passed her in the corridor only this morning and barely acknowledged her.

'Thank you,' said Ellen, slowly pulling back her hand.

Kerril's son, Palsus, broke through the crowd. He was handsome, bare-chested, as was the custom, wearing a leather harness of the finest harena hide inlaid with bright ceramics and jewels. He was flanked by four other men, the sons of other senior Suulvey lords. Together they dominated the politics of the young Suulqua. One of them was Halsur, who wore the red cape of a court messenger, a sweeping tattoo of a drakon spread across his toned pectoral muscles. Her friend since childhood, it was he who had brought her news of the attack on her father only hours ago.

'My lady, allow me to escort you,' said Palsus, reaching to take her arm.

She knew she should appear strong, as invincible as the stone edifice of the palace itself, untouched by grief, unbowed by the sudden responsibility of ruling Athria, but at the sight of him she longed to collapse into his arms and weep like a broken child.

She felt the warmth of his hand on hers and let him draw her forward. She embraced him, feeling a sudden weakness as a new wave of tears threatened. Ellen hugged him fiercely then pushed away, whispering, 'Thank you,' into his ear. Her unique bond with her father had always been two-edged, strengthening her love for him, while at the same time creating a distance in her other relationships. So many times she had longed to tell Palsus of her powers; awkward pauses where she had smiled unconvincingly and retreated into formality, longing secretly for a love without boundaries.

Ellen could say no more then, surrounded by the crowd.

She leant over and gave him a lingering kiss on the cheek. 'I will come to see you soon,' she said, walking past him. Despite her father's continued warnings, maybe the time had come to reveal herself. But would Palsus understand? No. She could not risk losing him too, not now.

Halsur smiled sadly as she passed, his face homely but kind. He had been one of her closest childhood friends up until she received her totem tattoo, at which time she was forced to separate from all males her age, except at formal occasions. He was now a follower of Palsus and always held back when he was with him.

The newest of the Suulvey Lords, Jorrel, bowed gravely to Ellen. His long face was creased with concern beneath his close-cropped black hair. The tall, thin Suulvey straightened. 'Athria has lost a great man, my lady. Let me know if there is anything I can do to aid you.'

Jorrel was the richest trader in Athria. The man had bought a Suulqua title decades ago, and had risen rapidly through the ranks of the Athrian Suul. Lord Jorrel seemed pensive, as well he might. Myan had been liberal where newcomers to the Suul ranks were concerned, recognising and rewarding talent. The old-guard of the Athrian Suul were not so forgiving. They resented Jorrel's wealth and his exulted position. Jorrel's enterprise in modernising the Athrian trading fleet had done much to restore Athria's flagging wealth, yet to many he remained a low-bred trader. Little better than a tradesman.

There were others, many others. She bowed and passed formal words of grief, the automatic mask of court life slipping over her like a shroud.

The crowd pressed in.

She pushed through them all. Outside the palace, the sharp chill of the night stung her skin. A reminder of the cold the Storm Season would bring.

She led her escort through the wide ground of Regent's Hill to the Cintros estate, dismissing them at the entrance. Here she had her own household guard.

She closed the door to her room and turned to greet the emptiness inside. She collapsed back against the door and sobbed, falling to the rich carpets as her knees gave out. The night around her grew deeper, colder as she finally gave into her grief.

Chapter Two

The room was warm and still.

Cedrin leant forward, his guarded grey-blue eyes scanning the karass board intently. He took a deep breath of the scented air, delighting in the smell of se-tobacco and sweet incense, which overpowered the acrid smoke from the oil lamps.

He looked up to his friend Marken, like him bare-chested apart from a well-used harness of dark leather crossing from shoulder to waist, fitted with a sheath for his razor sharp long-knife or calv. Both were calvanni – knife fighters.

The resemblance ended there. Marken was a head shorter, his carefully trimmed, long golden hair – unbraided in the current fashion – at odds with Cedrin's close-cropped dark brown. Cedrin was a fifth-degree. His Brotherhood tattoos began low on his abdomen and continued in a line to just below his pectorals, one tattoo for each degree of the calvanni. They began with a simple stylised bat, then the swift *efreet* messenger bat, the cavern-dwelling *jakkund* mount, the deadly *palgur* cat, then the fearsome *keerhound*, a beast bred for war: the fifth-degree that marked Cedrin as a senior member of the Brotherhood of the Night. Marken was new to the Brotherhood, and only had the first-degree bat tattoo.

And he was not concentrating on the game.

Cedrin followed Marken's golden gaze across the room.

Two women, both courtesans skilled in the arts of song, dance and pleasure, lounged comfortably in the shadows. One of them was a skilful lute player and began a peaceful air. It was the custom for women and men to go bare-chested within the privacy of their own homes, and Marken's eyes glistened with anticipation as he watched her play. She shook out her long brown hair, brought her lips together in a teasing pout and winked at him.

'There are few better ways to pass the cold of Storm Season. Hey, ami?' said Cedrin.

Marken looked back to Cedrin with a flashing grin of perfect, white teeth. His eyes were dilated, betraying the effect of the stimulant in the *se*-tobacco.

'You finished daydreaming?' asked Cedrin.

Marken shook his head and blinked. 'Too much *se*. May Larus forgive me,' he said, giving Cedrin a quick gesture of blessing with his right hand, then chuckling to himself. He sobered as he returned his attention to the game.

Cedrin had only known the merchant's son for two years, yet the depth of their friendship had grown rapidly. Both plied a dangerous trade as smugglers for the Brotherhood. Despite Marken's inexperience, his instincts had proven invaluable, as had his ability to move in the higher circles of Athrian nobility.

Marken had shown him unstinting loyalty, saving him from death's door when the rest of the Brotherhood would have left him to die.

As a young boy, Cedrin had loved his younger step-brothers and step-sisters, being highly protective of them all. But nothing came close to the bond he had developed with the gregarious, golden-skinned calvanni.

'I don't understand,' muttered Marken, his brow creasing as he studied the board. 'You. . .'

Marken was losing badly. Over the last hour, Cedrin had forced him to withdraw most of his remaining pieces to the neutral blue hexagon in the middle of the board.

'How about we raise the stakes?' said Cedrin.

'What did you have in mind?' asked Marken, swallowing.

'If I win, you have to answer one question about your life before the Brotherhood. I know you're too pretty to be a trader's son.'

Marken shook his head. 'I'm afraid you're going to have to be content with my coin.'

Marken's hands shook with excitement and se. He looked across at Cedrin, searching for some signal. Cedrin forced himself to remain expressionless; forced his hand to stay away from the good-luck piece that hung around his neck, the ancient signet ring of his father, Belin Kaidell – a man he had never known. Touching the ring was an old habit, one that had recently cost him dearly in games with Marken. For almost a week, Marken had won every game, forewarned of his killing moves. Fortunately, he had realised his error in time to win back most of the money, even using the signal to frustrate Marken's strategy until his friend twigged.

Marken advanced his ruby for the kill.

'Another opal! Ah, come to me, my love!' Marken pocketed Cedrin's coin with glee, the sea-serpent totem tattoo on his upper chest seeming to move over his golden skin as he leant across the board.

Cedrin launched into action, quickly taking the game.

'I should have known better,' said Marken as Cedrin slipped a ruby, an emerald and three of Marken's opals into his pouch. Each of the karass pieces were valuable coins of cast ceramic, each named for the gemstone whose colour they resembled.

Marken relit the se pipe and inhaled deeply, his eyes on the vacant board.

'Good thing its only money,' said Marken dryly.

Marken offered Cedrin the pipe. Cedrin lifted the narrow tube to his lips, drew on the tobacco and exhaled with a sigh of satisfaction.

Marken raised himself from the cushions, giving Cedrin a courtier's bow. 'To the victor the spoils! Sometimes I wonder why I bother playing you, Cedrin. I may as well just give you the money and have done with it.'

Cedrin laughed, nodding to Marken in thanks.

Cedrin raised himself to his feet, the well-honed muscles of his torso rippling like a flexing snake.

An urgent knock sounded at the door.

The congenial atmosphere vanished like smoke.

Across the room, the courtesans gave startled gasps. The playing faltered and ceased. Long, razor-sharp calvs of cast lanedd milkglass appeared in their hands. Their eyes met as they moved towards the door, ready for anything.

Cedrin signalled for the women to cover themselves and move into the adjoining room.

He moved to the doorway, motioning Marken to take position behind the frame.

'Who is it?' demanded Cedrin.

'Inyss!'

'Damn it,' muttered Cedrin as he reached for the bolt. 'What is it?'

'It's the Mouthpiece. He's on 'is way.'

The Mouthpiece of Smuggling was Cedrin's boss, a powerful and vicious thug by the name of Mat. For years, Cedrin had been forced to stand by and watch his senseless killing, until finally he reached the fifth-degree – and challenged Mat in the Circle of Blades. He would have died if the gem-ring had not fallen from its leather thong and thwarted Mat's blade, halting the lanedd edge just below his heart. Mat had left him for dead, but Marken kept him alive long enough to make it to the Temple, where the Druids had healed him.

Mat never trusted him again. Lucky for him, Mat needed their contacts. So far Cedrin had managed to outmanoeuvre him – so far he had managed to stay alive.

Cedrin opened the door slowly, always cautious of betrayal.

A dark-haired boy shot inside, his threadbare cloak billowing around his thin frame.

Marken came out of the shadows, visibly relaxing as he sheathed his weapon.

Cedrin slid his calv into his leather harness. He checked the landing and the wooden stairs that led to the narrow alleyway below. Both were empty. He carefully rebolted the door.

'He's got mainlanders with him. All calvanni,' said the boy, his eyes swivelling towards the plates of food on the small table.

'Here,' said Cedrin. He drew the boy into the light, offering him honey-cakes and watered wine. He needed time to think. Time to still the sudden flood of anxious thoughts.

He waited as the young boy gorged himself. Storm Season was only two days away and street-kids like Inyss had nowhere to go, no one to provide for them, so he gave what he could to help them. Ten years ago, it could have been him standing there in the threadbare cloak, driven and alone, living on the streets with other outcasts, the ancient ring and raptor totem tattoo the only things he could call his own.

'Slow down.' He drew Inyss away from the plate and sat him at the karass board. 'How many Calvanni does he have with him?' he said, taking a seat beside him.

'A lot.'

'How many, Inyss?' Cedrin tried to keep the sharp edge from his voice.

'Mor'n five. Don't know none of 'em.'

Cedrin leant back on his chair, forcing his mind into clarity through the drug haze with practised ease. He knew from harsh experience a clear mind could mean the difference between life and death.

Marken paced back and forth across the bare boards, driven by the se.

'What could he want this close to Storm Season?' asked Marken. 'He got his cut of the last job, we saw to that. It must be something different. Uros! Why now?'

Cedrin's eyes narrowed. Marken was a brilliant calvanni, a natural with the blade both at close quarters and thrown, but he still retained the impetuousness of his wealthy upbringing. Many times he had taken them both into danger because of his arrogance and contempt for the lowborn. Now was a time for clear heads.

'Marken, put away the se pipe.'

Marken extinguished the pipe and dropped it into a carved wooden box set with coloured glass. In the confusion, Inyss tried to grab some of the coins beside the karass board. Cedrin's hand whipped out, catching him by the wrist. He chose an opal and led Inyss away from the board. He could not blame the boy. It was survival.

'Here.' He gave him the coin.

The boy snatched the opal and moved back to the platter of cakes as though nothing had happened.

'Did you hear why he was coming, Inyss?'

'No, but it's big. Calvanni are 'ere from all over.' The boy paused, his eyes opening wide as he glanced around at Marken.

'It's all right, Inyss, he's a friend.'

The boy lowered his voice to a conspiratorial whisper. 'There's assanni. Scores of 'em. All from 'cross the Sea. Arrived with an army 'o black demons, they did.'

Cedrin smiled, dismissing the boy's exaggeration. The demons of Kallor, the Lord of Death, were said to rise from his realm of Llors during Storm Season, and were often uppermost in people's minds as the time of cold drew near. Now, with Storm Season only two days away, it would be easy for the imagination of a boy like Inyss to get a bit carried away. Assanni? Possibly. Demons? Cedrin shook his head, amused.

'Assanni!' said Marken explosively. 'One day Mat will go too far.'

'Disappear, Inyss,' said Cedrin, waving the boy towards the door.

They unbolted the door for Inyss, who bowed, pausing only to grab a handful of honey-cakes before he vanished into the night.

Marken shut the door behind him.

Cedrin tapped the heel of his drawn calv on the low wooden table, trying to tease out Mat's possible motives as Marken went back to pacing, no doubt trying to do the same.

A heavy knock shook the door.

They took up positions.

'Who is it?' asked Cedrin.

'Mat! Open the door, you blood-soaked mainlander,' he growled.

Cedrin cracked it open. The doorstep was crowded with darkened shapes.

Cedrin was the bastard son of a Bulvuran noble, the Anacian stock that had ruled the Empire for an age. He towered over the smaller, light-skinned Athrians and had run from his share of racist mobs intent on punishing another mainlander. His Brotherhood calvanni tattoos had put a stop to that, but not the continual provocation from harenas like Mat. The comparison with a harena, the tusked, bad-tempered omnivore of Kelas with its disgusting habits was an apt one. And yet, a harena tasted good to eat and produced useful leather – and there was nothing good about Mat.

Cedrin opened the door, his eyes sweeping across the seven calvanni with Mat, all strangers. Second and third-degrees, experienced and potentially deadly. None of them seemed the least bit intimidated by him, or the lacework of fine scars on his arms and chest.

Everything about this set Cedrin on edge. Why bring so many strange calvanni here in the middle of the night? Was Mat expecting trouble?

As he motioned them into the room, Cedrin could not help measuring the odds. In the close confines of the room, he was confident he could hold them off long enough to escape, but Marken would not be a match for any one of them. He would not leave his friend, or the women, at their mercy.

Cedrin turned towards Marken and shook his head slightly.

Reluctantly, Marken sheathed his calv. Shaking loose his long golden hair, he stepped forward into the light with the confident swagger of a courtier; arrogant, even contemptuous. Inwardly Cedrin cursed. The last thing needed now was to antagonise Mat.

The Mouthpiece turned to Marken, his small black eyes glowing in the light of the room. 'Ah, the piss-skinned merchant!'

Mat is in a foul mood tonight.

Like Cedrin, Marken also stood out amongst the folk of Athria, his golden skin and hair marking him as a Cioan – the ancient race of Kelas.

Cedrin could see the anger rise in Marken, sped and amplified by the se. Marken bowed in mock respect, using the motion to put his body into attack stance. 'Greetings, Oh Great One!'

Marken was a talented calvanni, but he had learnt his fighting skills in the Merchant's Quarter where duels were honourable. He was no match for men like Mat, who had perfected a repertoire of gutter-tricks before their first tattoo. Cedrin knew Mat was close to the edge, and would not stand for

Marken's flippancy tonight.

'Marken, get some bakta for our guests,' said Cedrin, breaking the impasse.

'My pleasure, Lord Cedrin,' said Marken.

Mat watched Marken disappear into the adjoining room, finally letting out a sigh as the tension left his stocky frame. Cedrin observed the vexation on Mat's face with satisfaction. The brutal sixth-degree could not compete with Marken's quick tongue.

One day Mat will push us too far. Then I will meet him once more in the Circle of Blades. This time Mat will lose. Cedrin resisted the urge to touch the savage scar that ran up the middle of his abdomen and stopped just below his heart.

'So, Mat, what can we do for you?' asked Cedrin, trying to appear relaxed.

'You and that perfumed piss-skin are wanted in the tunnels. There is a big job and we need you. Pack lightly and for a lengthy duration.'

Cedrin's fists clenched. 'You're mounting an operation in Storm Season? What sort of job? Where is it?' asked Cedrin, struggling to keep his voice level.

'You need to know nothing!' said Mat, his face flushing red.

He walked up to Cedrin, his ravaged face twisted with hate, his breath as foul as the harbour breeze at low tide. 'You will be at the Cavern within two bells or you'll wake up dead before the first dawn lights the sky. Do you understand me?'

Cedrin was conscious of the distance between them. He knew he could bury his calv into Mat's ribs faster than the ugly thug could move, but he could not match seven experienced calvanni. 'We'll be there, Mouthpiece. We're loyal Brothers,' he said levelly, silently vowing that when he gained the sixth-degree he would force Mat from the Brotherhood. Then he would lead the smuggling operations. His way.

The Mouthpiece grunted, arrogantly turning his back to Cedrin as he walked to the door.

Mat turned on the step. His eyes glittered in the lamplight like beads of dark glass. 'This is a big job. Say nothing to anyone.' He held Cedrin's gaze for a long moment, then smiled.

There was something in his eyes that left Cedrin cold. A promise . . . a deadly promise. What was it Inyss had said? *An army of black demons had come to Athria.*

Cedrin held his stare, looming over the smaller man.

Mat turned and walked down the stairs to the alley below, his men trailing behind.

Cedrin closed the door, slamming the bolt home.

Marken stepped from the shadows, a throwing knife held lightly in his fingertips. 'Mat came close to wearing this tonight,' he said. 'His colour, don't you think?'

'Something's not right about this,' said Cedrin. 'Something tells me we should take the last boat out of Athria and never look back.'

Marken sighed, replacing the knife in its hidden boot sheath. 'What choice do we have?'

'None,' said Cedrin.

* * *

Cedrin could feel the edge of coolness in the night. The latent Heat within his body stirred, waiting to awaken, but he resisted it. Again he cursed Mat.

He and Marken made their way covertly along the Way of the Worm, the twisting alley that ran across the sprawling mass of Lookout Hill, ending in the harbour like a frozen stream. Tonight they would leave it long before it met the sea.

They moved cautiously, slipping between shadows, pausing to listen for pursuit. There were seven ways to enter the caverns beneath the city. The six main entrances were all carefully guarded, the seventh hidden within a small Temple and known only to a few. Initiates were taken blindfolded until they obtained the first-degree. The Brotherhood guarded its secrets carefully, dispensing swift and final justice to those who betrayed it.

They reached the Kali, an old square shaded from view by massive trees whose roots had cracked the cistern. The vast underground chamber was now empty of water. In the distance, they heard the sound of the Nightguard and hurried towards the dry well, carefully lowering themselves into the opening.

Clenching their calvs between their teeth, they followed the ancient masonry to the silent cavern of the cistern below. As the trapdoor sprang open, a beam of ruddy yellow light cut into the dark, illuminating the cracked, graffiti-covered mortar behind them.

'Hold!'

Two calvanni blocked their path, calvs drawn. A second-degree Cedrin recognised from Theft and another first-degree Cedrin did not know.

'Relax, boys. It's Cedrin and Marken.'

'Oh, sorry, boss,' said the second-degree.

Cedrin let out a long, silent breath. Something had these men on edge.

All these new faces were starting to bother Cedrin. In the Brotherhood, your power was measured in the number of blades you could command, and he had yet to see any of his own.

They lit a torch and hurried on.

Now they began a different kind of game.

To an outsider, the caverns would be a maze. The tunnels, some man-made, others natural, wound without pattern deep into the island's bedrock. They passed though empty galleries and deep pools of darkness filled with the sound of bats sheltering from the coming cold. Stands of lungii flourished amid the droppings, their fronds and flowers faintly luminous in the darkness.

'What could they possibly be planning during Storm Season?' asked Marken.

'I don't know, but if Inyss is right about the assanni, we will have to move very, very carefully.'

He gripped Marken's shoulder, turning him into the torchlight. Marken's eyes were still dilated from the se. He was high on the drug. . . unpredictable. A wave of anxiety shot through Cedrin. His stomach clenched. Damn! It was the last thing they needed now.

'We will need clear heads for what comes ahead, my friend. No matter what happens, do not act. Do not answer back or question.'

Marken took a deep breath. 'I shall bide my tongue, Oh Lord of the Caverns!'

'This is serious!' snapped Cedrin. He was trying to save them and Marken was making jokes! He forced himself to remain calm. 'Promise me you will follow my lead.'

Marken nodded, his golden eyes searching Cedrin's. 'I will, my friend.'

'Good,' said Cedrin. 'Lord of the Caverns. Ha! We will be lucky to get out of this one alive.'

More than an hour had passed, and they still had at least half an hour to go before they reached the Cavern. *Assanni.* Cedrin shivered. There was no defence against poison – and the blowpipe was the assanni weapon of choice. No skill with a blade could help you then. You would die helpless, drooling like an old derelict, shaking with pain. . . As a young boy on the streets, he had watched a man die of poison. A big sailor, stabbed with a poisoned blade in a brawl. All arrogance, every ounce of dignity had gone by the end. He died, mewling like a baby, clawing at his own skin while the crowd watched. *When the time comes, give me a clean death.*

As they continued on through the dark, every pool of shadow transformed into the hiding place of a waiting assassin, blowpipe raised. . . Angrily, Cedrin forced the dark thoughts away. Mat needed them, otherwise why go to all this trouble?

'Come on, we have to move faster,' said Cedrin. They broke into a run, covering the last treacherous tunnels at breakneck speed, Cedrin relying on his knowledge of the pitted and worn path to keep from tripping in the dim light.

Finally, they neared one of the entrances to the Cavern. At a signal from Cedrin, they slowed to a walk and recovered their breath.

Cedrin looked across to his friend. Marken's eyes were *still* dilated. He shook his head. It was too late. They had to go on.

The Cavern was a natural amphitheatre where the Brotherhood met and where the Circle of Blades was formed at times of challenge.

The entrance was blocked by more than a dozen calvanni,

led by Vano, a fourth-degree from Smuggling who Cedrin trusted. He could see new arrivals being questioned by him and his men. Some were turned away while others were let through.

'Hey, Vano. What's going on?' asked Cedrin.

Vano would not meet his eyes. 'Let them through,' he commanded.

The ranks parted, and they were quickly ushered through the defensive ring.

'Vano! Talk to me!' said Cedrin as he was pushed forward into the Cavern. 'What's happening?'

Vano looked back, his eyes haunted. Cedrin saw the same look in all of them. Fear.

Cedrin had known this chamber all his life, and yet now it seemed like foreign territory. Hundreds were gathered, some of them calvanni Cedrin recognised from the Brotherhood, others strangers. All the exits were heavily guarded.

He walked through the crowd, greeting other calvanni as he passed through. He and Banis, who he nodded to across the room, were the only fifth-degrees.

The calvanni pressed in. Before long a crowd of around twelve surrounded him, all besieging him with questions.

'Do you know what's going on?' asked a second-degree from Smuggling who Cedrin had inducted into the Brotherhood himself.

Before he could reply, another first-degree cut in. 'What's going on, Cedrin?'

'What's being planned?' asked another first-degree with him.

Cedrin held up his hands. 'I know as much as you do,' he said, looking around at the small crowd. 'Now. One at a time.'

He spoke first to the second-degree, then to each of the others. Their story was all the same. Threatened with dire consequences, they were told to report for a big job in utmost secrecy.

More calvanni were still arriving, and Mat and his henchmen were nowhere to be seen. So his threats were bluster, after all.

'Where are the Mouthpieces?' asked Cedrin.

'Over near the harbour entrance,' said the second-degree.

Flanked by Marken and an entourage of experienced

calvanni, Cedrin pushed through the knot of excited Brotherhood men and circled the Cavern.

The Brotherhood worked in secret. The need to move quietly, unobtrusively through the tightly controlled society of Athria gave them all an instinctive caution. In prior gatherings here, the conversations had been in low tones, words carefully chosen. You didn't make a move unless you were fully committed – because moves could be deadly. Yet now the Cavern was abuzz with talk, high-pitched, panicked voices. Men on the edge, hands hovering near their weapons.

He heard voices raised in argument and turned to see three men trying to force their way back out of the room and being turned back.

That's when he saw them.

Assanni.

Dressed in plain grey trousers and open shirts, the mark of the teremb like a dark bruise on their chests. They were standing silently at every entrance. Watching. Waiting. Cedrin's eyes swept over them. He could see no sign of a weapon, but that meant nothing. They were experts in concealment. The four assanni standing closest to the three shouting men had their hands inside their open shirts, looking across the Cavern, clearly waiting for a signal.

Cedrin followed their gaze.

At first hidden by the uneven walls, the Mouthpieces – holders of the sixth-degree and leaders of the Brotherhood – stood together at the mouth of the sea-caves. He recognised Mat immediately, standing with Dresil, the Mouthpiece of Piracy. He also knew Kayleez, the Mouthpiece of Courtesans, his silk shirt straining against his bulging stomach, gimlet eyes concealed in his pudgy face. Tice, the whip-thin Mouthpiece of Theft, was also a familiar figure. There was another with them Cedrin did not know. A tall man with close-cropped blond hair and dead eyes. He bore the mark of the teremb. Cedrin drew in a sharp breath. This must be Stone, the Mouthpiece of Assassination. His attention was focussed on the altercation at the Cavern entrance. Stone shook his head slightly, and the four assanni withdrew their hands and stood back. The three men were roughly pushed back into the cavern and moved away by the other guards.

Standing with the group of Mouthpieces was a group of Cioan mercenaries dressed in black leather armour inlaid with studs of mought, a tough, almost unbreakable ceramic. They had greatscythes slung across their back in the old military style of the Bulvuran Empire.

Here was Inyss' army of black demons.

The hairs rose on the back of Cedrin's neck.

The warriors stood out among the blond and brown-haired Mouthpieces, their hair mainly gold to golden-red, their builds similar to Marken, of medium height yet compact and powerful. One scarred warrior towered like a golden giant over the whole room.

Cedrin's eyes immediately fixed on one man: a Suul warrior with long gold-streaked silver hair and pale skin. He was Cioan albino. Unlike the albinos of other races, his skin was pale silver, not white. He stood as though he owned the Cavern, and Mat and all the other Brotherhood Mouthpieces played court to him, their heads slightly bowed. Why?

The silver-skinned warrior met Cedrin's gaze.

Cedrin's hand twitched towards his calv. This was his home ground. The Cavern had been a haven for him since his earliest days with the Brotherhood. He gritted his teeth. The Brotherhood's strength was in how carefully it guarded its secrets, yet the Mouthpieces had brought strangers to its heart. If he had defeated Mat in the Circle of Blades, it would be him standing there as Mouthpiece of Smuggling – and he would not be playing court to anyone.

Cedrin held the warrior's gaze until he turned back to the Mouthpieces.

'Northmen,' said Marken. 'What are they doing in Athria? No Cioan has ventured from the Sardom of Armon in decades. Do you think they were washed down the Yasser?'

'I don't think so,' replied Cedrin.

He watched the silver-skinned warrior across the room as he dominated the group, the Suul mark a startling brand on his forehead.

Banis and his fourth-degree partner Cephor, both from Theft, joined their group, quickly falling into conversation with another two calvanni from Smuggling.

'Hey, Cedrin!' called a familiar voice.

They turned to see Skye and his partner Jaso striding across the room.

Skye had once been Cedrin's partner. Two years ago, he had taken a profitable offer to work with Kayleez. He and Skye, who had been inseparable since their first-degree, were to move together until he discovered the Courtesan's Mouthpiece did not want 'mainlander scum' working for him, claiming it was bad for business.

The group around Cedrin parted to admit the newcomers.

Skye wore trousers of the finest leather and a beautifully woven silk shirt, open to reveal his third-degree tattoo. His harness was immaculately worked with coloured mought. They greeted each other with a firm shoulder grip, Cedrin a full head taller than his friend yet no more powerful.

Jaso was a short Athrian, his slight frame possessing a wiry strength and endurance. His brown eyes were alert and amused, set in an angular face.

'By Uros, it's good to see a friendly face!' said Cedrin.

'You haven't washed that gold off yet, Marken,' said Jaso, his eyes flickering around the room in ceaseless movement.

'It's more of a tan than you'll ever have, Jaso, hiding in shadows like a mouse!'

Skye indicated the assanni with a nod. 'Watch them, Cedrin. I recognise a few and I've seen the tattoos on others. The mark of the teremb.'

'Assassins. There must be more than twenty of them,' said Cedrin.

'Yes. And I've heard it whispered the albino is the Traitor of Armon himself.'

'Raziin?'

'That's what I've heard,' said Skye.

Cedrin touched the signet ring, his finger playing over the cool emerald and the notch where it had stopped Mat's blade. He looked at the mercenaries and the man who led them with new interest.

Raziin was powerfully muscled, his face strong, cheekbones high like most of his race. His long hair was tied tightly in three braids, falling down his back in neat lengths. He gave off a sense of power, like barely suppressed rage. He would be dangerous, easy to provoke. Surrounded by his men he would be all but invulnerable.

Llors take them all!

Raziin Cinnor killed his own father, Sarlord Leith Cinnor, in a failed attempt to seize the throne of Armon. He was later exiled by his older brother Ralin, along with the leaders of the rebellion. He and his men had forged a reputation as some of the most fearsome mercenaries in Kelas. Tales abounded in the taverns of Athria of slaughtered prisoners, strange blood rites and worse – Sorcery.

Finally, Dresil, the Pirate's Mouthpiece, led the Brotherhood leaders and mercenaries into the centre of the Cavern. Dresil controlled shipping and was one of the most powerful members of the Brotherhood beneath the enigmatic and secretive Masks – the holders of the seventh-degree. He stood like one of the ancient statues the Cioans had raised along the course of the Yasser as he surveyed the crowd – stern, implacable.

Marken looked at Dresil, puzzled. 'Who's he?'

'The Pirate's Mouthpiece,' replied Cedrin.

Marken's jaw grew slack, undisguised hatred glowing like magma in the depths of his golden eyes.

'Seal the room!' commanded Dresil with a booming voice practised at fighting the howling gales of the Sea of Mists.

The calvanni guarding the entrances formed an impassable barrier. Stone raised his arm. The assanni fanned out along the rough-cut walls. They swiftly drew out hidden blowpipes and raised them to their lips. Even though Cedrin was expecting it, his heart leapt. He looked around wildly, his mind spinning.

The buzz of conversation was replaced instantly by tense silence.

Cedrin's fists clenched. The Cavern was where arguments were settled, but everyone always had their say. Assanni? Blowpipes? At a signal from Dresil, any one of them would be dead.

Skye's face was set like stone. Marken glared at Dresil with murderous intensity. This was out of character for his friend, but Marken turned away before Cedrin could question him.

The Mouthpiece waited, his small, cruel eyes watching the crowd with satisfaction. As the silence became uncomfortable, he began to speak. 'Each of you has been carefully selected for an important job. The profit will be more than you could ever imagine, for all of you.'

Dresil indicated the silver-haired Northman. 'This is Raziin Cinnor.'

A startled burst of conversation rippled through the crowd.

'Suul Raziin will be leading the attack,' said Dresil, cutting through the talk.

Cedrin's mind raced. Raziin's men were mercenaries, trained for open combat. Attack? Attack on what? Had the Brotherhood leaders gone mad! Their strength was in stealth.

The silver-haired warrior stepped forward. 'You all know of me,' said Raziin, his voice edged with menace as he searched the crowd. 'When I lead, I demand total obedience.'

Raziin let the silence stretch.

No one would be inclined to test him. A calv was no match for a greatscythe.

Raziin's lips curled into a savage leer. 'Together we are going to raid Regent's Hill.'

Regent's Hill!

Cedrin's eyes swept towards the exits. The calvanni guarding them drew their calvs. The assannis' merciless eyes watched the crowd, blowpipes at the ready. *No wonder the Mouthpieces took such a precaution, without them they would have had a riot!*

'You can't mean to raid during the Storm Season!' yelled Cephor.

Suppressed tensions flooded through the room in an explosion of voices.

Cephor raised his fist in defiance and two of the assanni swivelled their pipes towards him.

Cedrin and Banis saw the danger and grabbed hold of

Cephor to stop him from lunging towards Dresil. Like Cedrin, Banis and Cephor had often been vocal critics of Brotherhood decisions, but this was not the time.

'Shut your cursed hole and stand firm!' Dresil waved towards the assanni. 'Or you'll find yourself face-down in the harbour.'

Suddenly all the pieces fit. Assanni. An attack on Regent's Hill. The Sarlord was assassinated by the Brotherhood!

Fools!

Cedrin's grip weakened at the shock of his realisation. Suddenly Cephor lunged forward, pulling out of their grasp.

'You stinking harbour trash!' screamed Cephor, sweeping out his calv and pointing it at Dresil. 'How dare you bring these Eathal-fuckers into the Cavern! I'll have no part of this. And neither should anyone else with any sense! The–'

A poison dart appeared in his shoulder.

Cephor's eyes widened, and he collapsed without making another sound. He twitched for a few heartbeats, then lay still.

White with rage, Banis watched his friend die. To move to his side was to invite a similar death.

Silence.

Raziin stepped forward to stand beside Dresil. His eyes were shining with excitement. *The bastard is enjoying this!*

'Yes. We are going to attack in the middle of Storm Season. But it will be to our advantage, not theirs. We have a tunnel under the Wall of Sorrows, and the element of surprise. Together with the crews from Dresil's ships we have over 500 men.

'By the end of Storm Season, Athria will be ours. You will be rich beyond your wildest dream – if you obey without question.'

Raziin swept his gaze across the room, then stepped back to talk with his own men, satisfied.

Mat stepped forward. 'You will leave directly from here to Pirate's Cove. Each of you will be issued a heavy robe and supplies. We will be marching up the coast.' Mat paused, watching the shocked men. 'I do not need to tell you the penalty for disobedience. . .'

The Mouthpieces withdrew.

Gradually the Brotherhood calvanni relaxed, the buzz of conversation rising to fill the Cavern. The assanni remained in place around the walls, and only the exit to the tidal caves was opened. Carts were brought forward laden with supplies, and Dresil's men walked through the crowd handing out heavy woollen robes and rugged oilskin sacks filled with dried sea provisions. Cedrin took a set for himself and Marken.

'Here, Marken,' said Cedrin, offering him the robe and sack.

Marken's eyes were distant, his fists clenched at his side.

'Marken, what is it?' asked Cedrin.

He did not respond, his eyes turning instead to fall on Dresil, then sweep across to the assanni lining the walls.

'Gutter-scum, all of them,' Marken growled through clenched teeth.

Cedrin reached out and put his hand on Marken's shoulder.

'There's nothing to be done but follow their lead.'

Marken looked back at him, his eyes filled with a hunger Cedrin had never seen before. Then his face became guarded.

'Are you ready, my friend?' asked Cedrin.

'Ha!' said Marken, his voice thin. 'To march up the coast in Storm Season! To take on Regent's Hill with a dried biscuit! Of course I'm ready.' Marken took the robe and sack.

Banis knelt by his friend's body. Cephor's face showed shocked surprise, his eyes as dull as slate. Banis had time only to close his friend's eyes and retrieve his calv and pouch before Dresil's henchmen dragged the body away.

Banis' face was twisted with rage and pain. He silently disappeared into the crowd.

'This is bad,' said Cedrin. 'Very bad.'

'Nonsense,' said Marken. 'I bless the day I heard of the Brotherhood.'

Cedrin looked at Marken sharply, but the golden-haired calvanni just looked away. His face was expressionless but Cedrin could sense the strain beneath the surface. At least the effects of the *se* had finally worn off.

They were ushered quickly through a series of wide tunnels. As they drew near to the sea, the smell of salt and mud and the rotten stink of the harbour grew stronger. The air freshened as they reached a huge tidal cave. Scores of longboats were drawn up on the dark shingle. Far in the distance, dim moonlight betrayed the exit to the harbour.

Cedrin, Marken, Skye and Jaso stayed close together, forming a tight group. The shoreline was silent as the tense calvanni awaited their call.

'You! You're next. Be quick about it.'

Together they shoved off into the dark waters then leapt the gunnel, taking to the oars as the old seamen at the helm expertly guided their longboat towards the rock cleft guarding the entrance.

In the bay, a fresh wind whipped at them with a promise of the cold to come. Cedrin inhaled deeply, the last tendrils of se vanishing from his mind. He would need all his wits to get them out of this one. He had no doubt it would spell disaster for the Brotherhood, whether they won or lost.

Athria's harbour was magnificent, hosting almost a thousand ships. It was these ships and its position on the southern trading route that had made Athria rich, growing with the Empire from fishing village to a mighty city-state. Now, after the collapse of the Bulvuran Empire, it ruled in its own right.

'A good night to sail, eh ami?' said Cedrin.

Marken nodded. Above, the stars were outlined in brilliant clarity, the two moons hanging majestically amid the vault of heaven.

'Aye. It's a fine night,' said Marken.

Ahead, the trader-pirate's dark bulk loomed out of the night. The calls of sailors manning the rigging soon reached them in snatches on the strengthening wind. Once within hailing distance, curt commands were given from above and the longboat drew alongside. They scrambled up the rope-ladder to the swaying main deck, then were quickly led below to the crowded hold. Many calvanni were already there, as were off-duty sailors who were drinking and gambling. The crewmen eyed the newcomers with suspicion. Cedrin and his friends sat with relief on a rough wooden bench and shared a flask of bakta.

'Ah!' Cedrin exclaimed, the rough spirit burning his throat.

'Where did you get this harena-piss, Skye?' He looked at the clear spirit doubtfully through the glass.

Skye took a swig, smiling with satisfaction as he swallowed. 'Ahhh. That warms you alright!'

He passed the flask to Marken.

'How long till the Cove?' asked Jaso as he watched Marken take a shot.

'In this breeze we'll be there by first light, day after tomorrow,' replied a sailor who lounged against the ship's hull, easily moving with the sway of the ship.

'First day of Storm Season,' said Skye.

The sailor looked at Marken, whose golden skin glowed faintly in the guttering oil lamps.

'You a piss-skin, eh?' the sailor asked, giving a toothless grin.

'Yes.' Marken was smiling, but the smile did not reach his eyes. 'The gifted race with skin the colour of Larus.'

The sailor laughed and clapped him on the back. Marken's expression darkened as the sailor walked away.

'He's just a sailor, ami,' said Cedrin.

'Is he?' replied Marken. 'Or is he a pirate?'

Cedrin tried to read Marken's look, but it was impossible.

'What is it, my friend? What's on your mind?' asked Cedrin in a low voice.

'Oh, nothing,' said Marken. 'Just wondering how many innocents have died screaming beneath his blade.' He tried to make it sound flippant, but it came out harshly.

Skye and Jaso exchanged a questioning look.

Marken turned away towards the hull as though to rest, but Cedrin knew he would be wide awake. No one got to sleep after se. He stared at Marken's back for long moments, wondering what he could say to tease him out of his inexplicable anger, but could come up with nothing. Marken was evasive at the best of times.

Cedrin thought back to the first time he met Marken. Skye and he had already parted ways, and Cedrin had been working alone for months. He was approached by Mat, who told him of a merchant's son from the Quarter making noises in the Sea Serpent, the tavern stronghold of the Brotherhood on the docks.

Fearing a trap, Cedrin had reluctantly climbed through the tunnels that led to the Sea Serpent and met with Marken, a penniless and disinherited trader's son who had wanted to work in partnership with the Brotherhood, providing contacts in return for a cut of the profits. In time, Marken got his partnership, but not exactly the way he wanted it. The Brotherhood held most of the cards and he knew this. He was inducted into the Brotherhood and he and Cedrin became a team.

Over the past years, Cedrin had shown him a different side of life. A hidden one occurring under the noses of the aristocracy, and often, under their feet.

In return, Marken had shown him the carefree world of the upper classes as together they profited from the greed and wealth of the merchant class. They had drifted through the social life of some of the wealthiest and most influential traders on the island Sardom of Athria. They had been good years. But not good enough to break free of the Brotherhood's grip.

Cedrin shrugged his shoulders and joined Skye and Jaso in a game of dice.

Voices were raised on the upper deck, followed by the sound of running feet. Soon the ship was tilting, cutting into the wind, racing towards the Sea of Mist and Pirate's Cove.

Chapter Three

Ellen lifted the glowmetal higher, her hands aching in the cold of the tunnels. She had spent hours searching for any hint of the Temple of the Iris – yet she had found nothing. It was here *somewhere*. Years ago, her father had told her of it, yet he had never revealed its exact location.

Ellen had wandered deeper into the Cintros labyrinth than ever before. Taking a moment to concentrate, she reconfirmed the route she had taken in her mind, an inexplicable series of left and right turns, secret passageways and hidden stairs that would confound any other visitor.

Beyond the circle of the light, the dark waited; impenetrable, unknowable. Ellen shivered. She hated the dark, especially here underground. Her throat constricted at the thought of it, as though it had enough substance to reach into her, choking away her air. . . Nothing but childish fears, she told herself; yet only the intense, magical light of her platinum glowmetal, *Bluefire*, stood between her and the dark. Like all glowmetals, it had been unearthed as a single crystal of combined light and metal. Most were mere curiosities – unable to be melted, beaten or changed in any way. Yet there were those precious few that could transform. If *Bluefire* was fed with pure Fire – the essence of Sorcery – it would store the magical essence, releasing it as blue light a thousand times brighter than the dull glow of its natural state. Each glowmetal was unique. Some could take in heat and release it as sound, or absorb Moon-Essence and release it as Force – the combinations were endless.

Bluefire shook in its frame. Ellen looked up in surprise to see her hand shaking.

'Nothing but the cold,' she muttered. The dark pressed in on her, creeping towards her feet. . . The tension grew between her shoulders.

I must keep moving, yet where to now? She had spent days searching through the Cintros library to find only a single reference to the Iris 'sleeping in the belly of Kallor'. More than six hours ago, she had entered the labyrinth beneath the Cintros mansion, heading to the many small shrines to Kallor that she knew of, but they yielded nothing. Disappointed, she was forced to scour the whole labyrinth for murals, carvings, frescos – yet there were thousands of them – all sleeping fitfully in the dark. Her eyes ached from peering into the gloom, scanning the walls for a seam, some odd feature in the masonry, any sign or marking in the endless painted arrays of mythological creatures and stern gods that could point her to the Iris.

A few minutes later, her wandering brought her back to familiar ground. She knew of another depiction of Kallor nearby and pushed her weary feet onward. Another two turns left, then she depressed a small carving of the Sisters that opened a hidden stair. Soon she had emerged into the corridor where she had last seen it. The mural was distinctive, one of the oldest in the labyrinth, painted in the ancient Myrian style. *Damn! Where is it!*

Ellen leant forward to examine the wall, coughing as she pushed away the years of dust. She raised the glowmetal higher, the bright lines of blue that ran across its dull metallic surface pulsing with intense light. Dust had settled over everything like a fragile skin, covering both the walls and the bone-white marble of the floor.

'It must be here somewhere,' whispered Ellen under her breath, fearful to speak too loud into the darkness.

She moved along, the tunnel encased in a sphere of blue. Ancient torch-rings of cast clearglass glittered against the dulled paint of the walls. Minutes stretched to an hour and her eyes, already tired, began to ache and blur. Then her thoughts turned to her father, as though drawn, irresistibly, to the wound.

Three days had passed since Myan's death. The first day of

mourning she had spent in seclusion, grateful for the opportunity to vent her grief in private. The funeral service had been in the Temple of the Sisters the next day. Athria's Suul were all present to pay homage to a great leader. Standing in solemn rows, they were resplendent in simple white robes, chests covered for worship. The Druids in their golden silks, with their gem-encrusted sigils, filled the galleries above them. Their chants rose and fell in unbroken rhythm, swelling and cascading, surging over the assembly like the sea over the jagged rocks of Athria's coastline.

The ceremony was ancient, as old as the Suul class itself, dating from the first waves of Anacian settlers that later gave birth to the Bulvuran Empire. The Athrian Suul and their families – around 700 men, women and children – had rights of ownership to almost all the land in Athria, some owned outright, most granted through the Sarlord. With it, came the right to collect taxes. In return, they were bound to the will of the Sarlord, to defend Athria and the throne. Much of this wealth found its way to the Temple of the Sisters, whose Druids controlled not only religion, but most magic on Yos. No Sardom could function without the power of the Druids.

She had dressed her father in his clothes of office. Trousers of the finest black silk, harness of the best hide inlaid with precious gems. His drakon tattoo lay still and oddly impotent on his sunken chest, the golden Suul mark bright against his deathly pale skin.

Ellen was only vaguely aware of Torren as he came forward to the bier to accept the ceremonial knife. Her vision was filled with the shrunken shell of what her father had become.

She had come forward in turn to accept the knife. Grief twisted her heart, but she was now empty of tears. Her fingers curled around the gem-encrusted hilt as she slowly opened her robe. Without hesitation, she placed the point over her heart, her hands shaking. The sharp lanedd cut into her skin. The simple, physical pain was welcome as she inscribed the symbol of the deeper wound on the soft white flesh beneath her breast. The Circle of Larus. The symbol of life's journey; given birth in the loins of the goddess, finally sinking to the underworld Llors and the embrace of Kallor. The blood trickled down to stain her white robe.

The next day, she had awakened refreshed and cleansed. Following custom, her father would not be buried until after Storm Season. For once she was grateful for the respite from official duties. Palsus had been kind and gentle. He and the other Suulqua had arrived to show their support. Ellen found herself leaning on him heavily, her reserve broken down by weariness and grief. Palsus seemed the only friend she had now that her father was dead.

Torren had been trained as a warrior and had nothing but scorn for her scholarly ways. A full ten years older than her, he always treated her as a child. He kept a separate household within the mansion and even before her father's death their paths had rarely crossed. When they did, he was closed and unreachable, always surrounded by an entourage of senior officers, her attempts at forming a social bond rejected. After her father had chosen her for the succession, Torren had been openly hostile. She had tried to talk to him twice and he had rebuffed her each time, immersing himself in official duties, returning late to the mansion and leaving before dawn. Although no less than she expected, his coldness hurt her, the loss of Myan intensifying her need for family. *If only Estle was here.*

Ellen's thoughts snapped back to the dark of the tunnel, her eye caught by a slight difference in the colour of the wall plaster. She brushed away the dust slowly at first, then furiously.

At last! She stood back to examine the swirling depiction of Kallor. Unlike modern versions, his face was serene, almost kind. Her eyes travelled downward.

There it was.

Right in the belly of Kallor was a small eye.

The Iris sleeps within the belly of Kallor.

She ran her fingers over the eye and found that the iris was raised slightly. Excited, she pushed on the tiny stone panel. There was a groan as a series of weights moved inside the wall, then moments later, a door opened inwards.

She swung the glowmetal around in front of her and

cautiously stepped into the room.

After all the searching, the cryptic messages, she had finally found it.

The chamber was lined with chests and shelves. Glowmetals of every conceivable size, shape and nature were set across the walls and floor, each in its own stand of cast clearglass or polished wood. These were no useless trinkets. Each of these glowmetals were powerful devices, handed down for hundreds of years in secret within the Cintros line. Myan had hinted at them, but never would she have dreamed there were so many. The name of each glowmetal was written on its stand in large Cioan glyphs.

Below each stand was also a leather-bound manuscript. Ellen slipped *Bluefire* into a torch-ring and picked up one of the books, opening the mought clasps with feverish excitement. Each page of supple vellum was covered with ancient Cioan text, the flowing glyphs inscribed with impressive artistry. The manuscript described the characteristics and function of the glowmetal. One book for each glowmetal. They were priceless. Locked passages to great power.

With delight she deciphered the ancient Cioan glyphs. She replaced the book and scanned the shelf, her heart beating fast. All were in the ancient tongue. Hungrily, she read the names on the spines. *The Nature of the Fire*. *The Matrix of Shadows*. Irreplaceable texts on the art of Sorcery.

Here was embodied the lost knowledge of a secret art, and ancient Cioan was the key. Silently she thanked her father, at last understanding his insistence on Cioan scholarship.

She heard a whisper.

Ellen snatched the platinum glowmetal from its ring, her heart thudding as she turned towards the shadows.

A doorway!

Beyond it was darkness.

Ellen checked her glowmetal. Its bands of light were swelling, returning to their natural size, a sign that it was losing its stored power. It would soon need to be recharged with the Fire, but not yet.

Carefully she moved through the ancient arch, conscious of

her lack of weapons.

The sphere of blue leapt into the second room, dragging Ellen with it. The chamber was circular, the dark sunken floor carved out of the island's heart-rock. In the centre was a large mosaic, its thousands of facets gleaming like polished gems in the light. It was a pentagon, each of its five segments bearing an identical swirling hurricane of flame, smoke and fire. Each of the five whirlwinds tapered towards the centre, linking together to form a single shape.

The picture seemed to represent something just on the edge of recognition, vague yet powerful. Primal. The hairs on her arms stood on end.

'Who's there!' she demanded, her voice loud in the confined space. The room appeared empty, yet she knew the labyrinth well enough to know that someone could be lurking behind a concealed panel.

She edged further into the room, alert for any sound that would give away the intruder; the shuffle of a shoe, the scrape of a drawn blade on stone. She waited for long minutes, but the silence was total.

Ellen circled her shoulders, trying to lose some of the tension there. She drew in slow, even breaths. Perhaps she imagined it; perhaps the sound was simply the echo of her own breathing made strange by the small chamber. Slowly she examined the room, trying to find signs of another entrance. Nothing. She was alone.

As she neared the closest tip of the pentagon, she noticed that a short five-sided column, around a cubit in height, was set into the mural. She followed the outside perimeter of the pentagon with her gaze. An identical column had been set into a matching depression at each of the five points – except one. Here the column had been removed, the depression a gaping hole. She stopped on the threshold, her foot poised to step onto the glittering tiles.

As though through a mist, she saw the Iris, the great eye at the centre, the point that linked each of the five, identical designs. The eye of those five hurricanes consisted of fire and flame. It glared with malevolence. She cried out, her stomach clenching with sudden nausea. How had she failed to notice it? The Iris' presence dominated the whole room.

She felt blood tricking from her nose and wiped it away.

Her father must have removed the final column to break the symmetry. Instinctively she knew it would be foolish to replace it. The Temple of the Iris clearly possessed great power and would be beyond her ken until she learnt more. Ellen fought to contain her fear. She had found the Temple and was one step closer to fulfilling her father's dying wish. It would be much harder to find the Scion.

She turned to leave the room. Then she heard it again – a faint whisper, sibilant, echoing at the edge of her hearing. There *was* someone in the Temple. She spun around, holding the torch out in front of her to face the Iris, expecting to see someone standing there, perhaps emerging from a panel she had missed. She reached for the Fire, ready to move, to fight. . . yet once more the small room appeared empty.

The Iris was swelling, shivering with power, filling the room. The Iris *itself* had seen her. She quickly backed out of the Temple, shaking as she leant back against the wall of the first chamber. Without warning, her glowmetal gave out a last flare of blue then faded into dullness. Ellen gasped. The dark engulfed her greedily, the glowmetals like multi-coloured embers around her.

Her breath came in ragged gasps, her ears singing as blood pounded through her brain. Coming from the brightness of her glowmetal torch, she was blinded, unable to see anything in the dim light of the stored glowmetals. She tried to form a matrix in her mind, for an instant paralysed with indecision. Should she form a Shield? Recharge the glowmetal? Draw on the pure Fire?

Ellen tried to draw out the Shield matrix in her head, a spell that would easily protect her.

She heard a scrape, like a foot dragging across stone.

The matrix dissolved, lost in her churning thoughts. She was in the dark. Trapped in here with it!

She had to get out.

Anger surged through her. Fury that her own fears could overwhelm her so easily. She calmed her mind, opening the

Window, letting the Fire flow through her like a drug. The platinum crystal was now in its raw state, the tracework of blue light and the dull-silver metal existing in slumbering equilibrium.

Bluefire pulsed angrily as she forced it to accept the Fire, forcing the swirling blue light that threaded through the crystal to transform into metal, storing the power. Finally the crystal was fully metal. Once she ceased, the twisted glowmetal flared once more with an intense blue light.

Ellen advanced, once more examining the rooms. Empty. Clearly there was some magical power at work she did not understand. It was enough she had found the Iris.

She stepped outside into the tunnel and closed the panel, pausing in the dark of the corridor to collect her thoughts. Now the intensity of her fear seemed ridiculous. Was she a defenceless child? No. She was Ellen Cintros, trained Sorcerer and the next ruler of Athria. Taking a deep breath of the musty air, she followed the corridor back up towards the dungeons of the mansion, her tension easing as she neared familiar sections.

I found it! I found the Iris!

Something in the dust caught her eye. An old piece of cloth. She picked it up. A little girl's handkerchief, dirty with dust and musty with age. Ellen smiled as memories came flooding back to her.

Laughing, she sped through the mansion, her pursuers behind her. She rounded the stairs and fled deeper into the cellar, searching for a hiding spot. She was trapped. She could hear Halsur behind her, the five-year-old taking the steps two at a time.

'Ha, you're trapped now, Ella, you will be at my mercy!'

Frantically she looked for a place to hide, then she remembered the passages her father had shown her only months ago. *Never tell anyone about them, Ellen,* he had said, lifting her to his knee. *It will be our little secret. And never go in there by yourself.*

Ellen giggled as she ran to the wall, standing on a chair to activate the release. With a sigh, the panel slid across and she ran inside, locking it behind her. Suddenly it was dark and the darkness was frightening. She had beat at the door, finally running into the dark in panic, looking for the stairs that led to her father's study, the handkerchief falling to the dusty floor, forgotten.

Her father found her hours later, crouched in a corner of the labyrinth, her face streaked with dust and tears.

'Da!' she screamed as she ran into his arms. 'It was so dark!' she cried, terrified of her father's rebuke.

Instead, he took a small glowmetal out of his pocket and showed it to her. 'Put out your hand.'

Ellen stifled tears as he placed the small copper glowmetal on her palm, the red metal traced with threads of green light. 'It's pretty!'

Her father set her on the floor. 'Now close your eyes. Find the Window like we did before.'

Ellen channelled the Fire. Opening her eyes to see the copper glowmetal shining green without heat on her palm, illuminating the pride on her father's face.

For years they had shared a secret. She alone of the Cintros line had inherited the ability to wield the Fire. At one time, her father told her, all the Old Blood, the Suul, hereditary rulers of the Empire, had possessed the power. Each was a Sorcerer, practising their arts openly, working together in the pursuit of knowledge. Now many claimed the Suul title, but the Fire no longer ran in their blood. Only a handful remained, keeping their art alive in secret, fanning the flame of the ancient knowledge in their hidden enclaves as it guttered and threatened to extinguish forever.

Her father had shown her much, but in time she had surpassed him. The mysterious Erioth had come out of the Domains of the Verial to complete her training. The gentle, bird-like being lived secretly within the Cintros mansion for three years of intense study and startling revelation, finally returning to the unknown realms north of Kelas, beyond the Ranmyden range, his unspoken debt to Myan fulfilled.

With a sigh, Ellen came back to the present, opening the secret panel to her father's rooms. They would soon be hers, but she pushed the thought far from her mind, cherishing what remained of his presence. Soon, everything would change and she would keep the secret alone.

* * *

Hukum shrugged back his golden robe, freeing his heavily muscled arms.

Today was truly a day for rejoicing.

The news had just reached him. Finally, the last of the Sorcerers who defeated him at Raynor was dead. For years, the aging Sarlord Myan Cintros had defeated his efforts, working tirelessly to unite the fractured provinces of the fallen Empire; destroying his agents.

The massive stone door fell back into place with a boom, leaving his sanctum in darkness except for the soft light of a single glowplant. He was Sundar, supreme Sorcerer-Lord of the Eathal. Here in his sanctum, isolated from the factions of the Circle and the demands of rule, he was free to think, to plan.

He drew on the Fire.

At his touch, a single glowmetal blossomed into light. Scattered across the table were his original plans for the assault on Raynor thirty years ago. He had been so close to shattering the empire of man forever, yet in the end he had been thwarted.

Soon he would finish that task. Within a year, he would lead the Eathal legions across Kelas once again, and the Caverns of Maht would reveal their full strength at last.

Then, as now, Athria had remained a thorn in his side. The supply of troops and provisions from Athria had been a crucial factor in Raynor's past victory. In any second assault, he would be faced with the same problem. Athria, protected by a strong navy and safe from direct assault by land-bound forces, had to be neutralised. Yet Myan, most powerful of the remaining human Sorcerers, had always been one step ahead.

Now, at last, he was dead.

Dead!

The Brotherhood, with Raziin and his mercenaries leading their forces, would be unstoppable. Not a single Sorcerer remained in Athria to oppose Raziin. The Temple would shed no tears for the passing of the Cintros. As they had throughout Kelas, they would rapidly adapt to the new regime, thinking themselves secure in their positions.

Never before had Hukum had a tool like Raziin. Vicious. Powerful. Dangerous even to him. But the delicious irony! To have the son of Leith Cinnor, one of the three human Sorcerers to defeat him at Raynor, under his very power!

As the time drew near for the final advance into Kelas, strong factions were growing against him, vying for leadership. Purists who had criticised him from the outset for training the traitorous human – for using human agents at all. Yet if he did not, how could he have penetrated the courts of Kelas to such devastating effect?

Still, they had a point.

Humans.

The thick, grey skin of his mouth curled in disgust.

While the Sardoms and the Yasser States slept, their power all but gone, he readied his armies for the final conquest. Most of their own Sorcerers lay dead, persecuted by the arrogant, power-hungry Temple of the Sisters and their red-robed Templemen. *Fools. Too late they will see their own mistakes.*

The human Emperor Carris enslaved a generation of Eathal to build Raynor. Hukum would put the humans in chains for eternity, serving and sweating for their Eathal masters until the suns no longer rose.

He swept aside the old maps, drawing his new battle-plans towards him across the table. He viewed them with satisfaction.

Yes, today was a very good day.

Chapter Four

Cedrin's back ached with the weight of his pack.

He estimated Raziin to have only two score men. They were well outfitted, equipped with greatscythes and secure against the cold in their heavy insulated leathers. One of the black-clad warriors had been left to direct each division, while Raziin rode ahead on amelak with his lieutenants, the Brotherhood leaders and the assanni. The sturdy, long-necked animals with their woolly coats might be slow but they could easily outpace a marching line. Cedrin had long ago lost sight of them along the coast. The rest of Raziin's men rode behind them as a rearguard.

No chance of slipping away until dark, and even then they would be risking the Heat. Raziin and Dresil had planned well, keeping the calvanni spread over the force, watched constantly by their own men.

Cedrin ground his teeth until his jaw ached.

Trapped.

Now only a mistake on the part of the Pirate's Mouthpiece or the leader of the Cioan mercenaries would give them the opportunity to escape this madness – and judging by their efficiency so far, that seemed unlikely.

They arrived at the Cove just before first light, forcing a breakfast of stale bread and cheese into their uneasy stomachs under the watchful eyes of the assanni before crowding back into the longboats.

A heavy mist rose with the dawn, hanging like a cold, silver blanket above the grey swell, engulfing them as they rowed towards an unseen beach.

On the shore, Raziin's men formed them into divisions of thirty men and quickly marched them up a jagged stair cut into the dark, wet stone of the cliff. At the top, they set out along a path that wound east along the coast towards Athria. At first the mist still blocked their view, but they soon had their first glimpse of the Cove, a natural harbour concealed from the sea by the narrow channel at the entrance. The maintops of the three pirate-traders were just visible above the mist as they rode at their great round-stone anchors.

As the day drew on, the mists cleared to reveal hundreds of men marching across the bare expanse of the coast.

In the clear light of day, Cedrin could see the 'warriors' were sailors armed with an assortment of scythes, clubs, poles and knives; all fiercely loyal to Dresil. They marched without discipline in ragged groups. In contrast, there were few calvanni and assanni, and Cedrin guessed they must have highly specialised tasks to perform. *How does Dresil think these scum will take Regent's Hill, even with the element of surprise?* The Suul controlled almost a legion of guardsmen trained in the scythe and spear – over ten thousand men stationed around Athria and on her fleet. Dresil and Raziin may overcome the thousand or so that held Regent's Hill and the Wall of Sorrows, but the Brotherhood's hold would be temporary at best.

The eclipsed suns crept into a pale grey sky, their light bereft of warmth. It was a bleak day, the landscape washed of any colour. Even the wind had died. The red sun Uros had grown almost as large as Larus over the last two and half months and now stood before her yellow sister, blocking her life-giving warmth. The eclipse itself would last for little over a day – yet the intense cold would continue for days afterwards, then the storms would begin.

Yet for now, all was still.

No gulls wheeled in the breeze over the rocks, no raptors circled the skies. All were gone, sheltered safely from the cold. Only the timeworn boulders and softened hills of the southern Athrian coast remained to mock them. Anything living had fled.

Like any sane being.

Cedrin pulled the heavy woollen robe closer to his body.

Each of them struggled with the rise of the Heat, the survival mechanism triggered twice each year by the cold. It could save your life, but they were all familiar with the searing agony of its fever and the consuming hunger that followed – hunger that could send you mad if not appeased. The Heat was like a caged beast – once let loose it was infinitely harder to subdue. Keeping warm, and indoors, was usually enough to stave it off. However, once it took hold, the hunger became overpowering. If not fed, the Heat would continue to burn away the body, leading to agony and death. Only those with the strongest of wills, and blessed with a good constitution, could stop the Heat once it had started. Once it took hold, all inhibition fled.

Those on the streets without shelter were often doomed. The weakest beggar could become possessed with manic strength, killing for the merest morsel until he dropped. Riots, murder, madness. Everyone with sense stayed indoors and prayed to Larus for the demons of Uros, unleashed in their time of strength, to pass them by. Protective signs were painted on the lintel post: incense burnt to Larus the Protector. Those huddling within the warmth of sanctuary would wait for Larus to triumph, her pure golden disk finally winning free of the hunger of Uros.

Marken marched beside Cedrin in the centre of their division. Skye and Jaso were near the front with some Athrian sailors they knew. Banis was behind them in one of the last divisions. Cedrin had not forgotten the look of fury in his eyes after the death of Cephor, and it worried him. He did not want any more of his friends to die.

'You know, Cedrin,' said Marken, 'any wealth you derive out of this will soon be stripped away from you on the karass board.'

'Ha! The voice of overconfidence. You have a short memory, my merry trader. Your coins jingle nicely in my purse.'

'Live with success while you can, my friend. I sense the approach of luck.'

Cedrin laughed harshly. 'Your senses are certainly well developed, all I can sense is danger.'

'Luck is where you find it.' Marken looked up at the bleak

sky and smiled, although his forehead was creased with tension. 'What do you think Raziin intends?'

Cedrin squinted thoughtfully along the line of marching seamen. In a game of karass, they would be the sacrificial pieces, the unskilled front line. If so, who were they preparing the way for? And what was the calvanni's role and that of the assanni? He shook his head, weary of trying to reason the problem.

'Who can say? I'll tell you one thing for certain, Raziin and Dresil intend to get out of this alive – and rich,' replied Cedrin.

They marched on through the morning, then stopped for a brief lunch of salted fish and ship's biscuit beside the cliff-top path, sheltering behind a stand of boulders. The mercenary who led their division walked ahead to confer with Raziin, leaving them to rest.

A sailor called Rel, the second mate of one of the traders, emerged as the leader of the seamen in their division. He sported a well-made staff of solid mought and wore the discomfort of Storm Season easily.

Skye and Jaso had wandered to the cliffs and were watching the sea, rapt in some private conversation.

Rel dominated the conversation during the break. He abused his men continuously, trying to provoke them with course humour and wickedly barbed taunts. It seemed they were well-used to his treatment, all remaining silent and resigned as they ate their rations.

Getting no reaction, Rel turned on Marken. 'What about you, piss-skin, are you a golden fairy, eh? You like it on your knees like those Northmen?'

Marken fixed his eyes on Rel and smiled. 'No more than you sailors, eh? Out to sea with no women.' Marken paused, as though he had just seen something of tremendous interest in the second mate. 'In fact, you don't fancy me, do you, Rel?'

The sailors exploded with laughter for a moment before hastily growing silent and looking away as Rel glared at them. The mate's knuckles grew white where they gripped the staff.

'Now don't tell me, goldy, that hair is a wig, right? I seem to remember one of the whores on the docks losing a wig. She soaked it in harena piss for three days just to get the colour right.'

The sailors burst into another chorus of laughter, Cedrin joining them. It was not often someone gave Marken a run for his money.

Marken smiled, his eyes sparkling. 'Tell me, Rel, how did the amelak survive after you removed your face from its arse?'

The laughter began again but ceased abruptly when Rel surged to his feet, his face livid. 'You think you're so smart in your perfumed silks!' Rel swung the staff towards Marken and, with a click, released a lanedd blade that shot out from the end of the haft, turning the weapon instantly into a scythe.

The blade hovered inches away from Marken's throat. He froze, a piece of fish halfway to his lips.

Cedrin got to his feet, slowly. 'Put that up, Rel, before we all end up stuck with an assassin's dart.'

Rel fixed Marken with a triumphant gaze. 'Not so smart now, are you pretty-boy? Want a scar across that smooth cheek, eh? Your little faggots won't kiss you then, will they?'

Marken tensed, ready to grab the scythe. Cedrin caught Marken's eye and shook his head slightly. Rel would back off; he had to. To kill Marken would set the seal on his own death warrant.

Marken smiled at Rel, his unwavering stare filled with amusement.

Rel's hands shook with rage. 'What's the matter, goldy, lost yer tongue? Don't you worry, I've killed plenty of piss-skins in my time. You should have heard the bitch scream when I took this scythe off her then gave her some. Eh?'

Marken continued to smile back at Rel, undeterred by his taunts. Then Marken looked down at the scythe. His face twisted in fury.

There was a blur of motion, and the scythe was in Marken's hands, the butt striking forward to slam into Rel's unprotected solar plexus. The sailor collapsed forward, rolling to his side. Marken flipped the scythe and stepped in, laying the blade at Rel's throat, the lanedd beginning to draw blood.

Marken's eyes glowed with hatred and lethal desire.

He was going to kill him!

No! Cedrin cared nothing for Rel, but Marken would die in turn at the Brotherhood's hands.

Cedrin dived desperately, knocking Marken back as the blade surged forward, missing Rel's throat and slicing his ear.

Rel cried out.

Marken locked the scythe blade into the haft with an expert twist. Cedrin watched him warily, ready to block off Rel with his body, but as suddenly as it had come, the savage hatred was gone. In its place was a familiar smile.

'He almost cut his own throat, ami. It was instinct. Instinct.'

Cedrin nodded and turned away from Marken. It was more than instinct. Marken had paused, his eyes had burned to kill and the blade had slid home. One fraction of a second later and the seaman's throat would have been sliced wider than the Yasser delta.

Rel struggled to his feet and staggered to the far end of the camp. His eyes were wide as he looked back at Marken, his trembling hand on the haft of his belt knife.

Marken made himself a pipe of tobacco and drew silently on the aromatic weed, his eyes on the sea. He held the scythe-staff across his knees and looked down periodically at the haft.

Cedrin left him alone.

Could Marken have possibly fought Rel for the weapon? No. Impossible.

They finished the meal in silence and were soon marching again. Just before dusk they arrived at a long, sheltered valley. A fast-flowing stream cut through it to the sea, running parallel to its steep sides. Advance groups had prepared fireplaces and tents, and they eagerly built a fire and jostled for a place around the open hearth while cooks from the ships prepared hot stews and soups.

When they had eaten and cast off the chill, Cedrin and Marken gave up their place at the fire, braving the bitter cold to skirt the defences of the camp, the possibility of escape always in the forefront of their minds.

They circled around the guttering camp fires, climbing the narrow sides of the valley until they had almost crested the ridge. They froze when they saw two of Raziin's men standing guard duty on the rise, the warriors shuffling and stamping their feet in silence, listening and watching, their deadly twin-bladed greatscythes loose and ready. They tried to creep around them, but found sentries had been posted at regular intervals along both ridges.

They moved deeper inland.

They were almost on the black-garbed warriors before they saw them – standing still and silent in the reflected warmth of a concealed fire. Now that Cedrin knew where to look, he could see the glow of the fire on the rocks nearby, the flames themselves hidden by a natural depression. That way was blocked as well. Raziin and Dresil had them penned in.

Dispirited, the two calvanni retraced their steps, following the stream to the cliffs, where it cascaded down in a spectacular waterfall. Unseen in the darkness, the sea thundered on the rocks below.

They sat and rested, the clear sky above swollen with stars.

Cedrin took a measured swig of bakta from his flask, handing it to Marken.

'Ah. Thank you,' said Marken.

'Why did you attack him?'

'Why shouldn't I?'

On edge from the threat of the Heat, he turned on Marken. 'What's wrong with you? Are you that much of a fool? Rel could have killed you. It was only with the luck of Uros you got that scythe away from him. You were insane to risk it.'

Why did you almost kill him? What are you hiding?

Marken lifted the mought haft of the scythe. 'Do you really want to know why?' His voice was edged with anger and desperation.

Cedrin had never seen him like this.

'This is why,' said Marken, pointing to a crest that looked like a dull smudge of grease under the moonlight.

'Are you serious? You fought him for a scythe?'

Marken rubbed his sleeve violently over the haft. Cedrin tensed to dodge aside, thinking for an instant Marken had gone over the edge; but instead of lashing out, Marken held up the weapon.

In the light of the quarter moons, Cedrin could see the crest. Three golden towers on a background of yellow and blue. He leaned closer. 'A crest. I don't understand.'

'It's not just *a* crest; it's my crest. My family's crest.'

Cedrin laughed, incredulous. 'But you're Macil's son – a trader's son – what are you talking about?'

Marken lowered the scythe. 'I'm no trader's son. I'm Suul, Cedrin. Suul.'

Cedrin was silent, his mind inexorably fitting the pieces together. Marken did not look like a half-breed, he was full blood Cioan. Cedrin had always suspected there was something Marken was not telling him about his history, yet until now – despite the high level of trust between them – he had never been able to get him to open up.

'My father was a Suul Lord at the court of Althar. Sanil Kye. I am Marken Kye, his fifth son. His only living son.'

Althar had been razed to the ground by the Eathal thirty years ago and remained inside their territory.

Marken looked into the night sky, his face pale under the moonlight. 'He and my three oldest brothers stayed to fight the Eathal advance and perished with the city. My mother, sisters, six year-old brother and I left in a galley bound for Raynor, with a group of family retainers. We docked at the capital, but then it was decided to continue on to Athria when it was certain Raynor would soon be under siege. On the Sea of Mists, our ship was attacked by pirates. My mother and family were killed, the ship sacked and left to sink.

'It was one of Macil's trader-captains who found the galley drifting. My sister Aleshel had hidden with me in the hold. I was a baby, Aleshel only three. Neither of us was old enough to receive the Suul mark. Aleshel had a hastily written letter from our mother clutched in her hand, pleading with whoever found us to take us in. The ship was a wreck, stripped and slowly sinking, yet Macil took us anyway.'

Marken turned to him. 'The pirates took no prisoners. The bodies were left dismembered and mutilated. There is only one place Rel could have gotten that scythe. From that ship.'

Cedrin was drawn to Marken's gaze. Cedrin had never seen

those eyes burn with such passion, such strength of purpose. He realised Marken's flippant mannerisms were a shield. Within, he was driven. Cedrin's respect and affection for him deepened.

'Pirates,' said Marken, his gaze becoming heavy and lost, like a wounded raptor falling through a mist, waiting to strike the ground.

Cedrin's mind returned to the fight, just before Marken's explosive attack. *You should have heard the bitch scream.* He could have sworn the scythe *leapt* into Marken's hands.

'If we get out of this alive, I'm going to leave the Brotherhood. Leave Athria,' said Marken. 'Until now I have been stuck with Mat, trying to save enough to buy a Suul title, but it's not worth it. Smuggling is one thing – piracy, treason, attacks on the Suul themselves?' Marken shook his head.

Cedrin gripped Marken's shoulder. 'You know I have nothing else, ami, I can't leave the Brotherhood. But I'll do my best to see you out of it safely; that's a promise.'

'What will you do?'

Cedrin smiled. 'The sixth-degree. I have the numbers behind me. This time I'll be ready for Mat, and then I'll be Mouthpiece. In ten years, I'll be a wealthy man. Maybe even a Mask.'

Marken nodded, returning the grip. 'You're a good man, Cedrin. You deserve a higher station in life than dealing with these low-born scum. Come with me to Kelas.'

Cedrin winced at Marken's arrogance, then shook his head. 'No, my destiny is here.'

They released their shoulder grip and tightened their robes against the cold.

'I'd give six rubies for a good fire now!' said Marken.

They started back towards their fire. As they approached the outskirts of the camp, they glimpsed a ghostly figure.

They moved closer, stepping between moon-shadows, their boots making soft cracking sounds on the frosted ground.

It was Raziin.

He was stripped to the waist, his torso of solid muscle webbed with scores of military tattoos and jagged scars. He moved with machine-like precision, the greatscythe weaving a complex pattern, its arcs counterpoint to killing thrusts. They could see the Heat rising from him in steaming waves.

For long minutes they watched, the only sound Raziin's grunts of effort and the whistle of the twin lanedd blades as they spun in deadly circles. Abruptly he halted, locking the blades back into the haft with a savage twist of the mechanism. He looked directly at them, his pale golden eyes catching the light of the twin moons.

Cedrin sensed something else. Both familiar and alien at the same time. Despite the deep shadow in which they hid, he felt exposed and vulnerable. Cedrin tapped Marken on the shoulder and they carefully retraced their footsteps.

Raziin's eyes uncannily traced their path through the dark.

As they reached the circle of camp-fires, they could hear his laughter behind them in the darkness. Cedrin's heart leapt with a jolt of fear.

They headed for the closest fire, eager to shed the chill, and found Banis talking in low tones with a group of eleven other calvanni. They grew silent as they approached. Banis nodded gravely to Cedrin in greeting.

'Any way out of here?' asked Banis.

Cedrin scanned the group, wary of betrayal. Most of them had supported him in the Circle more than once.

Cedrin shook his head. 'Raziin's mercenaries have the place sewn up tighter than a sea-shroud.'

'We have talked this out, Cedrin,' said Banis, looking around the group. 'We are willing to fight our way out of here.'

Banis and his small cadre looked at Cedrin expectantly, waiting for his lead.

'I like this as little as you do, believe me, but the time isn't right,' said Cedrin. 'We can't take on Raziin's men.'

They sat in grim silence and watched the fire.

'When the time *is* right. Let us know,' said Banis.

Cedrin was both heartened and terrified by their trust in him. What if he led them out of here? What then? Would they have to fight the whole Brotherhood? He looked across the assembled men, noting their faces. How many would survive this bloodbath and how many could he keep alive?

'There may not be an opportunity before the battle – Raziin's men are too disciplined. But once it begins it will be a different story. If you can, break from the main force and make your way back to the Brotherhood caverns.'

The men nodded to each other in agreement.

'We'll wait for you there,' said Banis.

Cedrin and Marken went in search of their own fire. Out of habit, Cedrin scanned the camp. His heart raced as he saw Raziin watching them from the ridge above the valley, talking with two of his sentries. How had he tracked them in the darkness?

They reached their own hearth and jostled to the fire's welcome warmth.

'What manner of man is Raziin?' asked Marken.

'Crazy. . . and deadly,' replied Cedrin.

One of the seamen turned from the fire and looked through the dark at Raziin and his men. 'I say he's a demon. He has a face like a corpse.'

'No, he's a man alright, he's just possessed by a demon,' said a familiar voice fading into laugher. Skye moved around the fire towards them. 'Cedrin, where have you been skulking off to, eh?'

Marken laughed. 'Devout men need time for contemplation, my son.' Raising his hands, he gave Skye a blessing in ancient Cioan, feigning a solemn expression.

Skye bowed. 'Thank you, father Druid.'

Marken had spent almost two years as a novice in the Temple of the Sisters after Macil's death, learning the Druidic arts of Essence. He was an apt pupil, but by his own admission the life proved too frugal for him. It was after this that he approached the Brotherhood with his scheme.

They passed jibes and stories between them for a time, then a dice game started. Seeing there was not enough room around the fire, Cedrin, Marken and Skye gathered next to a large oval boulder nearby that had caught some of the heat from the open hearth. Jaso stayed by the fire, drinking bakta and joining his voice to the crowd's at each fall of the dice.

'What do you know about Raziin, Skye?' asked Cedrin, his hands buried deep within his robe.

'There are many stories. It's hard to separate fact from fiction.'

'I know about him. As much is there is to tell,' said Marken.

'Well, go on.'

'He is the second son of the Sarlord of Armon, Leith Cinnor. A twin by birth. His sister Razell lives in Armon with the eldest son, Ralin. Ralin is the Sarlord now.

'For some reason Raziin fell out of favour with the old Sarlord when he was still a youth. He was forced into the military to fight on the front lines on the Upper Plains against the Meadrel tribesmen.'

'Almost a death sentence,' said Skye, with a fierce grin. The thickset calvanni was half-Meadrel himself.

'Exactly, but he didn't die. He thrived as a warrior. Over the years, he was field promoted to Captain. He would have gone higher but his father prevented it.

'Soon he began to gather a following of highly placed warriors, Generals and Captains who believed he should sit on the throne, not Leith or Ralin. Fanatics who wanted Armon to march into Kelas and conquer the fallen Empire.

'So they struck and almost succeeded. Raziin killed Leith and brought an army to the gates of Osellen, but Ralin led the loyalists to victory. Scores of conspirators were executed, hundreds of officers sold into slavery, but in the end, Raziin and his close aides were banished. They have been mercenaries ever since, drifting between the wars of Kelas like the fiends of Kallor.'

'Men with nothing to lose,' said Skye.

'As if they weren't dangerous enough,' said Cedrin.

Cedrin probed Marken further on Raziin and his men, then they all shared a pipe of tobacco and speculated on the forthcoming attack. The camp was quietening, the noisy groups now sleeping in tents or close-packed around their hearths, the coals glowing with precious heat.

Cedrin drew on the pipe, staring into the clear sky. There was never a shortage of wars in Kelas. Since the fall of the Empire, the provinces had eagerly sought independence, the first border conflicts beginning even while the Eathal laid siege to Raynor. Not a glorious end to an Empire that had once ruled the known world, but then the end of Empire was never glorious.

Now Kelas was chequered with warring countries, from city-states to powerful Sardoms, each maintaining their own legions. The Imperial roads were full of bandits, and mercenaries drifted across borders. The Yasser States was all that was left of the old Empire. The three provinces bordered the Yasser river, bound together by the ever-present threat of the Eathal. And in the centre of the Yasser States, stood Raynor, the former Capital of the Bulvuran Empire. Its massive walls had turned back the Eathal. Like a bastion, it stood by the Yasser as though it still challenged the world.

The three stretched out on the rocky ground in the lee of the fire-warmed boulder. Above, the stars of Yos turned. The small moon, Rea the Runner, quickly overtook its brother Asic. Gradually the night grew colder and the sleeping men fought the rise of the Heat, many groaning as they lay in the grip of dark, Heat-spawned nightmares.

Through the night walked a pale apparition, welcoming the demons of Uros with a sensation akin to lust. His gaze fell on the sleeping figure of Cedrin, noting each of those with him through pale golden eyes that were predatory and without compassion. Then he was gone, swallowed by the dark.

* * *

The second day of Storm Season dawned even colder. There was no mist and a thick frost covered the grass. Larus had won free of Uros, but it gave them little cheer. The men mustered quickly, relighting fires and rubbing hands against the chill. Talk inevitably turned to the imminent attack and the riches awaiting them.

Cedrin stood quietly by the fire smoking a pipe, the talk surging back and forth around him.

Skye embarked on a fanciful tale highlighting his masterful skill with the calv.

'If you're so good, then why're you still only third-degree?'

asked Rel, sneering at Skye.

'Because I'm so fast, they can't see me,' said Skye.

The crowd burst into laughter.

Skye had speed and skill, but earning rank involved more than just fighting ability. To form the Circle of Blades, you had to have a following. Skye preferred to be led.

'Baah! No one is faster or tougher than an Athrian seaman,' said Rel.

The seamen gave a cheer, and Rel started boasting of his prowess as a fighter and the booty he would take from the Suul. Marken looked on with amusement.

During the night, one of the sailors had been taken by the Heat. He circled the camp-site like a ravening *palgur*, the big hunting cat of the steppes, waiting for the morning's baal broth to boil. His eyes were wild – fired with the exhilaration of the Heat – and he laughed at the men huddled around the fire. He had long ago thrown his robes aside, and his skin was flushed with the burning. Earlier they had given him the last of yesterday's stew and had watched him warily as he gorged himself.

The suns finally cleared the sides of the narrow valley, taking an edge off the bitter chill. Warmed by the broth, the calvanni threw back their hoods and moved away from the fire, both they and the sailors more relaxed in their own company. The sailors, in their woollen robes of grey, faded from sea and sun, now formed a solid mass around the hearth, all talking excitedly about the fight to come. In contrast, the calvanni seemed sombre in their new robes of dark brown and black.

A messenger entered the camp and made straight for the fire. Recognising him as one of the elite assanni that Dresil had surrounded himself with, the circle of sailors parted and grew quiet.

Cedrin tapped the ashes out of his wooden pipe, looking around at the calvanni. They regarded the approaching assassin with expressions ranging from suspicion to thinly veiled contempt, but kept their silence.

He was a thin man, his long face cut into grim lines. His grey eyes seemed so lifeless they could have been made of marble, yet a sharp intelligence lurked there. He casually warmed his hands over the fire, his eyes finally resting on Rel.

'What happened to your ear, Rel?'

'Cut myself shaving, didn't I.'

The assanni snorted. 'Where are the calvanni?'

Rel squinted at the assassin, a sly look on his face. The sailor brightened, his tone rising to gruff congeniality. 'Over there, my friend,' he said, waving at Cedrin's group.

The assassin gave Rel a cold smile then marched towards them.

'I'm looking for Cedrin, Marken, Skye and Jaso.'

'You've found them, assanni. State your business and be gone,' said Cedrin, glaring down at the assassin from his superior height.

'You've been summoned to the main tent. You are to follow me there. Now.'

His manner, and his assumption of authority, grated on Cedrin.

'Well? On your feet,' snapped the assanni.

Skye's hand rose towards the hilt of his calv. Cedrin caught the move and gave him a quick hand signal. *Not yet.*

'Lead the way, friend,' said Cedrin.

The assanni's eyes flicked between him and Skye. He turned and walked back the way he came, Cedrin and his friends following in his wake. The frost had disappeared from the grass and Cedrin loosened his robe. Cedrin had always known how dangerous and influential the assanni were, but up until now they had remained a much hidden part of the Brotherhood. It disturbed him to see them here, so openly part of this attack.

They wove through the camp to a marquee standing in the centre of the valley. The tent was of white canvas, with pale and faded geometric designs of blue-grey. Two of Raziin's men stood guard outside. It was surrounded by rows of smaller leather tents, each situated with military precision. Around them, Raziin's men lounged; many in conversation, some practising the greatscythe, others tending the fires set neatly beside their tents. They seemed to possess a sense of alertness, readiness, and their movements were sure and easy. None of them looked their way, but Cedrin was certain they were aware of them.

The assanni spoke in broken Cioan with the warriors guarding the tent, then waved them on. The black-clad mercenaries stood as fixed as statues, looking forward with unnerving intensity as the calvanni walked by.

They passed into an entrance chamber set with braziers of hot coals. The heat was stifling, the air filled with oily smoke, and they quickly removed their heavy woollen cloaks. Two assanni guarded the entrance to the inner chamber.

Cedrin was free of his cloak for the first time since they left Lookout Hill. It felt good to be dressed simply once more – leather leggings and boots, an open woollen shirt of coloured design over his harness. Skye and Jaso were similarly dressed, but Marken still wore his fine silken shirt. Conspicuous against the rough weaves of wool, it served only to make the golden-skinned Cioan look even more out of place.

From within they could hear the Mouthpieces talking with Raziin, the Northman's accent thick despite the years of his exile.

'Wait here,' commanded their assanni guide as he disappeared into the inner chamber. The talking ceased and a moment later the assanni reappeared.

'You may enter now.' The assanni looked at Marken as though he had never noticed him before, puzzled. He pointed at the staff in Marken's hands. 'Leave that.'

Cedrin led the way into the inner chamber.

Raziin was once more dressed in thick leather armour. He had somehow conquered the Heat, but his face betrayed strain. He watched them with interest as they entered, his brow creasing with curiosity as he took in Marken. Then his eyes met Cedrin's, and briefly there was some recognition.

Mat, Dresil and Tice were poised over a series of old drawings on vellum, each covered with fine detail. Kayleez was sprawled in a chair nearby, appearing bored. Skye and Jaso nodded to him and he acknowledged them with a wry smile. Stone was nowhere to be seen.

'That's the Wall,' whispered Marken.

Cedrin glanced down. He was right. They were sketches of the Wall of Sorrows. In the corner of each drawing the phoenix crest of the Bulvuran Empire showed prominently in coloured inks. The Emperor Odyss had built it eight hundred years ago after making Athria his vassal state. These looked old enough to be the originals.

Raziin turned to Dresil and waved at the calvanni.

'Are these the best you have?'

Mat fixed Cedrin with a triumphant gaze and answered for the assembled Mouthpieces. 'No better calvanni for the job.'

Tice swivelled his eyes towards Mat and laughed harshly. Dresil grimaced at Mat and Tice in annoyance. Kayleez looked straight at Cedrin, his smile cruel.

It was then that Cedrin realised why he and Marken had been chosen. Mat did not expect them to live. This was a neat way of removing Cedrin, his only threat to supremacy within his part of the Brotherhood. Banis had also been ready to challenge for the sixth-degree. *This whole force is expendable.* It was not just the sailors. They were all pieces to be casually discarded.

Raziin's mouth tightened in a grim line as he studied them. 'Do you know the Siren's Wail?'

'We know it,' said Cedrin, stepping forward. He had heard the legendary glowmetal sounded only twice before – its voice so powerful it made his very skull ache. Allowed to sing, it would rouse every fighting man in Regent's Hill in moments.

Raziin looked at him with a brief but intense gaze. He appeared eager for the conflict to unfold, but whether for personal gain or just so he could see some hapless enemy fall under his blade, Cedrin was not sure. Raziin continued, 'The Siren's Wail must be brought under our control quickly, and without anyone realising what we have done. For this, we must scale the Spire. Can you do it?'

'Of course,' replied Cedrin.

So that's why they need us. It must burn both Dresil and Raziin to have to trust us with this, yet they have no choice. Only the best calvanni could tackle something like the Spire.

'I'm surprised an elite mercenary group like yours does not

have expert climbers, Çinnor,' said Cedrin, his voice carefully neutral.

Raziin's eyes narrowed, but he did not take the bait.

The plan was beginning to come into focus. To take out the Siren's Wail, Raziin and Dresil needed calvanni who could climb a sheer wall and fight in a press once they had. Calvanni were expert fighters with the long knife, unbeatable in close quarters where the more unwieldy greatscythes were out of their element.

'So you understand the task?' asked Raziin.

'Yes,' replied Cedrin.

Raziin watched them carefully for a moment, then nodded. 'Good. Choose your equipment,' he said, waving at a pile of ropes and cloth-bound grappling hooks nearby, which had no doubt been lugged all the way from the city by Dresil's lackeys. 'We leave at sunset. Be here before then.'

Raziin turned back to the drawings that lay spread on the low table under the lamplight, falling back into conversation with the Mouthpieces.

'I take it we are dismissed,' said Skye.

They took what they needed from the pile, exiting the inner tent with relief. In the entrance chamber they dressed swiftly, eager to be away.

A few minutes later, Mat followed them into the entrance chamber. He faced them with the savage delight of a man who had bet on an arena fighting cock and now watched it rip the other bird to pieces. He approached with a swagger, deliberately making them pause in the heat of the tent.

Cedrin knew he had nothing to lose. 'Outside,' he said to his friends.

They looked at him with incredulous stares, but he urged them on. 'Come on, we're finished here. We don't have to listen to the yapping of Raziin's lap-dog.'

Lightly dressed, Mat could not follow without also donning heavy robes.

'*Uros-cursed mainlander scum,*' muttered Mat under his breath as they left. Mat shot a look back at the assanni guards, but they tactfully avoided his gaze.

Once outside, Cedrin turned and watched the flap.

'I hope you know what you're doing, my friend,' said Skye.

Cedrin clenched his jaw with determination.

Finally, hastily wrapped in a cloak, his face livid with suppressed fury, Mat emerged.

'. . . out into the cursed cold. I'll have you, by Uros' tits I will!'

Mat was brought up short, surprised to see Cedrin waiting for him. His faced creased in confusion.

'You three go on, I'll catch up,' said Cedrin. 'Got something on your mind, Mat?'

The four of them were needed. Cedrin knew that now. They were indispensable until the Siren was taken out of action. *Then* they were in real danger. For now, Mat would have Raziin to answer to if he interfered with them, or their task.

Mat walked up to Cedrin, his right hand inside his robe, no doubt gripping the handle of his calv, ready to draw. His face, twisted into a vicious leer, came to within a hand-span of Cedrin's.

'Watch yourself or you'll be bleeding, mainlander.'

For the first time since Mat had dragged them from the warmth of Lookout Hill, Cedrin felt free, released from the heavy restriction and uncertainty. At last he knew the rules of the game.

'You really are a floater, Mat. A parasite. A blood-sucking spawn of Uros herself. Why don't you run back to your masters, lap-dog? See what scraps you can get from the table.'

The Mouthpiece's jaw went slack with shock, his red-rimmed eyes glowing with fury. He swept out his calv, the naked blade gleaming wickedly in the light of the new day as he drew it back to strike.

The two black-clad guards at the entrance surged into motion, twin blades locking into place at either end of their heavy greatscythes as they took up position on either side of Mat, waiting for his next move.

Cedrin watched as a sudden realisation dawned in Mat's bloodshot eyes. His whole body shook as he fought to control his fury.

'Better put up that calv before they take you down,' said Cedrin grimly.

Mat had to use two hands to steady the calv so he could sheath it.

He looked back at Cedrin, his anger replaced with fear.

Still speechless, Mat stalked back to the tent and pushed back the flap. With parade-ground precision, the two warriors sheathed the blades of their weapons – each disappearing into the solid mought haft – and resumed their stations.

'Run away, old man. Before you piss yourself!' called Cedrin.

Mat halted in mid-stride as Cedrin's words caught him, then quickly disappeared inside the tent.

Cedrin let out a long sigh, turning to catch up with his friends. They had paused only a short distance away to watch the confrontation.

'I can't believe that ended without blood,' said Skye.

Marken looked at Cedrin and smiled. 'I had complete confidence in you, ami.'

Cedrin laughed, clapping Marken on the shoulder.

Around the camp, Raziin's warriors feigned disinterest, but they had no doubt watched the confrontation carefully, ready to step in if need be.

'You got the Heat, big boy?' asked Skye.

'No, Skye, just paying the first instalment on an old debt,' said Cedrin.

Skye shook his head and hefted the equipment. 'Cedrin, you have the luck of Uros.'

As they made their way back to camp, Marken and Cedrin hung back a little from Skye and Jaso, who had walked ahead, eager to return to the fire.

'What happened? What does it mean?' said Marken, his voice hushed.

Cedrin looked back at the marquee. 'It means we are safe for now. But after we take out the Wail – then we have to watch our backs. Do you think you could take out one of Raziin's warriors?'

Marken looked at Cedrin, suddenly serious. 'Not with a calv, but with this scythe I think I would stand a good chance.'

Marken lifted the scythe he had liberated from Rel. 'Or better still – this little garment accessory,' said Marken, taking a throwing knife from his boot sheath.

'Larus steady your hand,' said Cedrin. 'Be ready.'

They quickened their stride, cutting across the valley to their camp. Cedrin felt for his ring through the thick robe. *With luck. . . with luck we will escape the closing trap.*

They warmed themselves at the fire, and then passed the day in conversation and games. As the twin suns dropped to the western horizon, the whole army began to muster in the rising chill. Raziin's men handed out special rations of honey-cake and bakta to warm them on the march.

Cedrin watched the chaos with his friends, noting the occasional bare-chested man who had succumbed to the Heat. These waited with barely suppressed energy for the march to begin, demanding and receiving extra rations. They would be amongst the first to die. Although possessing strength and energy, they were supremely overconfident and would quickly give in to impulse. Such carelessness was deadly in a fight.

Just before sunset, the four friends, lugging their equipment and supplies, made their way to the main tent. Throughout the camp, fires were being extinguished and a great expectation filled the air. The tension and frustration of Storm Season were about to be given vent. These common men, some thieves and murderers, others devout followers of the gentle god Larus, all checked their weapons and thought of their foe. They were preparing to kill the Suul who had ruled them for millennia.

The marquee was being dismantled, Raziin's men mustering with efficiency and outward calm. One of Raziin's lieutenants, a huge man called Merceth, met them. The golden giant ushered them through the lines, six of Raziin's mercenaries taking position around them.

The suns fell. Torches wove through the dark like fire-flies, finally settling into ragged groups where they bobbed and flickered impatiently. Excited conversation and shouted orders filled the air as the commanders imposed order.

Cedrin and his friends quickly left the valley behind. They were soon marching over rough rock-strewn ground, cursing their heavy equipment as they struggled on. Eventually the ground levelled, and they realised they were on an ancient road, now overgrown. In the pale moonlight, it was almost indistinguishable from the grassland.

'What road is this?' asked Cedrin.

Marken paused to think. 'The old Lighthouse road.'

'The Lighthouse?'

Merceth turned. 'Be quiet,' he whispered harshly, the threat unmistakable.

Cedrin knew they would not use blades, but the solid mought of a greatscythe haft could still leave them bruised, bloody, and cowed; and they would stand little chance against seven.

They remained in silence for the duration of the journey. The stars burned bright and majestic in the clear sky, and Asic waxed low in the east. Despite the cold, the night had its own savage and desolate grandeur, and he was held within its grasp.

As the old road crested a rise, a great beam of light swept across them. From the ridge, they watched it follow an arc through the valley below. Looking back along the tight wedge of light, Cedrin sought out the source. There, sitting high on the coast, was the Lighthouse. A relic of the golden youth of the Empire, its massive mirror swept over the Sea of Mists; the golden beams welcoming traders who sped north from the southern Sardoms, their holds empty of grain, but full of gems and coin. By day it was the first part of Athria to be seen above the horizon.

Merceth pushed them harder now, casting his gaze above at the heavens as though measuring time from the dance of the stars. As they neared the slender tower, the beam flew across them with increasing intensity, until they had to shield their eyes.

The Lighthouse loomed larger until they climbed the final hill. Finally at their goal, they rested against the chill white stone of the building as Merceth disappeared inside. The door was guarded by Raziin's men.

The view was magnificent here. Cedrin wished he could see it during the day – and in more peaceful times. Behind them, a long line of torches signalled the arrival of the main force.

Cedrin stamped on the hard rock of the hill to keep his legs from freezing. *The tunnel must be here. It must be.* He looked towards Regent's Hill. From here he could see the lights of the Cintros palace and the many mansions inside the Wall of Sorrows. Suul, mourning the loss of their Lord, seemingly safe and invulnerable behind their wall.

The door to the Lighthouse opened and Merceth came out, his scarred face impassive as he stalked over to them, the greatscythe ready in his hands. 'Inside. Now.'

'Not one for words, is he?' asked Marken as they followed.

If Merceth heard him, he did not respond. Inside, they began to divest themselves of their heavy woollen cloaks, but Merceth motioned for them to leave them on.

Raziin and his lieutenants were there, surrounded by a score of assanni. They were standing with a tall man, his face completely concealed by an ornate full-face mask depicting the grim-faced god Kallor. The man looked across at Cedrin and his friends with an imperious gaze. His cloak was richly embroidered, the clothes beneath expensive. He smelt of perfume. *A Mask of the Brotherhood.* One of the unquestioned leaders who usually spoke only through their Mouthpiece. Cedrin's heart beat quickly. He was dressed like a Lord! A Lord of Athria . . . *a Mask of the Brotherhood?*

At a signal from the Mask, the assanni began to move. One by one they disappeared. The crowd thinned, revealing a narrow set of stairs. The tunnel.

Cedrin felt something heavy settle in the pit of his stomach. The assanni were being sent to their tasks. Death was on its way to Regent's Hill.

This was a game no longer.

The Mask followed the assassins into the darkness of the tunnel, flanked by four of Raziin's men. That they had been permitted to see this man, this Mask, did not bode well for their survival.

'Calvanni!' snapped Raziin.

Cedrin met his gaze. Pale gold. Hungry. Mesmerising like a snake. He refused to look away, resisting the negative charisma of the warrior, an aura that inspired fear and weakness. Their wills met, night and day, neither conquering the other. An instant dislike flared in Cedrin's chest like a small sun.

'The Siren must be taken quickly and completely. If not, each and every one of you will regret it,' said Raziin, his voice filled with deadly promise.

'We'll do our job, Cinnor. Make sure your own men do theirs,' said Cedrin, his voice hard and cold.

Cedrin swept out his calv, using it to gesture at the open tunnel. 'Let's just get this done.'

Raziin laughed. 'I love enthusiasm in my servants,' replied the warrior.

Cedrin grimaced. He knew he was a fool to provoke Raziin.

'You will not need your weapon. Yet,' said Raziin.

Cedrin slowly sheathed his calv, his three friends visibly relaxing as the lanedd blade slid home.

Raziin seized a torch and moved into the tunnel, flanked by Merceth and another of his lieutenants, Kyal, who shared Raziin's powerful frame. He paused at the top of the steps and motioned them to follow quickly.

Raziin was coming with them!

Cedrin had been planning for them to overcome four, perhaps five of Raziin's mercenaries, then somehow lose themselves in the battle, but fight Raziin himself? And his own hand-picked warriors?

Cedrin's mind flew back to the previous night. Raziin's laugh as he saw them through the dark, defying natural law.

A sheen of sweat formed on his brow, and he loosened his robe as they walked slowly to the steps. Below, the dark yawned, waiting to swallow them. He entered the honeycomb of caves beneath the Lighthouse, Marken, Skye and Jaso filing down behind him.

They soon left the cold behind, entering the temperate warmth of the upper caverns.

The tunnel was extremely well made, weaving between natural caves with vaulted ceilings and hewn passages as it sank into the heart of Athria. Torches burned along its length, revealing stained and faded murals and elaborate carved reliefs.

The attention to detail was astonishing. A window back in time to the height of the empire.

Cedrin quickly lost all sense of direction and stared out anxiously. Just beyond the circle of light things moved and called in the muted and unnatural voices of the underworld. Disturbed bats of all shapes and sizes squawked and fluttered above stands of lungii. A startled *jakka* fled deeper into the dark, away from the noise, giving a mournful cry at being forced away from its deathly pale pasture of lungii. These were unlike the tame passages of the Brotherhood. These caverns were wild.

Raziin looked back at Cedrin and laughed, the sound swallowed by the pressing dark.

Cedrin clenched his jaw and walked on. The real terrors lay ahead, in Regent's Hill.

Chapter Five

The calvanni and their Northmen companions spent long hours moving deeper into the heart-rock of Athria, the weird dance of the underground creatures continuing around them heedless of the Storm Season above. Finally they began to climb.

For the dark world, it was the time of crowded plenty. The millions of bats living in the caverns now stopped their nightly flights, living off stored fats. Their predators eagerly feasted, the fallen hardly missed among the throng.

In these wild caverns, teremb stalked their prey, and the calvanni remained wary. Deathly silent and swift, teremb could bring down a man easily, razor teeth snapping for the jugular. They were lean, intelligent creatures, and hunted by sound and scent. Although cautious of men, they had been known to attack during Storm Season, frenzied by the feast of sheltering creatures.

'Drakons, awake!' bellowed Raziin without warning.

Skye's hand jerked towards his calv and came back slowly. He smiled at Cedrin, shaking his head at Raziin's grim humour.

'No drakons have been sighted in Athria for four hundred years,' said Marken.

'Or none have lived to tell the tale,' said Cedrin grimly.

Drakons were massive armoured beings that lived deep in the lowest caverns, feeding off the heart-fire of the planet. They were still seen in the Mulisar and Ranmyden ranges on the mainland, emerging to hunt without warning, stretching their rock-like wings to the sky as they swept down to take their prey. Their breath could dissolve rock or set the insubstantial material of the upper world to instant flame.

Cedrin focused his thoughts. If Raziin and his closest aides chose to accompany them, silencing the Wail must be vital to the success of the attack. It also showed the arrogance of the three Northmen. Even outnumbered four to three by the best calvanni in Athria, they walked as though they were in the position of unquestioned authority.

Raziin's homeland of Armon was the only remnant of the ancient Cioan Empire that survived the scourge of Carris Cinanac. Perched high in the Ranmyden range, its very isolation had saved it. Carris, a powerful Anacian Sorcerer, had crushed the old order, declaring himself ruler of the new Empire of Bulvuran. Carris had never marched into Armon. Instead he accepted their submission and tribute. Now they gave tribute to no one. They were closed to the world, clinging to a culture that had vanished from most of Kelas thousands of years ago.

The ancient Cioans had come to Kelas before recorded history, building cities and temples along the length of the sacred river Yasser. From Ciofran-Ac in the broad delta to Osellen at the source, the river was life to them. Carris had broken the temples, defeated the cities and scattered the golden people. Some fled north into the dark wilds of Armon, others stayed to rebuild, as in Althar, taking oaths to new rulers, new gods.

Masonry lay tumbled on the path ahead, jagged remains of a crudely demolished wall that had once blocked the entrance.

Past the broken wall the tunnel narrowed rapidly, bringing them to a long chamber. The walls were constructed of smooth white marble blocks, which glowed yellow-gold in the torchlight. Regular depressions had been set into the right-hand wall. At first Cedrin was startled to see a neatly stacked pyramid of grey-white skulls. Beside them were a jumbled collection of bleached and brittle bones. Blinking against the bright illumination of the torches, his gaze slid across the sculptured shapes in the wall. Small creatures scrambled and scuttled within the display, startled by the light and movement.

They had emerged in a crypt. Around them stood the slowly decaying remains of generations of Suul. A single bat circled above their heads then fled deeper into the dark of the passage.

'Lovely,' said Skye.

'Charmed,' said Marken.

'Silence!' snapped Merceth.

Ornate caskets were set into depressions along the wall of the dead. Gems sparkled in the light, set deep within intricate designs.

Cedrin shivered as a cold gust rose about them, causing the torch flames to gutter and jump. Skye reached towards one of the caskets and ran his fingers over an inlaid pattern of rubies, his eyes gleaming.

Cedrin tightened his cloak and vowed he would not touch anything consigned to the world of the dead. He knew these crypts were a corridor to the underworld, built in caves so that the dead would not become lost as they struggled to find the entrance to Llors on their journey to meet Kallor, the Lord of the Dead. Some believed the dead would issue forth from these entrances during Storm Season, to claim followers for Kallor. A superstition reinforced by the fact that animals sometimes took refuge in the caves during the cold, and teremb would sometimes emerge to hunt in the dark depths of night, dragging prey into their deep lairs.

Rough-hewn stone rested behind the more recent dressing of white marble. Ancient designs were visible where the facade had fallen away. Marken ran his hands across it.

'It's ancient Myrian,' whispered Marken.

Cedrin nodded. The Anacian religion of the Sisters, brought by the Bulvuran Empire, had embraced and absorbed what had gone before. Myrian settlements had once dotted the coast of Kelas and remote islands such as Athria, and indeed most Athrians had Myrian blood.

The wall of the dead ended in a stairwell that led up from the crypt. At a signal from Raziin, the torches were extinguished and moonlight flooded down from above. The Northman motioned them up.

Cedrin carefully moved into the night, surprised to find the ground above the crypt sanctified with nothing more than an outdoor altar and simple shrine. The heavy stone block that had sealed the crypt lay casually discarded. Ten of Raziin's warriors guarded the shrine, silently standing at their posts, seemingly oblivious to the cold.

Statues of the Sisters flanked the altar on either side; dispassionate, detached from the affairs of the night. A lattice held a flowering vine, the petals and leaves folded against the cold to preserve moisture, yet still glossy with the natural oils that would keep them from freezing in the depths of Storm Season.

Cedrin and his friends looked out into the night, alert for any sign that they had been discovered, but all was quiet. Here the bitter cold was working in their favour. The gardens and gravel paths of Regent's Hill were deserted.

Raziin set out through the garden towards the palace, and they followed in a tight group, keeping to the shadows. The minutes passed and still they saw no one. Slowly Cedrin relaxed.

They were actually *inside* the Wall of Sorrows, the sacrosanct domain of the Suul. Until now, he had only glimpsed these palaces and mansions from the rooftops of Lookout Hill. From there, they seemed remote and unreal, yet now they glittered around him, the lamp-lit windows lined with precious clearglass.

Soon the Sarlord's palace towered above them, its massive outer wall a blunt refusal of carefully dressed stone. A second wall stood behind the first, rising even higher. The tall windows, now sealed against the cold, were worked with coloured designs and inset with gems. The roofs and swirling domes were constructed of brightly-coloured mought tiles – which Cedrin knew were hideously expensive. Thin towers soared, none identical in size or design, each constructed with a different colour of block. One squat tower was completely enclosed with clearglass, the panels dark and mysterious in the quiet night.

But one tower rose above them all.

The Spire.

Soaring from the inner wall, it rose to a height that rivalled the Lighthouse. It was constructed from dark stone, the sides sweeping in from the thick base to its narrow summit in a graceful curve. It was breathtaking.

'Hard to believe men built something like that,' said Jaso, breaking the spell.

Still safely concealed in the shadows, they followed the curve of the outer wall. Unlike a purely defensive fortress, the walls were not built as concentric circles. Instead they were nested ovals, connected at their apex by a series of stone platforms and walkways. They paused at that point, looking up at the sheer outer wall and the dizzy height of the Spire behind it.

The ascent seemed impossible.

But the Brotherhood calvanni were not daunted by a climb. This was their trade. Keeping their voices low, Cedrin rapidly conferred with Skye while Raziin looked on impatiently. They watched for sentries but there seemed to be no regular patrol. That was good. Both walls were lit at regular intervals by big oil-lamps, creating pools of dark and shadow – something they could exploit. There was not a guard in sight, but Cedrin thought, just for a moment, he caught a glimpse of a light moving on one part of the wall.

'Let's aim for the shadows,' said Cedrin, indicating a point some distance from where he saw the movement. Skye nodded, smiling broadly.

Alert for any sign of movement above them, Cedrin and Skye moved to the base of the wall. Marken and Jaso followed behind them with the rest of the equipment. Raziin and his warriors kept their distance, watching in silence.

Cedrin and Skye hefted the cloth-covered hooks. After a few experimental swings, they launched them up towards the battlements, Cedrin first, then Skye.

'Too high,' said Marken, his face pale with tension.

The heavy hooks fell rapidly from the top of the arc, striking their mark with pin-point accuracy.

Cedrin looked back at Marken with a raised eyebrow.

'Like swooping raptors to the kill,' said Marken, clearing his throat.

'You've forgotten my lessons already,' said Cedrin, recalling his efforts to teach Marken the cast with a wry smile.

Jaso and Marken came forward with the next hooks.

'Again?' asked Skye, taking his from Jaso.

'Aye,' said Cedrin.

They cast, all four calvanni watching spellbound as the hooks took flight, then fell, finding marks near the first with a series of dull thuds.

'OK. Let's move,' said Raziin.

They rushed forward, enmity forgotten. They were all intruders here, and all would meet deadly resistance should they be discovered.

Marken and Kyal were the first at the wall. They shimmied up the ropes as though the pit of Llors lay yawning beneath them. Seconds later, Merceth and Jaso were at the second set of ropes, the lithe Athrian quickly leaving the struggling giant behind.

Cedrin tied their equipment to two of the ropes and followed up, Raziin and Skye close behind him.

Soon all seven stood on the battlements of the outer wall, pressed into the shadows.

Cedrin looked around the wall. Four guardsmen huddled around a small fire some distance away, a pot of boiling broth the centre of their attention. One man leant forward to stir the pot. The glow of the fire seemed feeble in the pressing dark, yet it was these flames he had seen; and if not for that chance glimpse, they may have cleared the parapet to find scythes at their throats. He swallowed.

Raziin signalled Cedrin, Marken, Skye and Kyal to take them out of action.

Cedrin drew his calv. This was it. The beginning of the bloodletting. Many innocent men would die tonight in the name of Dresil's greed. He *had* to put it out of his mind. He had to survive. These guards would give him no quarter should they discover him. As soon as they had stepped up into the garden shrine, this moment was inevitable. He looked back to see Jaso fingering his calv with irritation. Raziin was mixing them up, keeping them deliberately off balance.

They moved swiftly and silently, flitting from shadow to shadow across the dark battlements. They quickly reached the fire and marked their prey. Cedrin said a quick prayer to Larus in his mind, asking that the man's soul would find a quick passage to the halls of Kallor, despite Storm Season.

Kyal leapt forward.

The calvanni came out the shadows an instant later. In one coordinated attack, their three calvs found their mark. The three guards were dead before they even knew it. Kyal took the last guardsman around the throat, trapping him in a lethal choke-hold.

The surviving guard began to struggle. Kyal twisted savagely, snapping his neck. He released the corpse, letting it fall to the stone. The Northman walked back towards Raziin, not sparing a single glance for his fallen foe.

Cedrin looked at the fallen men, their faces locked in expressions of shock and horror. He had killed before, in the heat of the fight, to defend himself, or in the Circle, but never like this.

Jaso appeared from the shadows, helping them to drag the bodies back into the darkness, away from the fire. Cedrin wiped the blood from his calv, again and again, a hot anger rising inside him.

'You all right, ami?' whispered Marken.

'No, my friend. I am not.'

Marken's eyes were haunted, lost. Cedrin knew that Marken had never killed before, even in self-defence. In the Temple, he had been under the tutelage of the Moon-Druids, the healers, helping the sick and infirm.

Cedrin sheathed his calv and gripped Marken's shoulder briefly. 'Let's get this done.'

As they moved back towards Raziin, Cedrin's thoughts went back to Banis and the other calvanni who had looked to him for leadership. Even now, they would be mustering to pass through the tunnel. With luck, they would all survive to reach the Brotherhood caverns.

The sudden deaths had brought back with startling clarity the peril they were in. Raziin and his men were killers. They cared nothing for life, nothing for them. Once they had taken the Wail, once the troublesome calvanni were no longer needed, they would turn against them.

Cedrin looked around at his friends. Marken he had warned, but Skye and Jaso suspected nothing of the danger.

Raziin was in whispered conversation with Merceth and Kyal. So far he had not seen them approach. It was an opportunity too good to miss. Cedrin motioned them to silence, and together they melted back into the shadows. Alone, Cedrin crept forward swiftly, using all his skill. Finally he was standing within earshot.

He heard Raziin laugh.

'. . . to die. The assanni, the calvanni, most of the sailors. . . small price to pay . . . Athria.' It was Raziin speaking, but Cedrin struggled to make out the words. Carefully he moved further in. He was close now. *Too close.*

Kyal, standing on the other side of Raziin, asked a question, his voice too low to hear.

'No. The new Sarlord could not let it be known he had resorted to such methods – not our little puppet. After the assanni have destroyed his rivals, after the calvanni have performed their tasks, after Dresil's force has all but taken the palace, he will swoop down, destroying Dresil's force and taking the Sardom. The surviving Suul will hail him as a saviour. Fools!'

Raziin looked up at that moment, directly at the shadows where Cedrin hid. Raziin tensed, and for a moment Cedrin thought he was going to attack.

'Where are the others?' demanded Raziin.

'Behind me.' Cedrin stepped slowly into the light.

'Bring them,' snapped the warrior.

Cedrin walked back to his friends, his mind reeling with what he had overheard. Not only were their lives in danger, Raziin planned to betray Dresil and the Brotherhood! There was nothing he could do about that now. His task was to keep them all alive.

When he reached them, he leant in close to Skye and Jaso. 'When the time comes, be ready.'

'When?' asked Skye.

'When the Wail is taken.'

Skye took Cedrin's wrist in a brief but solid grip. Cedrin had never felt life and friendship so precious – and so easily extinguished.

They rejoined Raziin and his men.

'Gather your equipment. Quickly,' ordered Raziin.

They ran along the battlements, then across the wide stone bridge connecting the inner and outer walls. They were soon below the wall from which the Spire rose. A solid wooden door was set into the wall, reinforced with mought strips. It was shut from the inside.

'They probably open it at the changing of the guard. There's no way we can force that. We will have to climb again,' said Raziin. 'Cedrin?'

He nodded, looking up the sheer face of the inner wall. Even here, on the battlements, it looked high.

Cedrin waved to his friends and they spread out their equipment, ready to make the cast. Once more, they picked the point where the shadows seemed deepest.

They heard the sound of marching feet on gravel and froze. Cedrin risked a glance over the edge of the bridge. A squad was passing through the courtyard below them, but the guards neither looked up nor loitered. Twice more they had to pause, waiting until the vast yard below was clear of troops.

Cedrin and Skye made ready. With a grunt they let both hooks fly, each describing identical arcs. Both found the tower top, but Skye's failed to grip. He hissed a warning, and they scattered.

The hook plummeted downward, shattering with a dull crack like breaking bone. Thankfully the cloth muffled the sound.

Cedrin walked to the inner edge of the battlement, looking down into the courtyard, then up to the top of the inner wall. Miraculously the sound had gone unnoticed.

Hastily they regrouped.

'There must be a thick wall. I don't know why it wouldn't grip,' said Skye anxiously, looking at the expectant faces. 'Someone will have to go up there.'

Raziin waved to Jaso. 'You are the lightest, and the fastest climber. Quickly. Take the hooks and rope with you.'

Jaso looked up at the rope, his face shining even whiter in the pale moonlight. Cedrin could tell he was terrified. The thin calvanni started gathering equipment, loading himself with hooks and rope, muttering a short prayer to Rea the Runner under his breath as he worked.

Cedrin smiled. Rea was the patron god of thieves. He had muttered a few prayers to Rea himself.

Jaso walked across to the rope dangling down the inner wall. The night was cold, the grey-black stone even colder. He looked up. 'It's a long climb. A long climb with all this extra weight.'

'You'll be fine. I'll steady the line for you,' said Cedrin, walking over to take the rope.

Jaso took a deep breath then surged up.

He began swiftly, but the extra weight slowed him. Cedrin knew how he felt, even on the climb up the outer wall his own muscles had threatened to cramp from the cold.

Halfway up, the hook at the top began to slip.

Jaso spun out of control. Frantically he reached a hand to the stone to steady himself.

Long seconds passed, all six of them watching Jaso as he dangled there, expecting him to come down on top of them.

'The hook has gripped again,' said Skye.

'Come on, Jaso,' said Cedrin. Long minutes passed, but Jaso remained motionless. Cedrin silently pleaded with Rea. *Don't desert him now!* But Rea was not listening. He had fled the sky.

After agonising minutes, Jaso started to climb once more, each movement smooth and measured. Finally he crested the upper battlements.

'Praise, Larus,' said Marken.

Raziin glared at Marken, his face twisted with anger. Cedrin's elation vanished. Raziin had sworn against Larus, that much was obvious. But what fool would make the goddess of life his enemy?

A few minutes later, Jaso threw two more ropes down to them.

'To the ropes,' barked Raziin.

First Marken and Skye, then Kyal and Merceth climbed up, leaving Raziin and Cedrin on the battlements, waiting for their turn.

Cedrin could feel the Arman's presence like an unwelcome guest. He turned to see the Northman watching him, his pale eyes deadly like a predator. Yet there was something more, something out of place. With a shock, he realised it was desire. He was waiting to kill, lusting to feel death beneath his blade.

Cedrin tore his gaze away and looked up at the ropes.

'They're clear,' said Cedrin.

They ran forward. Cedrin gripped the rope eagerly and began to scale the wall, putting every ounce of effort into reaching the top before Raziin. The Northman paced him effortlessly.

'Scared, calvanni?' asked Raziin.

With a surge of energy, Cedrin left Raziin behind, reaching the top a body length in front.

Cresting the rise, Cedrin pulled himself over the edge and looked around while he got his breath back. Suddenly he understood. The inside walls of the upper battlements were sloped to prevent grappling hooks gaining a hold. Jaso was standing nearby, his face ashen. He pointed at Cedrin's hook where it gripped the wall.

'Uros!'

The sharp edge of the hook was jammed into a timeworn crack in the smooth inside surface of the stone. It was the only thing that had given the first hook any purchase.

He looked back up to Jaso, who smiled. The lithe calvanni must have wept when he saw how little held his rope. It had been a miracle he survived the climb. Maybe Rea had heard their prayers after all.

Jaso had tied the other two ropes to the mought torch-rings that lined the base of the Spire. Nearby he could see an open doorway, unguarded, and sighed with relief. Cedrin levered himself over the wall and joined the other calvanni as they started drawing in the ropes.

Raziin cleared the wall. 'Leave the ropes. Kyal. Merceth. To me.'

The warriors ran to Raziin's side, unslinging their greatscythes and extending the wicked blades.

'Calvanni, you lead,' said Raziin, pointing at the open doorway.

The greatscythes were fearsome weapons, but within the narrow stairs of the Spire the calv would triumph.

Cedrin led his friends up the tightly winding stairs, expecting to be discovered at any moment, but the stairwell was deserted.

After an exhausting climb, they reached the top landing. The entrance to the Spire's top platform was only paces ahead, lit brightly from the tower top.

Still in the shadows, they swapped places.

Raziin and his men swept onto the roof, Cedrin and his friends following three paces behind to give them room to work.

He could see the Siren's Wail suspended above a huge mought trough of pitch, the big copper glowmetal shot through with glowing braids of green light. To the left, a set of narrow stairs led to an upper platform. Around the Wail, four guards gave a cry as the black-clad warriors came down on them.

Skye, Marken and Jaso rushed to join the fight, but Cedrin stopped them with a hand signal. With luck, the Sarlord's men would even the odds for them.

One guard reached for the torch to set the pitch on fire, but Kyal intercepted him. With a yell, the warrior sent his greatscythe whistling through a graceful arc that severed the guard's torch-bearing hand at the wrist. Kyal reversed the thrust and spun the weapon again. The severed hand fell to the stone only a split second before the guard's head flew from his shoulders. It sailed across the rooftop into the tar, sinking slowly into the dark fluid, the mouth and eyes still working.

Cedrin watched in disbelief as the deadly blades of the greatscythes fell. Three of the guards were down, severed limbs a ghastly rain on the stone, blood spreading over armour from opened throats.

The last man, a Suul, fought with great skill, his scythe matching Merceth's greatscythe blow for blow.

'Spare him, I beg you! You have bested us!' The voice came from above.

Cedrin looked up to see a Druid moving down from the

upper platform. He was a big man, but perhaps with more fat than muscle. His moon-face was smooth and unremarkable except for his golden eyes, which now showed disbelief and terror.

'Please, Lords!' called out the Druid.

'Stay out of this, Crephis!' yelled the Suul warrior.

Raziin took in the Druid with an amused expression. 'Step back, Merceth.'

The giant stepped back, his face expressionless.

Raziin turned to the man who had battled Merceth to a standstill.

'Good Sir, I can see you are a Suul. Lay down your weapon, and I will take you prisoner,' said Raziin, his face reasonable, his voice cultured and civilised as Cedrin had never heard it before.

The young warrior hesitated. Then, at a signal from the Moon Druid, he let the scythe fall to the stone. Raziin gave the barest hint of a smile then spun in place. The unnamed Suul had time only to flinch before his head fell from his shoulders. The body stood for a long moment then toppled like butchered meat.

The Druid staggered forward. '*Halsur!*' He turned on the Northman with fury. 'What manner of man are you!'

Raziin smiled and made for the Druid.

Cedrin had seen enough death. They had gained the Wail. He had to confront Raziin now.

'Leave him, Raziin,' said Cedrin, his voice low and menacing.

Kyal and Merceth spun to face him. He moved slowly towards them. Instinctively Raziin's men backed away, until a look from Raziin caused them to hold firm.

'What did you say, calvanni? A squeak, an Athrian squeak?'

Cedrin extended his calv, advancing towards the Druid and Raziin. Merceth and Kyal began to move, but Skye and Jaso were armed and facing them in the passing of a breath.

Marken stepped back into the shadows, reaching down to his boot.

Raziin regarded him with contempt. 'Do you really think you are a match for me, Cedrin?'

At the mention of his name, the Druid looked at him with

newfound curiosity.

Cedrin slowed his advance towards Raziin. He had no intention of getting inside the range of his greatscythe. *Come on Marken!*

Out of the corner of his eyes, he saw movement – Marken sweeping forward with his throwing knife.

That was it! He had won. With Raziin dead, the four of them could easily take Merceth and Kyal.

He looked back at Raziin, and his heart went cold. Raziin's eyes had begun to glow. *Sorcery!*

His cry of warning died on his lips as some intangible force leapt out from Raziin, surrounding him. Cedrin tried to move, but was fixed in position, his calv still poised for the attack. His eyes blazed at Raziin, but he could manage no more than a croak.

He swivelled his eyes.

Jaso was frozen in a stealthy attack on Merceth, knife poised inches from his chest. Marken stood like a statue, his right hand extended, throwing knife poised for the throw. Skye had paused in mid-stride, has calv at the ready. They were captured, and so simply.

Cedrin looked back to Raziin in mute defiance.

The Northman laughed, moving towards the Druid with casual ease. 'What exactly did you think you were going to do? Stop me? Stop this?'

Raziin shifted his grip and lunged forward at the Druid with the greatscythe as though it were a spear. The huge man could not escape the reach of the blade. It sliced through his woollen cloak, cutting deeply. With a savage twist, Raziin buried the lanedd into his heart.

The Druid sagged to his knees, blood flooding from the wound. Crephis gasped, then fell motionless to the stone.

Cedrin looked back to Raziin. His eyes still glowed with the power of his Sorcery, but now they contained something else – ecstasy. His face was twisted in bloodlust, that unholy desire growing by the minute. Cedrin suddenly remembered the look of disgust on Raziin's face when Marken uttered his praise to Larus. He was a worshipper of Uros! A devotee of the blood cult! That explained his mastery of the Heat.

He advanced towards Cedrin and lifted his greatscythe. For a long moment the blade hovered near his throat. 'No, not you. Not yet. First the vermin, then the pest.'

Raziin closed on Jaso. The small man looked up in fear, his knife still frozen in its death thrust. His mouth worked soundlessly.

Raziin stared at the small calvanni, his face twisted with contempt. 'It's all a bit unfair, isn't it? Perhaps, if you promise to run, I could let you go?'

The light of hope shone in Jaso's face.

Raziin suddenly laughed. He turned to Merceth. 'What do you think, my friend?'

The big Cioan remained impassive.

'I think not,' said Raziin.

Without warning, Raziin swung the greatscythe, the blade cutting Jaso from his groin to heart.

Almost casually, Raziin pulled his weapon free.

With a gasp, the calvanni fell to the ground. Released from the spell, his body shook and shuddered, his glazed eyes staring out without recognition. Within moments, his body had grown still, the spreading pool of blood around it steaming into the night.

Cedrin struggled to move, but was held fast. *There must be a way.* He could feel the force that bound him. It pulsed and shone, resonating, like a chant just beyond hearing. He focussed on it in desperation, his will channelled into finding a way to break the spell, to help him and his friends escape the slaughter.

Cedrin's vision turned black. Suddenly he was falling, spinning into an abyss. Naked, buffeted by a searing wind that came from everywhere. He looked into the dark and it deepened, becoming an emptiness so total his soul screamed in loneliness. As abruptly as it had come, it was gone.

He was in his old room above Tarral's glassworks. The bare boards of yellow wood stained with years of use and scrubbing, the bed tossed from last night's sleep. He looked around the room. There were no doors, only a single window, set in a triangular frame. He raised himself from the bed and drifted across the room. It seemed perfectly natural that he was floating, seemingly weightless in the air.

His foster-father Tarral had locked him in here, he was certain of that. He could not remember what he had done, but somehow he was a prisoner. Determined, he examined every plank on the floor, the rough stone of the walls, every inch of the cell enclosing him. There was no way out.

Only the window.

He drifted towards it. Beyond, a bright light waited, sending its searing tendrils through the inch-thick clearglass like a warning. This seemed strange. He should be able to see the street below, the crowds going about their business, but there was only the light. An endless landscape of gold and crimson. A boiling and surging sea, majestic and dangerous. Filled with an alluring power.

This is the realm of Fire.

The voice came from nowhere, but as he beheld the shifting patterns without, he knew it spoke the truth.

The room became constricting. He could not move . . . he was frozen. He had to escape, had to find a way out, yet there was only one.

The Window.

Desperately, he reached out, releasing the catch. Fire flooded into the room, roaring and angry. It sang as it filled him. He was lifted up on its power and he opened the Window further. Suddenly there was too much. There was an explosion, and he was lost in the light.

* * *

Raziin was enjoying himself.

After putting up with Dresil and his lackeys, those stupid and recalcitrant Mouthpieces and their undisciplined band of killers, this was a welcome relief.

And Uros had grown inpatient.

High time then, to spill some blood to her glory. His own pleasure . . . well, that was just a fortunate by-product.

He swept his gaze from Marken to Skye, then back to Cedrin.

That one – the fifth-degree – he would leave till last. He had led enough men in his time to smell rebellion, and this one could have cost him dearly. If not for this little exercise, he would have killed him yesterday.

Skye was glaring at him, his eyes rolling with fear. Good. It seemed the use of Sorcery had punctured his courage. Marken glared at him, his golden eyes filled with fury. The throwing knife poised in mid-air.

Yes. The Cioan would be next. He took a step towards Marken, but felt something stirring. Something that could not be. Fire was rising, *inside* the big calvanni.

He had time only to flinch.

A massive wall of flame exploded from Cedrin.

Raziin and his men were knocked from their feet.

Raziin's control of the Fire faltered, and all three calvanni were released from his Matrix of Binding.

'No!' yelled Raziin, struggling up from the stone.

Beneath the Wail, the pitch roared into flame, greedily rising higher. The Wail began to shift and change, the green tendrils shimmering, shifting from light to metal. The massive crystal rippled and shook like a living thing. With an unearthly groan, it gave voice.

He shielded his ears as the Siren's Wail filled the night. Its power was deafening.

Raziin leapt to his feet.

'You gutter-spawn! What have you done?' he screamed, looking across to Cedrin. But the tall calvanni had collapsed, overwhelmed by the intensity of the Fire he had channelled.

'Kyal! Merceth!' Raziin looked around for his men, but they were still regaining their senses. He would have to deal with these calvanni himself. The time for games was over. He hefted his greatscythe and ran at Marken.

A knife flew across the space, flashing like a diving bird to bury itself deep in his throat. He fell to his knees with a gasp. Pain and fear shot through him, threatening to overwhelm his mind, but a lifetime of discipline asserted itself. Carefully, he formed the Matrix of Form in his mind, readying to seal the wound.

He reached for the knife, pulling it out slowly as the tissue knit behind it. *Just a few more moments.* The knife was out. He threw it down onto the stone. A pulsing golden light started shining from his body, the power of the Matrix increasing as the wound closed. He had found the Matrix of Form only just in time, another moment and the calvanni's knife would have been his death. He smiled grimly.

Marken's face grew pale.

'Skye! That knife should have killed him!' shouted Marken over the din.

'Demon!' Skye's face was white with fear.

'Let's get Cedrin out of here!' shouted Marken.

The two calvanni lifted the unconscious Cedrin to his feet and fled down the stairwell.

Raziin used his greatscythe to push himself to his feet. 'Those bastard calvanni! *Damn them!* The Wail was to be kept silent.'

'Shall we go after them, my lord?' asked Merceth, who along with Kyal had regained his feet.

'No,' said Raziin, fingering the new scar at his throat. 'The damage has been done. Soon the wall will be swarming with guards.'

Raziin gathered his energy. Reaching within his mind, he channelled the Fire into Force, quelling the pitch, starving the flames of oxygen. Above the smoking pitch, the Wail pulsed and shifted angrily, sending its thundering screech across Athria. Despite the quelling of the flame, it would continue to send out its warning for hours to come.

Merceth was at his elbow. 'Your orders, my lord?'

'We must flee to the Shrine. We have failed here but all is not lost. We will regroup and advance; most of the assanni will have reached their targets by now.'

Raziin fixed the face of the calvanni in his mind. *Cedrin.* He gripped the haft of his greatscythe until his fingers were white. *We'll meet again, half-Blood.*

He turned away from the Wail in disgust.

It was too late to return the way they came. Even the calvanni were likely to meet death at the hands of the mustering wall guard now.

He would have to risk using the Matrix of Force. With delicate control, a Sorcerer could use the Fire to counter the rushing force of gravity. It was an imprecise art, and attempts to use it to fly or levitate usually ended in death or injury – which was why they had needed the calvanni for the assent. Now he had no choice.

'Step up on the battlements,' said Raziin, leaping up to the wall of the Spire.

Merceth and Kyal followed after the briefest of hesitations.

'We go!'

They stepped off the Spire, Raziin gripping them within a Sphere of Force. As the ground rose to meet them, he sent out tendrils of force to slow them. Even so they hit with stunning impact.

Minutes later, bruised yet unharmed, they were running towards the Shrine as the sounds of alarm spread through Regent's Hill.

Curse Larus! Curse Athria! He had restrained his hand long enough.

Tonight, Uros would feast.

* * *

Crephis struggled to rise, but he was too weak to stand. Blood still flowed from the wound, and he knew his Essence spell had given him only hours. His desperate attempt to heal himself had failed. Perhaps with at least one full moon in the sky, he may have had a chance.

With his last strength, he crawled across the bloodied stone towards the glittering prize. With a grunt, he brought it closer to his eyes. A black tower on a field of yellow. A vine of bloody thorns. *The crest of Kaidell.* It was Belin's ring.

'The ways of the gods are strange,' he whispered. Gripping the ring, he reached out to the Moons. Only Asic was present to lend its power and it would soon flee with the dawn. He drew on the feeble flow of Essence, striving to keep himself alive long enough to tell someone.

He had found Belin's son.

Chapter Six

Ellen was lost in a dream-city. Sometimes a carving, a facade, perhaps the graceful curve of a window or a particular hue in the stained glass would remind her of the palace, but just as often the cut and look of the stone would be alien. There was no horizon, the sky merging with the margins of the world in one continuous expanse of grey-blue. So far she had wandered alone.

A force – embodied within a spinning sphere of blue – urged her on, always hovering at the edges of her mind.

Ahead of her, a black growth spewed like a cancer from a square of grey stone.

Instinctively she backed away.

From the central axis of the growing monument sprouted five twisted limbs. They shivered, then swung towards her, reaching out, lengthening. Each of the tapering limbs had five sides, and at the end of each an iris flowered, glaring at her, unblinking. She tried to tear her gaze away, but could only back away further as those limbs continued to grow, a dark power pulsing inside them.

A sudden movement at the edge of her vision broke the trance. She saw a man, his dark woollen cloak fluttering as he turned and fled into a narrow alley.

'Wait!'

You must find the Scion. The voice came from nowhere into her mind.

The black monument dissolved into the dream, eaten by blue. The streets were empty. There was only the unreachable, spinning blue sphere and the fleeing man.

She began to run, fighting to match his pace. As she reached the entrance to the alley, she could see him waiting for her, his face darkened and unrecognisable. She slowed as she neared, triumphant, then an uncertainty flooded through her. There was something about him, a familiarity. A disturbing echo.

As she approached, he opened his lips as if to speak, but his mouth yawned impossibly wide. Something glowed within, and her eyes were drawn to it. Daggers of brightness exploded from it, stabbing into her mind.

Fire poured from his open mouth in a torrent and with it a wailing sound as loud as thunder. It reverberated off the buildings and they began to crack and crumble, falling to reveal only night where masonry had once been. A cool Storm Season gust gathered the dust, and stars glittered in the chill. The sound was painfully intense, the call of a great wounded animal, or the dying cries of multitudes.

She fell to her knees, clamping her hands over her ears. 'No!' she shouted. 'Make it stop!'

Ellen woke with a start, still screaming for the wailing to stop. She looked around her darkened room, trying to focus, but the wailing continued, mournful, thunderous.

The Siren's Wail!

She threw aside the covers and scrambled from her bed, a burst of fearful anxiety sweeping aside the last fragments of her dream. Taking up her scythe, she ran into the upper hall, still clad only in a light nightgown. The chill air swept around her legs and stung her skin.

She circled, then dropped into a low stance.

Something dark flew past her into the wood panelling. A dart. She dived and rolled towards a statue base, hiding in the shadow, listening as her heart beat like a galley drummer at ramming speed.

She waited silently, hardly daring to move, then smiled with relief as she heard the whispering of silk-covered shoes on wood. She knew where her attacker was. Gathering the Fire, she leapt at him, sending a flash of blinding white light as she went. The man cried out in surprise and threw his calv. She released a bolt of Force that sent his weapon flying wild. Then Ellen was on him.

She cut upward, her scythe-blade opening his throat. He sank to his knees then fell forward onto the woven rug at her feet.

Assanni!

She circled, searching for others, shaking with cold and shock.

Stupid! What was she thinking? Running out into the night in her gown? Heart clenching, she backed into her chamber and bolted the door. She dressed for the cold, then strapped on her light leather armour. A tremor of fear ran through her. She had been forced to use her powers of Sorcery. Had anyone seen her? A servant perhaps?

She slammed her fist into her palm, furious that her powers must remain hidden. Sorcerers faced death at the hands of the Temple, and such was the Druids' power that no one was safe – not even the heir to the Athrian throne. Her father had insisted on teaching her the martial arts of the Suul, determined that she would never need to reveal herself.

Ellen fought to clear her head. The Siren's Wail continued, which meant that Regent's Hill was under attack. She had to be prepared for anything. The estate could be surrounded by assailants. The assassin who almost found her may be the first of many, all moving through the mansion, seeking her.

Ellen moved down the sweeping inner stair towards the lower Hall. Lights were coming on in the mansion, and she heard the startled voices of servants as they lit lanterns and talked amongst themselves. The hall seemed empty, but she waited long moments in the dark to be sure, listening, her mouth dry. If the Siren's Wail had not woken her at that moment. . . she suppressed the thought. She was not out of danger yet.

She heard shouting, then the sound of running feet as a squad of family retainers marched into the hall, spears and scythes held at the ready. Servants followed with torches.

Ellen stepped into the light, hailing Escon, the Captain of her personal guard. A thickset man, Escon had devoted his life to protecting the Cintros family. He had once served on Myan's own bodyguard, and still retained his physical power, his balding head now covered by a mought helmet.

The old warrior's face flushed with relief. 'Lady Cintros.' His bow was brief and urgent. 'We killed two assassins fleeing the Siren, I feared for your life.'

Ellen shivered. Three assassins that they knew of. All for her.

'One lies dead above, outside my chamber.'

Escon winced. Ellen knew he would hold himself personally responsible for the breach of security.

'Are there any other attackers?' she asked.

'Not at the moment,' he replied, his light brown eyes glowing dangerously as he struggled to control his outrage.

Ellen paused in thought as servants lowered the huge hall lamps and lit the tallow, the bright light overpowering the smoky yellow flame of the torches. The Suul were prepared for this. If the Siren sounded, they were to meet at the palace with their personal retainers, to take commands from the Sarlord and participate in the defence.

A chill ran through Ellen as she realised why her father had been killed. There was no Sarlord. Kerril, who now ruled in his stead as Regent, would not be at the palace. *Athria had no leader.*

'The stables. Quickly!'

She ran through the hall and out into the night, Escon's squad at her heels.

'How many men can we muster?' asked Ellen.

'All told, perhaps forty men.'

'Rally them all. Saddle the amelak and prepare my narsiit. We ride for the palace!'

Escon's face was flushed with consternation. 'What of the mansion?'

'Forget the mansion, Athria is at stake.'

Escon gritted his teeth and nodded, issuing a series of curt orders to his lieutenants.

Moments later, Ellen and her retainers galloped from the estate, through a gate in ancient battlements that were once the walls of Athria's Citadel, but now formed the borders of a private garden. Ellen's narsiit towered over the sturdy amelak, her wings folded to her brightly-coloured body to conserve heat. Ellen had to continually pull her back so that the rest of the squad could keep pace.

They were barely half-a-league from the mansion when three riders appeared out of the night, also mounted on narsiit. She knew immediately they must be Suul. They reined in, their narsiit snorting and pacing impatiently at the check. Ellen rode forward to meet them and saw it was Torren, flanked by two Suulqua lieutenants.

Torren's grey eyes were set like stone as they regarded her. Habitually stern, he looked at Ellen from within a mask of authority. His sun-tanned face with its carefully trimmed beard would have been pleasant if not set with such hard lines, yet she had never known him otherwise. Her brother was a man who took duty seriously, and the long hours he spent honing his martial skills had given him a physical presence of power that warriors responded to immediately.

A tense moment passed, a moment of enmity put aside as they acknowledged a common duty.

Torren was the first to speak, his tone brusque and hard. 'The palace is secure. Aris is in command until the Regent arrives with his retinue. A force has mounted an attack on the Inner Garrison and we must answer, if only to discover their strength and pull back to the palace. I am here to take the retainers.'

Ellen briefly considered then nodded. 'Very well.'

Torren's narsiit stallion gave a cry and raised his fore hooves off the ground, displaying the impatience and tension his master held in check.

'These two will escort you back to the palace.' Torren indicated the two young Suulqua, who were clearly unhappy to be so easily dismissed from a fight.

'I understand your need for warriors, Torren, which is why I will come with you.'

Torren's face set harder, and his voice took on an edge of dangerous yet controlled anger. The kind only years of authority can cultivate. 'That's out of the question. I don't need a liability. My men will be constrained trying to protect you.'

'Remember who you are talking to!' snapped Ellen, her voice

like a whip crack. '*I am Sarqua. And every minute we delay means the lives of more men.*'

'You – ' started Torren.

'I am as accomplished in combat as you, Torren. Father saw to that. My blade will count as well as any other. Taking two Suulqua out of the conflict drastically reduces our strength. Think! We have four trained narsiit between us.'

They stared at each other. Torren clearly restraining himself with difficulty.

'Lead on, brother. I will not contest the fact that you are the best field commander.'

'So be it,' said Torren with finality. 'Form an even line! Scythes away! Spears levelled!'

Torren and his two lieutenants merged into the centre of the Cintros line. With parade-ground precision, the men quickly formed ranks.

A thrill shot through Ellen. Never in her wildest dreams had she imagined riding into battle alongside her brother.

'Forward at the gallop!'

The small division thundered through the wide gardens and paths of Regent's Hill towards the Inner Garrison, the amelak pushed to the limit to keep pace with the sleek narsiit.

'There are lights ahead,' said Ellen, noting a reflected glow in the sky above them. 'Have they lit the Wall beacons?'

'That's not the Wall beacons.' Torren squinted through the night. 'Damn these mansions! I can see nothing.'

They thundered around a squat Suul mansion, and the Inner Garrison came into full view.

'Larus!' said Ellen, the cry drawn from her involuntarily.

The Inner Garrison was in flames. Even as they watched, a section of wall collapsed as the flames surged higher. *They can not have fallen already!*

The galloping line faltered, many of the men as shocked as Ellen at the sight of the Garrison in flames. Behind the burning building, they could see the Gatehouse in the Wall of Sorrows. Its turrets were lined with raggedly dressed men. It too was held by the attackers. The Gatehouse was designed to be almost impregnable, capable of being held by a handful against a much superior force. She put aside her puzzlement at how they had taken it and focussed on the key conclusion: there would be no help from the Outer Garrison. Never could they have dreamed the Wall would be holding *out* their own forces.

'Keep steady!' commanded Torren, his voice like iron. The line strengthened and they swept onward through the night, the thunder of hooves lost in the increasing roar of the flames.

Ellen swallowed, trying to match her brother's composure. Even if all seemed lost, she must maintain a tight control over her emotions. Without strong leadership, the men could easily fall into undisciplined lines, becoming easy prey to a larger force. So Torren wanted her to cower in the palace while her own men were dying? She gripped the reins with grim determination. Even without her powers of Sorcery, she was a formidable opponent.

The burning building loomed ahead of them. Attackers besieged it, cutting down any man who fought through the flames. In the flickering light, she could see around one hundred dead guardsmen. The rest lay besieged within. Judging by the number of torches, the attacking force had considerable numbers, perhaps two hundred men. In contrast, she and Torren had little more than forty, but with the advantage of being mounted.

'How did they get inside the wall!' snapped Ellen, her question driven by outrage and horror at the number of dead.

'Hold your questions, Ellen,' said Torren. 'Ready your scythe and follow my lead.'

Torren studied the line of attackers ahead, seemingly undaunted by the odds.

'There!' called Torren. 'The weakest point in their lines lies close to the side exit. We have to take it. It's the only chance for those still inside. Wheel right! Wedge formation!' The whole line changed direction, thundering towards the gap Torren had pointed out. The men shifted into a wedge shape with the four narsiit at its tip, Ellen right at the top, galloping at breakneck speed beside Torren. The haft of her scythe felt slippery in her hand, and she gripped it tighter, her eyes wide as she scanned the attackers, alert for anything.

The night rushed past Ellen, images of shouting men, dead guardsmen and leaping flames spinning around her.

Torren stood in his stirrups. 'At my command, cast spears and draw scythes!'

At some unspoken signal, their pace increased. They now thundered towards the right flank of the enemy at full gallop.

The attacking force surrounded the building in tight knots. Ellen could see them jeering at the remaining guards inside the burning building, waiting for them to run from the building into their lines. Incredibly, they were so buoyed by their victory they had not yet seen them approach, the sound of the amelak and narsiit swamped by the roar the flames.

'*Cast!*' called Torren.

The volley decimated the group around the exit. One man caught a spear in the chest and fell backwards into the flames, his screams lost in the battle yell of the Athrian troops as they drew their scythes and closed on the remaining raiders.

The attackers broke and fell back, but black-garbed warriors in heavy armour quickly emerged from the nearby lines and led a furious counter-attack.

A warrior leapt at Ellen, yelling as he came. Her narsiit shied back as the big warrior spun a greatscythe towards her in a deadly arc, his golden skin and hair glistening in the flames.

She screamed her defiance and surged forward, her scythe blocking the greatscythe's deadly blades and cutting forward in a counter that slashed through the surprised warrior's guard and cut deeply into his shoulder. He cried out, dropping his greatscythe and Ellen swung again, decapitating him.

As the warrior fell, she looked across to Torren, who had similarly downed his black-clad foe. Only then did she register the golden skin, the golden hair. Cioans. Here in Athria?

The furious defence had halted the charge, and now the other attackers, taking heart at their superior numbers, pressed in. But despite heavy losses, the Athrian troops held firm and made steady forward progress. Soon they held the ground outside of the burning exit.

'Circle formation!' ordered Torren.

The men turned, the wedge dissolving into a half-circle

formation facing out from the exit with the four narsiit inside it, ready to act as a reserve.

'Good. Good,' said Torren. 'Well done! Keep at them!'

The men on the outside of the circle fought steadily, using the longer scythes and mounted height to their advantage. The attackers had an odd assortment of weapons and no armour at all. They soon grew wary of approaching the Athrian soldiers.

Torren turned towards her, looking down at her blood-stained scythe. 'It seems you weren't boasting after all,' he said. 'Well done, sister.'

Ellen tried to reply but found her throat choked with emotion. That was the first time Torren had ever spoken to her as an equal.

'Now it's up to the men inside to get to us,' said Torren. 'I hope they don't take too long.'

An amelak screamed as a well-cast spear found its mark, the mounted soldier lost under the mob that pressed them.

'Fill the gap!'

The two Suulqua yelled their battle-cries and urged their mounts into the breach.

They had lost seventeen men and they no longer had the element of surprise. Soon they would be forced to flee or perish.

Behind them, men began to struggle out of the garrison, many burnt or wounded. They looked up at the two Cintros Suul in bewilderment.

Torren scanned the men. 'Where is the Garrison Captain?'

A squad leader, with the rank of Crescent Razor by his insignia, limped to Torren and bowed, his faced creased in pain. His right leg was horribly burnt. 'The Garrison Captain was ordered to report to the Outer Garrison with the third and fourth divisions.' The Outer Garrison was outside the Wall of Sorrows.

Torren's face twisted with rage. 'Who was left in charge?'

The Razor paused as though perplexed. 'No one, Lord.'

'Any more left alive in there?' asked Torren.

The guard shook his head. 'None, my lord.'

There was a scream behind them. Another amelak had been pulled down and butchered, its rider with it. The formation tightened around them.

Ellen quickly counted the survivors. Just over fifty guardsmen had survived the attack and fire. Had they been prepared and led by an officer, and with the will of the gods, they could have routed the attackers. Instead, almost 250 men had perished in senseless deaths, cut down by a mob or left cowering in a burning building.

She heard a familiar war cry and turned to see Escon leading a furious counter-attack. Slowly the circle around them strengthened. Only the skill and determination of their men was protecting them. Torren's two Suulqua and their narsiit were facing more than ten attackers. They were holding on a knife-edge. If they did not break out soon, their formation would fracture, leaving them overrun.

'Torren. We don't have long,' said Ellen.

Torren nodded. 'Guardsmen! Form a fighting square. Shieldmen at the outer ranks. Spears!'

The men formed themselves as best they could, shields passed to the men on the perimeter. Some held scythes or calvs, many wore little or no armour, but they would be protected by the formation.

Ellen heard a narsiit scream. She turned to see one of Torren's lieutenants fall. The attackers pushed in, but the winged-mount struck back, protecting her rider with a blurred assault of hooves and teeth.

'Now!' yelled Torren.

Ellen and Torren urged their narsiit through the lines of infantry, taking position just in time to prevent the mounted line collapsing. The fallen Suulqua leapt back to the saddle and rejoined them, blood soaking his tunic, his eyes alive with battle fury as he gripped his scythe.

'*Fighting retreat!*' called Torren, hastily deflecting a cast spear that flashed past his head and into the burning building behind him.

'*Cintros!*'

Torren's narsiit gave a harsh cry as he charged straight into the lines of the attackers, holding onto the winged horse with his knees as his greatscythe whistled, raining death to the left and right of his mount.

Urging on their terrified mounts, they followed Torren into the enemy ranks, their rear protected by the fighting square.

Ellen's scythe came alive in her hands, blocking and cutting. Her world filled with wide, battle-crazed eyes and unshaven faces, limbs and faces sprouting blood as she let go her fury, screaming the Cintros battle-cry into the night.

Their men were falling all around them, but the formation closed and reformed smoothly.

A calv flashed past Torren, slicing his cheek. A moment later, his narsiit gave a cry of anger as a scythe cut its side. The winged mount responded with a deadly kick and sudden burst of speed, leaving Ellen at the head of the formation.

A black-clad warrior surged towards her. She met him head-on, exchanging blows until her narsiit kicked out his knee. Her blade darted through the distracted warrior's defence to cut savagely into his face and the warrior fell screaming.

Torren reappeared at her side. The fighting square was still intact, following at a half run.

The enemy ranks suddenly fell away and they burst through, pursued only by the bolder attackers, led by three of the black-armoured Cioans.

'Cavalry! Wheel!'

Torren turned the cavalry in a circle, thundering back towards the pursuers. The fighting square ran on towards the palace as Ellen, Torren and the two Suulqua once more plunged into the attackers.

Even the three Cioan warriors hesitated as they saw the line of cavalry bearing down on them, but bravely they stood their ground, yelling strange battle-cries as they came. The Suul urged their narsiit ahead, meeting fury with fury. The warriors fell quickly, disappearing under the hooves of the narsiit as they swept through. The remaining attackers scattered.

Free from pursuit, Torren turned the line back towards the palace, quickly overtaking the infantry.

'Slow to a trot!'

With relief the men slowed, the amelak panting for breath in the bitterly cold night. As they closed on the palace, they met with other guardsmen who had fled the Garrison or escaped the taking of the Gatehouse and Wall of Sorrows, all making their way towards the palace. Torren called a halt as the men straggled in. Ellen realised many guardsmen had run from the Garrison early in the melee.

The men provided a rough picture of the attack and Torren's face grew graver as he and Ellen listened.

They now had around fifty men, many of them wounded. Torren assessed them critically, looking back through Regent's Hill towards the Gatehouse then shaking his head.

Just as they were reforming ranks, a runner found them. He sprinted to Torren and bowed, sweat dripping from a face flushed red with the Heat.

'Suul Cintros!'

'Yes, man. Speak.'

'I was sent by Aris. Another force is descending on the palace.'

Torren's jaw went slack, and an excited wave of talk spread like wildfire through the troops, its undercurrent all too familiar. Fear.

Torren wheeled his mount. 'Silence!'

'How many?' demanded Torren, turning back to the runner.

'I am unsure, my . . . my lord,' stammered the man.

'*How many!*'

'Ah . . . hundreds. Two, three hundred of them.'

'Ellen. I'm going to try and re-take the Gatehouse. If I can win through, we could have two thousand guards to the palace in less than an hour.'

Ellen began to protest, knowing how well defended the structure was, but held her tongue. He was right. This could make a crucial difference. If they did not turn back these attackers, all their lives could be forfeit.

'I understand,' said Ellen. 'Take those you need, and I will lead the rest to the palace.'

Torren nodded gravely then rode through the ranks, picking out the strongest and best equipped of the Garrison infantry, maybe twelve in all.

'Escon!' called Ellen.

The old fighter cantered his amelak up to her side, blood streaming from a wound to his temple. His mought helmet had been lost in the fight.

'Give Torren's warriors your mounts.'

Escon nodded then passed the orders, and moments later Torren, his two Suulqua lieutenants and the twelve mounted men galloped back through the night.

Ellen silently wished him luck.

'Forward!' she called, feeling like an impostor. But the men fell smoothly into ranks and followed her as she urged her narsiit towards the Cintros palace.

Soon she could make out the attacking force, swelling like a creeping shadow against the walls. At least three hundred men including a squad of the greatscythe-wielding black warriors.

She swallowed.

This was no time for tactics. All they had to do was reach the gate.

'*Cintros!*' yelled Ellen, spurring her narsiit ahead.

'Form a line!' yelled Escon, and the remaining cavalry swept out on either side of her. Behind her, she could hear the Razor from the Inner Garrison urging his men on.

Ellen kept her eyes on the enemy lines. It was the armoured warriors, the Cioans, who were the danger. Her eyes immediately lit on the silver-haired warrior who led them. He exuded a sense of physical power, of threat, that sent her heart racing. He turned towards her. He carried the Suul mark!

'Stand your ground. Cut for the mounts! Archers let fly!' called the silver-haired warrior.

Ellen's heart clenched. They were completely exposed! Immediately the Shield Matrix formed in her mind. She looked up. The battlements were lined with faces, all watching them approach. The area below the wall was brightly lit. Should she use the spell, all would see the missiles stop in mid-air. They would know.

Archers raced from the enemy lines, launching a ragged volley towards them. Ellen watched the shafts as they swept up into the night, lost against the black sky, then swept down in a deadly rain.

It was too late!

Many of the arrows flashed harmlessly by, but screams behind her gave testament that others had found their mark.

'Shoot low! Aim for the mounts!' called the warrior again.

Ellen eyed the distance to the gate. *It was too far!* And they had used all their spears already. She must use her Sorcery or they would all die. She drew on the Fire, waiting for the best moment to use it.

The volleys came faster. The screams of amelak rose above their battle yells, but on they came, tightening their ranks, scythes held at the ready.

Ellen sensed something ahead, something familiar.

She looked up towards the silver-haired Northman. He was standing still, his face creased in concentration, his eyes on them as they approached.

Ellen thundered on, turning her narsiit towards him, her mount's wings extended as she raced forward effortlessly.

She could almost feel . . .

Screams erupted from the line of attackers. Men fled in agony as boiling oil was poured down on them from the battlements of the palace wall. The silver-haired warrior darted outside the radius of the splashing oil and hastily reformed his lines. Whatever she had sensed, it was gone. The threat of the missiles gone, she let the Fire fall away from her.

Then they were on them, cutting left and right as they came, amelak falling as the remaining attackers cut for their legs.

The silver-haired warrior ran at her, his greatscythe a blur in the night.

Ellen blocked and swung down with all her speed and power as she raced to the hastily raised gates, but he dodged the attack easily. The men followed her through the gates.

Once through the tunnel, she turned. Attackers were surging after them, but the silver-haired warrior called for them to stop, recognising the murder alley beyond. It was too late for the handful of attackers foolish enough to follow them through. The heavy gate closed behind them, and they were quickly cut down by a hail of arrows and crossbow bolts.

They had made it. Around her, the courtyard was full of men

and activity. Squads were being briefed while men tended vats of oil over huge hearths. Others rushed supplies and weapons up to the battlements. Escon had taken an arrow to the shoulder, but refused to be led away. He took the shaft of the arrow in his powerful hands, and with a yell of fury snapped the shaft just above the wound. He turned towards her, his chest heaving, as though daring her to take him from the fight.

For a moment, Ellen was lost for words. 'Es. . . Escon. Gather the men and join with our forces on the wall.'

'Yes, Sarqua.'

She dismounted, rubbing the flanks of her mount and praising her softly until a servant appeared to take her, then she rushed up the steps to the outer wall.

Archers and crossbow men began to shoot down at the press of attackers, and another vat of oil was poured over the outer wall.

The assailants retreated beyond bow range.

They had won a reprieve.

She scanned the crowd on the wall until she sighted Aris and moved hastily to his side.

He was deep in conference with two Athrian lords, both arrayed for war. When he saw her, his face set hard and he broke off his conversation, bowing imperceptibly as she stopped in front of him. 'Cintros,' he said curtly.

The Suul also bowed, backing away to leave Aris and Ellen in private.

'Has Kerril arrived yet?' asked Ellen.

Aris shook his head, his face grim. 'Kerril did not respond to the summons. I have sent a squad to his mansion, but have received no word.'

'And the attacking force?'

The Warlord responded mechanically. 'They appear to have numbered around five hundred in total. Somehow they gained the Wall of Sorrows and blocked the Outer Garrison. You were with Torren?'

'Yes, we rescued as many as we could from the Inner Garrison. Torren has taken a small force to try and re-take the Gatehouse.'

Aris nodded gravely.

'How did this force enter Regent's Hill without alerting us? Without passing the Wall of Sorrows?' she asked, venting her frustration.

'I can only assume a tunnel,' said Aris.

'But the palace guard numbers five hundred,' she said. 'We can hold.'

Aris' expression darkened. 'Usually.'

Her belly twisted and her heart beat fast as she waited for Aris to finish, hoping things were not as grim as she suspected.

'The main guard was ordered outside the Wall of Sorrows. We have three hundred men at best, including the ones you brought in.'

'How could this happen?'

Aris' single eye took on a deadly gleam. 'I don't know, but I mean to find out. *If* we are not already lost.'

She looked around the courtyard at the men who would fight for Athria. Die for Athria. There *must* be a way to help them. They needed more men, but how?

'If you will excuse me, I have a defence to plan,' snapped Aris, his tone patronising.

The Warlord was a powerful figure, and only days ago she would have eagerly stepped out of his way – but that was before Myan named her as heir.

'Have a care how you address me, Warlord,' she said, steadily matching his gaze.

'My apologies,' he said stiffly, giving her a short bow.

'You may go,' she said.

After Aris took his leave, Ellen paced the battlements, wrestling with the problem of increasing their strength for the defence. She snapped her fingers as it came to her. 'Of course!' The tunnel to the Temple of Sisters! Built three hundred years ago, it was a closely guarded secret of the Sarlord. Myan had told her of it only last year and it just may save them.

She rushed into the palace, her plan still forming.

Something nagged at her, something about that silver-haired mercenary, but she could not pin it down. She put it out of her head as she sought out the entrance to the tunnel.

* * *

'Straight up the stairs. We are almost there,' said Ellen.

She looked up through the dark, wishing there had been time to set torches along the roughly cut stairwell before she hurried to the Temple.

Behind her filed around forty Druids, and more importantly, hundreds of Temple Guardians. Expert in the use of the spear and shield, they would be invaluable for the defence of the palace. The whole force was led by red-robed Templemen, Druids of the Red Sun, Uros. Rarely were they called upon to use their power, but now, in the middle of Storm Season, they were at their peak. With this combined force, the undisciplined and ill-equipped attackers could be driven all the way back to the Wall of Sorrows, despite the black-clad mercenaries who led them.

Ellen let out a long breath of relief. She had sworn to her father she would never reveal her powers, and it was a promise she intended to keep.

As she worked her way up the narrow stair, the rough, cold stone leaching the heat from her fingers as she sought for handholds, his words came back to her. *This is a world where we must hide, Ellen. Even at the battle of Raynor I concealed the use of my power, using it only in the heat and confusion of combat, or in response to the Sorcerer-Lords of the Eathal. You must never reveal yourself – the Temple has become too strong. Your survival, Athria's survival, depends on it. We must work in secret.* Yet her father could never have imagined open war.

She thought back to the burning Garrison, to the dead who lay scattered around those flames, and the others who had fallen in her last desperate charge for the gates. How much death must she allow? How many must die before she unleashed herself?

Ellen shook her head. Thankfully that choice was removed from her. With the strength of the Temple, she would have no need to use her power.

Ellen thought back to the silver-haired warrior who had faced her. She had sensed something . . . something familiar

116

about him. No. Not about him . . . something familiar *in* him.

'At last,' snapped the Templeman at her elbow.

She looked up and saw the open portal to the Sarlord's day apartments. Bright lamplight flooded into the stairwell and lit the rough, dark stone around them.

'Come! Time is short!' said Ellen.

Now out of the treacherous and ill-lit stairwell she broke into a run, leading the Temple force through the winding maze of deserted palace corridors.

She led them out along a bridge connecting the palace's third level directly with the outer battlement. The men there looked around in stark amazement to find themselves suddenly reinforced by Druids and Temple guards.

Ellen quickly found Aris.

The Warlord was scanning the Temple forces with intense concentration. He turned to Ellen. 'So. How many more tunnels are there under the Wall of Sorrows? Should we expect more enemies to emerge from the other side of the palace?'

'Mind your tongue, Warlord! I have brought further strength to the fight. I suggest you use it rather than bicker with me.'

Ellen was stung. She had not expected praise, but she had not expected derision. She swallowed her anger. She knew how Aris must feel. The defence of Athria was his responsibility and he had almost seen the palace fall because of an unknown tunnel.

'How goes the battle?' she asked, looking into the darkened fields below the wall.

Aris turned with her and looked down at the forces below, which had once more retreated out of bowshot range.

'They have attempted to breach the wall twice, but we have turned them back,' said Aris, pointing at a score of dead attackers below the wall, scattered around the ruins of a make-shift ladder. 'Torren has returned from the Gatehouse. He met with no success.'

Ellen searched out Torren. He too was on the battlements, on the other side of the gate, busily organising men and supplies. Thank Larus he made it back alive. So, they were still cut off from the Outer Garrison.

She looked into the dark beyond the wall, searching out the silver-haired warrior. He was the danger.

There!

He was in the middle of the lines, surrounded by a knot of black-clad warriors, their solid, unwavering stance at odds with the other attackers, who stood in loose groups. He was standing next to another of the attackers, a short, stocky Athrian who was dressing down the Northman, pointing over at the walls, clearly demanding another attack.

'Their commander is a trader called Dresil. Uros-cursed traitor!' snapped Aris. 'We have sent spies to watch him for years, suspecting Brotherhood connections, but they had a habit of turning up dead in the harbour.'

The Northman halted the tirade with a curt word, then signalled to his troops. Ellen watched the man Dresil stalk back to the lines to marshal his men.

'Here they come again!' shouted Aris. 'Get ready, men! We have held them twice; we can hold them again!'

Ellen looked along the wall. Pitifully few palace guards remained. The Temple Guardians now outnumbered them. She searched for the Templemen. They stood together, aloof, watching the action from the bridge beyond the battlement. They seemed to have no intention of using their magic to help. In contrast, the Moon-Druids were already with the wounded, using their powers to heal.

At a command from the silver-haired warrior, the attackers formed up behind him. He now led the charge, running at the head of his Cioan warriors.

'They are charging the gate,' said Aris, incredulous. 'They won't break through there; it's suicide.' The gate was the strongest and most heavily defended part of the whole wall.

Ellen felt something stir.

Her eyes immediately went to the silver-haired Northman, and all at once, she knew who he must be.

'Raziin Cinnor,' she muttered. *The Traitor of Armon.*

Aris looked at her, puzzled, but Ellen's gaze was glued to Raziin. Apart from her father and Erioth, he was the only other Sorcerer she knew of in Kelas. And he was her enemy. Yet why had he waited until now? Why sacrifice Dresil's men instead of using his powers at the outset?

She felt him gathering the Fire, seeming to swell as he let it build within him to its killing crescendo.

'Aris! Send your men to the inner gate!'

'What?' said Aris. 'The inner gate is secure.'

'Now! Send your men!' screamed Ellen.

Raziin released his power as one massive bolt of Force. Like an invisible ram, it smashed through the first gate, reducing it to splinters as the mought reinforcing shattered.

The guards around Ellen screamed as fragments exploded into their ranks. She felt her hair flick upward as a shard narrowly missed her face.

Once more Raziin released his power, and the second gate smashed inwards in a concussion of wood and glass.

'Charge!' screamed Raziin.

The Northman led his men through the still stunned archers and crossbow men above the murder alley.

'Fire!' called Aris.

Their men rained missiles down on the attackers, but they bounced away, halted in mid-air. *A Shield of Force!* The first wave of attackers spilled into the courtyard. Above the alley, Torren was urging the Athrian warriors to attack the second wave, led by Dresil. Arrows and quarrels rained onto this second force with deadly results, but they were soon through, into the palace itself.

Running battles ensued, and the courtyard was full of fighting men and screaming animals. Raziin's men led a charge to gain the battlements, but were met on the steps by elite palace guards. Raziin could not use the Shield to protect his whole force, and soon dropped the spell, fighting greatscythe-to-greatscythe alongside his men. The defenders had the advantage of height, but Raziin's greater numbers were forcing them back.

Ellen knew that as soon as Raziin was free to work his Sorcery, they would be lost.

Ellen ran to the Templemen. 'You must use your powers now,' she said urgently. 'That is Raziin Cinnor himself! You must contain him, or we are all lost. Strike him now, while he is distracted.'

The lead Templeman, a tall, thin man with a long, lined face beneath his red hood, stared at Ellen. 'We will keep our own counsel on when we use our powers, Suul Cintros.'

Ellen swallowed her rage. Of course – they were waiting for dawn. Before the rise of the red sun, their powers would be less than a tenth of their full Storm Season strength.

'Yes, your grace.'

Without the Temple's strength of arms, they would have already been lost. She hurried back to the battlements and watched the fight anxiously.

Within minutes, Dresil had won the courtyard and Raziin's men were pushing hard up the steps to the battlements. Ellen's stomach tightened. Her own forces were steadily losing ground.

Torren directed fire into the press, reaping a grim harvest of death amid the attackers, but it was not enough.

Raziin gave a shout and soared into the air, aided by the Fire. He turned in mid-air, landing on the steps above the defenders with faultless balance. Before the palace guards could even turn, his greatscythe was cutting into their rear. The defence collapsed; in seconds they were overrun. With a great yell, Dresil's force surged onto the battlements, away from the falling death.

The Templemen raised their hands and began to chant.

Raziin reacted quickly, sending a wall of Fire into their ranks.

The lead Templeman screamed as he was incinerated, the others ran back into the safety of the palace in confusion, beating flames out on their heavy robes.

So much for Temple magic.

A Suul warrior ran at Raziin, and once more he was forced to abandon his magic. Ellen watched Raziin fight his way through the press. He fought like a demon, his men steadily carving a path through the defenders with deadly precision. Everywhere around her, men were screaming, dying. Even now, with the strength of the Temple to aid them, they could still lose.

Torren rushed past her, leading a desperate counter-offensive. If they lost the battlements, it would be all over.

She hefted her scythe and began to follow, but Aris' hand

came down on her shoulder.

'No, Suul Cintros. The heir must not be risked. Your duty is to protect yourself.'

'I know my duty!' She shook off his hand. 'Damn it!' she screamed, slamming the butt of her scythe into the battlement. She could do nothing but watch her men die!

She looked up anxiously at the balconies of the palace. The Templemen had reappeared and were sending down thin bolts of Force at the attackers, but for all their efforts they were less effective than the remaining archers. It was simply not enough.

The eastern sky was beginning to glow with the coming dawn, but time was running out. How much longer could she stand by and watch her men dying? The Fire was close – there at her command – in seconds she could send the attackers reeling with Fire and bolts of Force that would make the efforts of the Templemen look weak. But what then? Would she let herself be taken by the Temple? Or would she flee? Be reduced from Sarla to exile in one night?

Torren had halted Raziin's elite group, fighting greatscythe-to-greatscythe with the silver-haired warrior. Slowly her brother and the remaining defenders were pushing him and his men back to the stair, the remainder of the attackers forced back into the courtyard.

Raziin gave a shout of pure rage. He leapt once more, landing directly behind Torren's group. Taking a moment to concentrate, he released the Fire into their ranks. The guardsmen and Temple Guardians broke, some screaming as their very flesh took flame. Three tumbled back off the battlements to land in the courtyard, still crying out even as they lay burnt and broken below.

'No!' yelled Ellen. Had she taken on Raziin at the beginning, she could have prevented this.

'Suul Cintros. We must fall back!' said Aris.

'No. I will not run!'

The night was filled with the smell of burning flesh as Raziin's men broke through, Dresil's men following behind them.

Torren and his men fought on, but the battle had

degenerated to an undisciplined hand-to-hand.

Then Raziin turned and faced her. 'You!' he shouted.

Ellen felt the Fire build in him and hastened to match the flow. She felt for the Matrix, but sensed he was going to unleash the raw Fire once more. However powerful he may be, it seemed he had little finesse. She opened herself to the Fire, feeling the intense exhilaration of it as it filled her. She channelled the Fire into the Shield Matrix. The blast hit the Shield and cascaded around the invisible barrier with a roar, leaving her and those sheltering behind her – including Aris – untouched.

Acting on instinct, she let the Shield fall and sent a jagged bolt of Force at Raziin. Unlike the feeble efforts of the Templemen, this was a solid Wedge, travelling forward at tremendous speed, its form catching the light like a mirror.

She saw his eyes widen, and he leapt into the air. The Wedge missed him by a hair's breadth. He spun and tumbled to the courtyard below, landing on his feet.

Ellen leapt after him, shooting silver arrows of Force in a wide fan of death. He rolled but one took him in the side. He cried out as the silver bolt sliced through his leather armour.

Raziin sent a cascade of Fire towards her, its blossoming flame crimson and angry. Once more the Shield protected her, but when the Fire was gone, he had disappeared, hidden by the Matrix of Shadow. Ellen quickly channelled the Fire into the Matrix herself, becoming invisible.

This was a different sort of game altogether. Her own mind protected by the Barrier Matrix, she reached out for Raziin. She readied the Final Matrix, a form that, used delicately, could open up another person's thoughts to her – or applied with force could utterly destroy them. It was a dangerous ploy, but judging by his level of skill, one he would be ill-equipped to defend. She broadened her senses, readying herself to deliver the killing mental blow. With Raziin out of action, Athria would be saved, and Kelas would be free of a merciless killer.

There! She felt him, only briefly, then he was gone. The Traitor of Armon had fled the battle. Her instincts had proved correct. He had run to save himself. Raziin's men quickly followed, a huge Cioan warrior leading them back out the gates in a fighting retreat, leaving Dresil's men to fight alone.

Ellen released the Matrix of Shadow. She appeared within the deserted courtyard. With the loss of Raziin and his mercenaries, the battle had turned. The attacking force was withdrawing from the palace, archers loosing shafts at their retreating backs in the morning twilight. The Temple forces – and her own defeat of Raziin – had turned the tide. A giddy elation flooded her. They had won. She had saved Athria!

The courtyard was quiet for a time, then she heard Aris and Torren shouting at the men to remove the bodies and barricade the gate. The Temple Guardians helped amid the carnage, black-robed Moon-Druids healing where they could.

Men avoided her eyes as they passed her.

Ellen's stomach contracted with fear. *Larus! What have I done!* After all her agonising about the use of her powers, in the end the decision had been taken from her. If she had not fought Raziin she – and Athria – would have fallen.

Cold and alone, she searched the battlements for a friendly face, but the red-robed Templemen, the Druids of Uros, were the only ones to meet her gaze. They regarded her coolly. Not only had they been deprived of victory, she had outshone them in their time of strength; usurped them with her forbidden power.

Her life, which had seemed so solid, had been shattered like a delicate vase. *What have I done?*

Only then did the palace start to glow in the blood-red light of Uros, as first dawn broke. Too late. Soon Larus had also cleared the horizon, overpowering the light of Uros with her golden gleam.

Ellen forced her mind back to the present, searching for familiar faces. Kerril was still missing, and so was Palsus. Her mind fled back to the encounter with the assassin, stalking in the dark. She had been fortunate enough to wake in time, but what of the other lords of Athria? And where was Crephis? Her concern for herself was overtaken by a gnawing fear.

Aris took control of the palace guards while Torren formed ranks of stunned and wounded Guardians to pursue the fleeing attackers. Amid the chaos, the milling confusion of men, Ellen wandered like a lost child. Everywhere she walked, the living parted before her, men turning away with looks of superstitious fear.

The Templemen turned and re-entered the palace.

Ellen grabbed a wounded soldier. 'Where is Kerril? Crephis?'

The man looked at her in terror, mumbling incoherently and bowing in supplication. Ellen released him and he backed away over the blood-darkened earth of the courtyard. At the first cast of the Fire, she had entered another landscape, a strange limbo where she was an outcast. Ellen Cintros. Sorcerer.

* * *

As dawn swept across Athria, touching the empty alleys and cobbled streets, a weary and defeated group struggled across the manicured grass of Regent's Hill. Raziin struggled to keep up, his hand held to the savage wound in his side, where the arrow of Force had punched through the tough leather and mought. He could still draw enough Fire to call upon the Matrix of Form and heal himself, but he dare not. To do so would mean dropping the Barrier Matrix.

Fear kept him moving. Fear the bitch would find him and destroy him. He could feel the seeking touch of her mind, like a blind killer, feeling for a victim in the night. She had the Final Matrix, the only instrument that could seal his destruction! He lay defenceless before it, as his master Hukum had intended. The supreme ruler of the Eathal never gave his servants full leash, especially his despised human minion, Raziin.

The light of the two suns slanted across the Wall of Sorrows, touching the mansions and palatial homes of the rulers of Athria and the magnificent gardens. They had been so close. Now they fled. The Brotherhood would have had their day, but they would have only been puppets for the real power, the Court of Maht. The dark throne of the Eathal Sorcerer-lords.

They reached the Shrine in the full light of dawn. Raziin, helped by Merceth, called his warriors together as the remnants of Dresil's force fled the morning into the crypt. The once-Suul lord inspected his men, rearranging them into units, restoring discipline and order. Satisfied, he waved them into the tunnel.

Across the bright morning, Raziin could see the dark shapes of Temple Guardians marching in tight formation towards them from the palace. Cursing, he urged his men on. Anger surged through him, but beneath it, the fear remained.

He hurried into the tunnel. Supported by Merceth, he channelled a series of short bursts of Force, sending the columns of the crypt roof tumbling, tons of earth and rock falling to seal the only route of pursuit.

Laughing, Raziin channelled his failing flow of Fire into the Matrix of Form, shuddering with relief as the pain fled and the wound in his side healed. Now he was whole again, and free to leave this cursed rock.

But another fear now rose in him. It grew until it filled him like a fever. He had failed his impatient Eathal master. And what price would Hukum put on this failure?

* * *

Marken eased the dark velvet of the curtain back, allowing a stream of ruddy yellow light into the gritty darkness of the small alcove. The corridor was full of men, some bloodied, limping or holding wounds, others carrying the dead or wounded on stretchers. Here and there, amid the warriors, were Druids and Temple Guardsman, hurrying towards some urgent destination.

They had been hidden in the alcove for long, desperate hours. Fleeing down the Spire steps, they had found themselves amid chaos. Men alerted by the Siren swarmed everywhere, men made dangerous by fear, ready to lay about them with lanedd at the slightest play of shadow. Marken and Skye, supporting Cedrin between them, had no choice but to hide. Only darkness and luck had saved them.

Marken had covertly watched the movements in the corridor for all of that time, certain they would be discovered at any moment. Miraculously they had been left unmolested amid the confusion of the battle. But within the last few minutes, a change had overtaken the palace. Men no longer ran in the grip of urgency, but moved with weary and deliberate actions.

The friends had waited through the long hours of the attack for Dresil's or Raziin's men to enter the palace, hoping to join small groups of looters and make their way through the lines without being captured.

Cedrin was still unconscious, groaning in pain and shock. It would be only a matter of time before they were discovered.

Marken closed the curtain. Skye was supporting Cedrin's prostrate body, and he looked up hopefully. 'Anything?'

Marken shook his head, replying in a whisper. 'No. It looks as though Dresil and Raziin have lost.'

Skye smiled to himself. 'Any other time I would have welcomed that.'

They waited in tense silence, gripping their calvs with unspoken ferocity, listening to the traffic of soldiers who passed only yards away from them. Marken had attempted to rouse Cedrin, but he was in a deep coma. Although he had no visible wounds, it was obvious he was in great pain. He shook as though fevered and any movement would cause him to cry out, inviting discovery.

Marken was listening to the sounds in the corridor when something familiar caused him to break out of his resigned reverie. He crept to the curtain, opening it a crack. The light fell across Cedrin, and he groaned. Marken froze for a moment, then turned his anxious gaze to the corridor.

Moving along the passage was a group of three Moon-Druids. For the first time since the attack, the corridor was empty except for this one solitary group. They were deep in discussion, conversing in ancient Cioan, the *lingua franca* of men of learning, especially that of Druids.

As he listened, catching the meaning of the words in snatches, two startling realisations hit Marken with sudden clarity. First; these unsuspecting Druids could be the only way they would leave the palace without being captured and very likely put to death; second, the only way these Druids and Temple Guardians who had suddenly aided the defence could have gotten from the Temple to the palace so quickly was through a tunnel. A second tunnel. A second chance at freedom.

Thinking rapidly, he raised the curtain and stepped into the corridor.

The Druids started as they saw him, but he smiled cordially and bowed. 'If you will pardon me, Druids, we have a wounded man here, the son of the Overseer of Slaves. He has taken a very bad wound, could you spare a moment? The Overseer would, I'm sure, make a generous donation if you saved his only son.'

The foremost Druid took in Marken with a glance. The fine silk shirt, matched with well-worked harness and trousers, his golden Cioan skin. 'And who are you, good sir?'

Marken bowed. 'Just a humble servant of the realm. A lowly scribe, your eminence. All will be explained in time, if you will spare but a moment.'

With irritation, the Druids stepped into the alcove. When they saw Skye and the rough-clad calvanni he supported, they knew they were in danger. The leader opened his mouth to yell, but Marken had a calv at his throat in an instant.

'*Yuris salvaesis*, brothers.' *The river floods.*

They looked at Marken in surprise and curiosity. The ancient Cioan quote from the saga of the river-god had put them off balance. He smiled. 'Into the alcove quickly, and shut the curtain.'

They complied.

'Now, kindly disrobe. In silence.'

They pulled the robes of the unwilling clergy over their own while the warriors of the palace guard passed scant feet away. Marken concealed his staff beneath the robe. The Druids lay bound and clothed in their thick woollen sea-cloaks on the rough stone floor. Two of them were gagged.

Marken paused with the final gag in his hands, regarding the senior Druid with a deadly smile. This was the most crucial moment; they must discover where the tunnel joined the palace. Without the knowledge, their masquerade would not take them far. The palace would be recovering, and they would have to be far away soon if they were to avoid discovery.

'Now, brother, where is the tunnel?'

The Druid swallowed. A thin sheen of sweat grew on his

forehead and tiny rivulets ran down his ruddy, Heat-flushed face. 'Tunnel?'

Marken smiled and shook his head. 'You know as well as I that denial will not help you, brother.'

The Druid glared at Marken, but soon began to shake under his unwavering stare. He clasped his hands together. After tense moments, he gave in.

'The Sarlord's day apartments. A passage leads from Myan's chamber.'

The Druid looked at Marken in fear, his breathing ragged as he stared at Marken's calv, the edge of which glittered in the light streaking through the curtain. Satisfied, Marken put up his calv and gagged the Druid.

They lifted Cedrin to his feet, the sigil of the Moon-Druids swinging lopsidedly from his neck as he swayed.

'Curse the weight of this mainlander!' Skye said in harsh but restrained tones as they struggled to keep his bulk upright. 'Are you sure you can't rouse him, Marken? This would be easier if he could walk.'

Marken shook his head. His powers had been only meagre when he left the temple. It was well beyond his skill to seek the unconscious mind and bring it to awareness – that was the task of a master Moon-Druid at the time of his peak strength, when both moons were full in the sky.

Marken could heal minor injuries and perform some Force spells at night, but during the day he had never mastered the gathering of the slumbering Moon-Essence. The time with Rel had been different, the need had awakened something within him, focussing and sharpening his skills, allowing him to gather and magnify the Essence. He had drawn the scythe into his grasp with sheer will, but that unknown power had deserted him now.

'There is nothing I can do,' he said, knowing it to be all too true.

One of the Druids looked at Marken with a penetrating glare, recognition dawning in his eyes. Marken smiled, suddenly remembering the man. It seemed like a lifetime ago. The Druid had been one of the oldest of the Initiates at the Temple in

Marken's time, a taciturn yet vigorous man who despised those of lesser standing or ability; a category in which Marken was included at the time. It felt good to at last turn the tables on him.

The pale light of dawn had begun to filter through the long rectangular clearglass panels as Marken drew back the curtain, lightening the dull grey stone of the palace walls to bone white. The corridor was without adornment or marking, and Marken fought down a surge of panic. He was completely lost. How would he find the Sarlord's apartments? Ask the first Suul lord who came by? *Excuse me, sir, how do I find the secret tunnel?*

Pushing away doubt, Marken checked to see that the passageway was empty and led them out, carefully closing the curtain behind them. They kept the hoods close to their faces and walked boldly into the palace. Marken realised he would have to ask directions and fear grew despite his best effort to push it away. They were the enemy – impostors within the stronghold – and would be dealt with as such. It was only a matter of time before they met someone. As they walked through the corridors in tense silence, supporting the dead weight of Cedrin, Marken prayed it would be a group of palace guards. They would not question the enigmatic Druids. On the other hand, if they met Druids. . .

Marken was deep in thought as they rounded a corner to come face-to-face with a squad of Temple Guardians, led by a red-robed Druid of the Red Sun. A Templeman.

The Guardians rushed forward without hesitation. Marken fought panic as they were swarmed. He turned to see Skye reach into his robe for his calv. This was all happening too fast! He forced himself to think. There was no way the Guardians could have seen through their disguise so quickly. They were rushing forward to help them! With alarm, he saw Skye begin to draw his long-knife, his eyes murderous.

'Brother Skye. These Guardians will take Brother Cedrin for us.'

Skye looked wildly at Marken, comprehension slowly dawning on him and he nodded, his calv hastily returning inside the cloak. 'As you say, Brother Marken.'

Two Guardians took the prone Cedrin, and Marken prayed

to Larus the unconscious calvanni did not wake now or he would surely betray them in his surprise.

The Templeman stopped three paces from Marken, regarding the fake Moon-Druids with thinly veiled contempt on his severe and oddly angular face. The Templeman had wiry red-blond hair, tightly cropped yet unruly from being held within the hood. His eyes were pale yellow and the ruddy gleam of his skin revealed a mixture of Cioan and Myrian blood.

'Trouble, brother?'

Marken's mind worked rapidly, struggling to remember the politics that dominated the life of the celibate Druids. There was always antagonism between the Druids of the Suns and Moons, but none more so than between the Moon-Druids and the Druids of the Red Sun.

The Moon-Druids were dedicated to healing, learning only limited Force spells used mainly in defence. The Druids of the Red Sun worshipped Uros, specialising in spells of destruction and offence. In their time of strength, under the red sun of Storm Season, they could rival a Sorcerer and wielded much weight within the Temple because of their usefulness to temporal powers. There was a saying in Kelas. *Behind every throne a Templeman.*

Marken drew himself up in mock indignation and assumed his best court manner. 'No trouble, Templeman.'

He met the Templeman's glare, aware that with dawn well broken, the Uros-Druid could shatter his bones in seconds with crushing blows of Force.

Marken let his glance fall meaningfully onto the prone form of 'brother' Cedrin, his manner dramatic. 'Some give more than others in the service of the Sisters.'

The Templeman took the bait, fixing him with a furious glare. He took a step forward, his face flushing red. Marken feared he had gone too far. 'We all have our ways to serve, brother.'

Marken bowed slightly. '*Almus Carsicum*, Brother.' *May Peace surround you.*

The Templeman grunted and left, taking all but two of the Guardians with him. Marken shuddered and turned to the nearest of the Guardians. 'To the tunnel.'

'Yes, Moon-Druid.'

The Guardians were bound to obey any Druid, but Marken had clearly earned their respect by confronting the Templeman. He smiled inwardly. *If only they knew I had no choice.* If the Templeman had been allowed to question him, they would have been finished. Their ingenuity for causing pain was boundless.

Skye gave him a relieved grin as the Guardians carried Cedrin before them, leading them through a maze-like series of passageways and stairs. They were on one of highest floors of the palace when they neared the Sarlord's apartments. The plain grey stone gave way to elaborate facades, dressed with lustrous white marble and inlaid with detailed murals set with coloured mought tiles. Ornate torches lined the walls. Small statues decorated the ledges and fine pots dating from the Cioan Empire flanked the entrance to the apartments.

The Temple Guardians flanking the door gave way before the procession. With a suitably haughty air, Marken merely nodded as they passed. Within the apartments, a handful of senior Druids and Guardians were in informal conference with five Suulvey lords, the Warlord Aris distinctive with his eye patch.

The Druids regarded the three with curious stares but said nothing. A senior Moon-Druid was with the group, but was engrossed in conversation and Marken made a sign of greeting that he remembered from his days as an initiate, Skye aping him.

They descended once more into the gloom of the tunnels. The stairs were carved of dark stone and spiralled down through the darkness into the caverns beneath Regent's Hill, then on into a hand-hewn tunnel that cut directly towards the Temple of the Sisters.

Traffic was passing to and fro, but all were anxious about some errand and spared them little heed. Marken relaxed. The tunnel began to slope upwards, then turned.

Two Moon-Druids were walking towards them down the tunnel. The leader greeted Marken ritually, then began to speak to Marken in Cioan. His heart sank. Marken knew him. It was

Osis, one of his teachers from the Temple. He remembered him as a gifted healer, and a compassionate man.

'*Heyn mortis en eth compa?*' *What ails our brother?*

Marken smiled, struggling with the Cioan. He had to make a quick decision; to steer the Druids away from Cioan or attempt to hold a conversation. A tense silence developed as he tried to form a reply in the ancient language and failed. Shaken, he replied in Anacian, the common tongue of the Empire. 'He has extended himself.'

Osis was clearly offended he had not replied in Cioan and looked at him sharply. Marken bowed to conceal his face, letting the hood drop forward.

'I see,' said Osis. He studied Marken closely. 'Do I know you, brother? You are not immediately familiar to me and yet. . .'

Osis looked sharply at Skye, realisation dawning on his face.

'Impostors!' yelled Osis.

Marken swept out his staff and slammed it into Osis' midriff. He collapsed. The second Druid tried to run but Marken tripped him and delivered a stunning blow to the back of his head, leaving him unconscious.

The Guardians had been slow to react but, dropping Cedrin to the stone floor, they reached for the spears strapped to their backs. The two calvanni stepped forward, Skye quickly drawing his calv and Marken extending the blade of his staff, turning it into a scythe. The Guardians froze with blades at their throats, their hands halfway to their weapons.

Marken reversed the scythe, striking a neat blow to the first Guardian's temple. Skye hit the second guard in the jaw with a short, bone-crunching jab that snapped his head back. Both fell to the stone unconscious. Osis was only winded, and Skye paused uncertainly over his prone form.

'Leave him, Skye.'

Marken bent down to check Cedrin. His body had been seized by a new wave of trembling and he looked around with wide eyes at the tunnel and still forms on the floor. 'Skye, he's awake!'

'What...what is happening?' muttered Cedrin, reaching to touch his head. He groaned in pain.

'There is no time to explain. Come on!' said Marken.

Skye seized Cedrin's other arm and they ran on towards the Temple, dragging Cedrin between them as he struggled to regain his feet.

Osis got to his knees. 'Marken,' he croaked.

Marken turned. So Osis did remember him. The Druid looked at him sadly. A sharp pang of regret speared into Marken's heart.

'Look where you have fallen. See the blood on your hands.'

Marken tore his gaze away. The words left him in emotional turmoil, which he pushed aside. First he had to survive.

The tunnel turned again, and he had one last glimpse of Osis. The Druid knelt at the side of the fallen men, calling on the Essence, readying his art, love and life: healing.

They emerged into the inner sanctum of the Temple. It was packed with Guardians, but they did not question them and they moved quickly towards the outer chambers, passing amongst the Druids unnoticed. Once in the public chambers, they discarded the robes behind a statue and fled the Temple.

Outside, the street was empty, and they were conspicuous without robes to ward against the cold. The suns had risen to mid-morning and they ran across the cobbles to the welcome maze of Athria's back alleys. Home.

They paused, rubbing arms and stamping numb feet on the cobbles. 'Where to now?' asked Skye.

Cedrin put a hand to his head, wincing in pain. He looked terribly pale.

'I was at Tarral's, looking for a window, a way out . . . the Spire. I . . . Fire . . spilling from me . . .'

'Catch him, Skye!'

Cedrin sank into Skye's arms, unconscious again. His body began to spasm. 'Uros' blood. Now it's the Heat,' said Skye.

Marken looked at Cedrin's flushed face and knew it was true. Marken had never even seen Cedrin ill. He was always so self-contained, so in control. *Damn it!* They needed Cedrin to get them out of this mess!

'What do we do?' asked Skye.

Marken thought hard. The Brotherhood could not let them

live, the Temple would not show mercy and the Sarlord would hang them for their role. He considered his contacts and acquaintances in the Merchants' Quarter. No, they would betray him too easily, and they knew he was in the Brotherhood. His sister Aleshel was safely married into a wealthy trading family and he refused to put her in danger.

'What about Tarral's glassworks?' ventured Skye, still holding Cedrin's prone form off the dirty, ice-cold cobbles.

Marken nodded, warming to the idea, desperate to find any place of safety no matter how transient. 'All right. Anything to get out of the cold.'

They struggled through the deserted streets, wary of patrols. Cedrin had spoken little of his foster-father. Marken knew he had a glassworks near the docks, apart from that it was a part of his life Cedrin preferred to forget. What reception they would receive remained to be seen. At least a glassworks never dulled its furnace. It would be warm.

In his sleep, Cedrin reached for the ring around his neck, becoming frantic as his hand failed to find the familiar form beneath his shirt.

Chapter Seven

Jorrel led the warriors of the Outer Garrison through the open gate of the Wall of Sorrows at full gallop. Two thousand men, arrayed for war, prepared to destroy the attacking force without mercy. The Commander of the Athrian Outer Garrison rode to Jorrel's right, squinting at the battlefield ahead in the harsh light of dawn. The suns revealed a sordid harvest of death. Shattered gates, broken weapons and half-frozen dead. All lay quiet and silent.

'Highly unusual, my Lord. Why would the gates be held against us all night, yet left open at dawn?' asked the Commander.

'You should not question providence,' said Jorrel

'Of course not, my Lord.'

Jorrel scanned the ruins of the Inner Garrison with satisfaction. When the Siren had sounded, he had feared the Inner Garrison would resist, but his luck held. With the strength of Athria behind him, he already felt like Sarlord. In his mind's eye, he saw the remnants of Dresil's attacking force in the palace, easy marks for the full force of Athria's might. Dresil and the Brotherhood leaders would long ago have retreated to the safety of the tunnels, leaving unknowing lieutenants to face the wrath of Athria.

He would ride through the shattered gates, triumphant. Jorrel, the Saviour of Athria, would scour the palace of the roving looters who dared enter the inner sanctum of the Suul. Kerril, Aris, Crephis and the Cintros, all the supporters of the old rule would be gone – dead under the assassin's knife – and the surviving Suul would look to him for leadership.

He would reward Dresil for his part by giving him control of the Brotherhood Pirates, then he would exchange his Mask for the Sarlord's throne.

The palace loomed ahead, the gates little more than scattered fragments. His moment approached. He barked orders to the leaders of the force, who conveyed his commands through the immense line. 'Scythes ready!'

At full gallop, he led the force towards the gates.

The golden pennant of Athria still flew from the Spire, and palace guards and Temple Guardians manned the battlements. *Where was Dresil's force!*

The Outer Garrison Commander saw the pennant and called down the line. 'Slow to a canter!' He turned to Jorrel with joy. 'Thank Larus. Thank the Sisters. They have held!'

The bulk of the force was ordered to halt and stand ready outside the walls as Jorrel and the Garrison Commander entered the palace. On reaching the courtyard, he discovered the littered bodies of Dresil's force. *It cannot be, they outnumbered the defenders. Raziin the Sorcerer and his black warriors were fighting with them.*

The Warlord Aris and Torren Cintros stood on the bloody soil of the courtyard, flanked by Temple Guardsmen and Templemen. Ellen Cintros knelt with a group of Moon-Druids attending the wounded.

Both Cintros alive?

In one shocking instant, Jorrel knew his plan had failed. The premature voicing of the Wail had been the first ill-omen, forcing him to actively intervene in delaying the response of the Outer Garrison. The Commander had wanted to scale the wall, but he had overruled him, directing him to form ranks before the main gate and wait. He scanned those who filled the courtyard and despair grew within him. More than half the assassins had failed. Struggling to master himself, he dismounted and walked to Aris, bowing to the Warlord. The Outer Garrison Commander dismounted and followed him, also bowing to Aris.

'Lord Aris. I heard the Wail and mustered the Legion. If not for the attackers holding the Wall of Sorrows we could have prevented this,' said Jorrel.

Jorrel waved at the massive carnage around him, hoping his show of regret was convincing. 'Thank the Sisters you turned the attackers.'

Aris turned from Jorrel without responding and addressed the Commander. 'Bring four divisions into the palace to relieve the wall and palace guards. Leave another at the Wall of Sorrows, set roving patrols inside and outside the perimeter, and then return here to me with the Garrison Captains.'

The warrior bowed and left.

Jorrel feigned a grim expression. 'How did the attackers enter the Wall of Sorrows?'

Aris fixed him with a pale glare.

Torren answered, his anger all too apparent. 'Betrayal, Jorrel. Betrayal!'

Aris turned to Torren, his voice tightly controlled. 'Be silent, Captain.'

Torren's eyes glowed like molten glass, but he held his tongue.

Jorrel's mind was far ahead. He had to reach the harbour. He could be out of Athria within hours, with the bulk of his fortune. Any number of independent ports along the coast would be open to him. He had contacts in most of them.

He bowed, still feigning a show of regret, but his skin had begun to burn beneath his clothes. The Heat was rising! He must leave before it betrayed him.

'If you will excuse me. I must check on my interests, Lords,' he said, stepping back as though to withdraw.

'No, Jorrel, stand here by me,' said Aris casually.

Jorrel tried to reply, but could only manage a grim nod of acquiescence as he walked forward to stand beside Aris. He began to breathe heavily and, despite his best efforts at control, the Heat rose in a sudden fever, loosing the floodgates of his emotion. Trapped! *They know I am the usurper. Aris is only toying with me.*

His breathing grew ragged, and he loosened his fine cloak. The motion did not escape Torren. 'Losing control, Jorrel?'

The former pirate stood beside the Warlord as reports came in from all over Regent's Hill.

An amelak-drawn wagon appeared, moving slowly through the broken gates. Palsus walked beside it, along with Kerril's bodyguard.

Aris and Torren rushed forward, Jorrel following them.

Inside the wagon was the body of Kerril, twisted with the agony of his death.

Aris bowed forward with the shock, having to support himself against the wagon. Torren stepped forward, but Aris waved him away.

'Poison,' said Aris, almost at a whisper, turning to glare at Jorrel. 'First Myan, now Kerril. To die like this. . .'

Aris' jaw clenched and he straightened, walking slowly to Palsus and gripping his shoulder in silent sympathy.

Jorrel was truly shaken. The Regent was dead, but incredibly he was the only Suulvey to perish. Along with him, a mere six Suul had been killed. It was a disaster. It seemed Stone's assanni were overrated.

The wagon slowly drew away, and Jorrel took his place once more with Aris and Torren. His mind was spinning with the enormity of his defeat. As the minutes drew by, he could restrain himself no longer. 'Excuse me, Warlord. Exactly what do you want of me?'

The Warlord turned as though surprised to see Jorrel still there. 'Oh, to witness an interrogation.'

Jorrel's breathing was out of control, his body shaking while inside he was growing numb with fear. 'Whose, Lord?'

'An assassin was captured alive, he claims to know the architect of the plan. A pirate he says.'

Jorrel's voice quivered as he answered. 'A pirate? How curious.'

Aris' tight smile gave way to a look of unrestrained venom, anger twisting his face with terrifying intensity. 'Yes. How curious.'

* * *

138

Against the advice of the Moon-Druids, Ellen continued to use the Fire to heal as many as she could. The black-robed healers did not resent her gift, they welcomed any power that could preserve life, but they knew only too well of the consequences. Ellen was less worried. She knew the damage had been done, and was too overwhelmed with grief to care. Kerril was dead, his wife with him. Torn between sadness and hopelessness, she waited for more news, knowing Crephis was still missing.

Uros-Druids were the political power in the Temple. For centuries they had led purges against Sorcery, destroying any remnants of the Old Blood that surfaced in Kelas. They were now the supreme religious power. Even rulers like Myan, who had retained the gifts of the Old Blood, had to give way to them, practising their art in secret.

She was unsure how the Temple would react. They could not simply burn her, she was of a ruling line, nor could they let so public a display pass unquestioned.

A young Initiate of the Moon-Druids ran down the sweeping steps from the battlements.

'Brother Clavis! Crephis is on the Spire, he has taken a wound and is fading fast. He asks for Suul. . .' The young boy noticed Ellen and bowed, wide-eyed, embarrassed and a little fearful. 'He asks for Suul Ellen Cintros.'

Beside her, Clavis, one of the more senior of the Moon-Druids attending the wounded, looked up sharply from his work, first at the Initiate, then at her.

Ellen's heart leapt with sudden hope. She sprinted for the battlements leading to the Spire.

'Wait, Ellen,' called Clavis, but she did not.

Exhausted, she reached the top to find one young Initiate and four Temple Guardians flanking the prostrate Druid. The Guardsmen blocked her way.

'Let me go to him!'

She looked anxiously at Crephis, trying to gauge the extent of his wounds. Blood soaked his robes, yet even through his agony, she could see his relief that she had come.

'Let her pass,' croaked Crephis.

Reluctantly, the Guardsmen drew apart. Fighting tears, she

knelt at his side. Gathering the Fire, she began to form the Matrix of Form, but Crephis stopped her.

'Too late Ellen,' he said, blood dribbling from his mouth. 'I have bled too much inside.'

Stunned and disbelieving, she let the Fire seep away. She looked into his eyes, glassy with pain and impending death.

'Take this.' Crephis placed a blood-covered signet ring in her hand. A gushing flow of blood surged from his lips, sending him coughing.

'Cedrin,' he said, blood bubbling forth with the words.

Ellen understood. Cedrin had been here.

'Seek out Raphal.'

Raphal was Crephis' older brother, a kindly Larus Druid and Priest who had been confessor and spiritual guide to the Cintros family all through her childhood. In many ways, he had been a second father to her. An expert in the prophecies of the Scion, he had left Athria years ago to study in the Temples of Kelas. It was natural that Crephis should ask after him as he lay dying, so she pushed it from her mind.

He struggled to speak again, most of the words lost in a gurgling froth of blood. Only one word was clearly recognisable. *Calvanni.*

A sickening realisation dawned on her. 'Cedrin is a calvanni and was here as part of the attacking force.'

Crephis nodded, clearly beyond speech. His face was pale, and consciousness and life were fading fast. Ellen held him as he died. One moment he was there, the next he was gone; light and comprehension flickering out in the once-intelligent, charismatic eyes. Grief twisted her heart, yet tears were beyond her. Fate had taken all of them. All of those she loved.

Cedrin. He was one of the killers who had slain Kerril, who had left Crephis here dying. Was Myan's blood on his blade, as Crephis' surely was? How ironic. Myan had sought Belin's son as a key to salvation, but he was a killer. A Brotherhood calvanni.

The grief hardened her heart. She would follow Myan's will and find the Scion, but once she had discharged her duty, Cedrin would pay for his crimes. Justice would be done.

She cradled Crephis in her arms as the Moon-Druids crowded around her, panting from the climb. One by one they left her to her grief and sadness.

* * *

Cedrin woke with a gasp to find Marken and Skye restraining him, their faces weary and concerned.

'The ring. I've lost the ring,' Cedrin shouted, convinced in a dream sense he had to find it. He looked from face to face, delirious from dreaming, struggling against their hold on his arms.

'We're safe now, Cedrin. Relax. We've brought you to Tarral's.'

Slowly comprehension seeped into Cedrin's dulled consciousness. Memories of the long trek up the coast, the dark journey through the tunnels and the scaling of the battlements came flooding back. Their escape from Raziin was still hazy. All he could remember was the terror of being seized by the Northman's spell, Jaso's death, then fire. Fire swelling and covering everything.

He relaxed and looked around him. 'It's all right. I'm back on solid ground now.'

He was in one of Tarral's lower storey bedrooms, long vacant by the look of the disarray. Jagged blocks of glass and scattered tools lay across the floor. Roughly drawn designs for milkglass casts sat in a pile of paper nearby where they had been hastily removed from the dust-covered bed.

A wave of weakness overtook him, and he fell back onto the covers. 'How did we get out of Regent's Hill?'

Marken made a sign to keep silent as Emily, Cedrin's foster-mother, entered the room with a plate of food and a washbowl.

She paused on the step, meeting Cedrin's gaze. 'So you're awake, are you?' Her southern accent was still noticeable after all her years in Athria.

'Hello, Em,' said Cedrin, abashed even after all these years by a woman who only came to his chest in height.

She moved into the room with the casual grace of the dark-skinned people of the southern Sardoms. Her hair, once raven black, was now tinged with grey, her face lined with hardship and joy in equal measure. She placed the tray beside the bed as Tarral entered the room.

The thickset glassmith had hardly changed in ten years, possessing the powerful frame and sense of strength Cedrin remembered. His face was still deeply tanned, his light hair now shot with occasional streaks of grey that served to emphasise his mature strength. Cedrin was surprised to immediately recognise the traits of a warrior. The stance and eye, the confidence. Strange, he had never seen it as a boy.

'Cedrin. It's been a long time,' said the glassmith.

Once Cedrin had fallen in with the Brotherhood, he had left Tarral's roof for good. Yet the real trouble had started years before that, on the day of his manhood, the day Tarral should have confirmed him as apprentice. Until then he had dreamed of nothing more than making the finest lanedd blades Athria had ever seen; Tarral's mark, his father's mark, displayed proudly on each perfect cast. Instead he had been taken aside, presented with Belin's ring and abruptly told he was the bastard son of some forgotten noble; Belin Kaidell, Suul Lord of the Bulvuran court, ruler of the Delta province, First General of the Bulvuran Legions. The words meant nothing to him.

Tarral had told him what a great man Belin was, yet it seemed despite his promises to come for him, the old general was content to abandon his bastard in Athria. That told him all he needed to know of Belin, and the Suul. Tarral had arranged a commission for him in the garrison, using old contacts, but Cedrin had angrily rejected his plans, still stung by what he had seen as betrayal.

Ten years had passed, yet it seemed very little had changed here. He felt a pang of regret at the distance between them, but he would not have changed anything. Turning, he pushed himself to a sitting position. He began to eat the food on the tray, giving in to the hunger that came on the heels of the Heat. Tarral moved into the room to stand beside Skye and Marken.

'Sorcery, you say?' Tarral watched Cedrin carefully.

Marken nodded. 'A Northman called Cinnor. Raziin Cinnor.'

Tarral nodded gravely. 'Raziin. Hmm. Such a shame. His father was a great man. Without Leith and his power, the Legions would have never stopped the Eathal from taking the Empire after the death of Emperor Riin.'

Cedrin was surprised at Tarral's casual manner regarding Sorcery.

'Leith was a Sorcerer?' asked Marken, incredulous.

Tarral nodded. 'Leith was a powerful Sorcerer, and without him the Eathal Sorcerers would have destroyed Raynor completely.'

Tarral abruptly changed tack. 'How is he, Emily?' he asked, turning to his wife.

The small woman watched Cedrin critically. 'A touch of the Heat maybe. Other than that, he's all right. A lot of fuss over nothing, but he's always been like that.'

Cedrin smiled at Emily's jibe. He had missed her, missed Tarral. Living on the edge for so long, he had forgotten one part of him longed to belong; longed to be with those close to him without shields and defences. He pushed himself to his feet unsteadily.

'Thank you both,' he said, looking from Tarral to Emily.

Emily smiled and picked up the tray. 'Less than nothing,' she said, pausing to touch his face with a mother's care.

'It's good to see you,' she said, almost whispering. She paused briefly then left, her eyes moist.

Tarral turned to Marken and Skye. 'I need to talk to Cedrin, alone.' They nodded and left the room.

Once gone, Tarral regarded Cedrin with a smile. 'Well, you've grown into a fine figure of a man.'

Cedrin said nothing, struggling for words amid so many conflicting and long-buried emotions. In the end, he could find nothing to say.

'I knew the Brotherhood would come to ill for you in the end. In fact, I'm surprised you lasted this long. You must be pretty good with that calv,' said Tarral, indicating the long-knife slipped into his harness, and the five degrees of the calvanni tattooed into his chest.

Cedrin smiled. 'I get by.'

Tarral grunted. 'Come with me.'

Cedrin followed Tarral through the kiln room, looking round with nostalgia as they passed through to one of the back rooms. Inside, Tarral reached for one of the top shelves and took down a greatscythe. He hefted it with affection and looked at Cedrin.

'Once you said you wanted to follow my trade.' He handed Cedrin the ornate and finely made greatscythe. 'This was my trade long before milkglass and forges.'

Cedrin examined the haft. It was very old yet the mechanism was built with fine precision. He twisted the haft and the twin blades snapped smoothly into place.

'Belin never cared to give you anything but a name. Take my greatscythe.' Tarral walked forward, placing a hand on Cedrin's shoulder. 'Take it and leave your past behind. Wielding knives in the night is an assassin's trade. For my sake and yours, take this and walk under the suns, become a warrior. Follow the honour-code of the scytheman. Then you can walk without shame among men of high repute.'

Tarral offered Cedrin his forearm and they gripped. Man to man, they tested each other's strength, then laughed.

'Get to Raynor. A man named Kranor used to serve with me in the Legions. He'll get you honest work. Then move north. The Eathal are already on the move.'

They regarded each other in silence for a time, then Tarral spoke. 'You always were my son, Cedrin. In my heart.'

Cedrin felt something within him stir and come to life once more. He broke the grip and left the room.

The future lay ahead.

Chapter Eight

Ellen looked at the wretch chained to the wall, torn by conflicting emotions of pity and anger. For hours she had watched his interrogation, standing with Torren and Aris as the Templemen did their work. The Warlord and her brother had remained grim throughout, their faces lined with fatigue, yet showing no sign of mercy.

The room was lit by a scattered row of torches that left most of the deep, stone-hewn room in shadow. Two soot-blackened mought braziers had been set up nearby and glowed deep red, heating the air in the room to the point of discomfort.

The captured assassin, a thin, wiry man, was chained to the wall with ancient bands of solid mought. His clothes were blackened tatters, his face and torso bleeding from a score of cuts, his muscles knotted with pain to the point of spasm. His face, which had once held arrogance so easily, now showed only defeat. Given over to exhaustion, he sagged under his own weight; sometimes praying to Kallor for death, at other times weeping amid an incoherent torrent of words.

Standing within the dim circle of light, the two red-robed Templemen regarded the man with detachment and contempt. One held a red-hot rod of clearglass in a leather glove; the other a jagged crystal of silver glowmetal, its black light rippling with recent use. It was Aganus, the paingiver.

Further back in the shadows, Jorrel stood flanked by palace guards and two Temple Guardians. At first, Ellen had been puzzled by his appearance and the guard placed around him, yet as the interrogation continued, she began to understand. The assassin had made it clear that the Mask of Pirates was the Brotherhood leader responsible for organising this rebellion, and that this same man was also a Suulvey lord of Athria. If that was true – and she had no doubt – it could only be Jorrel. Yet the assassin had not been able to describe the Mask or reveal his true name.

The Warlord stepped forward. 'Enough, brothers.'

The Templemen bowed and withdrew to the borders of the light, clearly disappointed despite their passive demeanour.

Aris walked to the wall, regarding the assassin with distaste. He lifted his head by the hair and stared into eyes driven crazy by pain. Dropping his head, he stepped back and motioned to the two palace guards beside the door.

'Take him. Hold him for public execution with the others.'

The guards bowed and unshackled the assassin. He fell to the floor, barely conscious. They hauled him to his feet and dragged him away.

Torren left Ellen's side and stalked over to Aris, his face hot with rage. He pointed to where Jorrel stood in the shadows. 'What are we waiting for? It's obvious who was behind this,' he said, his voice barely contained.

Aris fixed Torren with a pale glare, his mouth drawn into a grimace.

'Jorrel was not a target of the assassins," Torren continued. 'Those marked for death were his enemies in the Council. You know this, Aris. And he was a trader before he bought his title. There is but a small step from trader to pirate.'

Aris nodded in agreement. 'He was more than a pirate, he was the pirate's Mask in the Brotherhood, one of their very leaders. How could such a man rise to the rank of Suulvey?' He raised his hand to his chin in thought.

'Why do we wait?' asked Torren in a harsh whisper.

'Because we have no proof. Yet,' said Aris.

Ellen looked back across the room at Jorrel, who had remained silent throughout the long interrogation. 'Have you noticed that although the room is as hot as a summer's day, Lord Jorrel does not disrobe?'

Jorrel stiffened.

'Yes. In fact,' continued Aris, 'I have never seen Jorrel without one of his fine silk shirts.'

Torren gestured to the two Temple Guardians who flanked Jorrel. 'Remove his shirt!'

Jorrel began to struggle, but two palace guards ran forward to restrain him while one of the Temple Guardians took hold of his finely pattered shirt and ripped it open.

A broad scar ran up Jorrel's chest, dividing the only remaining tattoo, a faded sea serpent totem. If there had been any other tattoos, they had perished beneath the wound.

'How convenient,' said Aris.

Jorrel managed a small smile. 'A fire at sea. Long ago. A burning spar fell across me. As you can see, it left me permanently scarred.'

'Warlord Aris,' said one of the Templeman. 'There are Moon-Druids who could heal that scar. And even though the inks have gone, the pattern of any tattoos would remain in the deeper skin and be revealed in the healing.'

Aris smiled. 'Summon your brothers.'

Jorrel suddenly shouted, twisting expertly out of the grip of the guards. In an instant he was armed with a calv, taken from the harness of one of the warriors. The Temple Guardians lunged forward, but Jorrel slipped inside their guard, opening one Guardian's throat and slashing viciously at the second. The first Guardian fell, the second covering his face and staggering backwards as blood sprouted from between his fingers. Jorrel lunged about him with the strength of the Heat. He downed another warrior and raced for the door.

Torren ran forward to intercept Jorrel, but was forced back by a deadly sweep of the man's calv. Like Ellen, Torren was unarmed, having put down his weapons after the battle.

The rogue Suulvey swept past them.

Ellen snatched up a spear from a fallen Guardian and raced after him.

Jorrel was almost at the door when she caught up with him. Ellen swept the spear down, hitting Jorrel on the shoulder with the haft. He cried out and spun around, calv drawn back for a thrust, but she was ready. The spear became a blur in her hands, the butt sweeping down to shatter the blade. Quickly she reversed the spear, the point pushing into the flesh of his throat.

Jorrel froze.

The remaining guards recovered and rushed forward to seize him.

Ellen passed the spear back to the wounded Guardian as he helped the others carry away the body of his fallen comrade.

Together they glared at Jorrel.

'What more proof do you need! He has the skills of a calvanni!' snapped Torren.

Aris motioned the palace guards to bring Jorrel forward. The Heat within him had risen uncontrolled and his once-fine clothes were soaked with sweat. His breath shuddered as he stood before them, his eyes flickering to the empty chains and filthy, blood-stained wall. He began to shake, yet remained silent.

'Take him to the wall,' said Aris with harsh finality.

'*No!* Wait,' pleaded Jorrel.

'What do you have to say for yourself, Jorrel?'

'I am innocent! I was merely trying to save myself from Torren's false accusations!'

Aris' eye bored mercilessly into Jorrel. 'You slay our own men and dare to profess innocence? We now know your Brotherhood was involved, Jorrel, but there is more to this. Why did you seek out Raziin Cinnor? He is an agent of Hukum. Where did the Eathal fit into your plans?'

'Eathal?' muttered Jorrel.

'Chain him!' commanded Aris.

Jorrel's eyes widened and terror ripped a scream from his throat as the shackles snapped around his wrists and ankles.

The Uros-Druids came forth, scrutinising Jorrel much like a painter would a canvas, readying their tools for art.

'I have rights,' shouted Jorrel. 'You cannot torture a Suulvey lord; the Council will not stand for it! As a member of the Council, you cannot order it. You must not.'

'How can you talk of rights when hundreds lay dead?' asked Aris, his voice as sharp as a knife. 'Your death is already certain, Jorrel. But there will be no simple public execution for you,

Mask. I promise you this: you will live long enough to know the real meaning of betrayal.'

'I still have friends in the Council,' pleaded Jorrel.

The Warlord looked at him with contempt. 'You have no friends anymore.' Aris signalled to the Druids.

The Templeman who held Aganus paused a moment to concentrate, drawing on the power of Uros, then channelled a precise flow of energy into the glowmetal. The silver lines thickened, the black light squirming as the balance of the magical crystal shifted.

Jorrel looked around, his eyes wild.

A flash of silver lightning lanced across the room to strike the Brotherhood Mask in the chest. He stiffened immediately with pain, his whole body going into spasms.

The lightning struck again.

Jorrel surged against the chains, this time finding his voice as a pain-filled scream echoed through the chamber. 'Aris, I have wealth, tremendous wealth; it could be yours. Galleys full of coin and gems. Anything. Anything.'

The Templeman with the rod of hot clearglass looked across at Aris expectantly.

Grimly, Aris nodded.

The Templeman began to advance towards the Mask.

'Think, Aris! The name of Cinev is no less ancient than Cintros. Your line has always been kept from supreme power in Athria by the same ruling elite. The Cintros. The bed-boys of the Cinanac Emperors. I know you secretly long to take the power! I can help you.'

The Templeman paused and looked across at Aris.

The Warlord's hands shook with fury. 'Do you confess?'

Jorrel began to sob. 'Please,' he pleaded.

'Do it!' commanded Aris.

The Templeman took the last two steps, and the hot glass sizzled onto his skin.

This time the screaming was truly horrible.

The rod was removed, and Jorrel sagged to the limit of his chains.

'Do you confess?' snapped Aris.

Jorrel was crying as the Templeman leant forward with his rod.

'No! *No!* I confess. . .I confess . . .'

'Enough delay. We have his confession. We must strike hard and fast at the Brotherhood!' stormed Torren.

'I agree. They must pay for their crimes,' said Ellen.

Aris nodded. 'Yes, they must; and here, within our grasp, is a man who can give us the Brotherhood's most intimate secrets.'

'And you will tell us, won't you, Jorrel?' said Aris.

Jorrel shook his head convulsively, yet he could not take his eyes from the clearglass rod, or the glowmetal.

The questions continued, and Jorrel endured much pain before giving up the secrets of the Brotherhood – yet he did.

Finally Ellen had the chance to ask her own question, one that had been burning in her mind since the battle.

'And why did Raziin hold back his power? Why didn't he simply shatter the gates and take the palace with Dresil's men?'

Torren and Aris' eyes met briefly.

Jorrel looked up at her. His face was a ruin of burns, twisted with pain and haunted with his defeat – yet his voice was calm, almost conversational now that the final barriers had been broken. 'The palace could not be taken too quickly – otherwise it would have spoiled the ease and triumph of my . . . my victory. The lives of Dresil's men were a necessary sacrifice.'

So she had been right. Raziin did hold back. A worm of doubt entered her. She had thought Raziin had fled from her, yet what if he had been merely taking the opportunity to desert Dresil, as he had planned all along? No, she had felt his mind. He had no defence against the Final Matrix.

Ellen had all the answers she needed. She nodded to Aris and Torren and took her leave. In the corridor, she paused in the dank cool, seeking to clear her mind, to push away the terror and agony she had witnessed.

She was streaked with grime and dirt. The blood of enemies stained her clothing, sent there by her killing blows. It was mixed with the blood of Athrian warriors she had held as they died. A sense of futility weighed on her with crushing intensity. If this was the reality of war, she was glad her father had shielded her from it.

Here, in the darkness of the palace dungeons, it would be easy to believe light had gone from her life; that all love, joy and laughter had been taken from her. Ellen longed to return to the Cintros mansion and clean herself, to wash away the memories along with the dirt and dried blood; but before she could, she had one more duty to perform.

Taking a deep draught of the cold, moist air, she walked deeper into the dungeons towards the holding cells.

She asked the gaoler to lead her to the assassin's cell. He asked no questions, but simply unbolted the door and held a torch aloft as she entered.

He was awake, lying prone on the floor, his eyes wide and unseeing, his breathing ragged.

'Assassin,' she said, conscious of the tremor in her own voice.

He turned towards her and a part of him recognised her, as though from a distance, as one of those in the torture room. He began to shake. Ellen forged ahead with her questions, conscious of the man's pain.

'Do you know a Brotherhood calvanni called Cedrin?'

Under the touch of the Templemen he had learnt to answer without hesitation and the words tumbled from him. 'Cedrin. Yes, I know him. Tall. He's a smuggler.'

Ellen felt excitement, relief and disappointment in succession. Now there was chance she would find him. She had expected, almost wanted, him to be an assassin, an easy target for her grief. Yet beneath her anger, she had secretly hoped that Myan's faith had not been misplaced; that this calvanni would be a good man, and that he really would be the key to the Scion. Ellen felt the ring in her pocket. Its touch was oddly comforting.

'Where can he be found?'

The assassin knew his trade and detailed the locations where he might be captured. Rooms in Lookout Hill, the Brotherhood's tunnels, the glassmith works of his father Tarral or the Sea Serpent tavern on the docks. She would try them all, and more, to find him.

The assassin tried to sit upright, but the shaking ruin of his body failed him and he sank to the stone. Ellen felt pity for him and experienced a strong desire to heal him. Unsettled, she withdrew.

'Thank you, gaoler,' she said with formality, striding into the dark, her mind in confusion. How could she feel pity for an assassin? One of Kerril's killers! She would not let herself. He had caused pain, he deserved pain in return, she reasoned. Yet as she made her way through the dark, Jorrel's screams once more haunted her thoughts, and her heart told her differently. She had seen too much pain and wanted an end to it.

* * *

At a signal from Cedrin, Marken and Skye lowered their hoods and pulled their robes tighter around themselves to conceal their harnesses and weapons. Head bowed, Cedrin led them past a crowd of supplicants into the small Temple of the Tree. The Tree, a sickly but ancient specimen, lay in the courtyard. Island legend imbued it with magical properties and many ceremonies were carried out beneath its skeletal limbs.

The Temple itself was a small building, squat and unremarkable, constructed of dusty, grey stone. Cedrin led them up the rough steps into the building, pausing as he saw a Priestess in robes of deep ochre setting incense around a marble carving of the Tree. The skilful depiction had yellowed with age and jagged marble stubs showed where limbs had been removed through heresy, accident or decay.

The woman straightened. She came forward with measured steps, the material of her robe stiff from the ground-sweeping hem of the skirt to the multi-coloured bands around the flared neck. She was of middle age, the grey in her hair lending austerity to her unlined face.

'Who comes to the Temple of the Tree?' she asked warily, her gaze sweeping across Cedrin and his friends. She knows we are Brotherhood, he thought, trying to remain calm. This Temple was their last hope of leaving Athria alive.

'Have you come to view the dead?' she asked quickly, her eyes calculating. 'Come with me.'

She led them down a narrow stairwell into darkness. Inside

the crypt, the Priestess lit a torch with a burst of flame from her fingers and rounded on them in fury. 'I told the Brotherhood I did not want them using this place. It is holy ground!'

Cedrin pushed back his hood. 'Priestess, we had no choice. The Brotherhood wants us dead, the waterfront is crawling with soldiers. Your entrance to the tunnels is the only way to reach the harbour alive. We have some coin, gems, they are yours . . . whatever it takes.'

'Be silent!' she snapped.

The Priestess' face became serene, distant. For a time it seemed she had forgotten them, then she changed focus, looking deeply into the face of each man.

'Women's mysteries make my skin crawl,' said Skye with a superstitious shiver.

'It's the Earth-Essence,' said Marken, his voice hushed with awe and reverence. 'I can almost touch it.'

Cedrin could feel nothing. He looked across at Marken and could see his face crease with concentration, then frustration. He smiled. Most Druids could not sense the flow, but early in his training he had been singled out as one of the few who could. Marken had once described the distant feel of the Earth-Essence; feminine, enticing; a feast set out of reach of his hunger.

The Earth-Essence varied not with time, but with *place*. Within their minor Temples, on holy ground, the Priestesses were powerful. Though their power was used for healing, vision and prophecy, they could also use the Earth-Essence for destruction. He realised immediately the folly of fighting this woman.

The Priestess closed her eyes and bowed her head. Suddenly they saw themselves through her eyes: three desperate men driven by fear, prepared to bloody their hands to win freedom.

Cedrin knew at once they had just been tested, a trial usually reserved for potential initiates.

Raising her head, she took a breath and met Cedrin's eyes. Her eyes were sad. She knew him now, better than he knew himself. She turned to Marken briefly, a smile tugging at the corners of her mouth, then to Skye. Inexplicably, she bowed to him. He awkwardly returned the bow. Without another word, she led them deeper into the crypt.

Obediently, they filed after her, finally reaching the back wall of the chamber. Without ceremony, she opened a section of wall. A flood of cool air gushed into the chamber from the darkness beyond, bringing with it the muted sounds and haunting calls of the underworld.

'Go,' she said.

Like the others, Cedrin struggled to form some thanks, but words were impossible, the moment too strong. At a loss, they moved into the dark and the Priestess handed them the torch she carried. For an instant, she was framed in black silhouette against the doorway, then she was gone as the vault closed once more.

Cedrin led them on through the maze-like tunnels, praying he remembered the way.

'Uros-cursed demoness. I am glad that's over,' said Skye.

'She was a powerful woman,' said Marken, his voice hoarse with suppressed desire.

They walked in silence through the endless caverns, engulfed in black. A gnawing fear was growing in Cedrin that they were lost, but finally he glimpsed a mark on the wall. He ran forward to touch it. 'At last!'

'Kallor will have to wait for us after all,' joked Marken.

'Now I know where we are,' said Cedrin, fingering the elaborate bat symbol chiselled into the rock.

'And now we have to be alert for Dresil's henchmen,' said Skye, looking around the dark chamber and adjoining tunnels for any sign of movement.

When they left Tarral's, they agreed they had to flee Athria. The Brotherhood leaders could never let them live. Cedrin and any allied to him represented too much of a threat. The Masks and Mouthpieces had plotted to use them as cattle, then destroy them at their whim. After the failure of their plans, they would be living in fear, twice as determined to destroy any opposition. By now word would have spread of the raid on Regent's Hill – and its failure. The Brotherhood leadership would be desperate to retain control and would have positioned strong forces of calvanni or assanni at the usual entrances with orders to kill the select few higher degrees they judged to be a threat.

They drew calvs, moving into the corridors that led to the Cavern and the tidal caves beyond, Cedrin's greatscythe and Marken's staff concealed beneath their robes.

They met their first group of Brotherhood men and greetings passed between them tensely, but without incident. The three passed on with relief, gaining confidence.

They walked on, passing more groups of men, drawing curious glances from many calvanni who knew them, but none challenged them. Eventually they came to the chambers below the Sea Serpent. Scores of men swarmed into the caves from above, some wounded, others loaded with chests and sacks of coin and contraband.

Cedrin halted one. 'What's going on?'

The calvanni looked at Cedrin in terror and pointed to the ceiling. 'Guardsmen. They are ripping the Sea Serpent to pieces. It's only a matter of time before they find the tunnel.'

The young calvanni broke away from Cedrin and ran to the safety of the deeper tunnels. They hurried on, joined by small groups of panicked men rushing towards the Cavern, a juncture for tunnels leading throughout the city. As they burst into the round chamber, a familiar voice reached Cedrin over the chaos. *Mat.* Cedrin spun towards the Mouthpiece, gripping his calv tightly. Mat had not seen them yet. He motioned to the others and they drew closer. Soon he could distinguish Mat's words from the general hubbub.

'Tell him to get down here. We have to call these guards off before they blow the whole thing,' said Mat. A calvanni sped away from the Mouthpiece, weaving through the press.

As he turned, Mat saw them, a grim smile spreading across his face. He called to his men. 'Boys, take them. Take 'em down. They're the ones who betrayed us.'

Eight of Mat's henchmen drew calvs and spread out.

Cedrin knew them and called to the leader, a third-degree from Smuggling, who he knew well. 'Retis, stop. It's Mat who betrayed us. Listen to me.'

The huge man shook his head. 'He's the Mouthpiece. Got to do as he says, mate. Sorry.'

An electric tension filled the room. Suddenly an invisible line was drawn. A small crowd surged across the room, led by Banis to back up Cedrin. His heart leapt with hope. Somehow he and his men had escaped the carnage. The fifth-degree calvanni nodded gravely to Cedrin. Now was the time.

As Mat's henchmen advanced, Cedrin drew the odds. They could make a good account of themselves, but the end result would be the same; they would end up dead. Here, in the middle of this chaos, with the Brotherhood in disarray, he would have to challenge and defeat Mat. It was the only way to get out of this alive. Cedrin pointed at Mat and shouted over the noise. 'He is not the Mouthpiece! He is a piece of harena-shit. I am the Mouthpiece here!'

The henchmen stopped advancing, the call plain.

Cedrin had enough men backing him to call a challenge. It had been the last thing Mat expected. Despite the chaos above, the calvanni spread out to form the Circle of Blades.

In the centre stood Cedrin and Mat.

Cedrin shrugged off his robe, passing it and his greatscythe to Marken. He swung his arms, loosening his shoulders.

'Kill them!' screamed Mat.

Retis kept his place in the Circle, looking at Mat quizzically. He would not budge. The rules of the Brotherhood were clear.

Marken's hand moved down towards the throwing-knife in his boot, but Cedrin shook his head sharply. Cedrin had to face Mat alone – anything else would end in all their deaths.

Cedrin repeated the challenge. 'Come on, you spineless piece of garbage. Come on!'

Cedrin had him. The men would go no further until Mat answered the challenge. That was the law of the Brotherhood. The Circle had been formed; there was no middle ground. Mat drew his calv, throwing his harness to the floor.

'All right, mainlander, you die!'

Mat surged at Cedrin.

The assembled calvanni turned their razor sharp calvs into the centre of the Circle towards the combatants. If either tried to flee, they would be killed.

The tension built until Mat leapt forward with a feint. Cedrin recognised the move – and he would not be fooled twice.

Cedrin blocked the feint and the stabbing attack, following with a riposte of blinding speed. As Mat hastily stepped away, Cedrin's leg lashed out in a powerful kick, meeting Mat's knee with a crack. The Mouthpiece cried out but pressed in, his knee affecting his mobility but not his skill.

For tense minutes the exchange swept back and forth until their forearms and chests were covered with thin cuts. Mat was tiring, Cedrin could feel it, the knee was giving him pain and it was slowing him. Desperate, Mat surged forward with a stabbing thrust.

Another feint.

Cedrin sidestepped as Mat's blade turned to slice at his throat, catching him across the shoulder. In a lightning quick return thrust, Cedrin's blade cut deeply into Mat's lower back. The Mouthpiece grunted in shock, then turned, his calv ready. Blood gushed from the wound.

Mat leapt forward once more but his knee gave way. He fell forward onto the stone. Cedrin leapt forward, his boot smashing down on Mat's knife-hand with a sickening crunch.

With contempt, Cedrin kicked the calv out of Mat's grasp. Mat struggled to rise, his body weakening from blood loss, but Cedrin kicked him savagely to the ground. Kneeling on his back, he pulled Mat's head up, his razor-sharp blade at Mat's throat as he readied himself for the death-thrust. He paused.

The tension built in the Circle. Was this the way to end it? Had they been allies, he may have let him live on as a fifth-degree under his command, but they were far from that. Mat had betrayed him and his friends to their deaths. Even so, there was no honour in this. Besides, Mat did not deserve a clean death. He pushed the old calvanni's head into the stone and took his right hand. Mat struggled as he understood.

'No. No. Kill me!' screamed Mat as the blade cut into his thumb. He gave a gasp and cried out in shock as the severed thumb fell from its bloody stump.

Now Mat was marked. Unable to wield a calv, he was finished in the Brotherhood. If he survived, he would be an outcast in the rigid society of Athria, to live each day with his defeat.

Retis put up his calv and nodded to Cedrin in acknowledgment.

Cedrin was now the Mouthpiece of Smuggling.

The irony of it cut deeper than any blade. Now, with the Brotherhood in ruins, his ambitions were finally realised. He sheathed his calv.

Mat struggled to his feet, clutching his hand. The calvanni in the circle stepped aside as he pushed through. He fled into the tunnels.

Banis walked over to Cedrin, gripping forearms. 'Well done, my friend.'

'Thank you, Banis. It's good to see you. How did you make it back alive?'

Banis smiled. 'We slipped away from the force and scaled the Wall of Sorrows. We did run into some of Stone's assanni in the Kali, but let's just say they'll not be troubling us again. What now, Mouthpiece? Perhaps together we can restore some sanity.'

Cedrin smiled grimly. 'Retis, have you seen any of the other Mouthpieces?'

Retis shook his head.

'Banis, have you seen Tice?'

Banis smiled. 'He knows better than to show his face to me. If he does, he will find himself in the Circle as well.'

Cedrin looked around the milling crowd, swelling every minute as calvanni pushed into the Cavern, fleeing the chaos on the surface. Apart from Banis and his men, there were only a handful from Dresil's attacking force.

'All of you! Gather around!'

Word was quickly passed around to the newcomers that Cedrin was the new Mouthpiece of Smuggling. It seemed every other Mouthpiece, and their Masks, had gone to ground following the failure of Dresil's plans, and the men were desperate for leadership.

Cedrin looked into the crowd. He knew many of the men well, others only by sight. Many of those he trusted, like Vano, were missing. For long years, these had been his brothers, his only family.

Cedrin raised his hands, and the buzz of conversation died.

'Do all of you know about the attack on Regent's Hill?'

There were nods and affirmations through the crowd.

'Good. All of the Mouthpieces and their Masks were in on it. What you need to know is that the Mouthpieces and the Masks never intended for a single Brotherhood man to return alive from that raid.

'The attack was never meant to succeed, just set the stage for a change of power. But their plans have failed, and now they have left you to die, just as surely as they abandoned the Brotherhood calvanni who entered Regent's Hill.'

'That can't be true!' yelled one fourth-degree.

'No? Then where are they?'

Cedrin let the question hang.

'The vengeance of the Suul will be vicious, and it will come swiftly. Already they will know many of our secrets. The caverns are no longer safe. There is nothing to be done but wait out the storm in the city above. Hide where you can, but all of you must go to ground and you must go now.

'Go!'

The crowd stood stunned for a long moment, then began to quickly disperse, but the blind panic had gone, replaced by resolve.

Banis and Retis and the men who had formed the Circle remained.

'I'm leaving Athria,' Cedrin told them. 'We all are,' he said, indicating Marken and Skye.

'My place is here in Athria, with my own family,' said Banis. 'We will look for your return, when the time comes.'

Retis' face creased in puzzlement. 'But why flee? There will be big changes now. You could be part of them. Stay and take the sixth-degree. We need new leadership, and you have earned it.'

Cedrin shook his head. 'No, Retis. The Mask of Smuggling will still want me dead. And Stone lives. Nowhere in Athria will be safe for me. I must go.'

Cedrin said swift goodbyes to other men in the crowd then

indicated the direction of the harbour with his head.

'Let's go,' he said to Marken and Skye.

First Banis, then Retis stepped forward and gripped forearms with Cedrin as a final sign of respect. Then the three calvanni left for the tidal caves, weaving through the dark passages. When they reached the dark shore in the harbour cavern, it was deserted.

Cedrin had not told those Brotherhood calvanni the whole truth. They could never conceive that the Brotherhood's time was over. The strength of the Brotherhood was in secrecy, in the unknown circle of men who directed and commanded it.

He had been so close – as Mouthpiece only one degree from becoming a Mask himself – but it was over. With the failure of the attack, the Brotherhood Mask in the ranks of the Suul would be discovered, his role obvious to the surviving Suulvey. Once the Mask was put to torture, the other Masks would be revealed and, with them, the most intimate secrets of the Brotherhood.

The raid on the Sea Serpent was only the beginning. The Brotherhood, and the power it now represented, was finished. In time it would rebuild, but it would be a generation before it regained a fraction of its former influence.

They pushed a longboat into the tidal lagoon and rowed through the dark twists and turns towards the opening, finally winning free into the harbour to join the scores of boats weaving through the calm waters.

The day was bright and chill. A pale blue sky crowned a magnificent vista of crowded ships, from galleys to sleek trading craft, waiting out the Storm Season before they stretched canvass to the winds that would carry them south. In the calm, the harbour was like a forest of masts, rising from sea-bleached wooden decks and the mirror-flat surface of the sea. Cedrin had seen this scene a thousand times, yet now that he was leaving it behind it took on a beauty all of its own. The suns' glitter on the water was like liquid crystal, the coloured stone of the harbour buildings nostalgic and buttressed with fond memory. The ships were majestic, like sleeping titans brimming with suppressed magic, waiting for a stirring breeze to awaken them. But the chill of Storm Season was here too, and it brought back the cold reality. Death was still on their heels.

They steered through the ships, making for the galley-trader, *Lusella's Pride*, which would leave on the tide, one of the last ships to depart for Kelas before the storms. Cedrin knew the captain well. They had smuggled regularly on his ship and would be treated with discretion.

Hailing the ship, they scaled the ladder to the deck while the longboat was hauled up behind them. The sailors nodded respectfully to Cedrin, a senior Brotherhood man, making obeisance to a power soon to be smashed into pieces by the Suul. Cedrin was careful to accept their obedience, even to appear to demand it; their escape depended on it. The Captain, Robic, offered him a berth in one of the cabins, but Cedrin declined. He wanted to avoid the attention he would attract by evicting some rich noble or trader, besides it would only be for him, not Marken or Skye.

He led the way down to the warm confines of the common-deck, and they eagerly satisfied their growing hunger with hot stew and hard ship's-bread from the galley.

At last it was over. They were free and alive, and the tide would bring them new days in distant Kelas. Yet they had left behind everything they had known, every skerrick of accumulated wealth, all but the weapons they carried and the clothes on their backs.

People soon set to drinking and gambling to pass the time, but Cedrin was not in the mood. As he sat waiting in the stuffy, overcrowded hold, he considered the people he would leave behind from his life in the Brotherhood and he realised with a shock that not one of them would shed a tear.

Hours later, the ship ran with the tide, aided by the sweep of oars. Cedrin had finally grown restive below and made his way to the deck. He found a spot by the rail, well out of the way of the sailors, and took in long, deep lungfuls of the cool sea air, clearing his head. The cuts on his arms and the wound on his shoulder throbbed, despite Marken's healing touch.

He looked out over the Sea of Mists. The dark blue waters lay as smooth as glass. No breeze rippled the surface as they pulled forward, the galley only gaining speed as slaves bent their backs to the task under the curses and cuts of the slave-master.

Cedrin watched Athria dwindle behind them as the suns fell. Absently he reached for the ring around his neck. Finding it missing, he looked instead at the heavy greatscythe that lay in his hand. He had to put his trust in this now.

Banis' words returned to haunt him. *We will look for your return, when the time comes.* There will be no return for me, Banis, he thought. Banis, Retis and the rest of those men had given him their loyalty, and now he was betraying them, leaving them to face their fate amid the doom of the Brotherhood.

Cedrin gritted his teeth. It left him with the bitter taste of guilt, but what was done, was done.

He turned to the dark shape of Kelas in the west. A huge and mysterious continent where his fate awaited him. The life of a mercenary was a hard one, yet there would be no shortage of work on the war-torn mainland, of that he was sure.

Twilight fell quickly, and he lost sight of the mainland. The *Lusella's Pride* struggled on, a single vessel crossing a dark sea, the oars pushing against the will of the gods, trespassing on the mystic stillness of early Storm Season.

The cold pressed on him.

He relived the terror of the Spire, watching as the Druid and Jaso were slain. Once more he looked into the eyes of Raziin to see his bloodlust. Then fire filled his mind. Fire. The images were blurred, and Marken and Skye would not talk of it.

There was a Window, half-remembered, beyond which the Fire lay. What did it mean? Some vision brought about by Raziin's unnatural magic? He shook his head, pushing the thoughts away and burying the images deep. They were the past, and he looked to the future.

Marken approached across the deck, swaying with the motion of the oars, his cloak drawn against the chill. 'Stinking Uros, it's cold. Where have you been, ami? They're playing dice below, and drinking wine. Someone even has a lute. Why are you here in the cold when there are fortunes to be made?'

Cedrin smiled, shrugging off the never-ending reflections of his life. He had learned to make the best of good times. 'By Uros, you're right. It's cold, and Raziin and Dresil can go to Llors if they aren't there already.'

Marken bowed drunkenly. 'Lord Cedrin,' he indicated, like a courtier, that Cedrin should precede him, 'the dice await.'

Chapter Nine

That morning, Ellen and Torren rode out from the palace, straight from the torture of Jorrel. She had forced herself to return after her hurried bath and had been there for the last of it. In the end, Jorrel had begged them to take his life. He lived still, a crippled wreck, awaiting his public execution as traitor. It had been vital they learned all that Jorrel knew of the Brotherhood. She wished there had been some other way, but if she had used her own powers to take the knowledge from him magically, she would have risked destroying his mind.

News of the attack on Regent's Hill spread quickly, yet not even the Brotherhood had been prepared for the scale of their response. Squads of soldiers swarmed into the Sea Serpent tavern – Outer Garrison men, eager to vent their anger and strike a blow at the enemy. Their scythes and spears were soon bloodied as fierce fighting erupted in the narrow confines. Ellen watched as scores of calvanni and shrieking women and children were hauled into the street. Bodies were laid in rows, cooling rapidly in the frigid air.

Torren coordinated the operation from a commandeered warehouse opposite the Sea Serpent, where the men were questioned in turn by Templemen eager to put their skills to good use. Ellen waited anxiously as he dispatched squads of soldiers throughout Athria, eagerly scrutinising each group of returning prisoners for sign of Cedrin.

The captured calvanni were chained together and made to sit on the docks before the splintered wreck of the Sea Serpent, while the women and children were held under guard nearby.

Ellen had hoped to find Cedrin in the first assault, yet as the morning wore on, he was still missing. She paced her narsiit back and forth along the dispirited line of calvanni shivering in their chains.

'Which of you knows of a man called Cedrin?'

Eyes lifted towards her, but no one spoke.

'Answer me and you will go free.'

Most of the heads lowered once more.

Overcome with frustration, Ellen swept out her scythe, urging her mount over to a fourth-degree who still glared at her, refusing to bow his head.

'You! Tell me what you know!'

The man simply stared.

Ellen raised the point of her scythe. Her hand trembled with exhaustion and rage as it rested on his neck. The blade was still stained from battle.

'Speak quickly, or you will join these,' said Ellen, jerking her head towards the rows of mutilated dead.

'Speak!' Her blade had begun to draw blood. She was filled with a reckless abandon and for a moment considered making an example of him.

'I know of no such man,' said the calvanni coolly.

She heard the sound of an amelak's hooves on the cobbles. Withdrawing her blade, she turned her mount towards the approaching rider. It was Escon, returning from Torren's headquarters with his report.

She cantered forward to meet him.

'Anyone matching Cedrin's description?' she asked as he approached.

'No, Suul Cintros. But informants have identified another smuggler, a second-degree calvanni, who must surely know him.'

'Well done, Escon. Take me to him.'

She looked back at the fourth-degree, her head spinning as she realised she had considered killing him in cold blood. Ellen swallowed as she returned her scythe to her saddle-sheath. What would her father have thought of her had she opened the throat of a defenceless captive?

Escon led her to a nearby building, packed with wounded. She dismounted and followed him through the miserable confines to a narrow cot. The man had lost an arm to a scythe-blade and the stump had been sealed crudely with pitch and bound with a blood-stained cloth. His face was creased with agony, but he was alert.

He returned her gaze steadily despite his pain.

'Do you know who I am?' she asked.

He nodded, unintimidated by her. Her anger surged up, yet remembering the man on the docks, she held it in check.

'Then you know I hold the power of life and death over you.'

She waited for the words to sink in.

'With a single word I could have the Moon-Druids attend you. You could be free from pain, free from prison, free from a painful death.'

'What is it you want?' asked the man, his voice hoarse.

'There is a calvanni called Cedrin. A smuggler,' she said.

Her heart quickened as she saw recognition flare briefly in the man's eyes. 'Do you know him?'

The man hesitated, then shook his head. 'No.'

Ellen's mood darkened. 'I could have you killed, right here.'

'I know,' he said. 'But I will tell you nothing.'

Ellen let out a long breath. She would have to wait until Torren and the interrogators from the Temple had done their work – but would that be too late?

She turned and walked away, Escon following her. Reluctantly she returned to the docks.

From the information gathered by the Templemen and other informants, a general picture had begun to emerge of the attack on Regent's Hill. It appeared that almost all of the calvanni had been unwillingly co-opted into the Brotherhood force, and some had escaped at the first opportunity. Most of the attackers were Dresil's pirates. The assanni operated as a separate unit used to keep the calvanni in line. For the first time, she admitted the real possibility that Cedrin may be innocent of Crephis' murder.

Some leadership must have remained, because just before noon there was a flood of Brotherhood men out of the tunnels, too many to hold. Most disappeared into Athria without a trace, but others fled the tunnels only to find they would have been safer below.

By noon the passages below the ruined Sea Serpent were swarming with heavily armed guards and Templemen, eager to put their talents to use. But the Brotherhood was not without defences. Squads of soldiers were ambushed deep within the dark of the tunnels. Without guides, the Athrian officers soon realised the futility of questing too deeply underground.

The captured calvanni claimed the Mouthpiece of Smuggling remained below in the tunnels, but this was later discounted as a ruse. Mat, the Mouthpiece of Smuggling, was found in an alley in Lookout Hill soon afterward, his body punctured by more than a hundred calv wounds.

Of the five supreme leaders of the Brotherhood, only the Masks of Assassination and Smuggling escaped their nets, having already fled Athria for the mainland in private galleys. The Masks of Courtesans and Theft, and their Mouthpieces Kayleez and Tice, were captured with their men even as they prepared to board their ships. Stone, the Mouthpiece of Assassins, was cornered in a warehouse in the Merchants' Quarter and took poison along with dozens of his men, but not before taking a devastating toll in the ranks of Athrian soldiers with darts. Dresil, the Pirate's Mouthpiece and Jorrel's right-hand man, was nowhere to be found. As the day wore on, scouts reported sign of a large force fleeing along the Lighthouse road and ships and men were sent to intercept.

By early afternoon, Ellen realised Cedrin had either slipped away, or worse – was already dead. She left Torren to his work and took her small squad of family retainers to Lookout Hill, searching for him. She found his rooms deserted and stripped. By the time she had searched them and the surrounding houses thoroughly it was almost dusk. Only Tarral's glassworks remained.

Ellen drew rein, patting her narsiit's sleek neck as she considered the maze of alleyways ahead of her. They had twisted and turned through a score of the narrow, cobbled streets and she had long ago lost any sense of direction.

'Are you sure, Escon?'

'Yes, my Lady. I grew up in Lookout Hill. Tarral's glassworks is close by.'

'Lead on, Captain.'

Escon had insisted on leading her guard, despite the tenderness of his newly-healed wound. Luckily the arrow had missed his lung.

The suns were falling in the west, and she drew her heavy robes closer around her. Despite the increased cold that came with dusk, it would be a relief when Uros sank from sight. The days of Storm Season were usually spent indoors, and it was strange to be out under the suns during the Destroyer's time of strength. The Druids of the Temple taught that destruction was merely part of the cycle of life, yet that was little consolation for those who attracted the dark blessing of the red Sister.

'There it is,' said Escon.

Ellen looked up to see another narrow and unremarkable street lined with identical two-storey brick houses, pushed together in a confusion of colours and decorations. Tarral's glassworks was set apart only by the three squat chimneys of dull red brick that climbed from the roof. Not the sort of breeding ground for Brotherhood calvanni that she had expected, with seedy taverns filled with whores and cutpurses in every shadow.

As she halted, Ellen could feel the eyes of the street upon her. Shutters moved slightly as people peered into the alley, those rich enough to afford clearglass pushing back curtains to watch. Was this another arrest? Would Tarral and his sons be dragged screaming into the cold? Although silent, the street possessed a heavy expectation as Ellen walked to Tarral's door, thumping on the solid oak with the head of her scythe.

'Open up in the name of Athria!' she called.

The door swung in, allowing a wave of warm air to escape. Framed in the doorway was a thickly-muscled man, sporting a solid wooden staff. A loose woollen robe of yellow and blue was draped from his wide shoulders. Beneath, she glimpsed a harness and heavily-tattooed chest. He leaned on the doorpost, his callused hands resting on the black mought bracing of the staff's end.

He did not speak. Instead, he regarded Ellen and her soldiers with heavy scrutiny. He made it clear he was neither cowed nor awed by them.

Ellen faltered under his steady gaze, but pushed on quickly, angry she could be put off so easily by a single commoner.

'I am Suul Ellen Cintros,' she declared.

She expected him to give way with a terrified apology, instead he blinked, the hint of a smile tugging at the corners of his mouth.

'What's your business with me, my Lady?' he asked, his tone flat, menace hidden within his civility.

Escon stepped forward and raised his scythe. 'You'll show some respect or you'll have me to answer to,' he said, his knuckles white as they gripped his scythe. The long night was taking its toll and Ellen realised even the stolid Escon was at the end of his tether.

Ellen waved Escon back. 'Are you Tarral the glassmaker?' she asked tersely.

He nodded slowly.

'I have to talk to you on state business,' she continued. 'And you can answer my questions here or in the dungeons of Regent's Hill, the choice is yours.'

Tarral sighed, pushing his weight away from the door frame and motioning for her to enter. 'Well, come in, Suul Cintros, but leave these louts outside. I have a lot of fragile things in my kiln-rooms.'

'Very well, but my Captain will accompany me.'

Escon followed her inside. He watched Tarral suspiciously as the glassmaker reached to bolt the wooden door.

'Leave it unlocked,' ordered Escon.

Tarral acquiesced and led them deeper into the house.

A short woman came forward uncertainly, bowing to Ellen.

'This is Emily. My wife,' said Tarral.

'Would you like something to drink or eat, Lady?' The woman possessed straightforward warmth, much like the nurse who had taken the place of Ellen's mother following her death. After the harsh cruelties of the night, the offer of hospitality was deeply touching.

Escon leant across and whimpered into her ear, 'Be alert for poison.'

Ellen knew Escon's concerns were well motivated, but she felt his suspicion a bit overdone. These were simple people, unlikely assassins, despite their son.

She turned to the woman with a smile. 'We would be happy to accept your hospitality.'

'But . . . ,' started Escon.

Ellen silenced Escon with a stern look. He suppressed his further protests.

Emily smiled and withdrew, clearly relieved.

Tarral led Ellen to a small table on the lower floor and offered her a seat. Pointedly, Escon remained standing.

They waited for a moment then Ellen began. 'You have a son. Cedrin.'

Tarral nodded, looking up towards Escon. He still gripped his scythe, ready to leap to her defence at the slightest sign of treachery. 'Yes, I have a son called Cedrin.'

Tarral had put aside his staff as he entered the room and Ellen could see he posed no immediate threat. Tarral was not unnerved by Escon, yet she realised immediately that he would be more communicative if her Captain were out of earshot.

'Escon, stand by the door,' ordered Ellen.

'Suul Cintros, I must protest. This man is dangerous.'

Ellen bristled. 'Do as I say.'

Escon bowed and withdrew. Once her Captain had gone, Tarral looked back towards Ellen.

'I have been waiting for the knock. Once news of the attack on Regent's Hill reached me, I knew it was only a matter of time. . . although I did not expect Myan's daughter to come calling,' he said.

Ellen hesitated, then reached into her pocket, opening her palm to show him the ring.

Tarral could not conceal his surprise.

'Does this belong to him?' Ellen asked, her heart clenching.

Tarral let out a long breath and sagged forward. He looked up at her, his eyes narrowing, then he nodded. 'Yes.'

Ellen smiled with relief and excitement. 'It's the signet ring of

Belin Kaidell. Did you know that?'

'That was his father's ring, given to me as a token when I took him in as a babe. Cedrin is Belin's bastard son.'

Ellen was filled with a giddy elation. 'Where is he, Tarral? Where can he be found?'

Tarral's expression was guarded. 'I haven't seen him in years. He left my house as a young man and never returned.'

She searched his face, but could read nothing.

Emily entered with a tray of simple cakes, hot oats and sweet mead. She smiled at Ellen nervously, laid the platter in front of them, then withdrew.

Tarral poured them each a cup of mead, then served out the oats and broke cake for Ellen before helping himself to the repast. She eagerly pulled the plates towards her, realising how welcome the food was after the long night.

They ate in silence for a time. When he had finished, Tarral drained his cup of mead and looked across the table at her. He seemed more relaxed, as was she.

For the first time, Ellen studied the tattoos on his chest. They were military degrees and honours, all from the Bulvuran Empire; some from the legions and others from the elite bodyguard of the Emperor himself. Here was a man who had served the old order with distinction. Her father would have liked him, she was sure.

'So, Suul Cintros. What do you want of Cedrin?' he asked.

Ellen took a mouthful of mead and collected her thoughts. Her own motivations were mixed. She was bound to find him, as a debt to her father . . . yet only hours ago, in the harsh dawn, she had vowed to make him pay for his crimes.

'I must find him, Tarral. It was my father's dying wish. He had searched for him for years, seeking to recognise him as Belin's son, but he was lost in the confusion of the Last Days.' Ellen paused, letting the words find their mark. 'Father never gave up hope of finding him. He thought it important enough that I should keep looking after he died.'

The Scion must stand in the Temple of the Iris.

For a moment her vision turned blue, and her head spun.

'Suul Cintros. Are you all right?'

'Yes. . .I'm sorry. It must be fatigue.'

Tarral looked at her with concern and offered her the cup of mead he had poured for her earlier. She accepted it with thanks and took a mouthful. She studied the ring she held in her fingers. 'Father said he would bear Belin's ring. When this was found on the Spire, it was a chance I could not let pass.'

Tarral's brow creased. 'But why now? Twenty-eight years ago, out of nowhere, Belin's lieutenant Kalyth turns up with the child, calling on old favours in the Legions to make me take him in. Only a few months, he said, a year at most, then he or Belin would return.

'After all that time, waiting for word, Cedrin is suddenly vital. Why? Can you give me the *real* reason? For all I know, Belin left a score of bastards behind him, scattered from the Plains of Poulos to the southern provinces. What makes Cedrin so special?'

Ellen's temper flared. 'I don't know why my father valued him so highly!' She took a deep breath and let it out slowly. 'I seek him because my father made me vow I would bring him under the protection of the court, and I will.'

Tarral regarded Ellen suspiciously. 'So you swear, by holy Larus, you mean him no harm? That you only seek to protect him?'

'How can I promise you anything?' she snapped. 'My father lies dead, the Regent and Crephis with him, all fallen to the assassin's blade. A score of other good men are also gone, many hundreds of soldiers with them – and he had some part in it.'

Tears fell from her cheeks. Without realising, she had tapped into the vast pool of her grief.

Tarral placed a hand over hers. She looked up and found only sympathy in his dark brown eyes. The simple gesture broke her. Tears flooded, her chest shaking convulsively as she sobbed.

Escon rushed into the room, then stood confused in the doorway. Ellen waved him back to his post.

She snatched back her hand and glared at Tarral.

'Cedrin was Father's hope, his dream; playing some obscure role in finding the Scion and the rebirth of the Empire.' There.

Finally she had said it. Her fool's quest was revealed. 'I did not question my father's wishes,' she said, looking back up at Tarral. 'Yet when I do find Cedrin, it seems he has blood on his hands. A Brotherhood calvanni, no less.' Ellen wiped away her tears. So much for finesse. How could she let herself lose control like this? It galled her.

'This much I swear under Larus. I will find him and seek to fulfil my father's will. Yet if he is guilty of murder, he shall pay for his crimes.'

Tarral nodded gravely. Somehow she had won his respect. She could see it in his eyes.

'Do not judge him on his past. The Brotherhood has good men as well as bad, and Cedrin is no killer. He left here many years ago yet has always been the son I knew. A good man. A man of honour.'

Looking at Tarral, she could believe it. 'Have you seen him?'

Tarral looked at her for a long moment, weighing something in his mind. 'He was here this morning.'

'Is he in Athria now?' pressed Ellen.

Tarral smiled. 'He should have taken the last galley for Raynor. Whatever his crimes, he is beyond the reach of Athria now.'

Gone!

How could she pursue him now? She had a Sardom to rule. Weariness and grief pressed in on her. It was time she returned to Regent's Hill. She had wasted enough time on this search for Cedrin.

Ellen stood, the mask of formality slipping easily into place. 'Thank you for your help, Tarral.'

'Myan was a noble man,' said Tarral, standing. 'I can see him in you.'

Ellen turned back to meet his gaze, surprised by his sincerity. He took her hands and she realised he was much like her father, possessing the same strength and integrity. She prayed she would find the same qualities in Cedrin.

'May the Sisters guide you well,' he said.

She took her hands from his clasp and left the glassworks, Escon in her wake as she emerged onto the cold street. Night had fallen, and the men were chilled to the bone, sheltering with the amelak in a corner out of the wind.

'To the palace,' she commanded, as though with severity she could stem the tide of sentiment Tarral had stirred to life.

Seated on her narsiit, she set the pace through the city towards Regent's Hill, her head buzzing with plans. She would have to send an agent after Cedrin. She would offer to recognise him as Belin's son, with the rank of Suulqua, if he came willingly. If he refused . . . he would be taken by force.

She could not allow this chance to slip by, for Tarral had been wrong; he was not beyond the reach of Athria. For the next few days, Cedrin would be easily caught. A war-galley could overhaul a slow galley-trader to Raynor long before it reached Kelas, and any sea-Captain would bow to the threat of a war-galley holding a full complement of warriors and archers.

Putting the problem of Cedrin aside, she turned her thoughts to avoiding the wrath of the Temple, and ruling Athria.

* * *

Ellen slowed her narsiit, her gaze sweeping the palace courtyard in search of Aris or his aides. She had sent her personal guard back to the Cintros mansion to take a well-earned rest and tend to their wounds.

Much of the carnage and destruction of the previous night had been removed and scores of carpenters and stonemasons laboured on the gates and battlements to repair the damage. Ellen was impressed how quickly Aris had organised this in the aftermath of the attack. That morning men had also started work on a new Inner Garrison, replacing the wooden structure with one of cut stone. A whole quarry had been reopened, men and Temple Druids who specialised in moving the heavy stones working non-stop in the Storm Season chill to supply them.

The Temple Guardians were gone.

As she dismounted and walked her narsiit towards the sweeping arches that gave entrance to the palace, a young Suulqua marched out towards her, leading a squad of twenty heavily-cloaked warriors. She recognised him as the son of one of her Suulqua scribes.

He halted his squad and bowed, smiling with relief. 'Suul Cintros, we have been searching for you since before dusk.'

'Well, what is it?'

'Suul Torren ordered that we escort you to the Cintros mansion. That was almost two hours ago. He requests that you wait there with us until he sends word.'

Ellen examined the faces of the men. They seemed tense. Surely not?

'You were ordered to take me into custody?' she asked, incredulous.

The young Suulqua's face blanched. 'No, of course not, my Lady. Torren ordered us to protect you at all costs.'

Ellen struggled to take it all in, her weary brain sorting slowly through the implications. Now was not the time to be sitting idly. Despite her fatigue she needed to be planning, readying herself to outmanoeuvre the Temple.

'Did he say why?' asked Ellen, her nerves frayed by the long day.

'There are many of us looking for you, Suul Cintros. I received my commands from another Suul coordinating the search. I was not told why. . . only that it was vital.'

'Where is Torren now?'

'Suul Torren and the Warlord Aris are with the Council. They convened quickly, just after dusk, with strict orders not to be disturbed.'

Ellen's heart missed a beat, a terrible expectation building inside her. The Council meeting without her? All her suspicions suddenly collided. *They are trying to remove me from power!* The suns had barely set on the day she revealed her Sorcery and already it had started.

Ellen's hands tightened to fists on the reins, but she held back her fury. The Suulqua would be too far below the politics to know anything.

Ellen looked past the Suulqua, her weariness forgotten. Torren could not even wait until their father's blood was cold to usurp the throne! *If he thinks I will simply lie down and let him overrule me, he is mistaken. I am Sarqua.*

'Return your men to the garrison. I am going to see Torren.'

'But my orders. . .'

Ellen bristled. 'Who will you choose to obey? The Sarqua or the Captain of the Wall?' she asked, staring him down.

'Very well,' he said. 'But at least let me come with you. My orders were to protect you at all costs.'

'I need no protection. Return the men to the Garrison.'

The young Suulqua was clearly upset, but said nothing more. He passed the orders, then bowed and led his squad away.

Ellen gave her narsiit to a stable hand, then hurried through the palace, climbing rapidly to the Council chambers on the upper level. She tried to think through everything that had happened, but somehow the pieces did not fit. She shook her head. Torren and Aris had no right to be convening the Council without her, of that she was certain.

Chapter Ten

Raziin reined his amelak to a standstill on the cliff above Pirate's Cove. He had pushed the animal without mercy, determined to reach the sheltered bay with his men before Dresil and his cutthroats. The beast gave out a plaintive bellow and tossed its long neck. It was breathing heavily, the big mouth with its rows of flat grinding teeth wide open as it sent its steaming breath into the air. Beneath its shaggy coat it was shaking with fatigue, its long thin legs trembling. He despised its weakness.

The cliffs were quiet, the sparse coastal grasslands around them empty.

Raziin was filled with rage, a hot fury at all those who had conspired to cause his defeat. Ellen Cintros, that blonde bitch with her tricks – no doubt learnt from Myan. That damn Athrian calvanni, Cedrin. Not only had he spoiled his fun, he, more than any of them, had lost him Athria. If not for him, the Wail would have remained silent; the palace would have been taken swiftly in Dresil's first attack and Ellen Cintros would have died in her bed.

Yet his real rage was reserved for Hukum, his treacherous master. Hukum had assured him no Sorcerers remained in Athria to oppose him, yet he had found not one, but *two* in his way.

Yes. The real blame for the defeat lay at the feet of Hukum.

If the Sorcerer-Lord had given him the Final Matrix as he had promised, then he would have been able to withstand the mental attack of Ellen Cintros. Then it would have been *her* fleeing the field, not him. *Curse her*. They would meet again, he was sure, and next time he would crush her beneath his power. His revenge would be a sweet delicacy, and how she would suffer before her end! He would keep that fantasy alive, dreaming of the day he could make it real.

Yet first he must contrive to slay his master.

How he hated Hukum, and the bonds he had forced on him. Raziin – the hand of Uros, privy to the thoughts of the red goddess herself – had been made a slave through Hukum's deceptions. From the first he had thirsted to kill him, yet he had always stayed his hand, waiting for the next piece of Sorcerous knowledge. Now his training was complete. . .except for the Final Matrix. Traditionally kept as the last spell taught an apprentice, it gave awesome power; the power to dominate – or destroy – the minds of others. How he had lusted for it. This alone had kept him in Hukum's service these last few months. Now he was certain that Hukum would never give it to him.

It was time for his master to die. He would have preferred to torture Hukum slowly, but it was impossible. Only a swift, unforseen attack would succeed. When next he reported to him, he would demand a private audience, alone in his sanctum. Then he would edge closer . . . and Hukum's head would fall to him, sliced away cleanly under his two long-knives.

Yet with Hukum gone, how then should he gather the knowledge of the Final Matrix?

He clubbed the amelak on the ear in frustration. Its cries of pain eased the tension in his chest.

He must not worry about that now. Surely there must be someone he could manipulate, one of the remaining human Sorcerers of Kelas, perhaps. Yes. He may find one hiding in Raynor.

But first he must survive.

He had pushed the defeated force hard from the Lighthouse, the badly wounded quickly falling behind. He hoped they would die painful deaths in the cold. They deserved nothing less for their weakness.

Raziin needed to get himself and his men as far as possible from Athrian retribution – and Ellen Cintros. Apart from his master and his brother, she was the most skilled Sorcerer he had come against.

Far below lay the three pirate vessels that had brought them to the Cove. Two were sleek converted grain traders, three-masted with only a single row of oars. These craft were swift hunters designed to run before the wind on open seas. They would be useless to Raziin now. The calm that came with the advent of Storm Season would last for at least another four days. Even with a lead of a day's sailing, the war-galleys of Athria could easily overtake them. The Warlord may already have craft at sea, scouring the coast for their ships.

Raziin eyed the last of the vessels. It was a true war-galley, with two rows of oars, each double-manned, the decks half-open to give the oar-master a better view of the rowers. The hull was thin like an arrow to pierce the water, its mought-tipped ram glistening just below the surface with gaudy paints. If any ship could get Raziin to Kelas before the storms, this was it. Yet here also was the problem. It would take a crew of more than a hundred rowers to man her properly; less could take her to sea, but she would never have the speed or manoeuvrability he needed. Apart from his own men – which he would never ask to do the work of slaves – the whole of Dresil's surviving force would barely be enough. He knew Dresil's mind. The old pirate would spread his men thin, seeking to put all three craft to sea and save his prize vessels. Dresil would head south-west, away from the trade-routes, hoping to avoid the Warlord's navy; looking to weather the fierce storms that followed on the heels of the eclipse at sea.

That would leave Raziin and his men vulnerable, mere passengers aboard one of the three under-strength vessels.

This he would never allow.

The conclusion was obvious. The three-masted ships would have to be abandoned, their skeleton crews – perhaps twelve men fresh for the oars – would need to be added to Dresil's surviving force to provide an adequate crew for the galley.

Yet how was he to convince Dresil to abandon his two sailing ships? He must give him no choice, yet he must also avoid open conflict. Every sailor slain was one less oar-slave. As tools, they were too valuable to waste.

Raziin looked up to the suns. They were out of eclipse now, but still close together in the sky, the swollen, blood-red disk of Uros falling first in the west, Larus behind her.

His rage boiled once more. This day should have been a day of victory.

'Why, Uros? Haven't I given you enough blood?'

Receiving no answer, Raziin looked away in disgust, his gaze sweeping across the jagged brown and black rock of the headlands towards the approaching column. Only twenty of his men had survived the attack. They ran ahead of the force in well-disciplined lines led by the tireless Merceth and Kyal. His heart grew heavy. These were his pride and joy, trained as warriors without equal, the cream of the Armon forces. He would have slaughtered a hundred of these Athrians to save one of them. What vengeance they had unleashed on the barbarians! Across Kelas they had seen the enemy scatter before them, cutting a swath through the most disciplined of lines. To receive the loyalty and adoration of elite warriors such as these was his due. And now there were less to revere him, to ensure his victory. That was a hard blow, and only increased his anger at Hukum. This was to have been an easy victory.

Some distance behind the black-clad warriors, stretching out in a long, undisciplined line, came the remnants of Dresil's force, now struggling to reach the cove before the ships sailed. Scarcely one hundred had survived, many wounded, and after the arrival of the Temple forces and the cursed Sorceress they were lucky to save this many. He would use these men until they dropped, until he was far beyond the reach of Athria. Beyond the reach of the Cintros Old Blood.

He was about to spur his amelak along the cliff to meet Merceth when a savage pain gripped the base of his skull. Tendrils of razor sharp silver stabbed into his brain. The cold brightness of the day dimmed as though sudden storm-clouds had hidden the suns. In terror he looked around, gripping the mane of the amelak. He looked up, but the sky was cloudless. The grey came from within. His master, the Eathal Sorcerer Hukum, sought his mind. The pain increased, the world sinking into surreal twilight as he slid from his mount.

He hit the ground with a painful impact.

Reaching for the Fire, he summoned the Barrier Matrix. He watched in his mind's eye as the swirling shield of mental energy surrounded him. Then the pain vanished. Outside the Barrier, he could see the reaching tentacles of Hukum's mind like frenzied limbs of grey, still seeking purchase within his mind. He could not let Hukum learn of his defeat. Not yet. He must somehow delay until he could get close enough to use his calvs to kill him.

Merceth ran to his side and helped him to his feet.

'What is it, Lord?' asked Merceth, ready to meet any threat to his master with sheer muscle and will. However, this was one enemy Raziin had to deal with on his own.

'It's nothing, my friend. Nothing.'

The pressure remained. His Barrier was weak, but for now it held. Hukum could reach him over any distance using the Bridge of Minds, the Sorcerous connection between master and pupil. Raziin had never resisted him before, and soon his master would wonder why.

He remounted his amelak.

How long could he hold out before Hukum gained access to his mind? He ruthlessly suppressed his doubts. He must take control of the galley first, then he would deal with Hukum's wrath.

'Merceth. Take half the men. Subdue the skeleton crews of the two traders, then burn the ships. Set the fires well, I want nothing left. Take the sailors and row for the galley with as much fresh water as you can carry. Go quickly, I want those ships in flames before Dresil's main force arrives.' Like each of the traders, the galley would be held by only five or six sailors; unsuspecting of an attack by their own forces.

Merceth picked ten men and set off at a run down the rough stair for the rocky beach and the longboats, his face transformed with savage zeal at this task of destruction.

'Kyal. Form the men into lines. Let no one come within five paces of me.'

The defeats of the night had not dimmed Kyal's ferocity. He barked an order and the men formed a square around their

Lord. Not a man among them had escaped without wounds. Some held broken greatscythes, or scythes and spears taken from corpses in the deadly press. Despite this, they formed the lines with precision and readiness. They would fight for him again, fight now if he gave the word.

He set out along the path towards the approaching force. Eventually the lines came together. Raziin halted his men, blocking the narrow path. Dresil, a raw scythe-cut across his face, reined in his amelak and faced Raziin. Behind the Mouthpiece and his aides the exhausted sailors staggered to a halt.

'What is this, Cinnor? Why are you blocking the path?'

Raziin feigned innocence. 'Look at your men,' he said, pointing back at the straggling line. 'We need all the crewmen we can get. You should regroup, give the stragglers a chance to form lines. An hour will make no difference.'

Dresil's face creased in concern. He studied Raziin and his men carefully then looked back into the empty hills. *He senses something is wrong, yet he still thinks he is invulnerable with his precious calvanni at his side.* Raziin smiled. He would soon learn differently.

'What madness is this, Cinnor? The Cove is only half a league below, the men can regroup while the ships ready for departure.'

Dresil's gaze swept the coastline, searching for the ships, but from this point on the path the Cove was hidden from view.

'Enough, Raziin! Make way!' bellowed Dresil, his face reddening.

One of Dresil's men pointed at the sky. 'Fire in the Cove!'

The shout was taken up by men down the line, panic spreading as they guessed their only means of escape was going up in flames.

Raziin looked back.

A column of smoke rose like a black tower in the still air. It was soon joined by another.

Dresil's mouth dropped open. He looked back at Raziin, his finger pointing in accusation. 'You have betrayed us, Cinnor!'

Dresil drew a scythe from his saddle and waved it at him.

'Stand aside.'

Raziin gave the order. His men smoothly moved aside as Dresil and his ragged men fled to the Cove, terror on their faces. There was a mad scramble and Raziin followed, his troops in close formation.

Raziin soon abandoned his mount, and he and his men followed down the stair and across the beach to the shore, a disciplined black knot amid the chaos. Dresil's men gathered the boats and surged into the water, rowing furiously, but it was already too late. The precious timbers were consumed beyond help, the masts set to topple amid the roaring flames. Merceth had engineered the destruction beautifully. Beside the two burning craft, the war-galley lay untouched.

Amid it all, Dresil, the old pirate, watched in disbelief as flames engulfed his two prize raiders.

Raziin laughed out loud as he signalled to Merceth. His huge lieutenant set out from the galley in the stern of a longboat pulled by cowed sailors. As it drew near the shore, Raziin and his men raced for the boat. Other men from Dresil's force also ran for the longboat, but they were savagely beaten back by Kyal and his men.

'Raziin!'

He turned to see Dresil behind them, but the Mouthpiece was too late. Raziin and his men were away, the rowers pulling hard under the harsh abuse of Merceth. He could see Dresil looking across at the war-galley, studying the deck of the craft. He shouted after him in fury, but the words were lost across the waves.

A few minutes later, Raziin watched from the deck of the galley as the last of the flames consumed the other ships, Merceth and Kyal at his side. The strain of holding the Barrier was taking its toll, but everything was going according to plan. Realising the fight to save the ships was lost, desperate men were striking out for Raziin's vessel, their last hope of fleeing Athria before the Warlord followed on their trail. Here were his oar-slaves, now desperate to join him.

Raziin allowed himself a strained smile. 'All the sailors and calvanni are to be disarmed as they board the galley and chained to the oars. If they resist, beat them into submission and chain them regardless, but don't kill them. We need every man we have to move this craft.'

'Yes, Lord,' answered Merceth and Kyal automatically.

'What of those too wounded to row?' asked Merceth.

'Kill them. Strip them of anything useful and put them over the side.'

'Yes, Lord.'

'I will be in the captain's cabin. I want four guards on the entrance.' Raziin surveyed the oar-deck. 'Get us under way as soon as we have a full complement of rowers. Allow the Mouthpiece to board with his lieutenants when his longboat arrives. Keep them under guard on the galley deck and wait for my orders.'

He turned towards the cabin, then felt the flow of Fire within him stagger and cease like a guttering flame. His Barrier Matrix dissolved into its own substance and the reaching tendrils of Hukum's mind speared into him. He shouted in pain as darkness descended like a curtain, threatening to sever his hold on consciousness. He felt Merceth at his elbow, but could see nothing.

'Quickly, Merceth, lead me to the cabin,' he gasped.

'Yes, Lord,' answered Merceth from a distance.

Raziin's legs gave way. He felt himself lifted into Merceth's arms then laid down on soft covers. He heard the door shut and knew he was alone.

Raziin was locked within himself, adrift in a vast black expanse. The feelers of grey had purchase now, seeking to master every corner of his mind. He felt the Eathal Sorcerer's presence pressing down on him.

Hukum had pushed his will on Raziin before, but he had never forced his mastery this far, cutting him off from his own senses. This was the power of the Final Matrix. Mental domination.

The rolling black cloud stilled, becoming a slumbering presence. Then through the darkness, Hukum's voice boomed like thunder, the words ripping at the insides of his skull like fragments of glass.

Cioan!

'Yes, master, I am here,' answered Raziin.

Why have you blocked me? Give me your report. Has Athria fallen to the puppet Jorrel?

Raziin tried to resist but felt his mind ripped asunder like a gutted fish. Images of his defeat flashed by him. Cedrin, the Anacian half-Blood and his cursed Fire; the angry pulsing of the Wail as it shattered the silence, destroying the crucial element of surprise. Templemen and the Temple Guardians as they entered the fray, turning the tide. The silver arrows of the Cintros bitch as they sped towards him while he ran in fear, fleeing with the scattered troops, shielded from sight by the Shadow Matrix.

So you have failed!

He fell into an abyss of pain.

'Myan and his councillors are dead,' he said.

Yet Athria is still in the hands of the Cintros. Worse, now his daughter is revealed as a Sorcerer.

You have failed me, Raziin. Failure was not acceptable, and you will pay a high price. You will return now to the Eathal camp at the Broken Tower. Within the Shattered Temple of Yosini you shall meet your death at the hands of the Eathal.

'No, Lord! Let me serve you! I have always been your faithful servant. Grant me the Final Matrix and I will return and destroy Ellen Cintros.'

Silence answered, yet across the Bridge of Minds he felt the determination within the Sorcerer-Lord to see him undone, to once and for all rid himself of the human servant who had been useful until now.

Hukum withdrew.

He began to hope for a reprieve as his spirit hung weightless in the emptiness, but then something approached him. It was a jagged crystal of energy, coherent and pulsing with angry red and orange. With unerring precision it hurtled towards him. He tried to flee but it struck swiftly. He could feel it eating its way into him, the crystal's energy wrapping itself around his mind and growing heavy with pain. For a small eternity he struggled, shouting wordlessly for Uros to take his life and free him from its agonising weight. But it grew. He began to fall, plummeting into the boiling, molten sea of his mind. As he struck the thing unclothed its essence.

Compulsion.

Then a blissful nothingness.

* * *

A knock at the cabin door roused him.

Raziin drank in the sights and sounds like a magic elixir, weeping like a baby with relief at the absence of pain. He could hear the oars and knew they had left the Cove.

He pushed himself to his feet. His mind was sound and uncompromised, despite Hukum's attack. Beneath it he sensed the Fire, once more ready to do his bidding. He was renewed.

The Compulsion had failed!

He laughed like a god and the knock came again, this time with Merceth's voice. 'Lord? Lord? Dresil insists he speak to you.'

Raziin laughed. He had nothing to fear now. He had taken the worst punishment Hukum could hand out, the razor edges and darkness of the Final Matrix, and survived intact. Hukum had used it to breach his defences and make him a prisoner within his mind, but the distance had been too great to use the Final Matrix or the Compulsion he sent to destroy him. He laughed again. He had never known the limits of Hukum's power, always afraid of what failure or disobedience would bring. Now he had tested it and lived. He was free!

The door flew inwards, turning on its hinges to strike the wall with a crack. Merceth leapt into the room with his greatscythe blades drawn. When he saw Raziin, he fell to his knees.

'My apologies, Lord. When I could not rouse you, I feared for your safety.'

Raziin strode forward, feeling benevolent. 'Rise, my friend. I am whole and well.'

As Merceth rose, Dresil also forced his way into the room, flanked by two calvanni lieutenants. They had been disarmed, but Merceth watched them carefully as Dresil came forward, his finger levelled in accusation.

'You had no right to burn my ships, Northman. I swear you will repay every coin of their value. This is *my* galley. These are *my* men!'

Raziin looked at Dresil with contempt. 'You're nothing now, Athrian. Your purpose has long expired. As for coin, do not delude yourself. Anything you had was stolen and paid for in blood.'

He walked forward until he was only inches from the pirate. 'You had better remember who is in control of this ship,' he said in low, threatening tones.

Dresil exploded, his fist lashing out to strike, but Raziin was faster, dodging aside. He stepped back as Dresil came at him, the pirate's rage towering as he advanced

'You were the one who failed,' screamed Dresil. 'You failed to silence the Wail. You failed to defeat the Templemen. You ran like a beaten dog from Ellen Cintros, soiling your trousers like a frightened boy!'

Raziin's anger rose and crested like a mountainous wave. He had been forced to accept accusations of failure from Hukum, but he would not take these insults from a petty pirate. He lunged, taking Dresil's throat in a vice-like grip. The pirate struggled in his grasp and almost won free, but hung limply as the Northman channelled Fire into the Force Matrix, strengthening his grip, cutting off the flow of air.

Dresil's two calvanni stepped forward, but they were halted by Merceth, his greatscythe blades poised and ready to cut.

With a shout, Raziin tossed Dresil through the door as though he was made of paper. Rowers on the deck were thrown into confusion as Raziin strode from the cabin, glowing with the Fire. The black-clad warriors guarding the rowers began to coerce them back to work, but Raziin halted them.

'*Stop!*' he shouted. 'Stop and learn who is the master of this ship.'

The sound of oars ceased and a flutter of excited conversation swept through the ranks. Men shifted in their chains, jostling for a better view. Rowers on the top deck stepped to the limit of their bonds, but the Armon warriors pushed them back, leaving the deck clear for Raziin and Dresil.

Taking in his audience with a triumphant gaze, Raziin continued. 'Once you were Athrian pirates, whores of the Brotherhood. No more. You are my crew. Your old masters now grovel to me.'

Dresil had been stunned by the fall and struggled to rise, but Raziin kicked him back savagely. Raziin's heart surged with glee. Too long he had been deprived of his fun. The pirate looked around him, searching for help from his men, then collapsed to the boards, waiting for what came next.

'Tell them, Dresil. Tell them all who is the master of this ship,' shouted Raziin.

Dresil looked around at his men. Raziin smiled. He could already see the contempt growing there. The old pirate had already lost their respect.

Raziin drew his calv, swiftly placing the razor-sharp blade at the Athrian's throat.

Pitched so only Dresil could hear, Raziin said, 'Tell them, or I'll cut your throat and drink the blood.'

They matched gazes for an instant, long enough for Dresil to recognise the truth of the threat.

'Raziin. Raziin is master of the ship,' said Dresil, bowing his head. The crew watched in silence, gazing from old master to new with resignation.

Raziin sheathed his knife. 'You're lucky I need all hands on the oars, Dresil,' said Raziin, his mind singing with triumph.

'Strap him to the sweeps on the upper deck with his lieutenants.' ordered Raziin. 'Where we can see him.'

Raziin stalked back to his cabin, the motion of the oars resuming behind him. Merceth followed. Once within the cabin, the huge Cioan, hunched beneath the low timbers, bowed to Raziin.

'We are on the open sea, heading for Kelas. I gave the helmsman orders to make for the Narrows, Sire. Should I tell him to hold course?'

Raziin walked to the window, which was set with diamond-shaped panels of clearglass. He pushed it open, looking out onto the flat surface of the Sea of Mists. The exhilaration of besting Dresil still pumped through him.

Despite Hukum's wrath, I can go anywhere. Yet even as this thought crossed his mind, a great pain rose his chest. Raziin gasped and gripped the sill. *What is this? I have won free of Hukum!*

Merceth had seen the change and stepped forward as though to support him, but stopped. 'Lord Cinnor?'

Raziin waved him back. *This cannot be.*

'What commands should I give the helmsman, Lord? Where shall we steer the craft? The Yasser? The Myrian ports on the Sea of Mists?'

A phantom hand gripped his chest in a painful vice. His body shook as he gathered every ounce of his will to resist. His mind screamed – *the northern ports, south to the southern Sardoms, anywhere but the Narrows.* Anywhere but the Yasser's mouth, the route that led to the Broken Towers, the Shattered Temple and death at the hands of the Eathal.

The shaking of his body became a violent tremor and Merceth rushed to his side, speaking words that were lost within the whistling torrent in his mind, a torrent that held him in its sway.

The Narrows. Come to the Narrows and enter the Shattered Temple.

The pain had risen from his chest to his throat and Raziin knew it was the Compulsion. His breath surged to be released, to speak the words that would steer him to his fate. His tongue and mouth ached to form them.

He could hold them back no longer.

'The Narrows,' he shouted. The tremors immediately reduced in intensity, the searing pain in his chest and throat gone with the breath that would condemn him. He stood shaking as Merceth backed away.

'I will tell the helmsman to maintain-course for the Narrows and the Yasser River beyond.' The giant bowed and withdrew, leaving Raziin with a silent denial forming on his lips.

He struggled to call after his aide, but once more the pain shot through his chest like a lancing blade and he fell to the floor in agony. He let the Compulsion have its way and the pain left him.

Breathing raggedly, he moved to the window. He was trapped. He knew that now. There was a Compulsion buried within him. He could feel it now. He opened his mind to it. The images filled his mind with shocking clarity. He watched as his dream self walked the path to where death awaited. There was no way he could prevent himself from entering. Yet even as he watched the image, it dissolved and he sensed it was incomplete. Hukum said he would go to meet his death, yet that part of the Compulsion had been unfinished; there was more to come. In this was his only hope. Despite his power, Hukum had his limits. Over this great distance, he did not have the strength to plant the whole Compulsion in one attack.

So. Once more Hukum would seek his mind, search him out across the Bridge that lay between them. Once Raziin opened himself to his master this final time, the last scenes in the play of death would be installed within the Compulsion and he would be doomed.

He reached for the Fire and the Barrier Matrix, fear growing like a cancer within him. Even as he did, he sensed the feather light touch of his master's mind leave his. The implications of what he had discovered struck him with full impact.

Raziin could not allow the Barrier surrounding his mind to fall. A single moment of weakness would give Hukum purchase. As he looked within his mind, he saw the scenes of a second Compulsion growing against the Barrier, like a shadow play, seeking entry. He would enter the Shattered Temple to stand before an Eathal lord with an axe of darkglass. He would walk like the spellbound victim of a blood rite, his gaze fixed to the axe in the Eathal's hands. Then, like the stunned prey of the drakon, he would lay his head on the block, calmly, meekly and without resistance. Then the axe would fall.

Over and over these scenes played at the protected edges of his mind, swirling and shifting within the orange-red form of the second Compulsion, growing in power beyond his Barrier. One slip and his fate was sealed. It would take the briefest moment, a time of weariness, the disorientation between the haven of sleep and the waking world. . . Raziin knew he could not let the Barrier fall. He could not sleep, could not rest until he found a way to destroy the Bridge between him and Hukum.

How long could he hold out? He fell to his knees, overcome by the weight of his fate. He raised his eyes to the suns, poised to fall below Yos into the caverns of Llors.

'Hear me, Uros. Give me an answer and I will let such rivers of blood you will swell to devour pale Larus forever. The land will be bathed in your colours for all time.'

Yes. The rites of Uros would lend him strength.

He ripped off his cloak and shirt, following with the harness. With his chest bared to the bitter chill, he allowed the Heat to awaken, welcoming its frenzy; the mark of Uros. He had until the end of Storm Season. Until that time, the Heat would drive him on, banishing sleep, giving him reprieve to find a power to help him.

With one flashing movement, he drew the calv from the harness at his feet. He smiled as he saw the glistening edge. So many good memories were captured in that blade.

The first was the best.

He was thirteen. His father had taken him hunting in the high forest above Osellen for the first time. With him were many of the young ladies and lordlings of Armon, many also on their first hunt. Raziin had not wanted to go, despising his peers for their stupidity and weakness. His whole life he had been forced into the shadow of his older brother Ralin while he and his sickly twin sister were hidden away, his family embarrassed by their pale silver skin. Yet it had not been his fault, it was his father's. If Leith had not married so close to his own line – struggling always to keep the Cinnor's Sorcerous blood strong – then Raziin would have been born with the golden skin of Cioa – instead he was cursed with the silver – usually a mark of physical weakness, or of a host of genetic disorders that left many of the Cioan albinos mindless.

For as long as he could remember, Raziin had been stung by the taunts of his peers, even though he could outthink them in classes and outfight them in training.

To encourage him to attend the hunt, Leith had given him a new lanedd calv of the finest edge.

The adults had left them on the crest of a forested hill as they quested into the deeper snow-laden valleys hunting down a giant harena who had so far evaded them.

Raziin had walked away from the group, aggravated by their pointless conversation. He hated them all. Yet most of all he had despised Lisis, two years his senior, blessed with deep golden skin and good looks. His father was favoured by Leith and he dominated the inner circle of his peers and was often at the centre of the campaigns against Raziin.

Raziin had been practising a knife-form, slashing his new blade through the air, lifted by the feeling of his own power; imagining the feeling of ecstasy as the enemies of Armon fell beneath his blade, their blood pumping from mortal wounds. He stumbled on a branch hidden beneath the snow.

Then he heard laughter.

He turned to see Lisis and the others laughing at him.

'Think you're some sort of warrior, do you?' said Lisis, and those with him laughed, their eyes mocking. 'You can't even keep yourself on your feet.'

Raziin's blood had boiled, a furious anger he had never experienced before – even in his darkest fantasies – coursing through him. And a shining thought took hold. A glorious thought. What if he could kill Lisis? Right here. Would they be laughing then? No. They would be cowering before him. Despite their confidence, he knew he was a match for any of them.

'Well. If you're the expert, Lisis. Perhaps you should show me how it's done?' said Raziin, his voice trembling with excitement at his plan.

Lisis stood up, turning to smile at those around him and shrugging his shoulders. As he thought, Lisis, bloated with his pride, could not reject the challenge.

Lisis drew his own calv. He advanced on Raziin, seeking to intimidate him with his superior bulk and height. When Raziin had been younger, Lisis had often beaten him, yet he had never feared him. Raziin was the greatest of them all, he knew it. He held his ground.

Raziin dropped into a stance, his left open, palm forward, his right drawn back, ready for a thrust.

Lisis was suddenly unsure, but he could not back down now. He stopped two paces from Raziin and also dropped into a stance.

'You need to keep your stance low, that's where the balance is,' said Lisis. 'Like this.'

Raziin felt his heart hammering. How many times had he fantasised about killing this stupid thug? Now he could *actually* do it.

Lisis stepped forward, executing a slow demonstration thrust. At the same instant, Raziin swept forward. He knocked Lisis' knife arm aside with his left, stepping forward and shifting his weight as he had been taught – and drove his blade to the hilt in Lisis' heart.

Lisis gasped. Raziin saw the pain, the surprise – the fear – in Lisis' eyes as he cried out again and fell backwards. Slowly Raziin's blade slid out, followed by a fountain of blood that splashed out across the snow.

His memory was clear as he looked at the blade in fascination, the bone-white covered with red, sticky blood. The ecstasy! Never could he have dreamed of the pleasure! Yet he had been unprepared for the intensity of the disappointment as the light finally died in Lisis' eyes.

He turned to the others. The desire to kill them all, one by one, rose like a glorious tide. If he did, he could live that moment, that beautiful moment again.

Slowly he advanced on them. Who to take first? Perhaps Terisa. She had often laughed the loudest, fawning on Lisis. He imagined her cries of fear, then the pale frozen gold of her face as it lay immobile and lifeless in the snow.

He was surprised by the sound of narsiit bursting into the thicket.

His father!

He turned quickly, assessing the scene. Lisis' body lay cooling in the snow behind him.

He suppressed his anger and looked at his father calmly as the Sarlord dismounted with his aides, horror showing on his face.

Lisis' father ran to his son's body. 'Dead!' he yelled, rapidly examining Lisis. 'This is a calv wound, Leith.'

His father's face had grown shocked, looking across at him and his bloodied calv in disbelief.

'Justice! I demand justice for this!' said Lisis' father.

'It was an accident, father,' said Raziin. 'Lisis and I were sparring with the calv. It was his idea.'

Raziin remembered his father's silvered hair whipping in the cold breeze as he stared at him, his golden eyes full of outrage.

'What have you done?' said Leith, advancing on him, his voice strangely harsh.

Raziin lifted the bloody calv. 'It was an accident. I swear it by holy Yosini.' It was amazing how many times those few words had saved him from punishment in the past. He looked at his father, trying desperately to suppress his triumph.

Leith had turned to the other children. 'What do you have to say?'

Terisa was crying. It was disgusting.

One of the boys spoke up, his voice shaking. Typical. Raziin was right about them all. They were all weak.

'He. . . he just stabbed him,' said the boy.

Raziin had not seen the blow coming, but he heard his father's outraged howl as it came, a cry full of grief and anger. Leith's powerful fist had lifted him from his feet, sending him three paces across the clearing to fall in the snow with a stunning thud.

'You are not my son,' yelled Leith, his face twisted, looking at Lisis' rapidly freezing body.

'What are you?' he asked, rounding on him. 'What are you? What demon has taken you?'

Raziin had rolled into a ball as his father beat him, the blows falling again and again, breaking ribs, smashing his young face. He was lost in a mass of pain, dimly aware of his father's aides drawing the Sarlord from him and the blows ceasing.

'My lord. He is only a boy. We do not know what really happened.'

Raziin's eyes were blinded by blood, and his cracked ribs made each breath agony, yet even in the pain there was excitement. He still had the bloody knife, and he carefully slipped it inside his fur-lined jacket. Dimly he heard his father.

'Take him out of my sight before I kill him. Take him to the northern battlefields. He is not my son. Not my son.'

He was lifted by strong arms as the darkness claimed him.

And there were other memories. . .

It was just before his march on Osellen, the capital of Armon. The time of his greatest military power.

Again he saw the blade, this time the blood on it was his father's. It was spring; he and his generals had ambushed Leith's party. Outnumbered, they had fallen quickly. The archers had their orders – fill the Sarlord with arrows until he could not draw breath. Raziin smiled. Old man, he thought, you were the one to die.

Leith's Sorcery had come too late to save him. Seven arrows had found their mark, driving him to the ground beside his dying narsiit. His bodyguards had fallen just as swiftly, arrows and javelins used to deadly effect.

When Raziin had reached his father, the old man was barely conscious, lying in a pool of his own blood. He was angry Leith had not recognised him in the end. He had wanted him to know – wanted to show him the knife before he used it. He remembered his father's hand, outstretched to touch the dying narsiit as though to soothe its passing. Weak fool. Raziin was glad he was not burdened by such emotions. They made fools of men.

Alone in his cabin, Raziin held the knife to heaven in entreaty.

'See me, Uros. I give you blood. My blood for your glory.'

He crossed his chest with savage cuts, opening a score of wounds in a frenzy of motion, the pain riding high above a surging tide of pleasure. Raziin felt himself aroused. This, the gift of Uros. His mistress had heard him.

Shaking with pleasure and pain, he felt the Heat rise, the blood steaming as it covered him and his trousers in a slick tide.

'The Heat cleanses me. Let it rise to cleanse me.'

Uros had heard his plea. The answer would come, he was certain. The dark path would open as it had countless times before. His strength was pain. Within it the glory of Uros had risen like a sun. At the height of his ecstasy, he gave Uros his pledge. *Kelas will bleed for you, Mistress. It will bleed not a river, but an ocean of blood. And the Empire of Cioa will rise once more from the pitiful remnants that remain. The Eathal, the shattered Empire of Carris, all will be swept away, and in this land only one goddess shall rule. Uros. The blood-goddess.*

Chapter Eleven

Ellen advanced through the cold of the ante-chamber, her angry steps echoing across the grey and black marble. Bone-white columns rose towards the ceiling, smooth and without decoration, mocking her with their passive solidity.

At the entrance to the Council chambers, four guards stood with scythes crossed, blocking her way.

She gathered herself in her best Cintros poise, then identified the squad leader, the Razor, by his insignia.

'Stand aside,' she said to the Razor.

The guard swallowed, clearly mortified. A flush of heat on his face betrayed his tension, but he did not shift his feet as he answered. 'We have strict instructions that no one is to be admitted, my Lady.'

'I am Sarqua!'

The Razor's scythe quivered in his hands, his eyes widened in fear, yet he remained resolute. 'The Warlord commanded that you not be admitted, under any circumstances. The order was passed to us by Torren himself. He said it was for your own protection.'

'My – ' Ellen's words choked in her throat.

With the Regent Kerril dead, technically the Warlord commanded Athria until she was formally installed as Sarla. Her assumption of the throne, and the formal announcement of her succession had been delayed because of Storm Season. Even so, she could not view this as anything but treason.

Aris, so vocal in his support of Torren, was trying to cheat her of the throne in favour of her brother.

'Do you want me to pass word to Torren, my Lady?' said the Razor.

Pass word? So Torren could leave her waiting. . .or worse, appear to gloat over usurping her power?

Never.

Her eyes bored into the man in a silent fury. Should she use her powers? She could not simply blast her way into the chamber in a blaze of Sorcerous Fire, injuring or killing an innocent man merely doing his duty. . . or could she? A smile touched her lips as it came to her. It was so simple!

She walked towards the guards, her determination fuelled by her outrage. It was time to take control.

'Stand aside,' she shouted, this time as a warning. She reached for the Fire and formed the Shield Matrix around her. She swelled with power. Involuntarily the guards inched back. No doubt they had heard tales of her battle with the Northman Sorcerer. She had heard other warriors whispering, talking of her like an angry goddess; one who flew through the air, shooting jagged bolts of silver from her outstretched hands.

Their scythe blades wavered despite their attempts to hold them steady, yet they held their ground.

'Enough,' Ellen shouted, forcing her way into their midst. They did not advance on her but levelled their scythes into her path. For an unarmoured warrior to advance onto the blades would have been to invite death, but as Ellen came forward the lanedd points met an invisible wall. The guards shouted in confusion as she pushed past them.

Realising his blade could not touch her, the Razor dived at Ellen with his full body weight, trying in desperation to take her to the ground and subdue her. His men followed, yelling battle-cries as they hurled themselves forward. Their hands slid off the unseen barrier, scythes and men falling to the floor in an unruly press. The guards gave shouts of alarm as she passed through the outer doors.

The guards picked up their fallen scythes and followed her. The Razor tested the unseen barrier with his scythe point as though trying to find a chink in her invisible armour.

Ellen passed through a short corridor, striding past two more guards who stared at her in disbelief. At the entrance to the Council chamber, she raised her hand and thrust the ornate wooden doors open with an unseen burst of Force. The soldiers pursuing her paused as she swept into the room.

The Razor raced ahead of her and bowed to Torren and Aris.

'My apologies, Lords. I could not stop her.'

Torren and Aris sat at a massive table with the eight Suulvey lords who formed the Council of Athria, many of them hastily elevated from Suul following the deaths of others. But Ellen's eyes were immediately drawn to a knot of red-robed men near them, and the one who led them.

It was the High Druid Kexos, the supreme power of the Temple in Athria. He was a Templeman, and his rich robes glowed a bloody red in the light of the oil lamps. Behind him were four other Templeman. These were no Initiates, these were masters of their art; and that art was destruction.

Kexos' eyes lit up with triumph.

'Brother Kiin. If you please,' said Kexos, his voice deep, low and charismatic.

Ellen readied the Fire for an attack, sensing the forces moving in the room, but Kiin merely reached into his sleeve and drew out a heavy object.

The room was suddenly alive with lights of brown and grey.

Kiin lifted up the object, caressing it lovingly as he swivelled it towards her.

It was lead glowmetal.

The magical device rippled, its light soaking into her mind like a dulling poison. Her sight grew suddenly dim. She staggered, and the Razor rushed forward to support her. Realising she was under some sort of attack, she reached for the Fire, forming the Barrier Matrix in her mind; yet when she opened the Window, searching for the burning energy of the Fire. . . there was nothing.

Through her blurred eyes, she saw the surface of the lead glowmetal thickening, the bands of dull twisted metal swelling as the gritty light shimmered. Hastily she closed the Window. Immediately the glowmetal stopped absorbing power.

Talons of fear clawed at her heart.

Many glowmetals could absorb the Fire, turning it to a myriad of uses, but this glowmetal *took* it from her, before even she could use it.

Her mind cleared, and she stepped away from the squad leader, at once realising her folly.

'What is the meaning of this, Warlord?' said Kexos, turning his pale, silver-grey eyes to Aris. 'You and the Suul Cintros assured me her whereabouts were unknown.'

'At the time it was,' said Torren smoothly.

'Then the Temple repeats its demand that she be given over to us immediately for judgement under edict of Purge!' said Kexos, his voice rising to thunderous command.

The Templemen standing beside Kiin reached into his robes and produced a stout set of mought shackles. Ellen began to back away, but at a gesture from Kexos one of the other Templemen raised his hands. She was instantly frozen in place.

'I am the heir of Myan Cintros!' screamed Ellen in panic.

Now was Torren's chance. He would deliver her up to the Temple and take the throne in one neat stroke. All her training, all her preparation, the quest for the Scion and Cedrin, all would come to naught under the crushing heel of the Temple.

She looked across at Torren. The brother who had always despised her because of the love Myan had lavished on her; giving her a special place in his life because of the power they shared, yet shunning him, his eldest son.

'Guards!' commanded Torren. 'Protect the Sarqua.'

The men from the corridor now surrounded her, forming a solid wall.

Her breathing came in ragged gasps.

Torren was protecting her.

'Kexos,' said Torren, evenly, yet with his characteristic command. 'Release her. Immediately.'

The High Druid of the Temple measured the odds. For a tense moment it seemed he considered taking her, then reluctantly he nodded for his Templemen to cease the attack.

Ellen staggered backward, released.

Kexos turned his pale gaze towards her. 'They call you Sarqua. Yet I assure you, Sorcerer, no one of cursed blood will ever sit on the throne of Athria.'

Kiin hid the lead glowmetal. She cried out as something ripped inside her mind.

Torren rose. 'Whatever my sister Ellen is, your grace, she saved Athria when the Temple's power could not. It seems to me that the only magic you excel in is that devoted to subduing Sorcerers.' Torren stared down the Templemen. '*And*, my sister is still a Cintros. Remember that.'

'Suul Torren Cintros,' said Kexos, pulling himself up to his full height. 'When you take the throne of Athria, the Temple stands to give you its full support – yet only if this Sorcerer is dealt with as we demand.'

Aris advanced on Kexos. 'The Temple needs reminding that they do not rule Athria,' he said, his voice deadly.

Kexos looked from Aris to Torren and smiled. 'You have one day to deliver her to us.'

Kexos turned and swept out of the room, his Templemen filing behind him. Kiin looked at her as he left, and she shivered, remembering only too well the skills of the Templemen who had interrogated Jorrel and the assassin.

Finally they had gone.

Ellen sank into a chair, her heart hammering, her hands shaking. Never had she felt so helpless! Had those Templeman come upon her anywhere else, she would even now be heading for the Temple's dungeon, bereft of her powers. She could feel the Fire returning, yet it gave her no comfort. Father had warned her of their strength, but never would she have dreamed that such a powerful device remained in their hands. She had no doubt it was a relic from the latter days of the Empire, when the Temple forced Emperor Jykor, himself a Sorcerer, to lead the Great Purge.

'My Lords, we will reconvene tomorrow, two hours after dawn,' said the Warlord.

The Suulvey rose and filed silently out of the room. Torren and Aris resumed their seats.

'Did my messengers not reach you?' asked Torren.

'Yes, but how did you expect me to react to an order of confinement? I was not told the *reason*,' said Ellen.

Torren sighed heavily. 'Kexos arrived here mere minutes after I returned from the docks. He demanded that the Council meet with him. He arrived not only with the Templemen, but with hundreds of Temple Guardians. He was here to take you, Ellen. I could not very well invite you to the meeting. I suspected they would have some means of subduing your powers, and I was correct. He was too confident.'

'At least we succeeded in ridding the palace of the Temple Guardians,' said Aris.

'Yes. Insisting on the removal of the Guardians also gave us time to discuss our options in the Council before we met with him,' said Torren.

How could she have misjudged her brother so completely? His face was lined, aged from the long night. Like her, he had not rested since the Siren sounded yesterday.

'Brother, I owe you an apology. I thought . . .'

He smiled. 'I am not conspiring against you, sister. But with the revelation of your powers, matters have become very complex. We need to consider all options.'

Ellen was relieved, yet anxious that matters had come to a head so quickly.

She turned to Aris. The Warlord had been against her succession from the outset. He at least would be eager to see Torren on the throne.

'Where do you stand, Warlord?' she asked.

The privations of the night seemed to have had very little effect on Aris. If anything, he seemed fiercer than ever.

'Ellen, you cannot rule Athria,' he said. 'The warriors call you a serpent of Uros, possessed by a demon.'

'How dare you!' she stormed.

Aris halted her with a gesture. 'The truth must be spoken,' he said. 'The Temple refuses to send Druids to the court until you are delivered to them for the Trial of Stone. Work on the new garrison has come to a standstill, with the Druids removed from the quarry.

'Myan's decree is meaningless now. Athria is in chaos, our leader dead. We need to give the people solid leadership. Anything less leaves us vulnerable at a time when we cannot afford to be.

'I don't need to tell either one of you how close we came to losing Athria. This will not be the Eathal's only attempt.'

He looked from sister to brother, his face set. It seemed to Ellen he had little love for either of them, or for any Cintros for that matter. Ellen remembered well his reaction when her father named her heir.

'Athria must live. And for us to prosper, we must have a leader who can work with the Temple. Your little display of power has forfeited you the right to rule. *That* is the truth.'

'And yet without my *little display*, we would now be ruled by Hukum's minions,' said Ellen. 'I am Sarqua, Aris, by Myan's decree. I will rule in Athria whether the Temple condones it or not, until I decide otherwise.'

Aris remained resolute. 'Torren is destined to rule.'

Torren shook his head. 'You go too far, Cinev.' Torren's face creased in concentration, and he rubbed his temples. 'Yet Kexos is opposed to any negotiations. It seems there is no way to satisfy the Temple without your abdication. Perhaps with pressure . . .'

Aris fixed his gaze on Torren. 'If you think the Temple will *ever* support Ellen, you are a fool. The Temple has persecuted Sorcery for centuries. They fear it. The people fear it. Many of the warriors would rather desert than serve under someone cursed with the taint of Old Blood.'

Surely Aris was overplaying the threat for his own ends. 'There must be a middle way,' she said to Torren.

'Believe me, Ellen. I have tried to find it,' said Torren. 'You don't realise how much power the Temple has. They are essential – and they know it. In a hundred ways, they have become indispensable to us; they control all healing, only the Druids can lift the great stones at the quarry, only the Templemen can defend us against the Druids of our enemies, they protect shipping. . . the list goes on.'

'Yet they failed to defeat Raziin,' said Ellen, determination fuelling her. 'All of those present saw how ineffectual they were against a true Sorcerer.'

Aris' face set even harder.

'What if I leave Athria to the Temple and Raziin returns? Or one of the Eathal Sorcerers?' said Ellen.

'Athria will come to a standstill without Temple magic,' maintained Aris. 'That threat is upon us *now*.'

'They cannot be allowed to dictate to the throne,' she snapped.

'The Council knew of Myan's powers,' said Aris gravely. 'But we also knew the consequences should he use them. Myan understood the balance of power.'

Ellen was amazed how powerful the Temple had become, demanding that she submit to this sham of a trial – a death sentence – even though she was uncontested heir. Even she had not believed they would go so far. Now that they had issued the edict they would not stop until they had her.

'You must flee Athria, and Torren must take the throne,' said Aris. 'You must put Athria first. If you do not give up the throne, Athria will be divided. The Temple, the people, will not accept you. There are rumours the attack was a curse of the gods, brought upon Regent's Hill because it harboured a Sorceress. Some even say you killed Myan. . .'

'*Enough!* You have had your say, Cinev. You were present when Myan declared me his heir. I am the chosen ruler of Athria. Seek to undermine me again and I will see you wear chains beside Jorrel.'

Aris stiffened. 'I am no traitor. I sought only to speak the truth – as harsh as it may seem.'

'I was chosen to rule, you can't destroy the truth of that,' she said.

Aris nodded. 'Yes, I admit you are Sarqua.'

How she despised Aris at that moment.

Ellen stared at the swirling design on the chamber walls. It was a depiction of Larus defeating Uros, the demons of Storm Season swarming behind the Red Sister like a black tide, their leering faces staring out at her in unholy glee, somehow sharing a secret knowledge of her defeat.

She returned her gaze to Aris. If not for the need for stability she would strip him of his title of Warlord right now, yet too much remained to be done to upset the chain of command.

'You may go,' she said.

Aris bowed stiffly, his jaw clenched tightly with suppressed tension. His eyes, livid with anger, looked to the floor, his gaze directed anywhere but towards her. Then he was gone.

She turned to Torren. 'What do you suggest now?'

Torren sighed. 'For now it seems we have little option but for you to leave Athria before the Temple seizes you. Although they are bound by their own edict, they know that if they take you it will pitch Regent's Hill against them. Not all the High Druids supported the decision. My spies tell me the High Druid of Moons wanted to exile you, in deference to your father.'

'How kind of them.' Ellen struggled for composure.

Torren smiled. 'Regardless, they realise it would be expedient to let you flee. Only the Templemen really want to get their hands on you. They voted to take you under edict of Purge and destroy you without Trial.'

'But what do I become, Torren. A fugitive?'

Torren rose from his chair and placed a hand on her shoulder. Ellen was surprised at this sudden show of affection. Hesitantly she placed her own hand over his and looked up into his eyes. She saw concern there and respect. She also sensed a burden had been lifted from him, and in a flash of insight knew what it must be. He had always been jealous of her special relationship with their father, taking it as a negative reflection on himself. Yet now he knew there was a reason. She and her father had shared the powers of Sorcery. It was not something that he lacked as a man, but instead a trick of birth that left her with the powers of Sorcery and her two brothers without.

'Ellen. Every Suulvey lord on the Council understands the debt we owe you. You would leave Athria with the rank of Suul. One of the options we discussed was to arrange a diplomatic mission to the Yasser States. With this attempt to take the Sardom, it is urgent that we maintain close relations with the Warlord's court at Raynor.

'You will always be a Lady of the Athrian court, a full Suul. It may take years for the Temple to be persuaded to rescind the edict, but we will keep the pressure up. If, in time, you can return, the Cintros mansion and its secrets will be yours alone.'

She would never give up her right to the throne. The Temple knew of her father's powers – yet never confronted him. Surely in time, they could be persuaded. For now though . . . her heart grew heavy as she realised Torren was right; for now it would be expedient to flee.

'If I am to leave Athria, to lay aside the throne for now, at the very least I must be given the rank of Suulvey. I must be recognised as a senior member of the court. A member of the Council in absentia.'

'The rank of Suulvey is not given lightly,' said Torren.

'I am the chosen ruler. The Council must agree.'

Torren nodded in agreement. 'Myan's decree is inviolate.'

It would be easy to give into her desire to defy the Temple, to pitch her power against them, bring them to heel under her throne. But as she met Torren's gaze, she saw Athria split: angry crowds massing outside the walls of Regent's Hill as the stranglehold of the Temple tightened. She had no choice.

'Ellen. I formally request you to release the Sardom to me. Not for me, for Athria. In return, you will have a place on the Council, the vote held by me until you return. You will be a Suulvey, that I guarantee you. Give the word and the papers will be prepared before dawn. Or . . . take the throne. If you so choose, I will follow you loyally. Whatever the cost.'

Silently they regarded each other.

'Choose for the people, Ellen. Not for yourself.'

She knew what she must do. Her heart twisted at the irony. Her first act as supreme ruler would be to remove herself from power.

'I agree that you may rule as Sarlord in my place, Torren. Yet only on the condition that you release power to me should I return. Until that time, I will take the rank of Suulvey.' It was done.

Ellen sagged forward against the table. Until she had been forced to give it up, she had not realised how much she had longed to rule. It had been a challenge, something grand to fill her life, replacing the things she had lost. It was as though, following her father's wishes, she would be clinging to what remained of him. Yet despite the losses, she had not come away from the disaster empty-handed.

She had broken through the isolation that had surrounded her like a curse since raising her hand against the Northman. Torren had proved anything but a betrayer. He was the same brother who had always been distant from her and there would always be a gulf between them, but he had proved to be a man of worth. He valued Myan's word and his own honour over the prize he had coveted for half his lifetime: the throne. Ellen had seen he was prepared to give it up. If she had refused to pass rule to him, he would have served her with complete loyalty. This was a remarkable insight into Torren. More than an ally, she had gained the respect of a man who had always given her only derision and contempt.

Inspecting the ruins of her ambitions, she realised her father's will had included more than the throne of Athria. Released from the constrictions of rule, she would be free to pursue Cedrin. What better place for Belin's son to learn the way of the Suul than at the court of Raynor? And what better place for them to search for the Scion together than the former seat of the Cinanac Emperors?

Ellen could now throw herself into the mystery of the Scion wholeheartedly.

She realised that one part of her, the small voice that always cried out against the restrictions of being a Cintros and a Suul, was actually pleased. Suulvey ambassador to Raynor. For many years it had been her greatest ambition, strange that now it should seem like defeat. Still, it was an honourable role. It was also a chance to see her brother Estle again. The second eldest – in between her and Torren – he had been Athria's chief ambassador to Raynor for more than five years. He and Ellen had always been close, and it would be good to see him again.

She looked across at Torren. His face was stark, impassive, grim. He was back to his old self, except now he had the rule of Athria. She pushed aside her regret. Nothing could be changed.

'What now?' asked Ellen.

Torren sighed. 'So much remains to be done. So many allegiances, alliances. Ahhh. . . Politics. Maybe I should have remained on the Wall.'

Ellen smiled. 'Nonsense. You were always too ambitious for that.'

Torren reached across the table and turned a large map of Kelas around to face them.

'We discussed this briefly in the Council before we admitted the Templemen. This will bear directly on your mission.'

Torren lifted a stylus and pointed at the map. 'The Eathal have launched a full-scale invasion of Kelas. We now know why they were so anxious to install a puppet ruler in Athria. With Raynor under siege, Athria is the only state that could get troops and materials into the city.

'With Athria free, Raynor could stay under siege for years. Without us, the Eathal would have starved the city in under four months.'

That made sense. They knew that Jorrel was being supported by the Eathal, Raziin and his warriors acting as the agents of Hukum and his Inner Circle.

Torren pointed at the map. 'They have two armies, each attacking on a separate front. Preliminary reports suggest they both number over five legions. One is attacking south of the Yasser, driving into the Sardom of Hend. Another has crossed the Yasser and is attacking north into Tupur.' Tupur was a former Bulvuran province, now ruled by the Temple of the Sisters.

'The Eathal have already scattered the border regiments of Hend with Fire,' said Torren looking up towards her. Ellen had known for years that Hukum was a Sorcerer, as were most of his Inner Circle.

'Some reports put the force in Tupur at over seven legions,' said Torren.

'Twelve legions! The Eathal have never had that kind of strength,' she said, her heart racing at the implications.

'It appears they did. Their first attempt to gain Raynor was no more than the initial stage of a well-planned conquest. They have had thirty years to strengthen their supply lines and have used that time well.'

If it was true, the Eathal could destroy all the cities of Kelas in less than a year. If they were not stopped, the destruction would be vast. . . and horrific.

'Your mission to the Yasser States is no sham. If the Eathal succeed in closing off the Yasser, the baal trade will be finished. Athria suffered badly with the fall of Althar and the eastern provinces thirty years ago. Now only the Yasser States and the farmlands along the north bank remain. They must be saved. Our economic survival depends on Raynor's victory.'

Torren tapped the stylus on the table. 'The Eathal claim they seek only the downfall of the Yasser States, but we have first-hand reports that the force in Tupur is heading for the City of Mirrors.'

'Olcis,' she whispered. The largest city in Kelas and the oldest in the former Bulvuran Empire.

'Olcis,' Torren said with finality. 'Then Kelas. The pattern is clear. Thirty years ago they claimed the lands south-east of the Yasser, now they plan to take the whole Yasser plain. They want to carve Kelas like a roasted harena, nation by nation. With no Empire to stop them, they will do it.'

'What about the treaty of Raynor?'

'The Eathal ambassadors have worked for years to undermine the treaty. The northern ports who signed it thirty years ago will not lift a finger to help Raynor now. The northern nations believe Hukum will stop at Raynor and the Sundar is sweetening the bargain with gems, rare tints and tinctures from his mines. To think even I criticised Myan for his policy regarding the Eathal. He knew them better than anyone.'

Ellen had never seen Torren so passionate and she realised Athria had gained a great leader. This man, her brother, would defend the nation's interests with every ounce of his determination and skill.

'The Yasser States are alone,' he said, gathering up the maps. 'They need our support.'

With characteristic control, he pushed the issue to the back of his mind. For Ellen it was not so easy. She saw thousands screaming and dying as the Eathal hordes advanced.

They walked together towards the doors.

'You will need a retinue. I will select two Suulqua to act as court messengers.' He paused, looking at Ellen. 'Of course, as

Suulvey you are free to choose your own retainers if you wish.'

'I'm sure they will be exemplary,' she said. She would leave Escon here to fully recover from his wound.

'I have already ordered a war-galley to be prepared for a diplomatic mission to Raynor. It has the usual complement of men. There are also documents to review and you must be briefed in detail on the mission. The papers allowing me to rule in your place and formalising your appointment as Suulvey ambassador must be signed and sealed with utmost dispatch. In addition . . .'

As Torren went on detailing preparations, she reflected on this twist of fate. *A war-galley has already been prepared.* It was as though some hand was guiding the way. If so, she would not question it. Her father's plea that she bring Cedrin under the court's protection and find the Scion was her only remaining link to him. She vowed to throw herself into the role with the same zeal that her brother displayed in embracing the rule of Athria.

Chapter Twelve

Twisting in ecstasy, the bat stretched his leather wings to the dark sky. He was an *efreet*, long and sleek, his muscled torso geared for flight. He soared above the budding shoots of Gimpessu forest regrowth, planted years before by human slaves. The message capsule on his leg rattled in the wind.

The efreet's ancestors were night-hunters. Rising from deep caverns they would range far, hunting under the moons, soaring high above the nightscape waiting to strike. Although the messenger saw prey far below, he had no desire to swoop to the kill. He had only ever taken sustenance from the hands of his masters.

Above the courier, the night sky was alive with light. The caverns rose ahead in ghostly clarity, outlined by returning echoes. He screeched as he fell, plummeting towards the great cavern mouth, an exultation of both regret and hunger. His master waited beneath in the warmth of the deepest caverns, and with him was the sweet flesh he craved.

Through the opening he flew, into the welcoming sights, sounds and smells of the home-caverns of Maht. He soared over the plazas and swarming caverns of the Upper Congregations, turning with unerring precision as he sped deeper below the surface of Yos. He passed through myriad caverns, all interconnected by stairs and bridges, tunnels and towers.

Thousands of Eathal swarmed below in markets and households, temples and squares. The underground cities were built of the heart-stone of Maht, a dull brown basalt, chequered and decorated with paints and pigments. The designs on some buildings were bright and new, while others had been despoiled by the continual rain of bat guano from the ceiling.

The messenger sped on, aware of both the mass of Eathal below and the squawking press of thousands of bats above. The city-dwellers were hardly aware of the bats. If they had looked up they would have smiled, revealing the sharp teeth of a predator, and muttered thanks to the Lifegivers; the winged children of Kallor who were the source of all prosperity, bringing the wealth of the suns from the surface to the dark bosom of Yos.

The air cooled. The carrier felt the thrill of expectation as the caverns became wilder, sparser, and more crowded with bats. He had to be careful, for there were predators that dwelled only within the caverns. Swift, solitary killers that would swoop, then fly with their prize to hidden, dark eyries amid the rough fissures of Maht's volcanic past.

The messenger saw a hunter plummet. The efreet stretched his wings and surged with all the strength that evolution and selective breeding had conspired to give him – leaving the pursuer far behind. The ancient Eathal had chosen well when they climbed the darkened walls to claim the first young efreet from their roosts to train and breed. Nothing short of a stalking drakon could best them in speed.

The caverns began to warm once more as he approached the Lower Congregations. The feast was closer now and the tireless flier added more speed. He hurtled through hundreds of caverns given over to lungii pasture, crowded with jakka, the docile beasts that fed the Eathal, tended only by their lonely keepers. These scenes fled and the messenger entered the most sacred of Congregations.

The wild, untamed Lower Congregations were protected by the edict of the Sundar. For any common Eathal to trespass was punishable by death. These were the haunts of the Eathal Lords, vast tracts of fertile but untouched ground; with private glades, hunting reserves and meditation groves. The grandest palaces and the holiest Temples were concealed here, within lush stands of lungii and decorative gardens.

They were fructive caverns, as were once those of the Upper

Congregations, and millions of bats, the holiest of animals, crowded the ceilings. Here they ruled. The unceasing rain of guano falling in a soft patter against the leaves and lush lawns of pale fungi grass.

Eathal gardeners moved amid the lush forests. Adapted to life within the caverns, the Eathal had excellent hearing and their sight had become extremely sensitive, dropping into the infrared range. To the Eathal the caverns were brilliantly lit by the stands of wild lungii, each glowing with bioluminescence. To a human, the caverns would have appeared to be in almost total darkness.

The palace of the Sundar stood ahead, the sprawling structure dominating an entire cavern. The fine walls and domes were built of the best quarried stone Maht had to offer, rising many stories high without apparent pattern. The bat raced for the roosting tower, which was carved from the cavern roof and dressed in fine marble, now heavily stained, and connected to the palace by an elaborate winding stair.

The messenger slowed as he shot through the vertical openings in the tower side, stretching claws to grip the roosting rod. The efreet gave a triumphant cry as he settled on his roost, dropping his head to the plate of shredded jakka, sticky with clotting blood. His reward of bloody meat.

The messenger's keeper loosened the message capsule from the bat's leg as the efreet supped on his reward. Like all Eathal, he was shorter than a human, hairless, with skin like creased leather the colour of grey-brown. His ears were large in proportion to the bald, dome-like head. The sparkling green eyes, irises slit, were hidden deep within heavy brow ridges.

They were a slow moving race, the hands claw-like for gripping ridges in stone, but they were massively strong. The frame of an Eathal bulged with raised muscles and was peppered with colourings of yellow and tan.

The keeper opened the capsule. 'Ahh,' he said, his voice strangely sweet and musical, considering the roughness and squat muscular power of the Eathal's build.

'A message from the forces in Hend.' He spoke in moderate tones, which would seem no more than a whisper to a human.

'General Yeffrij will be pleased. Hianer has been destroyed.'

'Runner!'

A young Eathal came forward, bowing. 'Yes, bat-master?'

The older Eathal regarded the young thal with satisfaction. 'Take this to the staff of general Yeffrij at once.'

The runner bowed, then shambled to the stairs. His progress would have looked awkward to a human, but for an Eathal it was the equivalent of a run. Their success as hunters relied on stealth, strategy and power, not speed and agility.

The keeper stroked the messenger bat. The sleek male raised his head in a screech, shreds of meat and blood framing the black, furred face. He was unhappy at the interruption of his feast and the keeper pushed the plate closer like an indulgent father. 'There, there my little one, feast. We shall feed you human flesh soon.'

The bat finished the meat. Lovingly, his keeper stroked the muscled back as the efreet's small, pink tongue darted rapidly to drink the blood remaining on the plate.

'Would you like that, little one?' The bat screeched as his feast came to an end, but the keeper took the cry of protest as an affirmation.

'You would?' He smiled as he took the plate away, still stroking the bat. 'My little one. Yes, my little one, we'll see if Yeffrij can get you some.'

The efreet squawked again as the keeper hooded him.

* * *

Hukum shifted forward in his chair, channelling more power into the uranium glowmetal. As his hands touched the glowing device, orange-red light blossomed within the triple spiral of its form. Slowly, meticulously, he constructed another Compulsion to send through the void to Raziin.

The glowmetal had been the secret pride of the Sundar's line for generations, passed from father to son in absolute secrecy since its discovery. There was no other like it – for it received the stuff of the Realm of Fire and transformed it into directed psychic energy: powerful, primal, emotion. And like his father before him, Hukum had used it well to dominate and subdue his enemies. Never before had it failed him. Yet now, the final phase of the Compulsion was failing to find Raziin. How could this be? What manner of being could keep a Barrier up for days without rest?

The light shed by the glowmetal wavered rhythmically in sympathy with the Fire that Hukum fed to it. It gave the dark grey skin of his arms and outstretched hands a strange touch of deep red, illuminating his features hidden within his hood. His facial skin was pale and gaunt, stretched between scars cut by greatscythe blades thirty years earlier as he battled to bring down the walls of Raynor.

There. It was done.

Hukum let the Fire fall from him. Satisfied, he rose to his feet. Sooner or later Raziin would succumb to his will. In the scheme of things the human was nothing more than a trifling annoyance.

His sanctum was lit by a single glowplant, fuelled by the finest grade of liquefied bat-guano. Its strong luminescence revealed a room furnished with a seemingly haphazard combination of the exquisite and the decrepit. Some furniture and sculptures represented the pinnacle of achievement for a court artist, others were ancient and rough, relics of Hukum's ancestors, still vibrant with the unseen imprint of Sorcery. The shadows were alive with dim, pulsing colours; reds, yellows, blues, greens and violets, other hues that defied the eye, some livid, some pale, others deep and rich, or strangely unsettling. Hundreds of glowmetals, set in their original frames of tough *lungii* stalks or ancient clearglass; each patiently waiting for their turn.

Masterpiece and heirloom alike, all rested on an undressed and uneven floor with only the most radical of protuberances smoothed. Jutting stone fluted from the walls and ceiling. The maker of the palace, the first Sundar, had insisted this most secret of chambers retain the characteristics of the original cavern as he had found it, the rock eaten by the hot breath of the drakon, his chosen totem.

Hukum walked across the chamber and left the room,

sealing the door with a heavy block of stone. It could only be shifted by a Sorcerer or Druid of Hukum's power, one who knew the unique Force-signature of the platinum glowmetal that moved the stone.

He emerged into his own chambers, deep within the heart of the Sundar's palace. His family had lived within these ancient walls for many centuries, the supreme rulers of the Eathal. They were still hailed as the saviours of the Eathal race; those who had led the survivors of the Great Destruction into the deep caverns of Maht, shielding them beneath the power of the great glowmetals housed here. The Eathal race had survived and prospered, despite the Destruction, and soon the circle would close. The time for the Vengeance was almost upon them.

His servants came forward, bowing.

'Ready me for the Inner Circle.'

In silence they went about the business of dressing the supreme Sorcerer-Lord of Maht. As they prepared him, he considered his good fortune. Of all those of his line, he alone would be entered into history as the avenger, the leader who destroyed the vile works of men. He would re-establish the great Caverns that Carris, the first of the Cinanac, had so ruthlessly destroyed, taking whole nations of Eathal to final destruction. He smiled as he imagined his armies marching through Kelas. There would be no simple death for these humans.

Carris enslaved a generation of Eathal to build Raynor. Hukum would put the humans in chains for an eternity, serving and sweating for their Eathal masters until the suns no longer touched the forests with life-giving light.

Still buoyed by the anticipation of victory in Kelas, he swept from his chambers; his dark brown-grey skin glistening with sweet oil in the luminescence of the glowplants, robes of deep red and gold draped from his solid frame in opulent falls.

His honour guard, elite Eathal warriors in hide armour, hefting solid maces and axes of darkglass, fell into step around him unnoticed, silently following his path to the Inner Circle. Hukum was used to their presence, and his thoughts were already on the coming meeting.

He reflected on the strategies, alliances, threats – and Sorcery – with which he had dominated the Circle. Easiest to manipulate had been the Druids of Kallor. He had merely fed and directed the living greed and thirst for power he discovered in their hearts. All of it was coming to fruition now. His policies were in favour, the Circle backed his conquest nine to three.

He entered the domed chamber. It was a remarkable feat of engineering that towered many stories and formed a flawless circle. It was a perfect parody of a natural cavern, complete with painted depictions of roosting bats on the distant roof. The elite of the Eathal had long grown to despise the continual rain of bat guano that fell on the common people.

The ruling class were called Junta, and all professed links to Sorcerous ancestors. In the decadent Empire of the Cinanac, the Old Blood had become careless with intermarriage. They had been so certain of their position that they had not suppressed the power of the Temple until it was too late. The Eathal had made no such errors. They knew the power of the Fire was the greatest of the three realms of magic; Heaven, Earth and Fire. Those with the Fire were admitted to the Junta, those who had lost the power for three generations were expelled. Marriage outside the Junta was strictly forbidden. Fire was power; Fire was strength, and Fire would be the instrument of the humans' destruction.

Slender columns rose to support the ceiling of the domed room, each a single carved tusk of a giant harena, brought from the surface. Apart from this artistic concession, the ceiling was supported only by the integrity of the conical arch it described.

The floor was decorated with thousands of concentric circles, constructed from tiles of ceramic, no two colours the same. A gradual rise in the vibrancy of the pigments reached a crescendo as the circles decreased in size. The observer's gaze was drawn to the centre of the room where the cushions and tables of the Inner Circle were set low in the style of the Eathal.

The members of the Inner Circle rose to their feet as Hukum entered the chamber and took his seat on the cushions. Then the Circle followed his lead and resumed their seats. They were silent as he regarded them, waiting for their Lord to set the agenda.

Hukum surveyed them. The thal and thel, male and female Eathal, who led the great civilisation of Maht. Soon they would join in ruling Yos and the Eathal would rise once more to their proper place. Nine Sorcerer-Lords sat within the circle of twelve, including his son Staraz; with them were two Druids of the earth-god Kallor, and one Druid of the ancient god Lidu.

Hukum's good humour faded as he met the gaze of Meaceth, the Liduin Druid. The old thel and her order were one factor he could not control. They had been against the Vengeance from the beginning, preaching the doctrine of peaceful Lidu, the Unseen Sun. They would be dealt with soon enough, thought Hukum. For the moment he needed their skills to heal the forests of Kelas. After that, they would not be so vital. New caverns needed new forests. This was an ancient rule. The Lifegivers – the bats – needed the great forests of the surface. It was there they fed, bringing the wealth of the suns back to the bosom of the earth.

Hukum steadily returned Meaceth's stare until she bowed to him. He smiled. Yes. He would use her then feed her and her whole religion to the Druids of Kallor. They would have no mercy.

He turned to his general, Yeffrij, who led the armies of the Vengeance. This one he had skilfully manipulated with Compulsions.

'What news, General Yeffrij?'

The general smiled, revealing the sharp teeth of the Eathal. 'Victory, my Lord. Our forces have destroyed Hianer, the capital of Hend.

'The city was predominantly wood and was easy prey for us. It has been reduced to ashes, the legions of Hend destroyed or scattered. News came only hours before, by efreet.'

Hukum's heart stirred. *You have done well, my marionette.*

'Excellent. Do any forces remain south of the Yasser to challenge us?' said Hukum.

'No, Lord. Hend's legions were destroyed. The fools ran from our Fire like frightened children. They have no stomach to fight at night and were easily surprised and vanquished. Only isolated outposts remain. These will be taken within the next few weeks. Then we can begin to entrench. The south of the Yasser is ours.'

Hukum gave a laugh of pleasure. 'What of the slave count?'

Yeffrij was apologetic. 'Unfortunately only three thousand, my Lord. Much of Hianer heard of the defeat of their Legions and fled north to Raynor and northern Kelas.'

Hukum was disappointed. Like his father before him, he had come to rely on human slaves to rebuild for the Eathal. Some grew grain for the legions, others replanted the forests their ancestors had cleared to grow baal; but most were turned to outfitting caverns or building new dome cities on the surface, sealed from the suns and stocked with proper life.

Overall, though, Hukum was pleased. More slaves could always be captured. More important in the short term was the military situation.

'What of the main force, Yeffrij? Are they in position in Tupur for the execution of our thrust into northern Kelas?'

At this, Yeffrij became animated, losing his composure like an adolescent, his eagerness for the northern campaign plain for all to see. Hukum was pleased the Compulsion he had secreted within the general's mind was working so well, yet he wished the thal did not have to act like such a gibbering fool.

'Our forces are ready to move on the city of Talis,' he said eagerly. 'With Talis destroyed, only the Tupur cities of Valleth and Kinass stand between our forces and the destruction of Olcis.'

Hukum watched Yeffrij with a secret satisfaction. Only months ago the general and his faction had opposed the full push towards Olcis. They had supported the destruction of Raynor and the Yasser States and another period of consolidation. But Hukum knew the time was right. *He* was the ruler who would see the final destruction of the abomination the humans had built, the Empire which had been founded on the death of Eathal nations. No, he would not pass that glory to another. He was the instrument of Vengeance.

Hukum schooled his features to stillness as he nodded to his general. 'Very good, Yeffrij. You may be seated.' Hukum knew if the Circle ever discovered he used Compulsions on them he would be ruined. They were his minions, but together they could depose his house from rule. That, he would never allow.

He was fortunate Yeffrij's talents lay on the battlefield. He was a weak Sorcerer, his perceptions dim. The Compulsion worked on him without his knowledge. Of all these Junta Lords, he had won his place on the Circle because of his brilliance as a general and his natural ability to lead. The humans were fools, he mused, allowing their Old Blood to weaken. No petty Druids of the Sisters could halt the coming storm. Humans. He snorted. Their own decadence and weakness had ruined them.

With the forces in Hend were the Wallbreakers, six huge glowmetals that had never been transported from the Lower Congregations before. Housed in chariots, they wreaked massive damage. Using them, his forces had flattened the proud city of Hianer in less than a day; the towers and palaces, built from the wood of the destroyed forests around Maht, returned to ash. The ruins of the city would be ploughed into the earth and a forest would grow in its place. More bats would be spawned and Maht would grow richer. Barren, darkened caverns would stir to life once more.

Hukum's gaze swept to Venan and Eith. Two powerful Sorcerer-Lords who, with Meaceth, were all that remained of his opposition. They argued the Vengeance should end with the destruction of Hend, that the Eathal should never again reveal their full strength to the men of Kelas. The Eathal should guard their secrets, they reasoned, and be content with the new surface forests and the underground prosperity they would bring. Hukum had defeated them. He was more ambitious for the Eathal. He saw a time when the Congregations of the Mulisar and of the Ranmyden ranges were regained, and the cities of men were once and for all cast from Kelas. Their curse would at last be removed, and the peaceful silence of the great forests would once again reign across the surface of Kelas. Only then could the Eathal turn their thoughts to the earth. The Eathal were the closest to the heart of Yos, it was their destiny to rule it.

Hukum was interrupted from his musing as Verst climbed to his feet.

'May I speak, Sundar?' His tone was impatient and demanding, as usual.

Verst was thin for an Eathal, but possessed incredible energy and great power. He had always supported Hukum in the conquest of Kelas, his bitterness and desire for Vengeance outstripping even the Sundar's. Verst wanted the annihilation of all humans. He was against even the taking of slaves, an important matter of practicality in Hukum's eyes. He was a purist and they had their uses, but Verst could occasionally be a splinter between his toes; as, Hukum guessed, he was about to become.

The Sundar nodded magnanimously. 'You may pose a question, Lord Verst.'

'What of Athria? Has the Island-State fallen to the puppet, Jorrel?'

Anger swelled in Hukum. His forces in Kelas were stepping from victory to victory. Now, when they were poised on the edge of Vengeance, he had expected the Circle to rejoice with him. Instead they could only point out his failures.

Lord Venan spoke up, the lazy scholar not bothering to rise. Hukum knew what was coming. Venan, that human-lover, could not wait to highlight the disaster. If this troublesome lord did not have the support of the scholar's guild, Hukum would have gladly posted him to the front line in Kelas. *See if he could maintain his scholar's detachment there.*

'No, Verst, the attempt to depose the Cintros was a failure. Worse, it appears the thel-spawn of the Sorcerer Myan wields the Fire,' said Venan.

Venan, his bulky body sprawled on the cushions, looked to the other Lords as though to strengthen the impact of his words.

'It was a fiasco. The traitor Raziin and his Cioan murderers made no difference. No, Athria is free and the attack on Raynor is bound to fail before it begins. When will the Lords of the Circle realise the humans will now reunify and repeat the Destruction with even more thoroughness?'

Coward, thought Hukum. The fat scholar had never raised a sweat in his life. He wants to cower here in Maht while another Empire rises from the ashes of the old one.

'Have you forgotten our duty to the Vengeance!' said Hukum. 'Do you want to wait for Raynor to grow strong again and destroy our only chance of obliterating the seat of Carris once and for all?'

'What of the Spear of Carris?' maintained Venan. 'Its fate was never determined.'

'The Spear is lost, the human Old Blood extinguished. Our enemies scatter,' insisted Hukum.

Venan was silenced, but Hukum could see the doubts he raised had fallen on fertile ground.

'Athria is of no consequence,' said Hukum, his voice now more subdued and persuasive. 'And what is one Sorceress to our strength? Her own people seek to destroy her,' he said, meeting each of their gazes in turn.

'We have taken Hend. Part of the force in Tupur will strike west into the Yasser States, destroying the cities like the cancers they are. One by one they will fall until Raynor stands alone in the smoking ruins of the former Empire. Then we shall bring its walls down in a mighty frontal assault. With the Wallbreakers, the issue of siege will never arise.

'Athria is a weak nation, isolated by sea. They have less than two legions and will not send more than a couple of hundred warriors to help the Warlord of Raynor.'

Hukum paused. He was beginning to sway them over once more. 'Do you think a few hundred human soldiers will make a difference? More than seven Eathal legions will assault the walls of Raynor. And it will fall, my friends. It will fall.'

Verst surged to his feet once more. 'What of Raziin? It is time he was destroyed!'

'Yes, Lord Verst. He is even now making his way towards the Shattered Temple. There he will be slain,' said Hukum.

Verst's eyes glowed in savage satisfaction.

Hukum smiled. Not a meeting of the Circle had gone by without Verst asking for the Cioan's death. Now he had his wish.

Staraz now stood and bowed. 'Sundar,' he said, his father's ferocity burning in his green eyes. 'Let me be the one to destroy him.'

Hukum felt a surge of pride in his son. He was strong and fearless, and full of the Fire. A fit ruler to stand in his place. When Raziin had entered the forbidden caverns of the Eathal many years ago, demanding to see the Sundar, Staraz had just begun his training with Hukum. Staraz had wanted to kill the human even then, for the sheer insolence of entering the caverns of Maht. But Hukum had seen the value in the Traitor of Armon and given him a few simple tricks to make him a better servant of the Eathal, always careful to leave him vulnerable to another Sorcerer. Staraz had been forced to wait for his training as Hukum taught the human of the Fire. How the hatred had grown between them! Hukum was happy his son would be the instrument of Raziin's destruction, it was the least he deserved.

He rose and walked over to his son, placing his hands on his shoulders. 'Bring Raziin's head back to the Circle on a lungii spike.'

Staraz smiled, a vicious grin revealing his pointed teeth. 'I will, Lord. That I promise.'

Hukum smiled at his son, a rare concession, and seated himself. 'Now, what other business has been brought before the Circle?'

Chapter Thirteen

The dead calm remained, and the *Lusella's Pride* struggled forward through a thick silver mist. Cedrin looked back across the ship, noting the tension in the men. Usually the crew sang, but not now. The oars rose and fell, the ship crawling towards Kelas and the reefs off the coast in silence. The melancholy strains of a faint flute melody reached them from below.

'Which way is west?' asked Cedrin.

Marken's face creased in concentration. 'You're in luck. Asic is in the sky. There,' he said, pointing over the prow to starboard. 'The suns are low on the horizon.'

'I'm impressed. Magic is not something I will ever understand,' said Cedrin. The suns had been concealed by the thick mist all the day. Somewhere, also behind that thick cloud, was the moon Asic. How Marken could sense its presence was beyond him.

Marken laughed. 'I did learn *something* in the Temple. Still, directions are one thing, reefs are another.'

They both looked back to the Templeman who stood by the tiller. Only his skills could guide the ship to safety.

All three calvanni had celebrated with a vengeance the night before, drinking wine, ale and bakta as though they had never seen a drop before and never would again. Cedrin's purse had suffered. He had discovered long ago gambling and alcohol did not mix, but, he mused, some are bound to repeat their mistakes.

The mist had risen with the dawn, billowing around them like the breath of a sleeping drakon, shrouding the sky.

None of the big trading ships would sail in the Storm Season without a Sun Druid, preferably a Templeman. All the Captains paid their dues to the Temple for the piloting service. Some of the wealthier Traders would also hire Druids for healing and protection. The smaller vessels had to make do with sailors' tricks and minor spells of Navigation known only to tiller-men.

Cedrin could see Captain Robic on the quarterdeck, waiting anxiously for the Templeman's direction. His straight, reddish hair lay dishevelled, a thick growth of beard on his wide face.

Thinking of the reefs that fringed the Narrows, Cedrin said his own prayers to the Sisters as they waited. Druidic magic had failed before.

Beneath the Templeman's hood, his face was a picture of concentration. His eyes were closed, and he was lost amid his inner vision. Defying the cold, sweat beaded on his smooth forehead as he worked. Moments later, he opened his eyes to reveal small, cruel eyes of dull blue.

'Turn two points to port,' he said to the helmsman.

The helmsman nodded, shifting the tiller. 'Aye, Templeman.'

Cedrin could see Robic was relieved, yet his fear of the Templeman was plain. Hands clasped behind his back, Robic gave the Druid a wary glance before leaving the quarterdeck and disappearing into his cabin.

'Let's go below,' said Cedrin. 'I think my appetite is returning at last.'

Below, in the crowded commons, Cedrin and Marken sat together on their bunks, holding bowls of hot baal, appeasing hunger long delayed by their hangovers.

Cedrin gingerly touched the fresh ink of the sixth-degree, a fierce sea-raptor clutching a calv in its talons, etched for all time into his skin. He had not been keen on receiving it, but when Skye found a master tattooist travelling with them on the common deck, he had insisted Cedrin wear the honour of his victory over Mat for all to see. There had been drunken applause from the crowd when it was finished, and confusion as Cedrin refused to speak of his victory. He was given a respectful distance after that.

The more ambitious of the gamblers had begun once more,

Skye among them. The noise was unwelcome and Cedrin found himself wishing for the quiet of his own apartment in Lookout Hill. Across the common-deck, the flute player, an old sailor whose gnarled fingers moved with surprising grace across the carved bone instrument, continued the haunting melody, fully absorbed in his music.

'Where to from Raynor?' asked Marken, laying aside his empty bowl.

Cedrin stirred from his thoughts. Without thinking, he replied, 'North.'

'North? Raynor's a big city.' Marken's eyes glittered with mischief. 'There must be some sort of opportunities for the two greatest calvanni in Athria. Why not stay for a while?'

Cedrin smiled. He knew what sort of opportunities Marken was talking about, and he had made up his mind to steer clear of them. He patted the greatscythe that lay across his legs.

'This is my trade now. No more knives in the night. I'm going north as a mercenary.'

Marken grimaced. 'Sounds like hard work.'

Cedrin smiled and concentrated on his belated breakfast.

Eventually Skye disengaged himself from his gambling and walked across the cabin to their bunks.

'So what do you want to do when we reach Raynor, Skye?' asked Marken.

The swarthy Athrian laughed as though Marken had made a joke. 'First I'd like a hot meal and a warm bed. Then I'd like to get my hands on Raziin. Sorcerer or not, I would make him pay for Jaso's death.'

At the mention of Sorcery, a couple on the next bunk ceased their conversation, looking up at the three with suspicion.

'Be careful, Skye,' said Cedrin, reaching unconsciously for the ring around his neck. Once more he realised it was gone. 'There is a Templeman aboard. We have not been questioned yet, but I'm sure a bored Templeman could make us uncomfortable when the mist clears and he is no longer needed above.'

'You worry too much,' said Skye.

Cedrin felt a pang of envy. Skye was the only one of them

who had taken the night in his stride. His Meadrel blood, inherited from a mother born on the steppes of northern Kelas, gave him a legendary capacity for over-indulgence.

Skye turned, his eye back on the game as it became vocal once more. The diffuse light of day had given over to the more intimate glow of lamps, and the gambling circle had been joined by the sailors from the day-watch.

'Well, looks like the game is getting interesting again,' said Skye, walking back to rejoin the game.

They sat in silence, Cedrin listening to the sound of the flute and thinking of Athria.

'Do you think Raziin and Dresil escaped the battle? The tunnel would have been still open,' said Marken. 'If so, they would have reached the Cove long before the legion and they would be on the Sea of Mists right now.'

Cedrin shrugged. 'The past is done. Raziin and Dresil don't mean anything to us now. Once we strike out from Raynor, we will be lost in Kelas. You would be hard pressed to find them in a lifetime.'

'You're right. With luck they will get caught in the storms anyway.'

Marken sat forward on the bunk and looked around the room. His eyes fell to the thick haft of Tarral's greatscythe. 'Give me a closer look at that thing.'

Cedrin smiled and handed the weapon over.

Marken inspected it with an experienced eye, turning the mechanism, running his fingers over the worked crest in the haft, and finally giving the scythe a spin to test the weight and balance. He nodded to himself. 'It's genuine, all right. You didn't tell me Tarral was in the Emperor's bodyguard.'

Cedrin nodded. 'He was one of the youngest ever chosen, that's how he came to know Belin. Belin was retired then, but he was still scythemaster at the Cinanac court. Tarral tells me Belin was never bested with the greatscythe.'

'I have never heard you talk of Tarral with so much . . . respect."

It was true. He had tried so hard to build a barrier of contempt between himself and Tarral, yet in his heart-of-hearts he had always loved his foster-father. As a boy, he had worshipped him. To regain that was like regaining a part of himself.

'Tarral is good man, Marken. A rare man.'

Marken looked at him, his golden eyes serious. 'So are you, my friend. You don't see it, yet everyone who follows you does. I see it.' Marken turned the greatscythe so the phoenix crest was rising. 'The crest of the Cinanac, the bird born of Fire,' said Marken. 'Some say it was the phoenix who first gave the races of Kelas the secrets of Sorcery.'

'They are a myth,' said Cedrin.

'I'm not so sure. Some of the old texts name them as the first race. Their very substance is linked to the Realm of Fire.'

Cedrin grew uneasy. 'Marken,' he said in warning, looking around to see who was listening; but the couple had left, and everyone else had joined the circle around the dice, or was on the other side of the common-deck.

The thought of Sorcery brought back their close call with Raziin. Despite his attempts to push the memories aside, Cedrin had found himself mulling over the events on the Spire time and time again over the last two days. There were pieces that did not make sense. Hesitantly, he came to the conclusion he needed another viewpoint if he were ever to lay the matter to rest.

Since the Spire, he had experienced strange sensations, his body humming, vibrating as though he stood within a great bell. At times he could feel something crawling beneath his skin, longing for release. The image of the Window, and the sea of crimson beyond it, would rise to consume his thoughts. Strange, inexplicable shapes would leap spontaneously into his mind like kiln-fired ornaments of multicoloured glass, yet with no possible use.

'Marken, do you remember what happened on the Spire?'

Marken looked up from his examination of the weapon and frowned. 'I remember it, all right,' he said, trying to smile. 'But I have been trying not to think about it.'

Cedrin took back the greatscythe, twisting the mechanism vaguely as he struggled to piece his questions together. He realised he did not know what he was after. There was something, but it was elusive. He drew back the blades with a final snap and looked at Marken.

'Tell me what happened. Action by action, until we fled.'

Marken was thoughtful, then in a low voice he recounted the events. The attack, the deaths, the slaying of the innocent Druid, despite Cedrin's attempts to save him.

'Then he killed Jaso,' said Marken, his voice thick with grief. 'I was next. Then, out of nowhere: Fire. Billowing out from you, engulfing everything, knocking all of us from our feet. We were released from the spell, but you fell to the ground unconscious.'

Cedrin was lost within the turbulent memory. There were images, scores of them, but through them all was that Window. He could see it clearly. Even now he felt the urge to open it, to let something flow from it towards him. What did it mean?

'Raziin's spell backfired, didn't it, Marken?' asked Cedrin, an unnamed fear clawing at him.

His friend looked utterly perplexed. Marken was usually so quick with the esoteric.

Cedrin prompted him. 'The spell backfired, and I was knocked unconscious.'

'His spell backfired all right, but if he had somehow bungled it, the effect would have centred on him.' Marken looked at Cedrin with sudden understanding. 'Not you.'

Cedrin did not like it. He had tried to clarify what happened to make it easier for him to forget. He had plans. He would reach Raynor, find Kranor, Tarral's old friend, and move as far north from Sorcery and the Brotherhood as he could. He wanted to put this behind him, he did not want complications, not now.

Cedrin was suddenly eager to play dice. 'Thanks, Marken. I'll think on it.' He stowed the greatscythe on his bunk and reached for his purse to count his money.

'Cedrin, listen to me.'

He looked across at his friend, a strange tension beginning in him. Slowly he put down his purse.

'I know magic. At least the principles of it. The source of the Fire was you, Cedrin. There can only be one conclusion: somehow, you channelled the Fire,' Marken said, staring at him steadily.

Cedrin's heart hammered and he gripped his money-purse tightly to keep his hands from shaking. The effects of the hangover, nothing more, he told himself.

'Belin Kaidell was Old Blood,' said Marken.

'What are you saying?'

'You channelled the Fire.' Marken shivered. 'And only a Sorcerer can do that. I can't believe I didn't see it before now!'

Cedrin shook his head. Marken's curiosity and obsession with magic had bent his thinking. He, a Sorcerer? It was absurd.

'You are wrong, Marken.'

'No. This changes everything. Don't you see?' prompted Marken.

'This changes nothing!' snapped Cedrin. He took a deep breath. 'I'm sorry, my friend. My nerves are frayed. . . but let's have no more talk of Sorcery, eh? It makes me nervous.'

Marken nodded. 'Very well.'

'Good. I've got better things to do, like regain my money,' he said, forcing a smile.

Marken watched Cedrin with unconcealed intensity, his eyes searching. 'All right, but I don't think you'll get any of those louts to play karass.'

Cedrin joined the dicing with barely concealed relief. He quickly forgot the matter amid the shouts and boasts of the gaming floor.

When Marken failed to join him, he looked across the room to see him lying on his bunk, shivering. *What's got into him?* He then turned his mind back to the game.

* * *

Ellen signed the formal documents giving right of rule to Torren, until such time as the edict was rescinded and she could return. Concurrently, the eight members of the Council, including Aris, had voted to elevate her to the rank of Suulvey. Then she had been formally accepted into the Council.

Ellen left the Council weary yet satisfied.

After this, she had returned to the Cintros mansion and threw herself into her preparations for departure. Ellen sent a hurried message to Palsus, telling him of her plans. Hours later, as the suns had fallen and things were well under way, her thoughts returned to him. The man who had been the only steady hand and soft voice through the long, dark time after her father's death.

Still there had been no word. Realising she would have to leave for the quay before the night turned, she sent another urgent message. She wanted, *needed* Palsus by her side and nursed a secret hope he would choose to come with her as the senior Suulqua in her entourage; and her lover. Less than an hour later, the messenger returned, claiming Palsus could not be found.

As the wagons were being loaded, she mounted her narsiit and sped towards Kerril's mansion. It was nestled against the Wall of Sorrows in the far southern corner of Regent's Hill; its single, squat tower distinctive against the pale black of the star-strewn sky. As she entered the courtyard, a groom ran to greet her, taking the narsiit into the heated stables.

The great wooden doors of the mansion opened before her and a nervous serving woman ushered her in. 'This way, Lady Cintros.'

Ellen had known the servant all her life. Erel was a kindly old woman who had served Kerril's family since her youth. Ellen could sense the reluctance in the woman and see the look of concealed fear in her eyes.

Erel led her to a waiting chamber, which was in itself strange. She usually went directly to the family section of the mansion and met Palsus there. Erel hurried away, her brusqueness barely concealing her eagerness to leave.

Ellen took a seat in the too-big room with its unlit fire. The wait seemed like hours, but finally, Palsus entered the room.

He was dressed severely, a dark coat of fine cloth covering his chest. Ellen smiled with relief as she saw him, but one look at his face was enough to check her welcoming stride.

This was the same Palsus who had courted her for years, the same Suulqua who had talked of betrothal as a certainty. The stance, the poise, the easy grace were there, yet the face was that of a stranger; hard, calculating.

Looking at him now, Ellen could not believe it was the same man. *Her* Palsus, always ready with a smile, words of comfort and a soft touch to the skin of her neck.

'Palsus?' she whispered.

'You should not have come here,' he said.

'Palsus, I leave tonight.' She took a step towards him. 'You could come with me. As senior Suulqua, you would be in charge of my staff.'

'My place is here.' He eyed her warily.

Ellen could not believe the change in him. If only he could see the plan, the old Palsus would return. It must be the grief of Kerril's loss, she thought. It must be.

'Palsus. Come with me. From Raynor I could petition Torren to raise you to Suul. It would be a new adventure. One we could take together.'

He stepped around her, putting distance between them. 'I am not going anywhere, not with . . . with you,' he said, turning to hide his eyes.

With awful clarity, Ellen realised *this* was Palsus. This, after all these years, was her first clear vision of the man's true heart. Suddenly she was angry.

'Won't go anywhere with what, Palsus? With a Sorcerer? With a demon?' She took a step towards him, her heart churning with need.

'Palsus.' He would not meet her gaze. 'Palsus,' she said again. 'For the sake of Larus, it is me, Ellen.'

Palsus kept his back to her, silent.

'What am I now? Cursed?'

'Yes. A Sorcerer. An outcast.'

Despite her anger, the words cut deeply.

'You had it all! I knew Myan would favour you. You had the throne and threw it away. We had Yos in our hands and now you. . .' He paused, looking at her with a disgust that made her feel naked and soiled. 'You were a Sorcerer all this time, tainted with the Old Blood. Cursed. To think we . . .'

Ellen backed away. Not from the words, but from this vision of the man she had loved. The years had been a sham. He had cultivated her friendship solely because of her link to the throne, so he could stand beside her in power. And now she had been forced to give it up, he had the nerve to call *her* cursed. Oh, it was clear now. Oh so clear.

'All this time. You were lying to me!' she screamed.

Palsus grunted. 'I gave you what you wanted.'

She realised what a fool she had been. She had wanted him, but their love was nothing more than the glitter of moonlight on the rushing tide. Unsubstantial. Unreal. And soon to flow away.

Ellen's heart was in ruins. She knew she had to go. The first wagons would be ready to make for the quay. The war galley would be awaiting her arrival. If she delayed any longer she risked being caught by the Temple.

She looked at Palsus. His stranger's face stared back at her as though she was a victim of the plague.

'We are finished,' she said, her eyes meeting his once more before she strode from the room, desperately trying to stop herself from running in tears like a girl. She would cry no tears here. Not under the same roof as Palsus. Ellen reached the door, then passed through it. Now she wanted nothing more than to leave Athria far behind her.

* * *

The night shrouded the quay in a chill blanket. Ellen watched distantly as men carried wooden chests, carpets, lamps and barrels onto the war galley in an unceasing procession. She had two Suulqua aides, Valdas and Mendor, both warrior sons of petty lords at court, who hoped to find distinction and fortune on the continent. They supervised the loading with an excess of zeal, their newly made greatscythes gleaming like bone in the torchlight.

The galley slaves finished unloading the wagons, which rumbled back up the docks to Regent's Hill for the last load. Ellen sighed, it was a pity she had to leave in such a mad scramble. Given time, she could have chosen more appropriately and brought more with her, enough to set up residence in Raynor as an ambassador should; as a Suulvey should, but this would have to do.

There were four maids from her household, a squad of thirty personal retainers led by a Crescent Razor with three Razors of lower rank beneath him; and two hired scribes to act as translators and record keepers. Torren had managed to find her a Larus Druid and a Moon Druid with no allegiance to the Athrian Temple, both eager to return to the mainland and willing to turn a blind eye to the edict. She also carried numerous letters and dispatches, including a letter she had written to Raphal, Crephis' brother, telling of his death. She would send Raphal's letter on to Olcis, the centre of the Temple in Kelas. If anyone knew where he was, they would.

A group of riders approached the quay, moving at pace down the harbour road, hoofs ringing on the cobbles. Ellen called to her Suulqua aides and moved towards the group. As they neared, Ellen could see all seven of the riders were mounted on narsiit, geared for war. As they drew up, Ellen recognised Torren as the leader. The other warriors were his elite guard, men he had surrounded himself with for years.

Torren swung himself from the saddle and walked to Ellen. 'You must board the galley,' he said urgently.

Ellen glanced at Valdas and Mendor, then stepped circumspectly out of earshot. 'What is it, Torren?'

Torren's face was grim, his tone bleak. 'It's the Temple.'

A shockwave passed through her, instantly banishing her fatigue. She gripped her scythe. 'What is it?' She feared the answer.

'The Templemen have swayed the Temple Council. They are coming for you under rules of Purge. Death without trial. They are coming to kill you, sister.'

Ellen cursed, turning to beckon Valdas and Mendor. The young Suulqua sprinted to her and bowed, all eagerness.

'Valdas. Tell the galley Captain to ready the craft with all speed. We will not wait for the last wagons.'

The tall Suulqua bowed and sprinted towards the galley.

She turned to Mendor. 'Gather the retainers and form them up on deck, bowmen to the front. The galley must be protected.'

The more level-headed of the two Suulqua looked from Torren to Ellen, his dark eyes curious, but he suppressed his questions and raced for the galley.

'How many?' asked Ellen. 'How long do we have?'

Torren was looking far up the quay where even now lights were showing. 'Not long, I'm afraid.'

She could hear the shouts of the slave master behind her as the rowers were roused and moved into position. It would be long minutes yet before they were all at the sweeps.

Torren gave orders for his men to dismount. 'I will hold them, Ellen. Even Templemen will think twice before tackling the new Sarlord.'

As her retainers emerged from the galley's hold, the Templemen arrived. They were riding amelak, their red robes dark like dried blood in the cold night. Ellen counted nearly twenty, three holding glowmetals which, even now, were pulsing with power.

Then she saw Kiin.

He too was holding a glowmetal, one she recognised all too well. The lead Fireseeker.

'By Uros,' said Ellen. She would not make the same mistake twice. She left the Window untouched.

Mendor ran to her and bowed, all eagerness and efficiency. If it came to a fight, he was ready. 'The men have been formed up, Lady Cintros.'

Ellen turned to see her retainers in neat lines across the deck, scythes held at the ready, bowmen ready to shoot.

The rowers were still not ready.

Torren's men had come into formation between the gang-plank and the Templemen, holding their greatscythes loosely, blocking the advance of the Druids. Her brother stood behind them, directing them.

Ellen started towards him, but Torren quickly walked back towards her, leading her back to the galley. 'You must go, Ellen,' he said urgently. 'Now.'

She looked back at the red-robed Druids. They had closed with Torren's warriors.

'Make way. We are about the Sisters' business!' demanded Kiin.

They had only a moment. Torren met her gaze, the grey

depths revealing sadness and hope; a complexity of feeling Ellen had never thought to glimpse in her brother. Torren pulled a golden gem-ring from his little finger, slipping it onto her ring finger.

'We are Blood, Ellen. Nothing can sever that tie.'

Ellen was torn between uncertainty and the new feeling of friendship that had grown between them.

'Now go,' he said, his eyes were once more like stone. 'Guard yourself well. Kelas will have need of your power before all this is done.'

Torren marched back to his warriors. The Templemen were demanding passage, growing steadily more aggressive, but Torren's arrival seemed to silence them.

She raced across the plank. Once aboard, Mendor ordered it raised and formed the retainers into a circle around her, as though to protect Ellen from the Templemen's magic with their bodies.

'Draw bows!' shouted Mendor.

Across the stern, her men drew their bows, taking aim at the Templemen.

The red-robed Druids surged past Torren towards the dock, but halted as they saw the archers. One of them raised a glowmetal, then another.

'Rowers, ready!' came the call from the oar-master.

'Cast away!' ordered Valdas.

In moments, the craft was speeding out of the harbour under oar.

Soon Torren and the Templeman were lost from sight in the darkness. Athria was now nothing but a memory.

'Well done, Suulqua. Stand down your men, Mendor, for now we are safe,' said Ellen.

Still trembling, she went below and ordered the maids to draw her a hot bath. She sank with relief onto the wide and richly coloured cushions set around her private rooms. She had only one more task to perform before she allowed fatigue to take her.

Drawing the green gem-ring out of her pocket, she stared at it for long moments. It was beautiful, carved from an emerald and set with precious coloured mought in an intricate design; a tower, circled with thorn vines, flowering red, all on a yellow background.

'You are my link to Cedrin,' she said, staring into the glittering green depths. 'My link to the Scion.'

From the pouch at her waist, she drew out a miniature glowmetal. A tiny sliver of silver, its dark light seemed to draw the colour from her hand. With a growl of protest she pushed herself up from the cushions, weighing the tiny glowmetal in one hand and the ring in the other.

She had work to do.

Chapter Fourteen

Raziin inhaled deeply.

The air was thick with the bittersweet smell of incense, a rare variety holy to Temples of Yosini. The precious scent had been lovingly carried across all the leagues of Kelas to serve this purpose. Streamers of the pungent perfume drifted through the cabin from scores of burning sticks, their lit ends like tiny burning eyes in the dark. Like the demons of Uros, thought Raziin. Beyond the swirling grey smoke was a deep blackness, which lay over the cabin like a blanket, hiding the touch of man, preparing the way for the doorways of mystery to open.

Raziin had thrown back the thick carpets, and sat cross-legged on the rough boards beneath. Outside, the oars continued their even stroke. All the windows had been sealed.

Raziin and his chosen sat bare-chested. Still, yet expectant. The golden skin of the warriors gleamed with oil and sweat, contrasting the ghostly silver of Raziin's chest, which was laced with newly-healed scars. All were covered with scores of tattoos, precisely intoned by the master tattooists of the Armon military.

Raising the calv at his side, Raziin held the point at his palm, slicing open the skin. He held his hand over a mought bowl, letting the blood run free. Each had given blood to the sacrificial bowl. Raziin was the last. Satisfied, he held the crucible up towards the ceiling, bowing his head in obeisance.

'Hear us, Uros. Give of your power,' he said.

He placed the crucible on the brazier in the centre of the circle, the red-hot coals cracking and spitting as he shifted them.

Soon their mingled blood would boil and their essence would take a new form.

He had but to wait, Raziin told himself, be patient. But for how much longer?

All day the galley had struck out across the Sea of Mists towards the Narrows and the Yasser beyond, taking him ever-closer to his appointment with death. A fate chosen for him by Hukum.

The galley had a full complement of men and was making excellent time. Raziin could not risk a mutiny by releasing them from the oars, so they had been left exposed to the elements. As a consequence, most had given over to the Heat. He knew from experience that in a press of men, once the Heat began, it spread like contagion. He was careful to ensure his appointed Captain, mates and the tiller-man did not succumb, giving them extra cloaks and rations. The water had gone, the food would soon follow, and then the men would start to go crazy from the Hunger and even the whip would not control them. Raziin knew he would have to get as much out of them as he could before that point.

Through the long hours of the day, he had been waiting for the answer of Uros. He had spent most of his time in his cabin drinking Dresil's wine while the fool trimmed the fat off his bones at the sweeps. He had fought his own battle against the excited carelessness that threatened below the Heat. So far he had managed to hold the Barrier against Hukum's compulsion, yet every hour that passed made the effort of containing it more taxing.

Waiting for the vision from Uros had stretched his control to the limit. As the suns dropped once more, he had begun to fear she had not heard him. Reluctantly, he realised Uros wanted more than his blood. It was time for the ceremony.

A new wave of Heat rose in him as the smell of warming blood filled the air. The Druids at the Temple of Yosini had once told him this was a rite of the Earth, that the forces unleashed were of man and not of the Gods, but Raziin did not believe them. It was Uros whose spirit filled the bowl, descending like a swooping bird to take the bloody prize; her spirit that stirred the visions, her spirit that had always shown him the way. Uros. Blood-goddess.

Raziin looked around him. Each of the warriors was beginning to breathe faster, her touch upon them.

He reached for his greatscythe. Noting his move, the men took their own weapons from the floor. Raziin nodded to Merceth. The giant raised his greatscythe and brought the blunt end of the haft down on the decking. Falling into time they followed, and the rhythm began.

These were his most trusted men. Merceth and Kyal were once generals under his command, each with a thousand men. The five other Cioans were all Suul, warriors of excellence, passionately devoted to his cause. They had all been inducted to these mysteries long ago on the high battlefields of the Upper Plains, where the cult of Uros had flowered out of reach of the Druids of Armon.

The beat was slow at first, geared to pace the rising Heat. Their minds soon became a frenzied whirl, the beat faster and more complex. They *were* the rhythm. They centred themselves on it, the falling greatscythes becoming something that existed apart from them. Into it they poured their passions, their hands moving like a blur as the energy that rose with the Heat was burnt away, leaving their minds free.

Show the way, Mistress, show me the way.

Before them, the bowl glistened dark with the blood they had shed. The men spoke the dark names of Uros, the secret and unknown names, calling on her to take the sacrifice, to draw Essence from it and so show her dominance over the Realm of Earth.

Their bodies wrapped by the Heat, steaming in the cold of the cabin, they began the chant in ancient Cioan. The blood in the bowl shifted and steamed, a mist of foul yellow rising as it was transformed in the crucible. The Earth-Essence circled faster and faster, looking for a way out of the circle, but it was trapped by the rhythm and the intense focus of their minds. Then, with an explosion of brown light, it expanded to envelope them. They cried out in pain and ecstasy as the whirlwind entered their minds.

Into the eye of this hurricane of Essence, Raziin once more yelled his plea. *'Show me the way, Uros! Show me the way!'* The images, which had been swirling like a maelstrom in his mind, now shattered like reflections in a broken mirror and were drawn into its molten core. Raziin gave a shout of exultation as he saw Hukum dead and himself glowing with power such as only one other mortal man had ever known. He held the Spear of Carris. The Realm of Fire, laid open, was his to command. The vision was sweet but brief, replaced with darkness.

In its place came dark memories.

He was running for his life. His attack on Osellen had been a failure, broken by his brother Ralin.

How was he to know his brother Ralin was such a powerful Sorcerer? That he would rip his frontal assault to pieces and rout his attacking force? He ran down a hill, flanked by the remnants of his scythemen. Suddenly, hundreds of archers fanned out of the trees at the base of the hill. They were trapped!

Thus had begun the greatest humiliation of his life. Captured by his brother, he and his generals had been put on trial for treason. The greatest warriors of the age – the cream of Cioa – displayed like common criminals. Waiting for his turn in court, his wrists and feet weighed down by heavy chains, Raziin had vowed never to be defeated by Sorcery again. He knew he had a talent for the Fire – all of his siblings did, even his weakling sister Razell – yet Leith had refused to teach him; squandering his attention on Ralin – always Ralin.

Finally he was brought forward to face his brother. The image of his father, Ralin sat on the Sarlord's throne, bloated with his own pride, smug, self-satisfied. Yet he was like all the others. When he met his eyes, he saw only weakness; the same softness that had them all crying in grief at the death of Leith.

'Why, brother? Why would you kill our own father in cold blood?' asked Ralin, his voice choking with sadness.

'His death was merely an accident of war,' replied Raziin smoothly. 'How could you think I actually planned it?'

Ralin's hands grew white on the arms of his throne.

'Oh, brother. How easily the lies flow from you . . . We have heard testimony from many of your surviving men. Your orders were clear.'

Raziin lifted his arms and turned to the assembled court.

'Aren't you tired of skulking in the forests of Armon? What of the glory of the Cioan race! I did nothing that any true patriot would not have done,' said Raziin.

'You murdered your own father!' said Ralin, surging up from his throne.

'What I did, I did for the good of Armon. If my desire to see us great once more is such a crime, then kill me!' said Raziin. 'I will go to my death gladly.'

Raziin knew Ralin's sort. He would agonise endlessly, unwilling to kill his own brother.

The court went into an uproar. The senior lords who had led Ralin's forces against him called for his immediate execution, while many called for mercy, impressed by Raziin's oration and stirred by sentiments of national pride. Those who had secretly backed his grab for power were most vocal in their support. They had been paid well for their appearance.

Eventually, after hours of debate, Ralin passed a sentence of banishment from Armon for Raziin and his senior generals.

So Raziin had set off into Kelas, determined to find a Sorcerer willing to teach him. His plan had been simple: once he had powers to rival Ralin's he would gather another army and march on Armon. Ralin, nothing more than a coward protected by the tricks he had learned from Leith, would be crushed beneath his boot heel.

Yet finding a master to teach him the ways of the Fire had not proved to be easy.

Where is the answer? Uros, I beg you, show me the way.

Spurred by his need, the images came faster now.

Years flashed past him, years of fighting, searching. . .seeking any who would teach him. Those few Sorcerers he found refused to teach him, others used him, yet in the end gave him nothing. All through that time he heard whispers, rumours of the Sorcerer-Lords of the Eathal, secure in their deep caverns beneath the peaks of Mount Maht.

Slowly he made his way south, drawn by the promise of power, the possibility of finding a Sorcerer willing to teach him, even if they were Eathal.

Two years after his exile from Armon, he left his men under the command of Merceth and walked alone into the caverns of Maht. He was quickly taken prisoner and marked for slavery. Yet when he told them he was Raziin, son of Leith, he was passed deeper into the lower caverns and brought before the Sundar himself – the Sorcerer Hukum.

And he kneeled before Hukum, pledging his allegiance and that of his feared mercenaries to the Eathal in return for knowledge of the Fire.

And Hukum had agreed!

He became strong in the Fire, strong in the knowledge of its use. He and his men fought through Kelas, taking pay from a score of Sarlords and petty Suul, merchants and Captains, all the time being directed by the unseen hand of Hukum. Raziin cared nothing for the purposes of Hukum, he cared only for power. But as the hold of Hukum tightened on him and he realised the Bridge of Minds had made him a slave to Hukum's power, his hatred of his master had grown steadily. Increasingly he sought ways to sever the Bridge, to escape Hukum.

'Mistress. Why do you torment me?' yelled Raziin.

The scene changed.

He was in Olcis, the City of Mirrors. He had waited long days and paid heavily in coin and gems for this audience. Each passing day had made Hukum's discovery of his treachery more likely, but at last he had been summoned.

The High Circle of Templemen had received him. They sat around him, austere, arrogant, and buoyed by their own power. The Hesguit, supreme leader of the Temple in Kelas, had leaned forward, his face framed in a red hood, the sigil of Uros hanging from his neck.

'What do you seek?' he asked. 'We have little time to spare for mercenaries.'

Raziin smiled, excited by the risk he had taken in coming here. These were the only men who could possibly sever the Bridge between him and Hukum – yet if they discovered he was a Sorcerer, it was doubtful he would leave the Hesguit's palace alive. Although not one of them would be a match for him in power, together they would be formidable; and he knew they had glowmetal devices that could subdue and destroy him.

He went ahead with his plan.

'I have been enslaved by Hukum, the Sundar of the Eathal. He has a Sorcerous connection to my mind. I am desperate to destroy his hold over me. I have wealth, tremendous wealth. Can you do it?'

Another of the Templemen, a small and officious looking man, spoke up in a high, thin voice, almost like a woman's. 'That is High Sorcery, Cioan. We cannot sever the connection without destroying either you or Hukum.'

Raziin grew angry. He had come so far, risked so much only to be denied? He surged to his feet.

'I came here because I thought you were powerful men. Have you no answer to this? Can you not even defeat one Sorcerer between you?'

Together they had channelled the Essence, flinging him against the wall, pinning him there with invisible bonds as they rose to their feet.

'We walk under the Light of the Suns,' said the Hesguit. 'We have no power to enter men's minds and nor do we desire it. Only a powerful Priestess or Sorcerer could sever this connection. And only one power in Kelas could challenge Hukum in his lair.'

Raziin held his temper in check. He longed to send these Druids flying with his Fire, but it would be unlikely he would leave Olcis alive.

'What power?' he asked in desperation. 'What power. Tell me, I beg you.'

The tendrils of Force left him and he fell to the floor. The small Templeman walked over to him. 'Ciofran-Ac,' he said. 'Ciofran-Ac has what you seek.'

They laughed together. Laughed at him.

'Just walk the Melaut,' another had said, mocking.

'Ciofran-Ac.'

'Walk the swamp.'

'Swim to the ruins of your ancestors, Cioan.'

They filed from the room laughing at him. No one had ever

sought the lost city of Ciofran-Ac and lived. The swamp that lay around it was deadly and impassable. Many believed the city itself, once the seat of the Cioan Empire, had sunk after the Destruction of Carris. That holocaust had shifted the Yasser's course, flooding vast stretches of land, creating swamp where once fertile land had stretched for leagues.

Eventually, only the small man remained. He looked at Raziin with contempt. 'You are doomed, Cioan, doomed. Such is the fate of traitors.'

Laughing, the Templeman left him.

Abruptly the beat came to a crescendo, the last of the whirlwind imploded and they cried out in pain. The beat became a ragged volley, the rhythm falling away. With exhausted gasps from the men, it ceased altogether. Some of them collapsed, others leaned on their greatscythes shaking with exhaustion, their eyes full of private visions. The images had gone, but one name rang out in Raziin's head. *Ciofran-Ac*. Uros had given her answer.

Shakily, Raziin climbed to his feet. The other warriors were too weary to move. The Heat had exacted a heavy price from them. It had faded for a time, but it would return with vengeance and only the lucky would be able to still it completely.

'Ciofran-Ac,' said Raziin, as though the words were a magic balm. 'Ciofran-Ac.'

He yelled the words at them, as though he wanted the wearied men to share in his discovery. Most did not hear him, but those who did looked back at him with glazed eyes. Merceth raised his head and met his gaze, pushing himself to his feet with the aide of the greatscythe.

'Ciofran-Ac, Lord,' said Merceth in a harsh whisper.

Turning from the men and the dim circle of light, Raziin staggered towards the deck. He swept the door open and a cool blast of air surged in on them, driven on the heels of flooding moonlight. They began to rouse in the cold, hastily pulling on woollen robes in an attempt to still the Heat before it rose again.

Once on deck, Raziin yelled to the rowers. 'Ciofran-Ac! Ciofran-Ac,' he cried, turning to face them.

Dresil and his aides still worked the oars and the pirate looked at Raziin with wild eyes as the message sunk in.

'What are you saying, Raziin?' asked Dresil, struggling to keep up the beat as men slowed to stare at Raziin.

He ran across the ship, leapt to the prow and pointed to the dark shape of the continent ahead. He knew from his boyhood lessons where the legendary Cioan city had been built - high on the Yasser River's ancient banks. 'Ciofran-Ac! That's where we are going.'

'You're mad, Raziin!' screamed Dresil. Cursing, he gave up his rowing and glared at him.

You think I am mad, thought Raziin, yet I am Uros' instrument.

He looked around the ship. The men milled in confusion, the stroke becoming uneven as some stopped in fear of Raziin and the name on his lips. Ciofran-Ac. The cursed city. As word spread they began to shout and cry out like condemned men. The rowing stopped completely and, if not for the chains, there would have been a riot. Men pulled at their bonds, surging to jump off the ship in an insane and Heat-driven frenzy of fear. The galley floundered as men ran and jostled in confusion. They soon turned on each other, beating, biting, tearing.

Raziin saw his men file out of the cabin onto the deck with their greatscythes. Merceth walked to the prow and shouted above the noise. 'Lord, we must stop this. They will kill each other.'

Raziin looked across the waters at the dark shape of Kelas, searching for the sand banks that marked the ancient Yasser delta. Around him hundreds of brawling men shouted and screamed in an insane melee.

'Lord, I beg you, we have need of them.'

Reluctantly, Raziin turned, jumping lightly onto the deck. His fatigue had vanished. 'You're right, Merceth.'

He stood in the centre of the rowing-deck looking at the chaos, his men immobile dark shapes on the quarterdeck, watching with exhausted and dazed eyes, waiting for instruction. Raziin sought the Window and drew heavily on the Fire.

With a yell, he released it as a Lightning Bolt, which arced up into the sky. A brilliant flash illuminated the whole ship and the sea around them for a league. It seemed as though day had dawned, then the massive crack of thunder broke over the ship, sending a shock wave through the timbers and knocking men off their feet. In the wake of the immense concussion, all was silent. Men lay where they had fallen, hands clasped to their ears, afraid to move.

'Hear me!' Raziin bellowed.

Men who were trying to kill each other scant moments before now turned frightened eyes towards him, awed. As they should be, he thought. He waited as the men struggled to their feet, shifting uneasily, still in the grip of the Heat.

'We are going to enter the course of the old Yasser,' he declared.

A murmur ran through the crowd, an undercurrent swelling once more with fear. Raziin channelled the Fire into a Matrix of Light, adjusting its form so that he became outlined in glowing tones of livid red. He had used this before to good effect. The men cowered, with a simultaneous intake of breath, as though Raziin were Kallor himself.

'Hear me,' said Raziin, his voice booming. 'I am the messenger of Uros!'

He expanded the nimbus of red, looking around him at the awed circle of eyes. Few doubted him. Most men had never heard of Sorcery except in conjunction with tales of demons and the underworld, Llors. They had certainly never seen a Druid stand like this, as though illuminated with the light of Uros.

Raziin pressed ahead. It was time they understood. He was the instrument of Uros, the hand that would give sacrifice to the blood-goddess as never before.

'This night I have been shown a vision,' he said, his voice hushed, full of ecstasy, making the listener believe they were privileged to share this with him. 'We are going to Ciofran-Ac, along the Yasser's ancient course.'

He began to sweat. A familiar tightness began in his throat. The Compulsion was rising to force his hand. But he fought it with logic. The Shattered Temple can be reached through the old course of the Yasser, he thought desperately. That was the beauty in his plan. Travelling this way, the Compulsion could be satisfied and, at the same time, he would have his chance at salvation.

The grip on his throat lessened. He had succeeded! For all its strength, Hukum's binding was a blind animal with little intelligence. To the magical construct, one trail was the same as the next. Oh, he would travel to the Shattered Temple all right, but only to kill his executioner.

'At Ciofran-Ac, the holiest of cities, we shall have salvation. Salvation!'

The men began to stir, responding to Raziin's fervour.

'Salvation!' they began to chant. 'Salvation at Ciofran-Ac!'

Raziin smiled. 'Back to the oars! Bend your backs and take us to the destiny Uros has ordained.'

Still chanting, they began to row once more.

Satisfied, Raziin let the glow fall away. He ran across the deck, climbed onto the quarterdeck and walked to the tiller. Merceth followed him wearily.

The tiller-man, who was one of the few not gripped by the Heat, looked wide-eyed at Raziin as he approached. Raziin did not know what this man believed, but he knew he could command his obedience.

'Steer us to the old Yasser mouth. We are going to Ciofran-Ac.'

'Yes, Lord,' the man responded, eyeing Raziin as though any minute he would transform into a black-skinned, horned demon and eat him alive.

The mists had cleared, and the helmsman had no need to use the minor Essence spells of Navigation he had been using throughout the day. He hastily looked up to the stars and changed course.

Raziin knew these sailors were well acquainted with the old mouth of the Yasser. It was lined with sandbanks and provided excellent fishing. There were also freshwater lakes across the old shore, on the borders of the vast swamp. The pirates had more than once stopped there to take on water, even venturing into the old Yasser mouth to avoid the Warlord's ships, but never too far into the Melaut. Ships had disappeared in the Melaut, and all sailors knew the stories of the demons there. Never would they remain there after dark. The tiller-man stared ahead anxiously at the coast, his eyes flicking fearfully at Raziin. *Perhaps he wonders who to fear more, the Melaut demons or me.*

Raziin walked to the quarterdeck rail, looking down on the rowers who were working in unison once more. The dark shape of Kelas loomed ahead as they turned towards it.

'Ciofran-Ac,' yelled Raziin, laughing.

The cry was taken up by some of the rowers below, but the ragged chorus quickly died.

Raziin laughed again. He would find his answers in the Melaut or meet his doom. If he had to take the whole ship to Llors with him, he would.

Outside the Barrier, the Compulsion waited for his will to weaken.

Chapter Fifteen

Cedrin placed his coins on the floor and shook the dice in his hands, breathing on them for luck. He was playing against a trader who had fallen on hard times in Athria and was returning to Raynor to rebuild his fortune.

All the gamblers held coins and purses, many flasks and bottles as well. They waited in an excited hush for the dice to fall.

Cedrin threw. 'Come on, you Larus-blessed bones of Kallor!'

All eyes followed the dice as they spun and skittered across the deck, stopping at the trader's feet. The man bent to the dice, his once-fine cloak parting to reveal a sea-shell totem tattoo and the Trading guild's eight-pointed star.

A pair of ones.

'Serpents' eyes!' He shouted with glee as he leapt forward to gather Cedrin's coins.

Those in the circle exclaimed at Cedrin's bad luck, some groaning, others laughing.

Cedrin threw up his hands. 'That's it for me, I'm out.'

'Not your game, my friend,' Skye said, grinning.

Cedrin grunted. 'My luck is not running.'

The companions second day aboard the *Lusella's Pride* had been much like the first, except they had escaped the harsh after-effects that had plagued them after their first night of celebrations. Like the other passengers, they had taken their fill of warm broth and spiced wine, and secure against the Heat and the Hunger, were happily settling into the routines of the common deck. They eagerly took part in the available distractions. Unfortunately for some, these could be costly.

Marken laughed. 'Remember, my friend, a light purse makes for a light soul.'

A cry went up from above. '*Ship ho! Ship ho!*'

The racket dropped to a hushed quiet.

There were shouted orders on the deck above and the sound of running feet, then nothing. As the minutes drew by, the gamblers began a new game and the noise rose once more, until abruptly the oars ceased. This time there was complete silence.

Every traveller on the Sea of Mists had the same fear: pirates. The gamblers looked up at the deck above. One man had paused in mid-throw, hardly aware of the dice clutched tightly in his fist. They had become used to the continual sound of the oars and the quiet was like a hurricane. Seconds stretched to minutes as they listened for the dreaded call.

The calvanni exchanged looks. Dresil's ships were somewhere on the Sea of Mists. Skye was grim, his hand unconsciously hovering near the handle of his calv, his dark eyes darting from the room to the decking above.

They were so close to Raynor, only days away.

Marken returned his coins to his purse. 'I'll go up.'

Scant moments later, Marken came racing down the ladder.

'What is it?' asked Cedrin, concerned.

'It's a royal Athrian war-galley, flying the Cintros crest,' said Marken, gasping for breath. 'Three longboats filled with retainers are heading for our ship. Whatever it is, they mean business.'

'They couldn't mean to turn us around,' said Skye.

'No.' Cedrin shook his head. 'They must be after something . . . or somebody.'

They checked their weapons.

Cedrin tried to relax, without success.

Skye looked directly at Cedrin. 'I'll not go back to Athria to hang.'

'Nor I, my friend,' replied Cedrin.

The buzz of conversation suddenly lessened.

Robic and two of his burly mates had descended the ladder to the common deck. They wore the thick black woollen coats of sailors, open in front of their chests, tattoos and scars lining their torso. They wore no harness, but charms and medallions of every sort hung about their necks. They were looking intently into the crowd.

A familiar thrill of fear and anticipation ran through Cedrin, and his heart raced. This is it, he thought, the next seconds would decide their fate.

The Captain pushed into the gamblers' circle, asking questions. The men stood tight-lipped, looking at the floor, but a woman of middle-years leapt up, pointing in their direction. In the quiet, they heard her words clearly.

'Over there. I heard them talking. I know it's them.'

Robic looked towards them, meeting Cedrin's eyes with recognition. *By Uros, they are after us!* Robic was going to betray him.

Cedrin gave the greatscythe mechanism a twist, the wicked twin blades shooting free to glint in the light.

The sudden image of a Window came into his mind.

'Here they come,' said Skye, sweeping out his calv. The long, thin blade gleamed in the dim light.

Cedrin stepped forward. 'All right, Robic, that's far enough.'

On his right, Marken extended the blade of his scythe, while Skye stepped out to the left.

Robic was a large man, born on the Raynor docks. He was wealthy now, but this had not taken the hard edge from him.

'The royal thel wants you, Cedrin. Ellen Cintros herself,' he said, his tone unforgiving.

On either side of Robic, his two mates held their heavy clubs at the ready, eager for the fight.

'Come on, fat-boy,' said Skye to the man opposite him. 'You think you're fast enough?'

Cedrin's mind worked rapidly. There was something here that did not ring true. The Suul Cintros had asked only for him. Why? And if Ellen Cintros had come to arrest them, it would be her own men he would be facing, not Robic. She had obviously told Robic to *ask* him to come.

Cedrin put his hand urgently on Skye's arm. 'Hold, Skye.'

Skye reluctantly lowered his calv.

Cedrin withdrew the greatscythe blades with a snap and stepped towards Robic. 'She wants me? Only me?'

Robic gave him a dangerous look, then some of the tension drained out of the old sailor. His two mates straightened from their crouch. 'She said she just wanted you.'

'What about Skye or Marken?' asked Cedrin.

His friends passed quick, bewildered, looks at each other.

Robic grew angry. 'She wants you, Cedrin. Just you, right? You can fight if you want, but she has a squad of retainers up there. I'm doing you a favour letting you go to her while you can still walk.'

'You must have some idea,' said Cedrin. 'What did Suul Cintros tell you when she boarded?'

Robic's face grew red. 'And why should a damned Cintros tell me anything? Every minute I spend here wasting time, Cedrin, the current drives us further from the Narrows. Do us all a favour and see what the thel wants, and quickly.'

Cedrin eyed Robic and his men. He knew they could easily deal with them, but Robic had a full crew. Would he fight every one of them, and the retainers of this Cintros woman?

'All right, Robic,' said Cedrin.

'Cedrin, what are you doing? We can't let them take you.' Skye was aghast. He had been ready for the fight and could not believe Cedrin would give himself up.

'There is more to this, Skye. I need to find out what the Cintros wants.'

Reluctantly, Skye put up his calv. 'Then we all go.'

Cedrin was about to protest, but he could see they were adamant. The three would stand together.

On deck they were whipped by savage cold. The sky was a clear blue, bleak and washed of colour, the suns standing high above, still close together in the sky. As they followed Robic, Cedrin gained his first glimpse of the royal galley. It was a huge craft with three rows of oars, the ram with its hideous head standing just out of the calm waters. The sleek lines were painted in gaudy golds and reds. Trailing limply in the calm atop the galley's single mast was a white pennant with the Cintros' grey raptor crest.

A score of well-armed men stood in formation outside the Captain's cabin, flanked by two young Suul lords, probably Suulqua.

The Suulqua watched them sternly as they walked forward. They pulled their coats tightly around them to conceal the degrees of the calvanni. The gazes of the young Lords moved to Cedrin as he led the calvanni across the deck. This gave him cause to wonder until he realised he still carried the greatscythe, the phoenix crest showing for all to see.

They too held greatscythes, and Cedrin noted – unlike him – they held the weapons with easy familiarity. Their chests were toned and oiled beneath heavy blue cloaks, fine tattoos etched in myriad colours. They both had the athletic poise of elite warriors. Despite this, their harnesses looked like they would be more suited to the court than the battlefield.

The shorter of the Suulqua pushed his greatscythe between Cedrin and his friends.

'Only the Anacian,' he said, his voice commanding.

At a nod from Cedrin, Marken and Skye reluctantly stepped back.

The Suulqua regarded Cedrin with a wary respect, noting the way he concealed the tattoos on his chest, and the harness' bulge beneath his cloak. His dark eyes came to rest on the greatscythe.

'Give me your weapons,' ordered the Suulqua.

Cedrin tensed. He saw the men shifting, Skye and Marken watching, ready.

Then the door to the cabin opened. 'Leave him his weapons, Mendor.'

Cedrin turned to see a slight woman framed in the doorway. Her hair was honey-gold, her eyes of the most startling green. Ellen Cintros. It could be no other.

'At least let me take the greatscythe. It has to be stolen, my Lady.'

Ellen looked at the weapon, her eyes falling to the phoenix crest.

'No, Mendor. That weapon is his.'

She looked up at him. Her white Athrian skin was smooth and flawless. Despite being much shorter than he, she managed to carry herself with poise and dignity. She was stunningly beautiful. The women he had known on the docks did not have a shadow of her grace.

'Thank you, Suul Cintros,' he said.

Despite her gesture of trust, the calvanni found himself on his guard. She regarded him with intense scrutiny, her intelligence obvious. *What does this woman want from me?*

'That will be all, Mendor,' she said.

'Are you Cedrin, son of Tarral?' Her voice was controlled and level, but her eyes betrayed a confusing mixture of hope and uncertainty. Around them the assembled men watched in tense silence.

'Aye,' he said, watching her carefully, uncomfortable with the greatscythe in his hands.

Her eyes showed triumph.

'Please,' she said, indicating he should follow her into the cabin. Mendor still hovered at his elbow, as though expecting trouble. Cedrin gave him a quick, wary glance before entering.

The cabin was much as he remembered it. Robic had entertained him and his friends many times aboard the *Lusella's Pride*. They had played karass, drank and laughed here. Never would he have believed he would be sitting here talking to a Suul. A Cintros!

Ellen motioned for him to sit. Laying the greatscythe aside, he sat at the solid wooden table that dominated the centre of the cabin. Ellen sat opposite, casually pouring wine from a flask into two fine crystal glasses.

Feeling awkward, Cedrin leant forward to take one of the glasses. As he did so his cloak fell open, revealing his tattoos.

As she saw the six degrees, she froze. Her eyes snapped back to his. Her hands trembled, but the tense moment passed and she smiled, also reaching for her goblet. Although she had identified him as one of the senior Brotherhood leaders, she had remained silent. Interesting.

He tasted the wine. Whatever was at stake here was more important to her than the attack on Regent's Hill.

She took a casual sip, watching him with cool green eyes over the rim of her glass.

'Ah, my Lady. Ahh. . .' he said, feeling himself go red as she regarded him, completely at ease, as though they sipped wine together every day. 'What is it you want of me?' He sounded foolish, his dock accent loud in his own ears. 'I don't want to delay your journey,' he added lamely.

She reached into the pouch at her side. For a moment her smile faltered, and he sensed that underneath her calm facade, she was unsure.

She drew something out of her pouch and held it up.

Belin's ring!

'I believe this is yours,' she said, her voice tight with tension.

Cedrin's face split into a wide grin.

'My lucky ring,' he said before he could contain himself. He immediately reached over to take the glittering emerald from her hands, but as he did so he saw her watching him, analysing his every move. Berating himself, he let his hand fall. 'Aye. . .ah, that is. . .was my father's ring.' His mind raced.

'How did you come by it?' he asked. Memories of the Spire flooded him. Raziin. Fire. Death.

'It was found on the Spire. The Druid Crephis identified you before he died.' Her eyes grew hard.

So she knew he was part of the attack on Regent's Hill, knew that he was on the Spire. There was no point denying his presence there. Marken had said that Crephis was a personal friend of the Cintros, and knowing he was a calvanni, she could only assume the worst. The hard truth was, she thought him guilty of the Druid's murder.

'I was on the Spire that night,' said Cedrin. 'Raziin was there, with two of his lieutenants. I was with three other calvanni. Our task was to silence the Wail.'

He paused, collecting his thoughts. 'I'm sorry to hear Crephis died. I tried to defend him as best I could. To tell you the truth, I thought Raziin's blow had killed him outright.'

It seemed she was about to speak, but she stopped herself. Her eyes glistened with moisture, yet when she spoke her voice remained hard. 'So you claim it was Raziin, not you, who delivered the fatal blow to Crephis?'

He looked her in the eye. For a brief moment he saw only a

young woman, bearing a burden of grief alone. Then, a moment later, the image was gone, replaced by Suul Ellen Cintros, intense, invulnerable.

'After the Wail was taken, Raziin intended to kill us all. It was sickening. He is a devotee of Uros, the blood-cult, something I realised too late. He killed the Suulqua in cold blood. . .'

'Halsur,' she said, her voice hushed. Her face grew pale.

'Then Raziin went to slay the Druid. I tried to stop him, yet he froze us with Sorcery and he stabbed him. It was a cowardly act.'

'If he froze you with Sorcery, how did you escape?'

Cedrin's heart skipped a beat. 'Raziin's spell . . . backfired, lighting the Wail. My friends and I managed to flee down the Spire in the confusion.'

Cedrin drew in a slow breath. 'What now?'

'I should have you and your friends arrested!' said Ellen.

'And yet, you will not,' he said coolly.

She glared at him, but did not contradict him. So, there *was* something else.

Ellen held out the ring to him.

'Take it,' she said. Her voice was uncompromising.

He accepted it gratefully, weighing it in his hand. It seemed heavier than he remembered, but he was glad to get it back.

'I never thought to see it again,' he said.

'It is the signet ring of Belin Kaidell,' said Ellen, noncommittally.

'Aye.' His eyes flickered from the ring to Ellen as he wondered where this was leading. 'Belin was my real father,' he said. 'I was his bastard son. He left me with an old friend in Athria during the Last Days.'

Ellen was surprised. 'So you knew of your heritage?' Her eyes fell on the greatscythe at his side and she nodded to herself. 'Of course you did. And yet . . . you did not come to Myan's Court.'

Cedrin was puzzled. Why should he, a lowly calvanni from Lookout Hill, think to present himself at Regent's Hill?

No one sought out a single man in the middle of the Sea of

Mists in order to return a lost ring, of that he was sure.

It was time he found out what else was involved.

'Lady Cintros.' He slipped the ring into his pouch. 'Why am I so important to you? What do you want from me?'

She drew herself up, her head raised slightly. 'Myan, my father, had been seeking you for years, Cedrin.'

He suppressed a laugh. By all accounts she was completely serious, and it baffled him.

'Myan was a close friend of Belin. Myan wanted you to come to the court, but you could not be found,' she said.

'But, Suul Cintros. I am a bastard son. Illegitimate. Unrecognised. The ring was the only thing my real father ever left me. I cannot believe the Sarlord of Athria would waste his time with a child Belin did not even remember.'

Ellen's eyes grew soft. She leaned forward to touch his hand.

'Believe me, Cedrin. Belin was in Athria only months before Myan's death. He told Myan it was vital you were found.'

He looked at her in amazement.

The feel of Ellen's hand on his was like silk, and he looked down, spellbound. His hand was callused and tanned, hers milk-white, almost like porcelain. He looked up at her, his eyes drawn to her lips. She was truly beautiful. Powerful. Yet for him, as remote as the goddess Larus.

He slowly drew his hand back.

Cedrin looked away from her while his mind turned. His father was alive? The man had been seventy at the fall of the old Empire, which would make him close to a hundred years old. Impossible.

What did this woman take him for, a fool?

'Belin disowned me long ago. The man was old then, surely he must be dead now,' he said, searching her eyes. There was a presence there, something elusive, almost familiar, making him cautious and attracting him at the same time.

'What is it you really want?' he asked.

Ellen's eyes grew hot, but she replied levelly. 'The simple truth of it is Myan wanted you at court. You have the blood of one of the greatest Suul of the old Empire, does that mean nothing to you?' She paused as though to gauge him. 'Myan wanted you to come to the court and gave me the responsibility of finding you, bringing you back under the Suul's protection.'

Cedrin wanted to rebuke her, but somehow he could sense her sincerity. Could it be? He looked at Ellen with new eyes, his heart stirring with a hope he had not dared let grow in all the years he had known he was Belin's son. All those lonely, lost years that he had hardened his heart, letting ambition fill him like a drug, fuelling him, giving him strength.

'You asked me what I want,' she said, her green eyes ablaze, her head raised like a narsiit poised for flight.

'I want you to come to Raynor as part of my entourage. I will give you what Belin did not, a place with the Suul. I have the power to make you a Suulqua, Cedrin.' He looked into her green eyes, intense, powerful, but still guarded. 'Trust me.'

It was lies, all lies. Belin was dead. Long ago he had made his peace with his father, the man who had left him at the mercy of the world.

It was time to force the issue.

He threw back his cloak, swiftly drawing his calv. He showed her the blade.

'Look at it,' he said. 'You do not know the blood I have on this calv. You do not know me.'

'I am a calvanni,' he said as though condemning himself. 'I have lived in the shadows of the rich and powerful all my life, supplying their needs and at the same time feeling their contempt. Most of my life I have despised the Suul and all they stood for, now you want me to step into Raynor on your leash.

'No, Ellen Cintros. I am the master of my own destiny.'

This woman wanted something from him. No Suul would offer to take him in, not without a deeper, hidden motive.

She looked back at him, blazing with anger. 'You would rather be a thief than my servant?'

'You want me to come to Raynor, playing some game like a performing dog. You dangle promises in front of me like star dust.' He sheathed the knife. 'I have my own destiny. I don't know what game you are playing and I couldn't begin to guess, but I know I don't want any part of it.'

She fixed him with a hot gaze.

'My friends and I were forced into that attack on Regent's Hill. I know you have no reason to believe me, but if you are satisfied with my innocence in the matter of Crephis. Let me go.'

She took a deep breath. 'I do believe you,' she said. 'And there are no tricks. My offer is genuine.'

'We are from different worlds.' He picked up his greatscythe and stood. 'You have your path and I have mine.'

He backed out of the cabin, and she let him go.

Outside he scanned the deck. Mendor looked at him in surprise and quickly re-entered the cabin behind him.

Here it came, he thought. Here is when the lies were revealed. His back itched as he waited for it. Any second now the Cintros' men would take him. It would be in Cintros chains that he learned the real reason she sought him.

But nothing happened.

He reached the ladder down to the common-deck and looked back towards Robic's cabin. There was no pursuit.

He hurried below, out of the wind, hardly believing his luck.

* * *

'The Anacian has gone below. Do you want me to apprehend him?' asked Mendor, his hands clutching his greatscythe eagerly.

Ellen reined in her anger.

What a fool she had been. How could this cut-throat help her find the Cinanac heir? Besides, Cedrin was right. How *could* Belin still be alive? She cursed herself, moving slowly to the door.

She had vowed to take him into chains, but that was when she had doubted his innocence. After meeting Tarral, her instinct was to believe Cedrin's version of events on the Spire. If she took him by force now, any chance of them working together in the future would be severely hampered by his antagonism. Damn him! Why did he have to make this so difficult? She sensed he and his men would fight her retainers and did not want any more blood spilt. She would let him go for now. Besides, she had another way of finding him . . . one he would never suspect.

'No, Mendor, gather the men. We are making for Raynor with all speed.'

He was shocked for a moment, then recovered and issued the orders to the men.

When she had seen the fresh ink of the sixth-degree, all the pieces of the puzzle slid into place, and they fit with his story well. The Mouthpiece of Smuggling, Mat, had been found dead. Jorrel had named him as one of the key organisers of the failed rebellion. It seemed there had also been a rebellion *inside* the Brotherhood, against the men who had led them against the Suul. Cedrin had defeated Mat and taken his place as Mouthpiece. . . only to flee Athria. The conclusion was obvious: he had left the Brotherhood.

Ellen's emotions churned as she stepped into the waiting longboat. First Palsus, now this. Cedrin had spurned her, thrown the offer back in her face as though it were the worst insult. Rejected her. So he wanted his own path, wanted to live life with the scum of Yos until he found a lonely grave. If not for her vow to Myan she would let him have his wish!

Even at the end, he had not believed her. What sort of a life could breed such mistrust in a man?

Her father's wish was that she take him under her protection. Well, she had offered and he had refused. She was certain Myan had never wanted him taken prisoner against his will. Ellen shivered as she remembered the drawn knife. *You do not know the blood on this calv.* The words echoed in her mind, along with the image of the razor sharp lanedd and the desperation in his eyes. Yet what warrior had not blooded his weapons? She herself had killed many times on that night and the memory chilled her.

As the small craft drew across the water towards the galley, Ellen's anger eased. She wondered what it would had been like to grow up on the edge, knowing you had been disowned; cast out to become hard before your time, nursing a bitterness like a cold venom within you and trusting no one. . . She cursed and vowed she would give him no sympathy, yet she could not forget the brief hope that had seemed to kindle within him.

There had been a moment when his grey eyes had sparkled blue, as though they glimpsed a rare joy. Then the darkness took over.

She could see how Belin might have been his father. His stature, the guarded intelligence, the strength so tangible within him. He could have greatness if he only allowed himself to trust her. She could help him find that greatness . . . in time.

For now, it was done.

Should she ever discover that he had a real role to play in her quest to find the Scion, she could find him easily enough. The tiny silver glowmetal she had inserted into his ring would act like a beacon to its matching glowmetal, the Seeker, which she had in her gear.

She smiled to herself. That part of the plan had worked well. She would be able to find him on the other side of Yos should the need arise.

Her war-galley waited for her on the gentle swell.

Raynor lay ahead. She was a Cintros, she was a Suulvey and she had a mission. To find the Scion.

* * *

Cedrin pushed his way through the crowd. The passengers had seized on the new distraction and gossip ran riot about the Cintros Suul and the mysterious calvanni she had summoned. As Cedrin passed, they plied him with questions, but he was too relieved, and baffled, by the whole thing to reply.

Perhaps what Ellen Cintros had really wanted he would never know. One thing he was sure of: the Suul never gave anything away. And they would never hand out a Suulqua title just because he was the bastard son of a forgotten general.

Skye and Marken flanked him, silent as they made their way towards the bunks. He was eager to put the whole affair, and the unwanted attention it generated, behind him.

As they reached their bunks, a hopeful knot of men gathered, waiting to hear why a calvanni would be summoned by a Cintros Suul; and what was so important the ship had to be overhauled in the middle of the Sea of Mists.

'Come on, Cedrin,' said a fat fletcher who had been visiting family in Athria. 'Tell us.'

Another echoed him, a man who had taken his son to Athria to be received into his totem in one of the minor Temples.

Cedrin smiled. 'You know those Suul ladies, always looking for a *really* long knife.'

The crowd roared with laugher, but they moved away when they realised he would be no more forthcoming. Skye drew his calv and absently spun it in the air, catching the handle, the twists became more complex as the blade climbed towards the ceiling.

'What did she want, Cedrin? How did you get away from her?' asked Marken.

Cedrin sighed, giving a short laugh. 'She wanted me to join her at court in Raynor.'

With a thud, Skye's calv lodged into the ceiling.

'What!' exclaimed Skye and Marken together.

The both looked at him in stunned silence.

'It must have been a trick,' said Skye, his face animated as he reached to prise the calv out of the ceiling. 'A trick to get us all.' He pulled the lanedd blade free.

Marken shook his head, deep in thought. 'I'm not so sure.'

'The strange thing was she seemed sincere. If she had wanted to take us, she would have. But me, a Suulqua in her entourage? It just didn't ring true. As good as it sounded, I just couldn't afford to trust her. It may have put all three of us in danger.'

'You should have heard what was said on the deck after you went inside. I got to talking to one of the retainers I knew,' said Skye. He paused, leaning closer to Cedrin in a conspiratorial manner. 'She is a spawn of Uros, they all speak of it. During the battle, she used Sorcery on the Northman. She barely escaped the Templemen on the docks. They ordered her death under edict of Purge. She is an exile.'

Skye leaned back, waving the calv at Cedrin for emphasis. 'She is demon-spawn, Cedrin. She was taken by a demon of Storm Season, they say. Arcane knowledge. You mark my words.'

Cedrin laughed. 'Skye, I've met her. She is no demon.'

Marken leaned across to Skye. 'Are you saying she battled Raziin and defeated him with Sorcery? Are you sure about that, Skye?'

Skye started trimming his nails with the razor edge of the calv. 'It's true, all right. Those retainers were there when it happened. They saw her fly through the air, calling down the silver demons of Uros on him. What's more, she stood amid a blast of Fire and was unharmed.' He looked from Marken to Cedrin. 'What more proof do you need? The woman's soul has been taken by Uros.'

Marken nodded, his eyes alive but inward looking.

Skye sheathed his calv. 'I hope she didn't put the demon's mark on you, Cedrin.'

Marken looked intently at Skye. 'He doesn't have any demon's mark, but there are some who would say he does.'

Skye gave Marken a puzzled look, then left to rejoin the dice game.

The oars began once more. Ellen and her men were gone.

'I'm going to get some air,' said Cedrin, ignoring Marken's comment. So Ellen Cintros was a Sorcerer, like Raziin. There were always rumours about Myan, but it was hard to separate fact from fiction where magic was concerned.

He strode through the crowd, leaving a chorus of fielded questions unanswered, then scrambled up the ladder into the cold above.

On the deck, Cedrin braced himself against the chill. Why had he let the woman get to him so much? He knew what he was going to do, he thought, hefting the greatscythe. He would head north, become a scytheman and in time he would Captain his own company. He would walk with honour and answer to no one. He would fight to protect, work to improve the lives of his men.

He would follow the Way of the Scytheman, as Tarral had done. The code that separated the killers like Raziin and his men from the true warriors of Kelas.

A sudden memory overtook him. He was eleven, helping Tarral in the kiln room. All the furnaces were running and sweat ran off his skin, soaking his simple tunic. He had burnt himself twice that day, and the skin of his hands still stung from the touch of hot glass, yet he did not care. He loved it, the art of it, the miracle of creating beauty and strength from nothing but coloured tint and plain glass stock. He had only been allowed in the kiln room since his last birthday, three months before, and he rejoiced in the chance to work alongside his foster-father.

'What is Kallor's Riddle?' he asked as he carefully measured one of the delicate fibres used in the complex lanedd cast.

Tarral eyes glittered with amusement. 'Kallor's Riddle? It's part of the Way of the Scytheman.'

'What is it?' Cedrin asked.

Tarral put down the tints he was working with and gave him a wry grin. 'I've followed the Way most of my life and I am still trying to answer that question. Now, hurry up with that.'

Cedrin continued to watch Tarral expectantly. Surely his father would know?

'I can see I will have no peace until I answer,' said Tarral. 'The Riddle is: to plant your feet firmly in Llors, yet take hold of Larus with every ounce of your strength.'

'What does it mean?'

'Well, you need to decide that for yourself.' Tarral looked at Cedrin and sighed. 'To me it means, at the very same time, to accept the worst that could happen and yet work with every ounce of your passion, skill and power for the best outcome.'

He must have looked puzzled, because Tarral continued.

'For a warrior it means to accept death, and yet use all his power to achieve victory.'

'What is the Way of the Scytheman?' asked Cedrin.

'You are full of questions today. Well. . .it's a way of living, a thing really only understood by living it. I could tell you in words and yet they would mean nothing. Now, hurry along. We have much to do.'

'Tell me,' Cedrin insisted.

Tarral's jaw clenched, and Cedrin expected anger, yet when he spoke his voice was soft. 'To never lie, cheat or steal. To devote yourself to the perfection of your martial skills. To empty yourself of emotion, become pure expression in the execution of your art. To conquer without cruelty, kill without hate, and only when duty or necessity compels you. To have the power and determination to kill and yet the wisdom to choose when. To embrace duty – to your commander, to your nation – yet never surrender your own will, your own judgement of what is right.'

'I'd like to be a scytheman one day,' said Cedrin. 'And follow the Way.'

'Alright, enough dreaming. Back to your work.'

Cedrin looked out over the Sea of Mists, his heart warmed by the memory.

It was a pity the Suul did not follow the Way. From what he had seen the Suul were born to wealth and power, spending their lives living off their own people, yet caring nothing for them. Kelas was ruined, and still the Suul bickered. The Eathal threatened, and still they jostled for position, seeking to line their own pockets. Where was the honour in that? Belin, his own father, had sworn to come for him, and yet he had not. Lies.

Before he realised it, he had the ring in his hand. He stared at it for long moments in nostalgia before laughing to himself. *Maybe now my luck will return.* He tied the ring onto a stout leather thong and hung it around his neck. It was cold against his chest, but it felt good to wear it once more. He would cast the Cintros woman and her subtle manipulations into the same abyss he had cast his other memories of Athria.

There was only one future he wanted. His own.

'I have no idea what you see in this cold deck, ami.'

He turned to see Marken beside him.

Cedrin smiled. 'The air is free from taint.'

Marken's eyes narrowed. 'Why did you refuse Ellen Cintros' offer, Cedrin? You are Belin Kaidell's son.'

'She lied about her real motivations. She must have,' he said harshly.

'I don't think she did. And what's more, I think you know it.'

Cedrin looked across at Marken sharply, a hot denial springing to his lips, yet he said nothing.

'Don't you think you are worthy to be a Suul?' asked Marken.

'Worthy? They are lying scum who care for nothing but themselves.'

Marken sighed. 'Many are. But not all. There are good Suul. Those who work for their people. Ellen's father was one of them.'

'They are all too few,' said Cedrin, his voice heavy with bitterness.

'Which is all the more reason that someone like you should become one of them! Kelas needs men like you, Cedrin. Honourable men.'

'It's done,' he said.

'Far from it. Ellen was headed for the court at Raynor. Go to her. Present yourself. Do it!'

Cedrin shook his head.

Marken looked out across the ocean.

'Whatever path you choose, my friend, I will follow it with you,' said Marken. He paused, then walked back along the deck towards the ladder, disappearing into the hold.

As the suns fell from the sky, a heavy mist covered the shapes of Kelas and the Narrows. The war-galley was already far out of sight and that was good. He did not want any Suul pulling strings in his life. Yet as he stared towards the Narrows, he did so with a feeling of regret. For a while it had been as though he had touched the edge of something enticing, something that lay concealed beyond his reach, both familiar and strange.

Angry with himself, he swept his gaze across the ship. He saw the Window again. For an instant he imagined sheets of flame, rising, engulfing everything, coursing, surging, boiling Fire. He gripped the rail as a wave of dizziness took him. He was not well.

He headed below for a rest. No more bakta, he thought, as he headed back to the common deck. It was giving him strange visions.

No more bakta.

Chapter Sixteen

Merceth passed a wary eye over the rowers. They were tiring fast. Many now slumped in total exhaustion, the all-consuming fires of the Heat having depleted their reserves. Rotating the able rowers to keep the stroke even and the ship on course had proved a challenge. He shook his head. They would not respond to curses or the whip. Soon they would lose them all if they did not rest.

The ship had stopped briefly at the old delta early in the day, and a squad of warriors had been dispatched in long boats to take on water from the lakes. Dresil had been released to supervise fishing with nets. Luck had been with them. The starved men had eagerly slaked their thirst and eaten their fill until the fish was gone, but Raziin would not allow them to net more. He pushed them instead into the Yasser's ancient mouth, a wide estuary leading to the extensive swampland of the Melaut, searching for the old river course.

Merceth turned to watch his master.

Raziin stood at the ship's prow, his limbs bare to the Storm Season cold, fevered and possessed by the Heat and the fanatical desire to reach Ciofran-Ac.

Night had fallen swiftly in the swamp, and they were somehow spared Storm Season's bitter edge. Clouds of hot, foul-smelling gas swirled over the water and stung the skin. Around them, the Melaut stirred uneasily, as though responding to their intrusion with primitive awareness. Squawks and screams haunted them; some like souls in torment, others utterly inhuman. The incessant gabble had begun with the sinking of the suns and gave the Melaut a dangerous presence.

They had twice been stuck hard on mud banks. Had they been a sailing craft, it would have meant their doom, but spurred on by the thought of being stuck in the Melaut, the men put their backs into the oars and pulled free. They were lucky the old course, originally running deep and wide, had not silted up completely. On either side of the deep channel, the Melaut was dangerously shallow.

Merceth looked into the dark swamp around them. His throat was raw from the harsh vapours, his stomach uneasy from the inescapable stench. The trees were stunted and skeletal, draped with clinging, mucous-covered vegetation like living tissue. The waters were dark with rot, lying calm until disturbed by the ship's progress. Then they would churn with a plethora of unseen forms, boiling as though in fury, slapping and thumping continually against the hull. Merceth feared a breach below the waterline, but so far nothing had managed to puncture the timbers. They had been lucky to find the Yasser's ancient course, but to follow it in darkness was madness. Still, their Lord urged them on.

Far back in their wake, the waters grew still.

Merceth was completely loyal to his master. Long ago, he recognised the mark of greatness within Raziin and had pledged himself to serve until death, as had many other generals and Suul. He shared Raziin's dream of the Cioan Empire's rebirth and was determined to share his master's glory when that dream became reality. Even after Raziin's defeat at the hands of his brother Ralin, Merceth had never doubted him. And Uros had granted Merceth a vision, Raziin *would* lead the armies out of Armon. The Anacian dogs who humbled Ciofran-Ac would suffer the revenge of a great people. He had seen it. It was Raziin who would lead him to this glorious future.

He reached down with his greatscythe to lift the head of a slumped rower. His face was hollow and drawn, eyes rolled back. *This one is not far from death.* He let the man's head fall once more, watching with contempt as the unconscious man's shackled hands moved with the oar's motion. The other rower struggled to keep the oar moving and eyed Merceth fearfully.

He waved to two of his men. The unconscious rower was taken away, to be laid out with the other incapacitated men in the lower hold, while another was moved to take his place. Many of the oars, designed to be double-manned, now only had a single rower. It was important to match them on port and starboard to keep the stroke even.

Merceth returned to the other warriors of Raziin's inner circle. They stood on the quarterdeck wrapped in heavy black cloaks, immobile and forbidding. Uros had visited them all in full measure, but despite this, they had all succeeded in stilling the Heat. Just as well. They would need clear heads if they were to survive the Melaut. Raziin's other men had all joined the oars, preferring to row rather than stand idle.

Kyal nodded to Merceth in recognition as he approached.

'We must stop to let the men rest, otherwise they will be finished by dawn.' Kyal spoke in Cioan and indicated the men with a wave, his tones clipped and short.

Merceth nodded slowly. 'Yes.'

Raziin was once more wrapped in the red glow, his gaze fixed forward as though, through his magic, he could see the ghostly spires of Ciofran-Ac through the dark curtain of the night. He had taken the station throughout the day, staring ahead at the waters, seemingly in a trance, but calling to the tiller with directions at regular intervals.

Merceth walked to Raziin's cabin, seeking a robe for his master. Alone of all those who had undertaken the ritual, Raziin had yet to subdue the Heat. For reasons known only to him, he had let it burn through the day and into the night. Raziin often let the Heat take him during Storm Season, welcoming the hand of Uros on him, especially in preparation for the ritual. But it was a matter of pride and strength, and a measure of his self-discipline, that he still it once more.

It was not like Raziin to let the Heat overtake him like this. They needed him alert if he was to lead them to Ciofran-Ac and whatever Uros had shown him there. Merceth had seen his master commit atrocities, destroy and pillage, even betray those who had been their allies, yet nothing disturbed him as much as this. Raziin was directed, always disciplined. Even his indulgence, in its excess, was a test of strength.

Gripping the cloak, Merceth walked across to the ship's prow, to Raziin's elbow.

'Lord?' Receiving no response, he laid the cloak across his master's shoulders. He must cover himself if he were to defeat the Heat.

Raziin stepped back and threw off the cloak.

'No,' shouted Raziin, looking with frenzied eyes around the deck. He took a step closer to Merceth. 'Hukum is tightening his grip,' he said. 'I cannot rest. I cannot sleep. We must push on.'

The Hunger had begun to show on him, his cheeks hollowing, his silver skin drawn and tight like parchment.

'We must stop, Lord. The rowers are near the point of exhaustion. If they are ruined, we will never move this craft again. We do not know how difficult it will be to find the city, or how many days will be lost.'

'NO!' shouted Raziin.

The warriors on deck cast off their cloaks and turned with greatscythes held at the ready, the force of Raziin's rebuke triggering an instinctive reaction. The rowers began to talk excitedly, breaking from the mind-numbing rhythm to stare fearfully around the deck. The warriors, seeing no threat, put up their greatscythes and recloaked.

The nimbus of red around Raziin began to pulse and grow, engulfing him, dripping from him like burning oil from a newly-soaked torch. The rowers near him backed away in fear, some crying weakly, 'Fire!' But they quieted when they saw that the strange flames burnt without heat on the wood. Raziin's eyes were stretched wide, like silver disks.

'We will not stop.' Raziin laughed coldly.

Raziin paced back and forth across the bow, as though having been immobile for so long the intensity of his energy could not be contained.

'We must push on. We can't afford to stop. Not for him,' he said, pointing into the darkness. 'Not for them.' He pointed to the rowers.

With a burst of explosive energy, he surged at Merceth, who saw him come but made no move. He had pledged his life to his

Lord. If Raziin chose to kill him, so be it.

Raziin stopped only feet away, shaking with the suppressed energy of the Heat, his mouth drawn into a snarl.

'It's what he wants. I will not stop. We will all die first.' Raziin nodded and laughed. 'He wants us to stop and rest. . . wants me to stop and rest.'

Merceth could see the edge of madness, and the Heat's fury, in Raziin's eyes. Yet he had seen madness in those eyes before and his Lord had always led them to triumph.

* * *

'We will not stop until Ciofran-Ac. Ciofran-Ac! Ciofran-Ac!' Raziin turned to the crew, striding the top deck between rowers as though to incense them to join his frenzied urgency. 'Ciofran-Ac! Ciofran-Ac!'

They simply stared at him.

Fear was the only emotion Raziin saw in them, though many simply stared, too exhausted to muster any response at all. Raziin turned sharply, looking around him. Why were they not responding? It was only hours ago they had shouted with him for salvation. . .

Raziin looked at the dark as though seeing it for the first time. In his fever-dream, he had not noted the fading light. His mind had been far ahead, probing the waters and planning his return to power in Armon when Hukum's power was broken. Denied for long hours, his Hunger rose with an intensity and pain that caused him to cry out and fall to the deck, doubled over. Like a snuffed flame, the red nimbus vanished and Merceth rushed to his side.

Spasms overtook his body, cramps from overtaxed muscles. He struggled to support himself but fell once more. He gasped in a quick lungful of air, his stomach clenching at the putrescent odour. Merceth helped him to his feet.

'To the cabin, quickly,' commanded Raziin, in a harsh whisper.

Raziin winced as he eyed the men, at last perceiving the truth. They needed rest now, and as many as possible should be rescued from the Heat. They were close to death.

'Stop the ship,' croaked Raziin.

His cry was quickly taken up. Rowers still alert enough to understand ceased rowing, falling with exhausted relief as far as their chains would allow. Others had fallen so far into the Heat, they rowed on, trapped by the rhythm, their minds lost well beyond the Melaut. Gradually the ship slowed and the anchor was dropped.

Once in the cabin, Raziin sat at the Captain's table, his body taken by violent shivers while at the same time burning. It was the Heat-fever, a sure sign his body's reserves were depleted almost beyond measure. Smashing one of Dresil's fine wooden chests with his greatscythe, he took a bottle of wine. He broke the neck open on the table and took a long draught while Merceth waited. He had gained a moment of clarity and he had to use it well.

'Unchain the men in small groups and give them what rations we have. Most have cloaks. When they sleep, make sure they are wearing them. We must stop as many as possible from going too far into the Heat, we need them alert.

'We will rest for two hours, then we will begin again. Then take one group off the chains every four-hours.'

He looked at Merceth, his determination rising. 'I mean to reach the lost city.'

Merceth nodded. 'Yes, Lord. It shall be done.' The giant's face was impassive, but Raziin could see his relief that he had taken control once more.

Another spasm wracked his body and he hunched forward on the table, the bottle falling from his numb fingers.

Merceth took a step towards him.

'See to the men,' he said.

Merceth nodded sharply and strode to the deck.

As he lay gasping, he checked the Barrier Matrix. The blue shield lay uncompromised, but the Compulsion that pulsed and moved like oil on the outside of the Barrier had strengthened once more. He had to be more careful, the Heat had tricked him, lulled him very close to a waking stupor. If Merceth had not roused him, he may have slipped fatally. Beneath the Heat, he sensed he was weakening, the Fire's flow gradually lessening as the long hours without sleep took their toll. How long did he have? A day, hours? He needed food. The pain of the Hunger had passed, to be replaced by a rising weakness and an aching need to consume.

A terror-filled scream rose from the deck. Soon others followed. Scores of men were shouting and yelling. Raziin grabbed his greatscythe and ran outside, fighting weakness.

Bat-like shapes dived down from the sky onto the chained rowers who were screaming in terror, unable to raise their hands to defend themselves. His warriors watched the sky, striking at shapes that shot towards them with blinding speed, slashing with razor-tipped wings and feet. The men were covered in bleeding cuts, which seemed to incense the attackers.

One man screamed as a bat wrapped itself around his neck with clawed wings and feet, razor-sharp teeth sinking into his throat to draw blood. Merceth swung his undrawn greatscythe at the shapes like a club and succeeded in bringing two or three of them down. Raziin ran to his side.

Merceth swung at a diving shape and missed, the huge form shrieking as it wheeled to the sky and disappeared.

Raziin ducked, barely avoiding a slashing wing-tip. 'Unchain the men on the top deck. Bring up the nets!'

As a boy in the wilds of Armon, banished with the frontier troops, he had often gone to set nets at night. If the net was placed in the right spot, scores of bats could be captured as they soared out of the distant Ranmyden Ranges to the forests to feed.

Nets were brought onto the top deck and lifted into position. The sailors quickly grasped the idea and a brave few clambered into the rigging to secure them. One sailor fell to the deck with a dark shape on his face, his screams muffled.

The bat's soon became entangled, to be quickly dispatched by Raziin's warriors. Sailors fell on them with bare hands and any weapons they could find. Some strangled them with the chains on their wrists.

Eventually the winged attackers faltered. Alerted by the screams of their captured brethren, they circled warily above the netting, shrieking in anger and frustration, sensing the warm blood below. They rose and circled above for long minutes, then were gone.

Raziin stepped forward and pulled one of the shapes free, carefully holding its wings back against the body. It eyed him with dark glittering eyes and shrieked in frustration and hunger, its mouth working, the razor-sharp teeth stretched forward towards him, the claws gripping air. He held it above him for the men to see. It shrieked at the movement.

'Here is your demon,' he shouted.

He looked at the beast once more, a savage animal with a hunger so like his own. All on board were watching him, but he was lost in the Hunger's grip and the familiar ache of blood-lust. The animal was warm. . .

With a savage cry, he ripped out the animal's throat with his teeth and drank eagerly on the hot blood, the red spilling and splashing. His body shook with need. He drained it as the bat's struggles grew weaker. With a shout of triumph, he threw the bat to the deck and fell onto another. A low moan went up from the Heat-fevered sailors.

Across the deck, his cloak drawn tightly around him, Dresil watched Raziin with horror. 'Sweet Larus, Raziin. You *are* the spawn of Uros!' He made the sign of Larus at him.

Raziin laughed. 'Larus has no power on this ship, you pitiful Athrian.'

The Heat-starved rowers surged forward, eager to join in the feast of blood, fighting over the corpses of their attackers. Blood spilled and splattered the night, tracing arcane glyphs across the deck, over arms, cloaks and chests, faces and beards, and over men's souls.

Dresil turned to Merceth, who was watching impassively. 'If they don't sate their Hunger before a man's blood is spilt, the result will be madness. Chaos and death!'

Merceth looked across at him. 'I am watchful, have no fear. Although if you want to invoke your god, pray that we don't meet the beasts that these bats usually feed upon, for they are sure to be fearsome.'

The feast continued. Around them, the Melaut stirred and

babbled like a restless killer, the continual racket punctuated by distant screams.

Amid it all was Raziin's laughter.

Chapter Seventeen

A touch woke Marken with a start. He reached for his calv but a heavy hand restrained him.

'Marken!' It was Skye. 'Cedrin has the demon-mark. We have to call the Templeman.'

As Marken struggled awake, he could hear a chorus of excited whispers around him. He was on the top bunk and, as he threw off his blankets, he noted a lurid yellow glow outlining Skye's features. He shook his head and rubbed his eyes, but the light remained. It was coming from below him.

'What?' muttered Marken.

'Cedrin has a demon in him. I knew that cursed Suul was possessed by Uros. She did it to him.'

With shocking clarity, Marken realised what was happening. He dropped from his bunk. Cedrin was wrapped in a sulphurous yellow glow that pulsed and rippled with his breathing. *He was channelling the Fire!* The blankets and bedding were beginning to smoke and char. If not for the fact that the nimbus appeared mostly above his sleeping form, the ship would already be ablaze. Flickering tongues of red snaked through the glow, red-hot. If he reached through the nimbus to rouse Cedrin and one of these whipped back onto his arm . . .

The crowd was growing, awoken by friends or the increasing murmur of conversation. They stood in a fearful circle around Cedrin, drawn by their curiosity, yet careful not to get too close.

One woman pointed her finger. 'He is a Uros-spawn.'

Many in the crowd nodded in agreement.

A sick feeling grew in the pit of Marken's stomach. *Cedrin is in danger.*

A trader came forward, the man Cedrin had been dicing with only the day before. 'I say we call the Templeman.' He earned cries of agreement from the crowd – and from Skye.

'We have to, Marken,' Skye said in a low voice, gripping his cloak. 'Or we will all have the curse. It must be stopped before it spreads.'

Marken had seen enough. He had always known people were ignorant of magic, but never had he realised the fear of Sorcery, driven into the people by the Temple themselves, ran so deeply.

'Be silent!' Marken shouted. The crowd backed away. 'Go back to your beds or you'll have me to answer to.'

They murmured angrily.

Marken drew his calv, rounding on them. 'Uros may be powerful, but I have a better reach. If you don't move away, I'll cut you where you stand!' he said in a low, dangerous voice.

At this, the mob dispersed, some returning to their beds, others drifting into the shadows to watch with suspicious eyes.

'And if any of you go for the Templeman, I will slit your throats and eat your hearts for breakfast!'

Marken was angry. Angry at the ignorance of these people. He was also disappointed he had been reduced to making physical threats, but violence was the only language they would respond to.

Skye gripped his arm roughly. 'Are you mad, goldskin? He has been possessed.'

Marken shook out of Skye's grip. 'Just be quiet and I may be able to help him.' He was not about to try and talk Skye out of his superstition. 'Just give me a few minutes. I used to be a Moon-Druid Initiate. I ahh. . .' he thought quickly, '. . .know a way to reverse the curse.'

'You do?'

Marken suppressed his triumph. 'Yes, a special prayer to the Moons and Larus. Just give me a moment.'

Skye waited apprehensively as Marken began a low chant. The prayer was actually a blessing for a newborn child, but Skye would never recognise it and he certainly could not translate the ancient Cioan. As he murmured, Marken felt through the night for the Moon-Essence, gathering in the flow. It was strong and he tapped into it, letting it pass through him. Wrapping himself in the threads of the Essence, he let his hands fall onto Cedrin.

Three red tongues flicked across his hands, hissing. If he had attempted this without an Essence-Shield, they would be charred stumps. If the flow ceased only for a minute. . . He pushed the thoughts away, breathing calmly as he concentrated. As his hands passed through the shimmering yellow cloud, they were outlined in a pulsing, ghostly silver: the Moon-Essence. Dimly, he could sense the Fire within Cedrin, like a raging inferno glimpsed down an infinitely long tunnel. There was no doubt now, Cedrin was Old Blood; born with the ability to access the power of the Realm of Fire. Marken tried to reach the Fire burning inside his friend, yet it remained far beyond him. He felt a vague disappointment at this discovery, but continued. Marken had hoped the Old Blood also ran in him, but it was not so.

When his hands reached Cedrin's chest, Marken shook him. His friend began to wake, and for Skye's benefit, Marken ended the fake ceremony with a plea to Larus.

'Larus. Cast the demon's mark off this soul!' *What rubbish.*

* * *

Cedrin woke with a gasp and the sheath of Fire shrank into him like a withdrawn tentacle.

Cedrin saw Marken and Skye, their eyes fixed on him, and he struggled upright. He had been lost in a strange dream. In it, he had reached for the Window, which had been hovering near him, and he had thrown it open, breathing in the very fabric of the Fire itself.

Cedrin shook his head to clear it, looking at each of his friends in puzzlement.

'What is it?' asked Cedrin. 'Has the ship passed the Narrows?'

Skye clapped Marken on the shoulder. 'Larus be praised. You have the favour of the Sisters, Cioan.'

Cedrin blinked and looked around him. A handful of people still watched from the cabin's dark corners and he could sense their hostility.

His nose twitched at the smell of burnt cloth and he looked down at his bedding.

'What the. . .?' Cedrin leapt up off his bunk, staring at the charred cloth in disbelief. 'What's going on?'

Skye stepped forward, his face drawn, yet relieved. 'The Cintros Sorceress put a demon-mark on you. Marken knew a way to stop the curse, but I think you should see the Templeman just in case it lingers.'

Cedrin looked sharply at Marken, whose jaw was clenched in anger.

Skye reached out to clap Cedrin on the shoulder but his hand dropped short, his face betraying fear and uncertainty. 'We almost lost you to the demons of Uros.'

'Don't give me any of that superstitious rubbish, Skye. I'm in no mood for your foolishness,' said Cedrin, still on edge from the abrupt awakening.

The swarthy Athrian backed away from Cedrin, making a sign of protection. 'You must see the Templeman.'

'Have you lost your wits? The Templemen work with the Suul. That Uros-Druid would betray us as soon as look at us.' Cedrin looked at Skye in confusion, noting the man's fear and hesitation. 'What has gotten into you, Skye? It's me, Cedrin.'

'I do not see Cedrin,' Skye said. 'I see a man claimed by the demons of Storm Season.'

Skye gathered his belongings into a bundle and faced Cedrin, once more making a sign. 'I will not sleep beside a demon.' His face was grim as though the decision pained him, but was necessary. 'Take my advice, Cedrin. See the Uros-Druid. For you will have no peace until the demon is cast out. If not for this goldskin, we would have already summoned the Templeman and it would be out of you.' He left with a parting glare at Marken.

Cedrin watched him leave with a sinking feeling. He regretted his harsh words. Skye was his oldest friend, and at the very least he had deserved a hearing.

'What happened, Marken?'

Marken looked around at the crowd, who were still watching them, wary.

'Come up on deck and I'll explain. There are too many ears here.' He pointed to those who still watched and others who pretended to be sleeping in their bunks.

Cedrin groaned. First the Cintros woman with her strange promises and now this. He reached beneath his bunk for his cloak and threw it across his shoulders. Then, hefting his greatscythe, motioned for them to move to the deck above.

The deck was bitter cold, with slick ice underfoot. Responding, the Heat strained within them. Cedrin pulled the cloak tighter and they rubbed their hands and stamped their feet.

The sailors on duty were wrapped in sea-cloaks and insulated leggings, special spiked soles on their sea-boots to grip the treacherous planking. They looked at Cedrin and Marken as though they were mad, wanting nothing more than to be in the warmth of the ship's hold.

'This is ridiculous, Marken. Coming up here in the cold of night.'

Marken led Cedrin out of range of the sailors' hearing and gripped him by the shoulders.

'Listen to me carefully, Cedrin. When I woke you, you were encased in a nimbus of power.'

Cedrin looked at Marken's earnest face. He swallowed. 'Surely you are mistaken?'

'I think not,' said Marken. Cedrin had rarely seen him so serious. 'If I had not woken you, the Templeman would already have you.'

Cedrin's disbelief gave way to an aching fear. A nimbus of power? What did it mean? After all that had happened to them, why this?

'Maybe Skye was right. Perhaps I am possessed. The Templeman may be able to help me. . .'

'By Uros, Cedrin! Demons infect the soul. This is a malady of the body, something else entirely, and that cursed Uros-Druid will know only too well what it is.'

'What then?' Cedrin was suspicious and fearful at the same time. 'What is it?'

Marken looked Cedrin in the eye. 'Sorcery.'

Cedrin did not know whether to laugh or cry. Everything around him was suddenly alien; the ship, the mast, the rigging. Marken, this friend he had known for years, was a stranger, talking about Sorcery and demons. He felt lost, like a blind man fighting, pushing away bandits in a hopeless attempt to keep his life, yet knowing the fatal blow was close.

'Marken,' he said, almost in desperation. 'You know me. I am no Sorcerer. How could I be? It *has* to be something else.'

Marken produced a flask of bakta and downed a warming shot of the spirit, passing the flask to Cedrin. His soft golden features relaxed.

'I know you, Cedrin. You are a good man with a great heart. This is something you do not want, but you must know the truth of it. Druids are taught, Cedrin. Despite all the Temple's talk of their Chosen, most men and women can be shown how to find the Essence. Sorcery is a different matter. The talent to touch the Realm of Fire lays only in certain bloodlines.

'You are Old Blood, Cedrin. It's Belin's legacy to you.'

As much as Cedrin wanted to deny them, he felt the truth of Marken's words. It was a complication he did not want. Not now.

Cedrin looked out into the darkness, thinking it through. What worried him most was the danger he was now putting his friends in.

The whole thing seemed insane.

He had lived most of his life without a single clue of what flowed through his veins – the Old Blood. Now this.

Perhaps his confrontation with Raziin had brought it to the surface. If so, its appearance may be temporary. He clung onto that hope. If he stayed on guard, worked to suppress it, to push that strange Window from his mind, it may become dormant in him again.

'You must go to Ellen Cintros. Only she can train you as you must be trained,' said Marken.

Cedrin turned to his friend, saw the love and concern there, and his heart warmed.

'Marken, I cannot. That road is closed to me.' He had made his plans, and he intended to carry them through.

'Cedrin, for the love of Larus. Swallow your pride!'

'Just. . . let me think on it.' He did not want to be a Sorcerer. The mere thought of it terrified him. He needed time – time to see if he could control these strange new powers – and somehow return to the simple calvanni he had been only days ago.

Marken nodded grimly. 'Very well. For now I will say no more. But please be wary.'

As they turned and walked in silence back towards the ladder, Cedrin did his best to push the whole affair from his mind. Yet as he reached for the top rail, the Window once more leapt into his mind. Beyond it was a landscape of boundless power. What surprised him was not the vision, which he had experienced several times now, but the sudden desire to reach into that Realm, to draw the Fire into himself – and release it.

As he descended the ladder, he remembered that in his dream he had opened the Window. With a shock, he realised it had been real: his burnt bedding was testament to that.

He had already channelled the Fire.

* * *

Cedrin and Marken watched Raynor from the cold deck of the *Lusella's Pride* as the fat-bellied trader stood-to off the Asog River, waiting for entry into the sprawling river port. They had waited for two hours as the bitter cold of morning passed to the mere bone-numbing chill of day.

The Yasser was over three leagues wide here, but was alive with traffic. Grain traders, huge and sleek, lay anchored by the score, dwarfing the sea-going galleys beside them. River craft teemed on the waters; small river galleys, sailing craft, flat-bottomed punts loaded with barrels and sacks, rafts from as far as Armon loaded with timber cut in the high forests. All found their way through the confusion in seemingly miraculous fashion.

The port lay at the junction of two rivers, the Yasser by far the greater. The mighty Yasser ran wide and untamed, while the banks of the Asog, running down from Olcis in the north to meet the west-flowing Yasser, were alive with the colours of a vast water-borne city. Hulks of every description lay anchored or lashed with heavy rope to massive pylons. Even across the leagues, they could see the hundreds of small row-boats weaving through the floating city like bees on a flowering bush.

The small war galleys of the Warlord, which patrolled as far as the borders of the Yasser States, were distinctive in their blue and yellow colours. They roamed between the larger craft, herding like dogs at the heels of amelak, the crossed spears and shield banner of the Warlord flying above their masts.

Robic had drawn the ship into the still waters that verged on the far bank, the oars almost touching the barren islands that sealed the Melaut from the Yasser on the southern bank. The islands were little more than exposed banks of mud and sand, covered with ambitious mangroves and long-legged wading birds. In times of high flood the islands were submerged, the surging flows carrying all the debris of Kelas into the dark expanse beyond.

Cedrin and Marken had passed the morning like any other aboard the craft, supping eagerly on broth and spiced wine. Cedrin would have given anything to have had Skye join them, but he remained aloof.

As the dawn arrived, Cedrin and Marken had shuffled into the cold to watch from the deck as the massive twin pillars of the Narrows passed them by. The two of them pointing with awe at the blasted rock, laughing over a pipe of Se-tobacco. Enough strangeness had passed during the last few days. Cedrin was glad to relax. The two of them would soon leave the Brotherhood and the Eathal far behind them, travelling north to begin a new life. He was still hopeful Skye would join them.

Raynor was set well back from the intersection of the two rivers, high on the Asog's western bank. It was surrounded by a mass of two and three-storey dwellings and sprawling market squares which, in turn, were circumnavigated by a sea of baal, stretching as far as the eye could see along the Yasser's northern banks. The baal crop was like a vast yellow ocean above the muddy river, small villages appearing as islands in its midst.

The main docks were on the eastern side of the Asog. Seven bridges crossed the small, fast flowing river, linking Raynor with the bustling Docks District. They were the drawbridges of Raynor, representing the pinnacle of the Empire's architectural prowess. Each bridge rose hundreds of fathoms above the Asog, supported on pylons and great arches, each with massive towers rising from the banks. Gazing across the leagues, the bridges looked spectacular, but Cedrin knew the reality was very different.

Like Raynor itself, if you looked closely you would see the decay. One bridge had been damaged beyond repair during the last Eathal invasion and a light bridge of wood now spanned where the massive cast blocks once met. Three others had fallen into such disrepair that great sections of them had tumbled away completely. The wealth and expertise to maintain them no longer existed.

The walls of Raynor were massive, built from cast blocks of dull red mought. Behind them rose hundreds of spires and towers. Some were twisted, others straight, shooting skyward like a mismatched flight of arrows, rising amid domes and roofs of golden tile and glittering glass. From a distance, the city was truly magical, like a vision of paradise.

Perhaps it is for some, thought Cedrin, his eyes seeking out the majesty of the Warlord's palace, the palanac, rising like a jewel, its colours stunning. Inside the walls of Raynor, the palace was sealed further within a Suul district known as the palastrada.

The Outer City, as it was called in Raynor, stretched from the walls to the Asog in some places. Official craft had their own dock, a neat and orderly stone quay nestled into the fringes of the Outer City, sealed from the rest of the sprawling mass by a garrison wall. Cedrin could make out the shape of the Cintros galley amid the craft tied up at the Suul docks.

This contrasted sharply with the chaotic scene of the main docks that lay roughly opposite. Built of a combination of wood and stone, extended and improved only at the whim of the rich traders who owned each wharf, it was a strange mismatch of architecture and colour, crowded with ships and people. Rising like a slender arrow from the confusion of the docks was the flag-tower from which the dock traffic was controlled. It was a single massive wooden pylon, topped with the flag-wavers cage. It was rumoured to have fallen twice, taking the flag-wavers within to untimely deaths.

Everything was much as he had seen it before, except a new city of tents had risen on the fringes of the baal crop and the docks, well below the flood line. Refugees. Cedrin turned to see Marken studying the tent-city.

'The weather must be nice here at the moment,' said Marken, his voice thick with irony. 'Lots of visitors to admire the splendour of the Empire.'

Cedrin grunted. 'I wonder where they've come from?'

'The Eathal are marching into Hend, laying waste to everything.' They turned to see Skye behind them, neither had heard him approach.

It was the first time they had seen Skye since the angry words of the night before. He seemed amiable enough now. Cedrin searched his face, but his old friend gave no indication of how he felt about the strange magical happenings.

'I talked to one of the slaves of the customs official who boarded us. A scribe he was,' said Skye. 'He said Hianer has already been destroyed. Most of the people fled before the Eathal arrived.'

Cedrin looked towards the sprawling mass of tents. They must number in the tens of thousands. *Who will feed them?*

They were interrupted by a cry from the mast. The *Lusella's Pride* had received the flag signal to enter the docks. Robic shouted orders from the quarterdeck, the commands relayed below to the rowers. Gradually the beat began and the ship turned into the current, striking out for Raynor, weaving between the traffic. They were forced to full stops repeatedly by other craft, and finally reached the mouth of the Asog almost an hour later.

Approaching Raynor, they were absorbed in the sounds and sights of the city. The closer they came, the more it lost its quality of majesty. Closing on the docks, the view was dominated by the floating city, the Outer City and the Docks District. All that could be seen of the city itself were the massive walls, rising above them like dirty red cliffs.

As they passed the floating city, the sounds and smells of a mass of humanity assailed them. The powerful stench wafted towards them from the hulks with the bitter-sweet scent of cheap incense.

The floating city was a jumble of colour, faded tarpaulins and flags, banners and clothes hung out to dry. Across the water, they could hear shouts of abuse and the sound of a woman singing rising above the babble of talk.

In the Dock District, men shouted and called to each other as the ships were unloaded and loaded in unceasing rhythm. Counterweighted cranes swung above the heads of the crowd to the shouts of the teams operating them, the creak and squeal of pulleys never-ending. The calls of traders and peddlers, loud and coarse, were punctuated by the screams of women and angry voices of men. Ships bosuns and customs officials shouted above all of this, trying to keep the docks working.

As they approached the docks, Cedrin could see the tent city was guarded by the Warlord's men. The mostly old men, women and children held within the barricades looked miserable and hopeless. Once rich men in fine cloaks and trousers stood with beggars and slaves, all as helpless as each other. A whole society torn up by its roots. Those who could not afford the entrance fee into Raynor were all beggars in the eyes of the law, and desperate refugees had potential for trouble.

'Nothing for them but the chain, now,' said Skye.

It was a horrifying thought. To be free one day, yet forced to accept slavery the next. Many of them would take the chain, Cedrin knew, rather than starve or face an uncertain future.

They docked alongside an old wooden quay. Crowds were heavier than usual, despite the Storm Season, and the usual excited buzz was replaced with a panicked urgency.

The fear of the people of Raynor was almost palpable to them as they waited their turn to disembark, queuing with the other passengers from the common deck – waiting for the richer passengers who had taken their own cabins to make their way up the steep companionway. The docks were built to rise above the worst of the floods and now stood well above the deck, a stair and rail lowered from above.

At last they were in Raynor.

All that remained was to make the trek into the city, find accommodation and locate Kranor. Then, in days, they would be heading north, the three calvanni together, good pay and good food, adventure and fresh air. Cedrin felt more hopeful than he had for days. What he would give for a bath, a good fire and a meal!

They waited to disembark, absently watching the minor Suul and wealthy traders make their way into the press with their retinues. Cedrin became aware of the stares on his back and the whispered comments, the authors of which were as elusive as mist. He heard 'Uros-demon' and 'Kallor's curse' whispered by a dozen different voices and caught the accusing stares of others before they looked away.

He could not help but notice Skye edging away from him. It doesn't matter, he told himself, we three will be well away from them before long. Almost grudgingly, the bosun gave his men the order to let them pass. They surged with the rest, clambering up the stairs to stand, finally, in Raynor. They had done it. They had escaped Athria and the Brotherhood, everything lay before them. A life of adventure. A life.

Once on the wharf, the calvanni shouldered their bundles. The docks seemed to change on every visit to Raynor. Buildings torn down and replaced, others destroyed by fire; great piles of crates and barrels everywhere, guarded by gangs of toughs with clubs. To meet Kranor they would have to enter the city and take some rooms inside the walls.

They would get no serious work on the docks, not with so many willing hands ready to work for nothing, or accept the chain of slavery for a meal. That meant making the pilgrimage over the bridges into the city, a costly and time-consuming business. Beside them, Skye was eyeing the sprawling dock district, its rough gambling dens and whorehouses. A talented thief could do well here, where the law could be bought.

'Welcome to the heart of Empire,' said Marken, eyes glowing with humour. 'Shall we go straight to the palace or dally first in the bordellos of the palastrada?'

'Straight to the palace,' said Cedrin. Why not go straight to the top?

Cedrin looked across at Skye and almost missed a step. His old friend's face was like a death-mask.

'We are heading into the city to find a place on a caravan heading north. Are you coming with us?' asked Cedrin.

Skye looked around at the docks. 'There are lots of opportunities here, and there will be too many soldiers in the city.' He hesitated. 'Our paths may be different.'

Cedrin nodded. So things were not so simple after all. They had never agreed they would all go north, but after being through so much together, he always thought they would stay together. If Skye wanted a different path, good luck to him. They would part friends.

Cedrin put out his hand. 'May our paths cross again.'

Skye looked at Cedrin's hand as though he were offering him a poisoned cup; his dark eyes flickered to Cedrin and back towards the docks. He extended his hand briefly, yet short of gripping his friend's, he let it fall again.

'Larus be with you,' said Skye. He turned to hurry into the crowd.

All had not been forgotten. In Skye's eyes, Cedrin was infected with the curse of Uros, to be avoided like a plague ship.

Is this what life comes to? The betrayal of friends? The destruction of everything you had built? In Athria, he had a life, had been rich in most men's eyes. He had owned an apartment and lived comfortably. Now where was he? Alone on the docks in a foreign city, shivering in the cold of Storm Season while in Athria thugs and thieves looted what had once been his. *Damn the Brotherhood!* Why had they been so greedy!

He turned towards the bridges, not looking back. Marken walked silently at his side as they pushed through the dirty streets, crowded with workers and slaves who hurried with their burdens.

The climb up the bridge ramp was steep and hard, the cost of the crossing outrageous, but they had no choice but to pay. The suns were already starting to drop and they could feel the Hunger stirring. Cedrin paused at the crest of the bridge and looked down. His gaze fell by chance on the crest of the Cintros galley, tied to the Suul docks far below. Ellen's face, framed with honey-blonde hair, flashed into his mind.

The dream of heading north started to seem foolish, the reality as hard as the stone that kept the privileged Suul like Ellen Cintros from the peasants like him. Yet he was free, and the master of his own destiny. What more could a man want?

The day drew on, and they struggled through the Outer City towards the southern gate into Raynor, becoming lost amid the mass of humanity. By now exhausted, being the master of his own destiny seemed a small consolation.

When they finally entered the city, it was dark. They had paid two tolls and were forced to bribe three officers to skip forward in the queue or face a night outside the walls. Their money was running low and they had not found an inn. They paused for a meal on the outskirts of the palastrada, the district that enclosed the palace and the mansions of the Suul. Cedrin could not help but look up towards the sheer palace walls and wonder what Ellen Cintros had really wanted.

It seemed the price of freedom was high.

Chapter Eighteen

Ellen followed the court functionary through yet another set of doors and into yet another long corridor faced with pale marble. The air inside the Warlord's palace was warm, almost balmy. She had forgotten it was heated against the Storm Season chill. Ahead of her, a Trader and his scribe followed close on the heels of the functionary. *The Trader must have important business with the Warlord.* So many other delegations had been forced to step aside for Ellen's audience. Her war galley had reached the Suul docks only that morning. She had scarcely had time to bathe and change.

The court functionary passed through another set of open doors, then abruptly turned to face her. *What now?* A question died on her lips as she saw the man's cold eyes.

The doors behind Ellen shut with a slam. She could hear the angry protests of Valdas and Mendor, trapped on the other side, through the heavy wood. Then the court functionary disappeared from view as he shut the doors in front of her as well, sealing Ellen inside the short corridor with the Trader and his scribe.

A thrill of fear shot through her.

The Temple has found me!

Immediately she swung towards the two others with her, who, seemingly, had also been waiting patiently for court.

The trader, heavily dressed in rich golden robes, swiftly drew out a long jagged glowmetal of white metal and begun to chant in Cioan. Beneath, she saw the sigil of Uros. A Templeman!

The dim corridor came alive with fierce lights of orange and red. She gasped as an icy spear sunk into her mind, dulling it. The Window was unreachable. Unlike the Fireseeker, this device did not take the Fire, merely blocked it. The result was the same.

'Quickly, fool!' snapped the Templeman. 'Attack her while her powers are subdued!' His accent was Athrian.

The other man beside him, who had posed as the Trader's scribe, threw aside his board of parchments. He drew a pair of thin calvs. He closed on Ellen quickly, his eyes searching eagerly for a place to strike.

He struck out with the calv in his left hand. Ellen dodged it, only to face a simultaneous attack from the right, which she blocked with her forearm.

He was fast and skilful. Even with a blade, she would be hard-pressed to match him.

He attacked again. Ellen kicked out expertly for his groin, but her foot was hampered by the dress, and she hit his knee instead.

She swayed, a narrowly avoided thrust cutting through the fabric of her heavy black gown. She took a hasty step backward, only to slam into the faced marble of the hallway wall. The impact knocked the breath from her lungs.

The assassin struck out again. Ellen dived into a roll. She came up in a crouch, facing both men. She reached under her skirt to her inner thigh, where she had secreted a small throwing knife. Ellen pulled it clear. She drew her hand back.

The calv-wielding assassin flinched, but he was not the target.

Ellen had been surprised by the Temple and their tricks once too often.

The knife flew across the narrow space.

The Templeman had time only to widen his eyes before the knife embedded itself in his right eye.

He gasped, the glowmetal tumbling heavily to the thick carpet. The lights vanished immediately, and Ellen wasted no more time.

She swiftly drew on the Fire, forming the Matrix of Binding. The assassin tried to flee, but was quickly caught. He grunted in surprise as the Sorcery took him, freezing his running form in an instant. His forward momentum sent him straight over. He cried out in pain as his head struck the wall. His eyes rolled and he went limp in her magical grasp.

She released the Fire.

Hastily she stepped across the carpet and took the knife from the eye of the Templeman. She wiped it quickly on his clothes before replacing it in its hidden sheath.

The doors behind her opened with a rush of commotion, and she swept up the glowmetal, hiding it in her sleeve.

Valdas and Mendor rushed to her side, greatscythe blades extended.

'Suul Cintros!' said Mendor. Valdas was too furious for words.

'Two assassins,' said Ellen, breathless. She looked down at her gown. The blade had narrowly missed her left side. She folded the billowing cloth across the hole, holding it in place with her arm.

They were soon surrounded by a crowd. Ellen searched for the court functionary who had sealed the doors on her, but he was gone.

A court officer pushed his way through, followed by a squad of Raynorian soldiers. His eyes widened as he saw the dead man, and the other unconscious man beside him.

'What is going on here?' demanded the officer.

'We could ask the same!' stormed Valdas, facing down the man.

Ellen raised her hand, giving her Suulqua a warning look. The surviving assassin would need to be questioned, descriptions of the others given, but for now she was content just to see the surviving assassin in custody. She had no intention of being side-tracked from her court appearance.

'These two men tried to kill me,' said Ellen, pointing at the men. 'Fortunately, my own men intervened. This one,' she said, pointing at the unconscious man, 'is still alive and should be questioned.'

The officer eyed her warily. 'And who are you?' he asked bluntly.

'This is Suulvey Ellen Cintros,' said Mendor, his voice level, yet edged with threat. 'You will address her with the proper respect.'

The officer's eyebrows shot up and he hastily bowed. 'My Lady.'

'See that the man is taken into custody. I will be making further enquiries into this matter through my consulate,' said Ellen. 'I intend to see justice done,' she finished, her voice hard.

The officer blanched, and waved for his men to pick up both the unconscious man and the dead Templeman and let her pass.

Ellen swept into the main entrance chamber, Valdas and Mendor flanking her. Behind them her four ladies, as nervous as ornamental birds, had resumed their positions. She had sent the scribes and retainers ahead to her apartments earlier; they were hired men, not courtiers.

'Are you all right, my Lady?' asked Serel, one of her ladies. She was smaller-bodied than the others, her dark hair stark against their long blond Athrian tresses. Serel also lacked their curves, but her eyes were sharp. Ellen suspected a keen intelligence.

'Are you unharmed?' asked another, not to be outdone in concern.

Ellen patted their arms. 'All is well. Now, back in line.' Her voice was harsher than she intended.

She smoothed her dress, trying to still her hands.

In Raynor less than two hours and already the Temple had tried to kill her.

'Mendor. Keep this safe,' she said, passing the glowmetal surreptitiously to the Suulqua.

A court functionary asked her name, and she was quickly ushered to the front of the crowd of supplicants. Many eyed Ellen and her group with envy and not a little hostility. Some of those pushed aside for the Suulvey from Athria had waited weeks for an audience.

Moments later, she was standing at the doors, waiting to be introduced.

The Warlord's court was huge. The whole Cintros mansion could have fit comfortably beneath the massive dome. She remembered gaping at it like a country girl when she first travelled to Raynor with her father at the age of six. Now, with her heart still hammering from the attempt on her life, she had little time for details.

Her two Suulqua stood to attention beside her, perhaps a little too close. She could not blame them for being protective after that attempt on her life. Mendor's face was impassive, yet underneath she could sense his rage that he had not been there to defend her. Valdas was less cool. He looked around the room, his jaw clenched, his eyes hot, looking for any threat. As for herself, she was surprised by her own calm.

The court was lined with galleries and all but the highest were filled with minor Suul, their servants and slaves. The ground floor of the court was partitioned on either side. Behind the scarlet ropes and mirror-finish poles were the most exulted of the Warlord's Court. This was the public court and the Suul gathered here for the entertainment. The pursuit of gossip in Raynor was second only to the pursuit of ambition.

'Ambassador from the Athrian court, sister to Sarlord Torren Cintros, Suulvey of the Athrian Council. Lord, I present Ellen Cintros!'

A stir went up from the assembly and she advanced slowly.

As she walked across the polished marble, she was conscious of hundreds of eyes upon her. She could just imagine their critical assessment of her. They would see her as a Provincial upstart. 'This is Ellen Cintros?' they would whisper. 'The one they say inherited her father's powers? She looks so slight, poor thing, are you sure she faced the Traitor of Armon. . .'

'...Suulqua Mendor Ores and Suulqua Valdas Nema.'

The Steward raised his ornate staff, cast cleverly with a fluted end in all the colours of the rainbow, and struck the floor three times.

Ellen set out into the hall, across the vast floor where the glories of the Bulvuran Empire were immortalised in sweeping murals. *Not too fast. Steady, steady.* A sweat broke out on her forehead. The severe gown, lined heavily against the chill of Storm Season, had been chosen deliberately to show public mourning for the death of her father. She had not expected to be fighting in it – and the Warlord's court was heated to the temperature of a summer's day.

She examined the rows of Suul who flanked her at ground level through a mask of formality. The men wore ornate harnesses of fine leather or silk, garishly coloured and inlaid with the rarest gems and tints. Their trousers were looser than the fashion in Athria and billowed around their legs, draping to their slipper-clad feet. The trousers looked effeminate against the profusion of coloured tattoos on their torsos. She felt certain some were for decoration. Tattoos for decoration? The idea was absurd.

The women wore tight-fitting skirts that draped to the marble in billowing folds, the colours bright and vivacious, the patterns geometric. The fine silks that covered their chests varied from thin to almost see-through, some with a thin parody of a man's harness crossing between their breasts. Scandalous – to show themselves in public – everyone knew breasts were only to be bared with close family or friends.

She kept her gaze fixed ahead. She was here as an ambassador and had more important things to think about than fashion.

Daran, the Warlord of the Yasser States, sat on the Cinanac throne. He was at ease within the embrace of the massive seat of carved emerald. As the youngest and most brilliant general of the Court of Riin Cinanac, he had led three of Bulvuran's legions in a fighting retreat from the Eastern frontier to save Raynor and the remnants of the Empire from total destruction.

Unlike the court dandies, Daran was dressed in heavy boots and leather trousers. They were crafted to project austerity and heighten his warrior's image. Beneath the ornate harness, the Warlord's torso was covered with dull blue military tattoos. His totem tattoo, a simple tree, was of poor quality, revealing to all he was not born a Suul. A more conceited man would have had the tattoo reworked, but the Warlord seemed to like reminding people of his origins in Raynor's poorer quarter, the son of a Legion Second Captain – commander of a division of around one hundred men – who had worked his way up from the lowly rank of Blade.

Ellen's entourage reached the base of the dais. Her Suulqua bowed from the waist and her ladies prostrated themselves. Ellen bowed her head. Daran may be the leader of the most powerful country in Kelas, but if not for her father the Eathal would have razed Raynor twenty-eight years ago.

Daran straightened in his chair and Ellen regarded him critically. He was a man still in the strength of his middle years. Despite the plumes of grey touching his temples, he exuded an energy and alertness that marked him as younger. His dark hair and pale skin revealed a mix of Anacian and Myrian ancestry. His dark eyes were set into a face that was well-proportioned, but too strong for beauty.

'Worthy Cintros,' said Daran warmly. 'I am grieved to hear of Myan's death. He was a friend and ally to the Yasser States.'

The silence in the room was emphasised by its sheer size and Ellen had become even more conscious of the eyes upon her. She had accompanied Myan many times to the 'Capital' as he still referred to it. It seemed scant years ago she was sitting on Daran's knee.

'You are kind, Warlord. May I reassure you of Athria's continued friendship under Torren Cintros.'

'We must, however, leave our grief for another time,' Daran continued in a low voice, his sorrow sincere.

A courtier rushed up the dais, whispering quickly into Daran's ear. His eyes flicked towards her and he nodded.

The courtier withdrew, bowing.

For an instant, the brown eyes searched hers deeply. He had just learnt of the assassination attempt. She was sure of it. Yet that was not something he would announce to the court.

'You may be assured that you are most welcome here, Suulvey Cintros.'

His eyes met hers meaningfully. He was trying to tell her the attempt on her life was none of his doing.

She bowed her head briefly. 'Thank you, Warlord. I hope you will always view me as a friend to Raynor.'

The brief searching gaze was gone and, once more, he was all formality.

He raised his voice to fill the court. 'We are soon to be under siege in Raynor. Are you aware of the Eathal invasion of Hend?'

Years ago, when the Eathal had assassinated the Imperial family and swarmed from Maht to engulf Raynor, Hend had betrayed the Empire, withdrawing its legions to leave the city defenceless. Every child in the street knew that much. What was known only to a few was that Ternacus, the Governor of Hend, had actively led the assassins into Raynor with his legion months before. The people of Raynor had lined the streets to cheer as they marched into the south gate, but with them was an Eathal shapechanger, Maht's ambassador to Hend, now posing as a human general under Ternacus' command.

Ternacus killed the Steward of Raynor and set the shapechanger to take his place. While Emperor Riin lay with his legions on the Eastern frontier, his trusted advisers were one-by-one beheaded. The First legion marched out of Raynor to the east under the false-Steward's orders. Ternacus had but to hold Raynor until the Eathal legions reached it, open the gates, and it would have fallen. Yet when Leith Cinnor led his forces south, and Daran his legions from the east, turning the First legion back towards Raynor, Ternacus lost his nerve. The combined forces of Leith and Daran would both arrive before the Eathal. Hend's forces fled back across the Yasser, leaving Raynor to Daran – who, as the most senior surviving general in the Imperial armies, was raised to Warlord.

The aging Ternacus had perished at Hianer only days ago. The betrayers were betrayed, a poetic justice.

Ellen was impressed with Daran's calm. He apparently considered Raynor impregnable.

'We are certainly aware of the threat. I have communications for you from Torren and the Council of Athria regarding these developments,' said Ellen. She began to relax into her role as the formal proceedings continued. She realised her long hours taking Cioan dictation in the courtrooms of Athria and later supervising the court records had prepared her well for this role. Court life had a rhythm. Formal parleys that waxed and waned across the hours in an elaborate structure of etiquette and formal language were nothing more than a verbal dance. Once you had the step, the words whirled away, almost of their own accord, to some hidden rhythm.

As she continued, the court's magnificence was once more impressed on her. Built at the Empire's height, the known world was once ruled from this room. The wealth of Yos had been laid at the feet of the Cinanac as tribute flowed from all corners of the Empire. But piece by piece, the vast civilisation had crumbled.

Three hundred years before, the Southern Empire, beyond the Gimpessu, had won free from Raynor. No sooner had the ancient land, comprising Cioa, Myria and Anacia, cast off the bonds of Empire, than ancient rivalries began to tear it to pieces. The Southern Empire was now divided like Kelas into a score of Sardoms, each with a distinct culture, all warring incessantly. When the Eathal had risen like a dark tide, they did not lift a finger to save Raynor.

In Kelas, the Northern provinces had been eager to see their Cinanac overlords fall. Sensing the Empire's downfall, they refused to send their legions south. Only Armon, which had never been conquered by Carris but had a treaty with the Empire; and Athria, the oldest and richest of the Myrian settlements, had come to Raynor's aid.

'. . . and how many ships will Athria send each month? We intend to fill our storage houses to brimming,' said Daran, as an adviser in a full-length robe whispered in his ear.

Ellen studied the Warlord's adviser. He was a Cioan, overweight, with shots of silver running through his long golden hair. His eyes were the colour of honey, his face rounded and unremarkable. It had to be Uran Cinnel. A refugee from the destruction of Althar, he was one of the most powerful men at the court. Reputed to be a Sorcerer, he and the Warlord had worked closely together to rebuild the strength of Raynor in the years since the Empire's fall.

Uran regarded her with intense interest.

'We have worked out a schedule, Lord Daran,' responded Ellen automatically. 'As you see in the first dispatch.'

'I see the Athrian Temple has seen fit to send only ten Druids to aid in the defence, and the Court only three hundred warriors. I had hoped. . . ,' continued Daran.

As Ellen explained the tender position of Regent's Hill, her attention was drawn to the two Druids who flanked Daran's throne, cowls drawn deeply over their faces, hands concealed within their robes. Their garb was not familiar. She searched for the identifying sigils that Druids of the Sisters always wore and found none. Instead they wore a round pendant, hollow in the middle. She had heard of it. The Hidden Sun. The Druids of Yosini here at the court of the Warlord? She was so absorbed by her discovery she missed Daran's last words.

Ellen stifled embarrassment as Daran repeated himself and the conversation flowed on. Then came the rap of the Steward's staff on the marble. Who would dare to interrupt her audience? Few would possess the rank. A visiting Sarlord perhaps? She had not heard of any.

A stir went through the balconies above, and for the first time she was aware the upper galleries were filling rapidly. Whoever was going to present themselves had let rumour go before them.

A group of Druids swept into the room. The ornate robes and heavy sigils of the leading three denoted them as High Druids, two of them, including the leader, wearing the red of Templemen, the third in the black of the Moon-Druids. Ellen was instantly on her guard. Each held a jewelled staff of office. They came forward with regal bearing, the Templemen attended by more of their number, the Moon Druid was flanked by a yellow-robed Larus Druid and a brown-robed scholar wearing the sigil of Larus. Behind them, towering over the Druids, was a man in a fine white robe of embroidered linen, open in front to show a superbly muscled chest intoned with fine tattoos.

The entourage defied etiquette by coming forward without waiting to be announced. The disconcerted Steward struggled to speed the introduction.

'High Druids Ranlan, Esel, Manel, by providence of the Sisters and the Hesguit's seat in Olcis, and Osterac of Olcis, Suul, Ward of the Hesguit's seat.'

They were ambassadors from the Hesguit, the supreme Druid of the Temple of the Sisters. So far the Hesguit and the Temple of Olcis had not issued any edict against her. The

Athrian Temple was acting alone.

As they approached, she could not help but stare at Osterac. Palsus had been a miracle of proportion and grace, but Osterac outshone him. He was a tall, wide-shouldered Anacian, his dark hair curled above a face cut in the classic features of a Suul warrior, and he moved with the easy grace of an athlete. But above all this, the man had a natural charisma that made every expression seem profound. He swept his pale blue eyes across the assembled Suul as though they were beneath him. When he paused for an instant to study her, her heart thudded under the intensity of his gaze. Then he turned to Daran.

The Warlord straightened on his throne as they came forward to stand before him, his eyes gauging them and the High Druid Ranlan in particular. Ellen moved closer to the throne to give them room. She had learnt to be wary of Templemen.

Ellen could not help but study them for any trace of glowmetal devices as she met Ranlan's stern and righteous gaze. He spared her only the briefest of glances, and she let out a long breath of relief. They were not here for her.

Uran bent to whisper in Daran's ear and Ellen was now close enough to hear. 'This is the Hesguit's delegation. They entered the gates this morning.'

They came to a halt in front of the Warlord.

The buzz of excited conversation that had sprung up as the delegation had taken the floor now faltered and gave way to a stunning silence. Ellen was sure a cough in the highest galleries could be heard where she stood.

'Strange times to come calling, Ranlan,' said the Warlord, his manner casual, as though he were talking to an old friend from the Legion.

Ranlan suppressed his anger and kept his bearing, pitching his voice for all in the court. 'We have journeyed here in the height of Storm Season on the most holy and urgent of missions.'

Ranlan raised his hands and turned back to the audience like a stage performer. Behind him, the other Druids were as still as statues, each striving to maintain their poise. In their midst,

Osterac was all arrogance, the slight contempt beneath his manner as palpable as an insult. Whatever they were doing, they were playing a dangerous game.

The Warlord turned away from Ranlan as though bored and talked to Uran. Each laughed as though sharing a private joke.

Ranlan faltered for an instant but pushed on, his fury plain.

'Now the foul Eathal once more spill from dark pits of Llors, this is the time of Yos' great need. This is the time the call shall be answered.' Daran looked at his fingernails, seemingly unconcerned, but Ellen could sense that beneath the affected manner, he was listening with sober intensity.

'It was the Hesguit's vision that this time would come. That at this time, we would give to Yos what had been left in our keeping.'

Ranlan's voice trailed off, as though the weight of his duty in the service of Yos was hard to bear. In the pause, a low buzz of excited conversation filled the galleries. Daran's other advisers talked heatedly amongst themselves, but the Warlord remained still and silent, as though he were in the great hall alone.

Ranlan signalled for Osterac to come forward. He advanced slowly, as though at ease with this immense crowd.

Daran leaned forward, raising his voice for the court to hear. 'Well, Ranlan, don't keep us in suspense. Lunch is waiting.'

The stifled laughter broke the dramatic poise that Ranlan had attempted to build. His anger finally surfacing, he turned on the Warlord. 'It is not for me to declare!'

This silenced the laughter.

Osterac pushed past Ranlan to stand mere paces from Daran. He raised his voice to the room, his tone rich and imperious, as though the assembled gathering were his to command. 'I, Osterac of Olcis, by the grace of the Sisters and the spirits of my ancestors, declare myself Osterac Cinanac, son of Riin Cinanac and Evylin Kaidell. Direct descendant of the line of Carris and rightful heir to the Cinanac Throne!'

There was a thunderous roar from the crowd.

The Suul on the floor of the court pushed forward, shouting questions. They jostled to get a better view of Osterac, who was standing like a god, brimming with elation as he met Daran's eyes across the floor.

A ragged cry began in the upper galleries and was quickly taken up by others, until the whole court seemed to be shaking at its very foundations.

'*Scion! Scion! Scion!*'

Osterac held up a ring to the throng. A heavy-set ruby that glittered between his fingers.

'This is the ring of Riin Cinanac, given to me against this day.' Osterac turned to face the crowd as they cried out together in a thundering chorus. '*I am the Scion!*'

At this, the crowd burst through the barriers and surged forward. Ellen stepped towards the rear of the dais as the palace guard tried to halt the press. She was in a daze. Her eyes locked to the tall form of Osterac, who nodded at the crowd's cries as though it were the least recognition he deserved; his bearing regal, faultless, every inch the Emperor. He was magnificent. The search was over. She had found the Scion.

Daran stood, his voice cutting through the mob's frenzy.

'*Silence!*'

The crowd fell back, the chorus of 'Scion' becoming ragged and dying away. Daran blazed with anger. He glared at the crowd like a raptor about to strike. Even Osterac was subdued.

'Clear the court,' commanded Daran.

'I never would have dreamed the Hesguit would go this far,' said Uran softly.

'Enough damage had been done,' said Daran in a harsh whisper to his advisor. 'We must withdraw.'

Daran stormed from the court, his entourage and guards following. Ranlan and Osterac made to follow but were blocked bodily by the portly Steward. 'The Warlord of the Yasser States has declared the court at an end. If you wish to see him, you can make a formal application to his offices,' said the Steward.

'He will see us,' said Ranlan in fury. 'Or the people will tear down the palace walls!'

The Steward bowed then followed Daran. He slipped easily past the same impassive guards who blocked Ranlan, Osterac and the remainder of the Hesguit's delegation.

Ellen was left standing by the throne, forgotten.

Ranlan turned to the Druids. 'Everything has gone well. Within hours, the word will have spread throughout Raynor. Daran, that Uros-cursed usurper, will have to act. If he does not officially accede the throne to Osterac, the mob. . .'

Ranlan suddenly noticed her watching him and became silent. He did not need to finish. The Storm Season mob, already half-crazed with fear at the impending Eathal invasion, would seize on the declaration like a banner of salvation.

'We shall find our apartments and wait out Daran's next move,' said Ranlan.

Ellen watched Osterac and the Druids leave as she and her group were guided from the court by a young Suulqua. Her eyes fixed to the swaggering shape of Osterac as he moved away with the delegation. How could her father have been so misguided? Where better to find the Scion than the seat of the Cinanac? To think she had bothered chasing some cut-throat calvanni across the Sea of Mists! If the Scion was to be found anywhere, surely it was among the Suul?

The Suulqua leading Ellen's delegation was reed-thin, his long, lank hair falling from a pale oval face that seemed perpetually concerned. He introduced himself as Nacius, bending his thin body so low to her as Suulvey she thought he would snap in half. Nacius was also the name of a hero of the early Empire, an Anacian warrior who reputedly had held off the Meadrel tribesmen from swarming into Kelas single-handedly. The warrior's name only emphasised the man's emaciated appearance.

'This way, my Lady,' said Nacius, standing at the juncture of two corridors. He had the look of a scholar about him, an inward-looking intensity that sought other worlds.

'Very well, Nacius.'

Although she had taken up her father's quest to find the Scion, she had never really joined in his vision of the Empire's rebirth. It had always seemed a backward-looking dream, a longing for what had been lost and was never to be regained. But as she followed the thin Suulqua, she could imagine what it must have been like as a young Suul, striding these corridors when the Empire spanned Yos; the feeling of standing at the nexus of the known universe, the grand centre of civilisation and rule.

'This way, my Lady.' Nacius paused at the juncture of three identical corridors and waved towards one.

'Just lead the way.'

'Yes, my Lady, of course, my Lady.' His face blanched as though she had just threatened him.

Awkward at taking the lead, the young man continued on, pausing to look back occasionally to check he had not lost the entourage. Mendor and Valdas snickered, muttering depreciating comments about scribes. The young Suulqua pictured themselves quite the young warriors and could not pass up the opportunity to poke fun at the nervous, lanky, Raynorian.

'Empires are built with both pen and scythe,' she said. Mendor's eyes lit up, and Ellen guessed he had just realised that Ellen too, had once been a scribe. 'You may, one day, owe your life to the written word. Do not mock it.'

After many twists and turns, they entered the Athrian consulate, an obscure corner of the palace that had been given over to the Athrians and their representatives; three floors of a squat tower that had only one entrance. The polished wooden doors, set into the corridor, were closed and guarded by Athrian soldiers. Once they sighted Ellen, one of them left his post and disappeared inside.

Nacius bowed low once more, then met Ellen's gaze for the first time. She was surprised she had not noticed his eyes before, by far his most striking feature. The blue shone vividly, almost violet, the colour of the deepest sea, engorged in the sallow face and shining with the strength that had been drawn from the rest of him.

'If I may take my leave, my Lady,' he said.

Ellen felt something in him, and acting on intuition, probed the nervous young man. 'What is your family name, Nacius?'

He took a shuddering breath. 'Cin. . .Cintar. . .my Lady.'

Cintar. One of the ancient lines of the Old Blood.

His pale face reddened with embarrassment.

'What do you do, Nacius?'

He shuffled nervously. 'I work with Uran Cinnel. Ah, I . . .' He looked at Mendor and Valdas nervously. 'I perform many duties.'

Ellen nodded. So he worked for the Cioan Sorcerer. The answer seemed only to raise more questions. 'Thank you, Nacius, you may go.'

'Thank you, my Lady.' Relieved, he hurried away.

The door opened and a familiar voice filled the corridor.

'Dear, Ellen.'

She turned, looking for her brother, and could not believe the change in him. He wore billowing trousers of bright yellow silk, orange pointed slippers, a belt of dyed red leather inset with curious coloured panels, and a harness covered with gems and coloured glass. His yellow-blond hair was flowing across his shoulders in waves and the cunning silk shirt could not conceal his growing paunch.

'Estle. You painted dandy!'

Estle beamed as though complimented and took a bow. 'Well, you look quite meek and subdued for the powerful Sorceress.'

She lost her good humour, casting nervous eyes around the corridor for listeners.

'Don't be so stuffy, Ellen. You are in Raynor now. In fact, you are the talk of the court! At least you were, until *He* arrived.'

Of course, thought Ellen. That explained Nacius' nervousness.

Estle took her by the hand and led her into the consulate.

'Things are different in Raynor. The Temple does not rule the roost.'

Estle signalled for servants to come forward. 'Take these people to their quarters,' he said, indicating Ellen's entourage. The valets led them into various chambers and corridors while Estle steered Ellen deeper into the tower.

'You heard of Myan's death?' asked Ellen.

'Of course,' said Estle. He looked around the corridor at the servants. 'Come, Ellen. My chamber is better than the corridor.'

Ellen silently raged. How could he be so flippant? Myan was their father! She kept a stiff silence until they entered Estle's apartments.

'Bring some fruit and wine,' he ordered a young female slave. Ellen frowned. Estle's tastes were the same.

When the slave had gone, he reached for Ellen's hand. The carefree manner now gave way to concern. She could see how tired he was, as though he had not slept in weeks. Ellen was ashamed of herself, his conviviality had been nothing more than pretence.

'Are you unharmed? Did the assassin's blade break your skin? We must be alert for poison.'

Ellen shook her head. 'I am fine.'

'Are you sure? I can summon a physician.'

'No. Really. I am fine.'

Estle nodded, searching her face. 'I have already had a preliminary report from the guards. The surviving assassin confessed. He was hired by the Athrian Temple. The other man was a Templeman in disguise.'

So Ellen's suspicions were correct. She should have realised Kexos would not give up so easily. It would have been a trivial matter for him to communicate magically to his brethren in Raynor and have assassins lay in wait for her.

'Do you think they will try again?' she asked.

Estle shrugged his shoulders. 'Personally I think it unlikely. Yet, who can say? The Temple has less power here than in Athria, and these rooms are amongst the safest in Raynor.'

Ellen told Estle about the attack, and the glowmetal device.

'Interesting,' said Estle. 'We must get it to Uran. He will want to study it.'

He summoned a scribe to take down her descriptions of the two court functionaries and sent the man to the palace guard with the dispatch.

Finally, they were alone once more.

He studied her for a long moment, rubbing his temples. 'How did father die? I have read the official report, but it told me little of consequence. Apart from that I have heard nothing but rumours.' Estle's pale brown, almost yellow eyes were sorrowful. Estle had always been the sentimental one, the poet who defeated her father's attempts to make him a warrior.

Gripping his hand, she told him, omitting nothing except the Bridge between her and Myan. She let the tears flow, feeling safe for the first time since his death; the events distanced from her by time and space. Here, with the brother she had always felt closest to, she could begin to probe the wound. Estle was a misfit who always had a soft spot for her. In many ways, he had been her strength, and she his champion with Myan.

Estle frowned as Ellen explained Myan's cryptic quest and grunted in disbelief as she told him of her confrontation with the calvanni Cedrin. When she had finished, Estle shook his head.

'Myan's quest. The resurrection of the Empire.' His voice was heavy with sadness. Taking Ellen's hands once more, he met her eyes. 'Ellen, it was nothing more than Myan's dream. You don't have to find the Scion or this bastard, Cedrin. A calvanni? He would just as likely cut your throat! That you went so far as to find him. . . *that* is tribute to your faith in Myan. But let it go. Let this stupid quest die with our father. Start anew here in Raynor. Let the past take care of itself.'

Ellen withdrew her hands. How could she ever explain how their minds had been joined at the end? How she had felt the certainty, the truth of his will?

'Do you think Osterac is the Scion?' she asked, picturing Osterac, his bearing so regal, the booming power and command in his voice as he held up the Cinanac ring to the assembled Suul. It seemed so right he was the Scion.

Estle eyed Ellen as though she were mad. 'It doesn't matter if he is.'

'What!'

'He is just a pawn, Ellen. The Hesguit's puppet. That much even a fool could see.'

'What of the Cinanac line?' she asked.

Estle stared incredulously then began to laugh, reaching to grab a piece of fruit as the young, nubile slave returned to lay down a platter, then withdrew. He bit into it, the juice running down his chin.

One day his appetites will ruin him, thought Ellen.

He poured himself a glass of wine.

'Ellen, this is all about power,' he said, swallowing the fruit and wiping his chin with a brightly coloured cloth from his sleeve. 'This is the Hesguit's most ambitious gambit yet. He must feel the Temple is losing its final grip in the Yasser States to resort to this.'

Another slave-girl ran into the room and whispered in Estle's ear. He nodded and waved her away.

'We are about to have a visitor,' said Estle, his eyes glittering with mischief.

Ellen started to ask who, but Estle held up his hand.

'So how was your passage across the Sea of Mists?' asked Estle, taking another sip of his wine.

Ellen had only begun to reply when a man entered the apartments, his golden hair and skin shining in the light.

'Uran. I wish you would stop creeping up on me,' said Estle.

The large Cioan bowed to Ellen. 'My Lady. You made quite an impression on Nacius. The boy was all elbows and legs when he returned to the Eastern Tower.'

Ellen was charmed. 'You have me at a disadvantage.'

Uran grinned, which gave his face a predatory look. 'I doubt that very much.'

'Uran Cinnel, chief tongue-twister of the Warlord's court, mighty Sorcerer. . . meet my little sister,' said Estle.

Ellen could hardly believe one of the most important men in Raynor had casually walked into the room and made himself at home.

From the sarcasm, Ellen guessed they were old friends. Or at least old sparring partners.

'Thank you, noble Estle,' said Uran.

Uran took Ellen's hand in formal greeting, kissing it with great ceremony, and sat at the table, reaching to pour himself wine. 'I heard about the assassination attempt. I apologise, Ellen. We should have been more vigilant. Yet in a city the size of Raynor, it is difficult to watch everyone.'

'Fortunately they underestimated me,' she said, staring steadily at Uran.

'I can only assure you that you have nothing to fear from the Warlord. We value you as a friend of Raynor.'

'Thank you.'

Uran had the Warlord's ear and could command most of the palace. Raynor would have to be the only place in Kelas where a man such as Uran could openly declare himself a Sorcerer and stand so close to the seat of power. How had Daran succeeded in loosening the Temple's grip?

Without asking, Uran poured Ellen a glass of wine. It was a thick red, very dry, as was the fashion here in Raynor. She sipped it carefully as Uran downed his in great gulps.

'It proved to be an eventful court today. With some unexpected visitors?' asked Estle.

Uran snorted. 'Indeed. The Hesguit's delegation. I would not exactly call them welcome guests. And that pumped up pretty-boy they dragged along for the show. They could be difficult.'

Ellen held her breath. She desperately wanted to know what Daran's next move would be. She waited for her brother to question him, but he seemed content to refill his wineglass.

Ellen could not contain her impatience. 'He had the ring of Cinanac.'

Estle shot her a warning look. Ellen gritted her teeth and remained silent, waiting for Estle to lead.

'Yes, I wonder how they got hold of that. It was lost with Emperor Riin's party when they were ambushed by the Eathal,' said Uran.

Estle reached for a piece of fruit. 'I wonder what Daran will do now.'

To Ellen's surprise, Uran laughed. 'Why, dear Estle, he has no choice. What can he do but grant him the throne?'

Estle and Uran laughed hysterically. Ellen managed a small laugh. How can they treat this as though it were comic?

Estle refilled their glasses, tipping the decanter over Ellen's even though none was poured. 'Did you hear your cousin from Armon was in Athria cutting heads for his Eathal master?' he asked casually.

Uran sobered. 'He is the one who will have his head cut. Hukum does not tolerate failure. My spies in Maht tell me the Inner Circle have given orders for his death. Raziin's fate is sealed.'

Ellen's mind reeled. Spies in the court of Maht?

'But Raziin is free,' she blurted out. Giving Estle a defiant look, she pushed on. 'And he is not a weak Sorcerer. I believe he is still alive, and still a threat.'

Uran sighed. 'Such a pity Hukum reached him before me,' he said almost to himself, then turned to Ellen. 'Hukum's reach is long, my dear. He has tools we could not begin to guess at. Glowmetals that make those hoarded by the Temple look like sideshow fancies.'

There was so much Ellen wanted to ask this man.

'I came to enquire if you would care to visit my apartments for the evening meal?' said Uran, sweeping on past the topic of Raziin.

Ellen inclined her head pleasantly, as though she would love nothing better, her eyes flickering desperately to Estle for guidance. He suggested yes with a slight nod.

'I would be delighted, of course.'

'Good. Shall we say, eight chimes?' said Uran.

Ellen nodded and he rose from the table, bowing stiffly and leaving as abruptly as he entered.

Estle's jovial manner evaporated as Uran left. He turned towards her, shaking his head. 'You have much to learn, little sister. Never let what you want show in Raynor. Uran is a powerful ally, we must keep him on our side. And I must tell you, he has no sympathy for the Scion. He is the Warlord's man.'

Ellen was confused. 'What does he want?'

Estle laughed. 'Why, he wants you, little sister. He wants you.'

Chapter Nineteen

Raziin cut the man's throat and pushed him over the side of the ship. The swamp churned and then he was gone.

'Row!' he screamed. 'Row or join your mate in the swamp.'

Nearby, Dresil glared at him, his dark eyes glittering with malice. Raziin looked away. He had little time for details.

His will to fight Hukum was weakening.

As he passed Dresil, one of the Mouthpiece's lieutenants leapt at him. He wrapped his chains around his neck, pulling tight.

Weakened by lack of sleep and the continual strain of holding the Barrier, Raziin fell to his knees. Other rowers surged at him, screaming their hatred, smashing their chains down onto his head while Dresil's man pulled ever tighter, cutting off his air.

Their cries of victory were short-lived.

Merceth and Kyal came wading in, slamming the butts of their greatscythes down onto the men, scattering them. Relieved of the weight, Raziin pushed himself to his feet and took hold of the chains at his throat. He crouched forward, then using his hip, threw the man over his head, loosening the grip. He unwound the chains, gasping for breath.

Kyal was screaming, bringing down the darkest curses of Uros onto the stunned man as he rammed the blunt end of his greatscythe into his head again and again.

'No, Kyal!' commanded Raziin.

Instantly, the attack ceased.

'We need all rowers,' croaked Raziin. He was beyond

revenge now. 'He is still strong. Take him back to the oars and revive him. Get the ship moving.'

'Yes, Lord.'

A bucket of the foul-smelling water was drawn up from the side and thrown over the man. He spluttered back to consciousness and was soon coaxed back to work under the threats of Raziin's men.

The beat resumed.

His head throbbed with pain, the skin of his throat burning where the chains ripped into it, yet these were mere trifles. His power was almost gone. He had scarcely more than an hour, perhaps two, before Hukum's Compulsion overtook him.

His hands curved into fists.

I need an answer now!

He looked out into the Melaut. The dark trees and never-ending landscape passed by as though through a translucent screen. A steamy mist had risen hours ago and the men wore cloths over their eyes and mouths to stop the stinging vapours from reaching them.

They rowed on, seeing nothing but the endless swamp, hearing nothing but the slow beat and the calls of the depth throwers.

Raziin now lacked the strength to feel the ship's way through the mist with his mind. Yet still he pushed them on. He *had* to survive. He had promised Uros a feast of blood and he intended to deliver.

The forgotten lookout, perched high on the mast, gave out a cry. Raziin blinked. Could this be it? Was this the sign he had waited for?

Raziin ran to the rail and looked forward through the cloud. A dark shape was forming in the mist ahead, coalescing from the formless grey.

'Faster,' he yelled.

The hollow drumming of the beat-master quickened and the men struggled to match it. Raziin paced impatiently, kicking away the drained corpses of bats that still littered the deck, scattered carelessly amid the wild brush-strokes of spilt blood.

The dark shape won free.

It rose from the swamp like a dark god, surrounded on all sides by the vast Melaut. What seemed to be massive quays, still intact, jutted out into the swamp.

The shattered city of Ciofran-Ac.

The legends do it justice.

It was massive. Set high on a rocky isle, the scale of it dwarfed anything in Kelas. As they approached, Raziin could see much of the Lost City of Temples lay under the swamp. Before the Destruction of Carris it had stood on a hill, above the Yasser and the fertile plains below. Now it stretched, league after league, stone and rubble, shattered columns and fallen idols.

Raziin motioned to the Captain, a hard-faced old pirate who had once been Dresil's mate.

'Can you take us into the quays?'

The Captain eyed the city carefully, rubbing his chin. 'Aye, if we take it right slow. We don't know what's under the swamp.'

Raziin would not be deterred by sunken rock. 'Take us in,' he said harshly. 'And if the ship comes to grief, you will be the first to suffer.'

The Captain nodded, his face grim as he gave orders for the galley to turn.

Raziin left the quarterdeck and walked to the bow, where he was joined by Merceth and Kyal.

As they approached the city, they left the old course of the Yasser and began to pass over the sunken ruins of the city itself.

Raziin felt an unease growing inside him. He had found the fabled Ciofran-Ac. Yet what could such a devastated ruin offer him that would defeat Hukum?

What he had thought were quays were actually massive causeways that had run from the city to the now vanished bank. The depth callers worked frantically and twice the ship had to stop to avoid jagged stone heaps that lay just below the surface. Once they passed so close to a ruined temple the broken columns could be heard scraping the hull.

The vision *must* speak truly, thought Raziin. *I must be alert for signs.*

The tumbled ruins were now an endless sea of broken, red-brown rock. As they drew near, they could see the structures had not just been shattered, they had been blasted with a massive heat and lay melted together like cheap glass in the camp fire. Twisted and frozen.

The scale of the destruction awed them to silence.

The oars rose and fell to the beat, a rhythmic creak and groan that transformed to the torment of lost souls, trapped around them in melted ruin.

As the galley drew closer to the rising island, they began to hear fragments of a distant song. At first they laughed, joking about the sirens of the swamp and the wind playing in the shattered hollowness of the great temples above, but the song did not fade like a fickle gust, it grew in strength. The sailors made signs against evil and whispered amongst themselves, some earning the whip as they faltered at the stroke.

When the galley could go no further, the distant song had become a wailing, an eerie screech that bordered on melody but seemed to fall short. . . or go well beyond. Amid the silence of the ruin, it was strangely out of place. It gave the sense they intruded here.

As Raziin looked around the city, he could see that no living thing had returned to claim it. No birds had made their home amid the high perches of the debris, not a single tree had taken root. Nothing.

Yet, that song. . .

It gripped him at the base of his neck, setting his teeth on-edge. Around him, the men's eyes were wide with fear. Not so Raziin. This strange cry. This must be it. Somehow *this* would lead him to his salvation.

'Merceth, you and Kyal guard the ship. Be wary, we don't know what lays around us here. I am entering the city.'

Raziin picked four of his warriors and ordered the crew to lower a longboat. He did not bother with provisions. What lay hidden in the city would reveal itself to him quickly, Raziin felt sure of that. It must. He had no time left. His blood-goddess, Uros, had been here ahead of him. She had opened the way.

Raziin and his warriors rowed through the Melaut to the jagged beach.

They leapt from the long-boat, landing lightly on a smooth surface like dark glass.

At once, Raziin led them deeper into the city. Even though he had no idea what he was looking for, he could feel the power behind that eerie wail, and it drew him onwards.

Moving over the rubble was hard going. Once wide streets and alleys were now only frozen tides of melted rock. They soon reached the high plain that had once been the centre of the city. Here, the destruction was less, and for the first time they could walk, rather than climb.

And the voice grew.

Soon it was throbbing and crashing around them like a turbulent sea. One of the warriors screamed and ran from it, fleeing from unseen terror. The others dropped their weapons and pressed hands against their ears. They could feel the stone beneath their feet and the walls around them vibrating. The wail seemed like a great animal, giving voice to a burden of power it could not contain.

Raziin pushed forward towards the source, vaguely aware of one of his warriors falling unconscious to the stone, blood trickling from his mouth and ears. Raziin screamed, but his voice was lost amid its power.

They turned from the alley, moving towards the source. Ahead was a wide, ruined plaza, its broad steps rose, flanking shattered fountains, and debris lay everywhere. He followed the sprawl of a ruined building that lay across the stone and saw it end in blankness. Intrigued, he staggered towards it, discovering an invisible wall of force dividing the ancient destruction like a neatly drawn line.

He moved towards the wall and saw the rest of the plaza, intact and shining ghostly with faced marble, beyond it. He reached forward to touch the barrier, shouting with pain as the sound's full force struck him. It was dark like night, smooth as a mirror, and he knew it. It was a Shield. A massive construction of Force that encapsulated the heart of Ciofran-Ac.

The Temples had survived.

Gathering what Fire he could, he hurled bolts of Force against it; then pure Fire, but the attacks were like pebbles against a mountain.

Raziin raged against the Shield. *'Do you hear me? I am Raziin Cinnor. Let me pass!'*

His ears, his whole face was blazing with pain, as though scores of red-hot needles had been thrust into him. His determination let him rise above the pain. He was close now. Close to his answer.

Two of his men were still with him. All were deafened by the force of the wail. Their bodies shook and vibrated with its force like rag dolls in a gust. With signs and shouts, he managed to make them understand that what he wanted lay beyond the half-glimpsed barrier. With hands clasped over their ears, they searched for an entrance.

* * *

Deep within the Citadel, Marina watched the three warriors in her viewing device. The chamber was dark, lit only by the wan light of the screen and the dim golden flicker of a lamp. Marina's hand touched the copper glowmetal lightly, channelling power. Streams of light shot towards clearglass lenses set cunningly to receive them. She watched the three swollen pieces of clearglass with detachment, without passion, as the song slowly destroyed the warriors.

A second figure, a dark, hooded shape, entered the room. The feeble, distilled light from the lenses played over his wide nose and heavy brow ridges, the dark skin, the not-quite human face. Son of a human slave and an Eathal craftsman, sterile and yet strong, he was a Minitil. The unlucky fruit of an unnatural union from which so many were stillborn, others surviving yet wishing they were dead. He was one of the lucky ones.

'The Northman has reached the outer boundary of the Earthsong,' he said in ancient Cioan.

Marina withdrew her hand.

Like a dying animal, the glowmetal shuddered and gave out its last, the light flickering to extinction. The room was now illuminated only by a single lamp-flame. She turned.

Her face was serene, ageless. Her slim form concealed by the fall of her blue cloak. In the soft light, her golden skin gleamed, the bronze hair shot with crimson. The servant cowered back, grateful for the darkness. He did not want to see those terrible red-gold eyes, those glistening irises that could overwhelm so easily.

'Breach the barrier. I want only the Northman. I am not concerned for the others.'

The servant raised his heavy, almost bald head, the broad shoulders shaking with fear. He was only too aware of her powers; of what she could inflict. Yet he would never have another opportunity to question her wisdom. Once the barrier was lowered. . .

'May I speak, Great One?' asked the Minitil.

Marina's gaze was upon him and he averted his eyes.

'Let him die, Great One. The Evil cannot be raised again, it must not be. We are in grave danger.' He felt her power growing, knew he could turn away no longer. Slowly, his head rose. Soon his gaze would fall into hers. He would be lost within the red-gold, dying in bliss.

'No. It must be done.' She turned from him. With a gasp, he dropped to the floor, relief and disappointment driving him close to tears.

'We lay cowering, dying through the centuries. The Evil will remain, regardless.' She began to pace, her delicate hands raised as though in struggle. 'It is growing even now – and we lay here impotent. It is coming to a second birth, rising with a will of its own.' Her gaze returned to the now empty clearglass lenses. 'Jykor was a fool.' The Minitil cowered before her. 'Only the Blood of the Three will end it forever.'

The servant rose, chastised.

'The Serpent must awaken, and no mortal man could resist it. Who better to be bound by its coils than another viper?'

'Raziin is perfect.'

'But in the Scion's hands. . .'

'Do not question me.'

The Minitil was silent.

'Go. Bring him to the Chamber of Shadows.'

Raziin hurled himself at the barrier. Blood trickled warmly from his ears and his body was in spasm, as though in the throes of some violent fever. He struck it and fell back once more. One of his warriors was kneeling near him, hands clasped to his ears, the other had fallen, eyes glazed and staring.

'Why do you torment me?' he screamed. 'I promised you rivers of blood and you shall have them.'

As if Uros had answered his call, an iris-shaped opening formed in the barrier. Through the gap, Raziin could see the ghost-plaza beyond bathed in dim twilight. Enthralled, he walked through, his warrior following. Behind them the opening closed and they were encased in total silence. Ears ringing, they walked forward as though granted a vision of paradise.

The plaza was wide and spacious. Even in the strange twilight, Raziin could see statues and fountains, the half-moon shape of an amphitheatre, and an ancient, stunted tree spreading limbs towards the light beyond the barrier. As they walked, the gloom around them deepened and they were soon in total blackness. Raziin called out to his remaining warrior, but half-dazed and deafened, they could not find each other in the pitch black.

He wandered on and the dark began to shift, weaving itself into his mind. He was stepping, moving between worlds, his substance dissolving, reforming.

'Raziin!'

The voice was stern and admonishing, all too familiar. He turned in anger to face his father.

'I killed you!' said Raziin.

Leith stood above him, as he had when Raziin was only a child and his father had seemed formidable, a giant. He pointed a huge finger at Raziin in accusation, his face looming large like a magistrate.

'Yes. You killed me. Yet I was not the first,' said Leith, pointing to where Raziin's childhood companion Lisis stood beside him in silent solidarity. Leith put a fatherly hand on Lisis' shoulder. Lisis looked at him sadly, pitying him.

Raziin turned, tried to run, but they were always before him.

'You killed us, but you were the one who died, Raziin. You died in your soul. You are a walking corpse.'

He screamed, but made no sound. A clawed, fluttering bird of fear came alive inside him, ripping into him. He was going to die! To die here and become nothing.

'You are nothing,' said Leith.

He reached out, but was suddenly alone. Nothing more than a point of awareness, suspended in infinite space. Time stretched, becoming an eternity.

Help me!

With intense shame he recognised his own need.

He wanted something. Somebody. Anything.

Don't let me feel. I do not want to feel.

Distantly, he heard the screams of his remaining warrior. A soul in torment, the sounds of terror. The cry stopped abruptly.

'Raziin?'

He turned again. His twin sister Razell stood in front of him. Her face thin and childlike as she acted out a scene they had played long ago, a scene in which he was now the observer.

'Raziin, what are you doing?'

He watched, cut off, detached, as her face filled with fear and the blows came, knocking her to the ground. Then unseen hands were tearing off her clothing. Her thin, pale face was frozen in shock as he watched himself rape her. Afterwards, she lay like a broken doll. He had laughed at her weakness.

She was always so weak. *I hated her.*

The image dissolved. He could feel his body again. He was whole. The twilight was returning. Half-glimpsed through the borders of the dark, he could see towers and columns, vast buildings, intact and rising majestic towards a canopy of unknown stars.

The haft of a greatscythe struck him in the solar plexus. Gasping, he doubled forward. Hands seized him, snapped a collar around his neck. He struggled, but they held him fast, dragging him into the foreign city. He worked one hand loose and struck a dark shape in the face, only to be struck behind the knees and savagely kicked to the ground.

His face was scored by gravel. He gasped, his ribs and back alive with pain.

Instinctively he reached for the Fire, ready to scatter these bastards, whoever they were. He drew greedily, ready to release it, yet immediately lost control. It turned on him, searing the nerves at the base of his neck like a hot torch, sending him into the dark.

When he rose to consciousness, he was being dragged through the thronging streets of a darkened city. Scores of people had gathered to watch.

His body, his head, throbbed. He drew in a breath, wincing as a sharp knife of pain lanced into his right side. A snapped rib.

'It's the Priestess' men,' said one.

'Looks like they are making for the Temple of Yos,' said another.

He lifted his eyes to see a great Temple above him.

In a daze, he looked around at the crowd. They were a mixture of human, Eathal and strange half-breeds, some hideously deformed. Was this another illusion? He looked down at the circlet tight around his throat. It was clearglass, filled with rare liquid glowmetal. It glistened silver and crimson, a heavy weight around his neck. Any Fire he drew would be returned by the glowmetal in equal proportions. This was real. This was happening.

He struggled to his feet and his captors let him walk. He saw occasional mixed couples, regarding him like he was a ghost or some kind of demon. They were afraid of him. *Good.* In the distance, flashes of blue lit the sky, followed by dull rolls of thunder. At first he thought a storm was coming, but the sky was clear and cloudless.

The architecture was vaguely reminiscent of Osellen and the other Cioan cities in Armon, the buildings supported with huge square slabs of quarried rock. There was not an arch in sight. Everything was built in rectangles, in the ancient style. He could see now that the buildings in Armon were only echoes of the originals.

This is Ciofran-Ac. He had done it! His heart quickened. He was close now, surely.

They began to climb towards the Temple, drawing closer to the lightning. In the regular flashes of brilliant blue, Raziin could see an extensive garden of twisted trees and lungii, flowering in luminescence. As they left the more populated parts of the city, Raziin saw men leading *teremb* on leashes, patrolling the dimly lit outskirts bordering the darkness.

The Great Temple was as tall as the walls of Raynor, the massive grey columns, monoliths formed into the shapes of the river-gods, towered above them. Roosting in the Temple's eves were scores of black shapes, engorged, their razor wings folded as they rested. Raziin eyed them with wariness and suspicion. Pets of the Priestess.

The lightning came like whip-cracks, striking from the clear sky into the Temple. Raziin eyed his captors as they led him up the sweeping steps to the Great Temple's entrance. Two were Eathal, three human, the leader was one of the half-breeds, a Minitil.

The Temple was a darkened maze of chambers and corridors where the Minitil seemed to have authority. He spoke to the guards and officials in an archaic form of Cioan from which Raziin could gather only a few words. They took him to a chamber in the centre of the Temple, open to the sky.

A bolt of lightning shot from the sky to the floor of the chamber. Involuntarily Raziin struggled back, awed by its power.

Raziin had a fleeting glimpse of fluted columns, equal in size to those that faced the city. Beneath them were gathered a crowd of hundreds, waiting silently, watching as he was dragged towards a vast depression in the floor. Within it, he could see lines of blue light, pulsing and shifting, a dull gleam of silver. . .

The lightning struck again; the jagged arc lancing into the biggest glowmetal Raziin had ever seen, the size of three wagons put together. Instinctively, he guessed this was the source of the voice, the power that fuelled the barrier. He was aware of the shapes of figures clustered around it, some winged and feathered; others spiders the size of harena. They regarded him through alien eyes.

His captors threw him to the floor before the glowmetal. He winced in pain and pushed himself to his knees. The flash came again and Raziin's stomach clenched in anxiety. That thing was powerful! He looked up towards his captors. They stared back at him, eager to do their work. He knew that if he tried to move he would be dealt with harshly. He steeled himself to remain still and looked around him. He saw a birdlike face, peering at him from the congregation around the glowmetal. He recognised it from the ancient drawings in the Temple in Osellen. It was a Verial. The huge, spider-like form was that of a Tahistill, the beings that inhabited the sprawling Gimpessu jungle to the south.

'Vermin,' said the Verial, his wings quivering with distaste.

He glared back at his captors, his eyes slowly adjusting to the soft blue light given off by the glowmetal. Another bolt of lightning shot down out of the sky into the glowmetal. He flinched back and was immediately knocked flat by a blow to the back of the head. The pain flared like a small sun, paralysing him. Slowly he regained control.

'I am Raziin Cinnor, I demand to be heard!'

Those around the glowmetal laughed. The melodic tones of the Verial joined by human and Eathal laughter and the dry rasping of the Tahistill.

'He is filth,' said a Cioan man, dressed like a Druid of Yosini.

'We all viewed his mind,' said an ancient thel, her skin wrinkled like dry leather. 'He is possessed of the greatest foulness.'

'Marina should have let him be consumed by the Earthsong,' said the Verial with irritation. 'He is contamination here in this last bastion!'

Raziin heard murmurs of agreement and feared for his life, yet discerned he had an ally in this Marina, whoever or whatever Marina was.

His captors returned with heavy chains of mought and proceeded to bind him hand and foot. The room had subsided into silence, the dark and quiet broken only by the sharp, irregular crack of lightning strikes. As he was hauled to his knees, he sensed they were waiting for somebody. He did not have to wait long.

A long sonorous note sounded through the expanse from an unseen trumpeter. He did not see anyone approach, but heard the sounds of hundreds falling face-forward to the marble in obeisance. Even the congregation around the glowmetal were cowed, most on their knees, some in prostration. All looking to the floor.

He stood, the chains rattling as he struggled up. As he looked around, he could dimly see his captors face down, not daring to move. Who was it that inspired such fear?

A shaft of lightning pierced the gloom with another whip-crack and Raziin saw a single woman approaching over the darkened mural of the floor. *A single woman.*

His laughter echoed in the dark.

These fools, if I were not collared, I would shake this Great Temple to its foundations. Raziin felt the realisation of his dreams only a hand's breadth away. The lightning struck again. She was only a pace away. Close enough for him to see her eyes.

Marina stood before him. Watching calmly as his arrogance dissolved.

He tried to gauge her appearance, fix a picture of her in his mind, but beyond the bronze hair and golden skin all he could see were her eyes. He matched her gaze, determined to stare her down. It was as though he had fallen into a sea, a vast red-gold sea.

He was a point of insignificance beside the vastness of the power in which he was lost, a shadow of nothing. She was the incandescent flame that lit the universe, filling him with light and life, aching need. Still lost, he fell to his knees. His vision vanished, replaced by a blinding vibrancy, a frightening force of life that threatened to destroy him as easily as a snowflake on the spring ground. It was melting his being, destroying him as surely as he stood living within his own pyre, yet its magnetism could not be denied. Blind, lost, he struggled across the marble towards Marina like a newborn baby, whimpering, crying. Pity touched the corners of her eyes and she turned away.

As though a barbed spear had been withdrawn from his heart, he gave voice to an agonising scream.

His body shook, his head throbbed as though he had been drugged, but his vision cleared. Beneath it, all was emptiness, such an emptiness he had never felt before. An aching void within where something should have been, something he had lost. He curled himself into a ball, praying to Uros to take away his weakness.

Marina signalled to her men and he was stripped naked. Lacking clothes and dignity, he lay face down in the dusty stone at her feet, still whimpering.

'I cannot lead you from the darkness you have chosen,' she said. 'Or your corruption. Your thirst for power. . .'

Raziin got control of himself. Holding his fists tightly, he suppressed his feelings. Slowly the cold, dark emptiness and cool rationality returned. He could feel his strength, the Fire that lay beyond his reach. He would kill if he could, but he faced more power than he could hope to challenge. This woman, this Priestess, was filled with Earth-Essence and Fire. An Enchantress.

Marina turned. 'You are the Traitor of Armon?' She looked at Raziin.

He began to tremble, his strength failing. The cool darkness within could not resist her. His head began to rise, seeking her eyes, seeking the flame once more. He could not fight it. His awareness of the emptiness was sharpening.

'No, please. Anything,' he heard himself whimper.

She turned from him and he eagerly embraced the numb darkness. *Darkness was strength. To feel is weakness.* He must state his case quickly, before she destroyed him.

'Please, let me speak. Spare me.'

'Speak.'

'I seek to sever the Bridge. To be free of the bonds my Master has placed on me.'

Contemptuous laughter rose around the room and Raziin realised he was naked, grovelling before her like a worm.

He struggled to his feet. 'I am a Suul of the Old Blood, not a slave to abase myself here before you!'

The shadowed audience laughed anew, as though a fresh joke had been made.

'Silence,' said Marina softly. Immediately the sound ceased. Sensing her near, he fell back to the floor.

'Only Hukum's death will sever the Bridge, Northman.'

'But I must. . .'

'I know what you seek. Escape from your own destruction. I cannot destroy Hukum from Ciofran-Ac, we lay a world away. Yet there is a way to cheat your fate.

'The Bridge cannot be severed but it can be blocked.'

The Priestess motioned. From the shadows, her Minitil servant came forward, on his knees, to hand her a pendant and chain.

'This is what you seek,' she said, her manner severe as she held it out to him.

Raziin dared to lift his eyes, enough to glimpse what she held. It was a small, golden glowmetal, traced with violet light and set into quartz by a trick of nature. He saw Hukum's defeat in his mind's eye. Saw the blade fall, the blood spurt. . .

'I will bring you gems and coin, precious glowmetals, the heads of your enemies, anything.'

'I want nothing from Yos,' she said.

Raziin gasped as though he had been hit in the stomach. The force of her words had a physical presence of their own. Breathing fast with the anticipation of victory and sensing Marina was going to free him, he pushed on. 'How can I pay?'

Marina laughed. The sound chilled him. 'You will pay. First and last, you will pay. First with Blood, then with blood.'

Raziin was confused. His blood. Did she mean to kill him after all?

Marina clapped her hands and the room began to clear. Raziin could sense something about to happen between them. He began to rise but strong arms pushed him down.

Marina began to undress.

'It has been long centuries since one of the Blood walked Ciofran-Ac, even one whose line is as tainted as yours. Those who were with me originally are dust, long gone. Memories in the shadows. I am the only one left.'

Marina stood naked. Her body was supple yet strong, the breasts small and high, her hips shapely. Even though she stood revealed, none who remained dared to raise their eyes towards her.

'You cannot mean. . .'

'I have lived since the fall of Ciofran-Ac,' she said.

He could feel her presence like warm radiance and, despite himself, was drawn to her, his whole body responding.

'I was the only Priestess of Yos to survive. There were others, Sorcerers, but my arts could not keep them from death forever. Even I must fail. There shall be another after me. Another of my Blood and your Blood.'

His gaze was drawn to her, he had only moments before he was lost once more. 'Why are you helping me?'

'I have seen your death, it is not at the hands of Hukum. You have a destiny, cousin, and I will speed you to it.'

Raziin may have rejoiced to hear those words from another seer, but from her they were a prophecy of doom.

She reached out a slim hand and touched his shoulder, breaking his last resolve. He looked up, hoping to catch a glimpse of her face before he was claimed and engulfed by her, but the eyes were all he saw. Crimson irises, shot with flecks of gold. They were fixed for that one instant before they began to expand.

Beneath him, the cold stone leached away the heat from his back. The chain bit into him, his broken rib stabbing pain into his side as she began to ride him with an almost violent fury.

His thoughts were swept away on a tide of ecstasy.

He could see nothing. He was consumed, lost within the flame of her essence.

He reached up, hearing the chains move beside him, seeking to touch her skin, her breasts, but her power flared over him, pinning him to the stone. He tried to cry out, but the breath was taken from him. It was though he was being crushed beneath a great weight. He could feel the warmth of her thighs across him; the hot pleasure of their coupling, the feeling of her wetness. Despite the pain and exhaustion of his Heat-ravaged body, her essence stoked the fire of his lust higher and higher, until finally – immobile and helpless – he released himself, shuddering as for a few moments more, she rode on.

Then it was over. She was gone, and darkness claimed him.

When he woke, he lay in soft cushions. The chains were gone, but the circlet of liquid glowmetal remained. He was dressed in his harness and leathers, his memories of the dark hall like a dream. Beneath the collar lay the golden glowmetal pendant, a heavy and welcome weight. He was in a small, private chamber, lit with lamps and decorated simply with hung paintings and tapestries. The faint smell of incense lingered.

He sat forward on the cushions. His body was drained and weak, muscles stiff and sore, as though he had slept for a month. It was agony to move but he forced himself to work life into his limbs. He thought he was alone until Marina stepped from the shadows. Hastily, he covered his eyes.

'Look at me,' she said.

Raziin watched as she came into the light. She was a beautiful woman. Her face fine, her skin gold. Her bronze hair was braided and fell across her right shoulder, ending at her waist. Her power slumbered.

As striking as she was, her mouth was set hard, as though she had an unpleasant duty to perform.

'You will return to Yos and seek the Power.'

'The Power?' he asked.

Her eyes flared and he was held transfixed, like a speared fish. She had tricked him! Her words took on a compelling weight, resonating within him as though he stood inside a huge bell.

'You are destined to hold the Power. You must seek it.'

Visions filled his head. Indistinct at first, they began to resolve. He could see the Realm of Fire and, within his hand, he held the key to it, a golden shape. Metal, forged by the hands of men. An artefact so powerful it could unleash the Fire's fury without limit. Ultimate power for the hand that held it. The vision faded and Marina stood before him once more.

She touched his forehead.

A spinning shot of power entered his head. Like a white-hot branding rod, it forced its way into his mind, to expand like a hot flower. It was the Final Matrix. *She has given me the Final Matrix.* With it, he was defenceless no longer. He was free to match wills with another Sorcerer, and to dominate and destroy the minds of ordinary men.

'You must seek the Power,' she said again.

Remembering the first vision, he sat forward eagerly. 'How?'

'The calvanni, Cedrin. He holds the key to the Power.'

Raziin grunted. Yes, the half-Blood. He will perish quickly now. With the Final Matrix he could reduce him to a quivering simpleton. He could make him a slave, as Hukum had made him a slave.

'He will stand within the plaza of Cinanac in Olcis at the feast of the Asic's Blessing.' Her eyes blazed. 'You must stand with him in the Temple. You must reach first for the Power. Do you understand?'

'Yes,' he whispered, once more lost within her eyes.

He held the visions of power like tokens as he fell towards darkness.

* * *

The sound was deafening and Raziin ran from it, dazed, hardly aware of his surroundings. When he reached the lava and rubble-filled streets on the edges of the upper city, he slowed, reaching for his neck. The circlet that restrained his Sorcery was gone. In its place was the pendant. He opened his mind and saw the Barrier he had held for days was not in place, yet the Compulsion Hukum was sending towards him was blocked. Its power was being consumed by the glowmetal pendant around his neck.

Victory!

With the golden glowmetal around his neck he was invulnerable to the Compulsion. It absorbed and ate the energies as though starved, the violet light shimmering. Slowly it began to give voice, like a smaller parody of the wail that cried from the centre of the ruined city. The glowmetal was transforming the Compulsion's energy into sound, incoherent screeches and moans. For Raziin, they were the sounds of freedom.

He would travel to The Shattered Temple, fulfil the first part of the Compulsion – which was already in place in his mind – then he would have a surprise for those who waited.

They would be the first to give their blood to Uros.

* * *

Marina watched Raziin stumble through the ancient capital's streets towards his galley. She could feel his seed growing within her and knew it would be a girl. *Yosini be praised.* Another Priestess. One of the Old Blood, the Blood of Cinnor.

As Raziin left the range of her screen, she fell to her knees in prayer.

'Yosini. Hidden Sun. Mystery. You lend your heat to everyone, even in the greatest dark. Let the visions speak truly.'

After a silent moment of doubt, she stood and turned from the darkened screen.

'The Evil rises.'

Chapter Twenty

There! She had him.

Cedrin was in the city, not two leagues distant. Ellen concentrated, focusing on the image. Through her Sorcerous connection with the silver glowmetal in her hands, the Seeker, she could see crowds, markets. . . The tiny glowmetal she had implanted in Belin's ring was working perfectly.

She held the Seeker between her two hands, the glass sphere that encased it cool to her touch. By using a simple Matrix she could see the light falling into its smaller twin, now hanging around Cedrin's neck. It was very useful, yet it had one drawback. Although it would always tell her his location, it could only transmit images: not sound, smell, nor any of the other senses. If he wore it in pitch black – or if it was covered by other cloth – she would see nothing. Now with the suns high in the clear sky, conditions were ideal.

So, Cedrin had come to Raynor.

Perhaps he had changed his mind? Maybe now the rebellious calvanni would come to her. With the Scion declared, they could work together to fulfil her father's quest. Larus knew, she needed an ally. She had tried to convince Estle, but after hours of exasperating conversation he had become openly hostile. He refused to support her quest, or make any formal overtures towards Osterac.

In the matter of the Scion, she was on her own.

She had risen early, eager for the day. It had taken scarcely an hour to complete the pressing diplomatic work, leaving her bored, and with no way of progressing her quest.

She had tried to gain an audience with Osterac, but the Druids were scrupulous about those who met with him. Although there was no edict from Olcis against her, her reputation had preceded her. The Hesguit's officials refused even to take her applications.

Even though she was Suulvey, and reputedly a Sorceress, she had discovered that here she was a minor token on the political board. Her rank within the court of Raynor was honorary, not actual.

There was a knock at the door. Ellen hastily hid the glowmetal. Her connection to Cedrin broke, the images fading from her mind.

'Here is the green dress, my Lady.'

She had forgotten the time. The dinner with Uran was scarcely an hour away.

'Thank you.'

Once her maid had gone, she hid the Seeker.

She critically examined the dress: a severe yet practical gown of light green that would highlight her eyes. Uran was a powerful man, and one to cultivate as an ally – yet she did not want anything too provocative. She was no unmarried daughter for sale.

She dressed quickly and walked to a private, glass-enclosed balcony that overlooked the inner courtyards of the palace.

Ellen saw this meeting with Uran as a chance to find out where he stood regarding Osterac. If he really was the Scion, she was bound by her promise to her father to support his claim. To do that she needed allies.

This dinner was more than just a casual affair. Uran had no wife. She had no intention of marrying him, yet how was he to know that? She had unwittingly begun to play the game, yet what choice had she? Her minor diplomatic role aside, she was essentially a powerless exile.

With longing, she looked past the palace walls. The suns were setting beyond the intervening restriction of stone and she looked down eagerly into the crowds surrounding the palastrada, looking for the tall, rough-cut calvanni and his Cioan friend. He was there. Somewhere. Should she send Mendor to find him? To repeat her offer?

'Damn it!' She slammed her palm into the rail, surprised by her own anger. Her father's quest to find the Scion – and Cedrin – was the only thing she had left, and yet there were nothing but obstacles in her way. First Cedrin refused her offer, then, with the Scion himself in Raynor, she could not reach him. Worse – all her allies refused to join her cause.

She re-entered the apartment, frustration boiling inside her. Without thinking, she reached for her scythe. She gave it a test swing, then began to move through one of the forms her weaponmaster had taught her. She began to work faster, one form flowing into another, joined with powerful whirls and strikes.

There was another knock at the door. Ellen paused, panting. She was covered in sweat, her fine gown dishevelled and slightly twisted on her supple body, her face flushed with exertion.

'What is it?'

Her maid entered, startled as she saw Ellen with the weapon. Her hand moved to her mouth as though to stifle her surprise.

'A messenger has arrived from Uran. He says if you are. . . ready, he will receive you now.'

Ellen put aside the scythe and straightened her gown. It was useless now. 'Run a bath. Quickly.'

The maid withdrew, her face despairing. Ellen felt a pang of guilt. Why was she so hard on her maids? They should not bear the brunt of her frustration. She thought it was because they were a little too eager for her to embrace the games of Raynor. A little too enthralled by the whispered intrigues and gossip.

She stripped off the gown, standing naked before a mirror as she waited for the maid to fetch her robe, looking critically at her white skin and less than ample bust. She turned from the mirror, covering her breasts with crossed arms.

She missed her father. The shallow pleasures of life as Suulqua had vanished to leave her nothing, no one. She was alone, clinging to her father's quest as though it were the only thing in her life. Was it?

She broke from her thoughts at the sound of the door

opening. The maid placed the robe around her shoulders and led her to the bath.

Dressed in another green gown, slightly less severe, the bodice low, she followed Uran's messenger through the endless corridors to the Eastern Tower. She had expected the messenger to be Nacius, but it was a silent Anacian, dressed in plain robes. He introduced himself as Medis. Ellen was content to follow, lost in her own thoughts. In her hand was a padded leather sack containing the glowmetal the Templeman had attacked her with. She intended it as a gift for Uran and hoped it would win her some favour.

Ellen was surprised at how heavily guarded the Eastern Tower was. By the time they arrived at Uran's apartments, they had passed scores of elite palace guards armed with greatscythes. Other stern men were dressed like Medis, some with the hollow sun-symbol of Yosini around their necks. At the guarded entrance, Medis bowed and left her to Uran's servants.

Once inside, she was impressed by the luxury Uran lived in, no doubt inherited from a deposed Suulvey. Raynor had for centuries been the centre of the world and, even though it had declined, that wealth remained. Statues and ornaments carved from precious gems and horn lined the walls and floor, carefully set against tapestries and rugs.

Ellen was examining the pieces when Uran's First Consort entered the room. She was a Cioan, the faded Suul mark showing her to be one who fled the Eathal invasion of Althar, one lucky enough to find a place in Raynor.

'Suul Cintros,' she said, bowing low.

Uran had obviously told her to impress. She was dressed in a shimmering robe of worked gold and red that hugged tight to her body and swept behind her, leaving the shoulders bare.

'Welcome to my house,' she said with genuine warmness. 'I am Ersta.' Her hair was a light honey-gold, her eyes so deeply red they were almost black.

Behind her, framed in the doorway, were two small, golden heads, eyes peeping. Ersta turned and spoke rapidly in Cioan dialect, too quickly for Ellen to catch the meaning. They disappeared.

'Please,' she said pleasantly, beckoning her to follow.

'Thank you,' said Ellen, entering the main apartments through a set of heavy curtains.

The style of furnishing was undoubtedly Cioan. Uran had no shame about his origins. Through the curtains they entered a wide, simply decorated chamber. Cushioned steps descended to a central table.

Uran rose from his pipe, exhaling a breath of pungent se-tobacco. 'Ah, Ellen.'

He greeted her formally, with a bow, then kissed her hand. He was richly dressed in trousers of heavy linen, patterned and set with diamonds of coloured glass. His chest was bare, the torso lacking in tone and decorated by only two tattoos; his totem tattoo, a finely crafted spiral, and a smaller insignia of the court, a small diamond decorated with precise scrollwork.

Ersta waited until the greeting was completed then came forward to give Ellen a sister's kiss, on the cheek. Her eyes were warm but sad, the meaning was obvious. Whatever union Ellen and Uran wanted, Ellen had the First Consort's blessing. She blushed as Ersta withdrew, wondering awkwardly if she should bare her breasts as she would for family.

'Sit, please,' said Uran.

'I brought something for you,' said Ellen, offering him the leather sack.

Uran took it with interest, drawing out the strange white glowmetal. Bands of red and orange light wound themselves through it.

'Excellent! Estle had told me of it. The Blocker. I had heard rumours the Athrian Temple possessed it. They will be furious at the loss.'

He looked up towards her and nodded his thanks. 'I will study it with interest. Thank you.'

He dropped it back into the sack and put it casually aside.

Disappointed at his reaction, and wondering if she should have kept the powerful artefact, Ellen lowered herself to the cushioned steps.

Uran poured them wine. His hair was braided tightly away from his face in the style of a warrior and Ellen noted for the first time his eyes were silver, not pale, but bright and glistening. His face was rounded from good living, but retained the high cheek bones and square chin of his race.

'I was sorry to hear about your father, Ellen.'

She paused, her hand on the wine glass, unsure how to respond.

'He was a fine leader, a friend to Raynor and a powerful Sorcerer. He will be sorely missed in the fight ahead, I can assure you. On the other hand,' said Uran, eyeing Ellen and taking a generous mouthful of wine. 'We had no idea his daughter was so . . . talented.'

Ellen raised the glass to her lips, her heart beating rapidly. How much should she reveal? With studied slowness she lowered the glass, surprised to see she had taken a mouthful in the excitement. She always pretended to drink, but she never actually drank. It was good wine. Deep, rich and red, not too sweet.

'Thank you, Uran.'

This intimacy seemed odd to her. He was a stranger, after all. But things might be different here in Raynor.

Dinner was served and, throughout the many courses, they passed formal pleasantries between them, as though they were at a state dinner. When the last plates were taken away, Uran looked at her for a long while before speaking. Ellen was becoming uncomfortable. What was he after? What did he want?

'I understand you fought Raziin in the attack on Regent's hill.'

'Yes,' said Ellen warily. 'The battle was pitched.' She reached for the wine glass, raising it to her lips to hide her thoughts, taking another sip. Just a little wine, she thought, to calm her nerves.

'A battle of Sorcery.'

Ellen replaced the wine glass on the table, surprised to see it was empty again, and laughed lightly, waving her hand as though to pass off Uran's probe. He refilled her glass.

'Groundless rumours, of course. Sorcery is myth,' said Ellen, trying to seem casual.

Uran laughed with so much gusto Ellen became embarrassed with her guarded responses.

'Ellen, this is not the backwoods of Athria, this is Raynor. I do not have a Templeman lurking in the next room, scribbling down the damning words. Not even the Hesguit's edict would carry weight within these walls.'

Ellen was abashed. *The backwoods indeed!*

Uran reached across the table and took her hands affectionately. 'Ellen. I want no barriers between us, we are too few.'

He withdrew his hand and became stern, his face taking on an expression of studied concentration. Ellen thought he had grown angry, until she began to feel the familiar tug of the Fire. He was opening the Window, drawing the substance of Fire into himself. Uran formed a Matrix to shape the flow. Fragments of light began to form, like pieces of glass floating in oil, each holding an image of what lay behind it. Gradually they coalesced and Uran vanished from sight behind the Matrix of Shadows.

Ellen, giddy with wine, watched in wonder. It had been so long since she had shared this secret part of herself. With a sensual sigh she filled herself with Fire, forming a small bulb of light in the air before her, at the apex of a hidden geometry. She began to subtly change the delicate Matrix, twisting and reforming it like a play-thing.

Uran let the Shadow Matrix fall away, the shards splintering and flying into nothing, insubstantial mirrors of sugar-glass dissolving as they spun. He watched with amazement as Ellen sent the bulb spinning and soaring around the room, sweeping through precise arcs, cascading through the spectrum as it went.

Uran clapped his hands with appreciation, laughing. Ellen had become so absorbed in her task the sound startled her. She broke her concentration and the ball paused in mid-air, rapidly expanding like a spent sun to explode with a green-white flash.

'Oh!' said Ellen, in a startled exclamation.

They laughed together, drinking more wine. Ellen drank freely now, relaxed for the first time since her father's death. It felt good to laugh, felt good to let this secret part of herself free.

Yet even as she proffered her glass for more wine, she heard her father cautioning her. *Never be free with Sorcery, keep it close to you. Only in desperation reveal it.*

Uran took the bottle and moved around the table to sit next to her. 'I heard rumours, but I could not know for sure. You don't know what this means to me, Ellen.' He placed the bottle on the table and took her hands lightly. 'Shall we drop the formality between us?'

Ellen tilted her head. Why should she be so formal at this intimate dinner? Feeling like a young girl revealing her breasts for the first time, she opened her gown to the waist. It was the custom on Yos that chests are bare between close friends and family.

For men, it served an even more practical function. Chests revealed, men knew each other's history as surely as if they had read a book. Each tattoo had meaning. A covered chest was a sign of deceit or shame among warriors. For women, it was a chance to show their womanhood. Only girls covered their chests, as a sign of mysteries yet to be revealed both to themselves and others.

Uran was a gentleman and his eyes did not touch the slight swell of her breasts, the delicate pink of her nipples, except in fleeting appreciation. A woman would be insulted if she were ignored completely. His arm reached between the loose fabric of the gown and her skin to encircle her waist.

She looked up demurely to meet his gaze and her head swam with wine and excitement. One of the most powerful men in Kelas, touching her like a lover.

Uran took her gently into an embrace, his chest hot against her breasts as they kissed. First slowly, then with increasing passion. She was breathless as Uran broke away, his hands lingering on her waist, awakening her desire.

'The Temple's Purge has taken so many of us,' said Uran.

Suddenly, too conscious of his presence and aware the wine was leading her down the path of abandon, she pushed him gently away. A Sarlord's daughter was taught never to let desire rule. Her head swimming, she wondered how she had come to drink so much.

Uran became animated. Taking a newly opened bottle of wine, left by an unobtrusive servant, he climbed to his feet.

'I have something to show you,' he said, taking a gulp from the bottle. His capacity for wine was clearly enormous. 'Come,' he said with a conspiratorial manner, taking her hand to help her to her feet.

Uran led her from the room, along a silent corridor. Ellen was wary, but relaxed as they entered his private study.

The walls were lined with books and scrolls placed carefully in shelves and pigeon holes. She was drawn by the books, they had been her life up until now, and examined the titles with interest. Military, botanical, ancient poetry, the subjects were diverse, most were in Cioan but some were also written in Anacian. The range of titles was extensive, yet the shelves were without anything pertaining to Sorcery or magic. This piqued her curiosity.

Uran produced two black robes, handing one to Ellen. 'You will need this.'

Ellen put on the robe, the wine warming her, her bodice still open. It was Uran's robe and it billowed around her like sailcloth.

He turned to watch her gather up the draping folds and they laughed.

A section of wall opened to reveal a dark corridor. Uran seized a lamp and led them from his study into the cool darkness beyond. The whole affair had taken on the atmosphere of adventure and Ellen looked around eagerly as they made their way through the dark, Uran's arm around her.

They climbed a set of steep, spiralling stairs, Uran saving her from falling as she tripped on the oversized robe – an occasion for more laughter. It seemed they had climbed for hours when, finally, they left the passages through a small door, entering a vast domed chamber. The floor was a detailed mosaic, only partially revealed in the flickering light of the torches on the curving wall. As Uran led them across the space, Ellen traced the familiar form of the mosaic. A pentagon, five parts, each reflecting the other, and in the centre. . .the Iris. Ellen stopped, looking at the depression in the floor where the Iris was depicted.

'A Temple of the Iris,' she said, incredulous.

'Yes, one of the Five Faces. But look at the rupture through it. We are trying to repair it, but it's a life's work in itself. The Opening Matrix has been lost for years. With that and enough power – perhaps it would be useable. Otherwise it's useless.'

Five Temples of the Iris? Looking closer at the floor in the dim light, Ellen could see a great force had hit the centre in massive concussion. Cracks and lines ran throughout the pattern of the mosaic and it looked lifeless and dull compared to the one in Athria. Ellen wanted to tell Uran so much. About the Scion, about the Temple of the Iris she had found beneath the Cintros mansion; but he tugged her along with him, across the floor towards another series of rooms, which were lit by the yellow brilliance of a small glowmetal. It had to be Fate, she thought, a Temple of the Iris, here in Raynor, and the Scion. She was elated. The fulfilment of her father's wishes seemed so close now.

Ellen looked around the room, astounded by the collection of glowmetals that littered the floor in myriad shape and colour, and the precious books on magic that lay in haphazard stacks, some of which she had never seen before. *On combination of Realms. Matrix of Transformation.* Here again, the precious light of knowledge had been preserved.

Uran turned, the light of personal vision burning in his eyes. 'We are rebuilding the ancient knowledge, birthing a new age. There are four of the Old Blood training under me. You have already met young Nacius.' He approached her, touching her shoulders with his hands as though to overwhelm her with his intensity. 'Two could already match the Sorcerer Lords of Maht. Soon our Druidin will match the Temple's power.'

'Druidin?' Ellen had never heard the word before.

'Yes, Druidin. For too long the arts of the Druids have been kept secret by the Temple. We are training workers of the Essence who have no link to religion, skilled and powerful men with an allegiance only to Raynor.'

'No link to religion?' asked Ellen, astounded by the idea. 'Many follow the way of Yosini, but they are no more than craftsmen of magic. We leave the religion to the Priests and

Priestesses. That is why the Temple is so desperate to put a stranglehold on us, we intend to destroy the power of Olcis over Kelas. Soon we shall cast them out of the Yasser States like the fakes and power-mongers they are.'

'But what of the Religion of the Sisters?'

Uran's eyes lit up. 'The way of Yosini, the Hidden Sun, allows you to worship any gods, or none. It is the pursuit of Enlightenment. We will absorb the Temple of the Sisters and take a great weight off the backs of the people.'

Ellen was caught up in the excitement of the vision and walked with him as he turned to examine the diagram of a Matrix on a low table. Something Ellen had never seen before. *A new Matrix!* He turned back to her.

'We are rebuilding the strength of Raynor, the power of the old Bulvuran. When the time is right, Daran will take the throne as Emperor.'

Ellen was suddenly brought back to cold reality.

Daran take the throne? The people of Kelas had long expected it, yet what of the Scion? Uran spoke as though Osterac did not exist. The pleasant glow of the wine was fading to a dull ache in her temples. Uran stepped forward and slipped his hands through the robe, seeking her soft waist. His eyes were inflamed, his breath strong with wine.

'You could share in that power. Together we could form a strong alliance of Blood, a marriage of power. Our children would be the inheritors of Bulvuran's greatness. Sorcerers.'

Ellen pushed away from him, conscious of her open bodice and the fevered touch of his hand on her skin. She tightened the robe around her.

'My apologies,' said Uran. 'You are so desirable. In so many ways.'

Ellen blushed as he looked her up and down. The wine had finally had its way with him, and men were dangerous in this mood of unrestrained desire.

'What of the Scion?' she asked a little too abruptly, buttoning her bodice, seeking to put some distance between them.

Uran laughed as though Ellen had made a great joke. He placed a hand on her cheek, as though she were a child to be pacified. She stepped back from his reach, coldly.

'Why do you laugh?' she said.

Uran was sobering, but was still humoured by Ellen's question. 'You mean Osterac?' He gave a short laugh. 'Ellen, he is not the Scion, he is an Olcis puppet. We will soon have him dancing a different tune.'

Ellen's heart sank. What if it were true? What if he was not the Scion but some pretender? Where did that leave her? Until now, she had not realised how much she had counted on Osterac being the Cinanac heir, an easy release from the quest her father had set her. Her doubts began to grow, but she would not surrender to Uran easily.

'The declaration . . .what if he is the Scion?'

Uran responded patiently, as though explaining to a child. 'The Scion is a myth. Do you seriously think the Warlord would give up his power? He held Raynor against the Eathal, held it together when the Empire's own provinces rebelled, waiting to see if the walls would fall, careless of the people of the Yasser valley and the refugees from the Eathal advance who sheltered here.

'We are rebuilding power, regaining knowledge. You can be part of it or not, as you choose. But do you think for one minute we would give away all we worked a lifetime to achieve?'

Ellen held her arms crossed in front of her. How could she have been so naive? Estle had warned her Uran was the Warlord's man. Facing each other in the stark brightness of the glowmetal, the last effects of the wine left them. Ellen remembered their intimacy with a sick feeling of violation. She was not even sure she liked him. It was dangerous to press him further, but Uran had trodden on stony ground when he attacked the Scion. Like it or not, her father's dying will had made her the Scion's champion.

'What if the Scion lives? What if Osterac *is* the Cinanac heir? If not him, another?'

The last traces of humour had left Uran. He faced Ellen with cold calculation, realising for the first time where her sympathies lay.

'There is no heir,' he said, his voice cold. 'Belin Kaidell

escaped through the Iris with the child, but they both died, of
this I am certain. It has been twenty-eight years. Belin would
have shown his hand by now. The Scion would have come.'

Uran folded the Matrix design on the table with finality, as
though he did not want Ellen to see it. Once more he met her
gaze. 'They died. He, the Eathal shapechanger Gesil, and the
newborn. They were in the Iris together when it collapsed. The
explosion would have destroyed a drakon, you yourself saw the
damage. They are dead, Ellen.'

The finality and certainty of Uran's words cut her deeply.
Could it be true? Myan's dream, now her dream, nothing but an
illusion?

'What of the prophecies of return?'

'There have been a hundred prophecies. Rantings of old
women. There have been a hundred false-Scions. In the
beginning we investigated them, but in time we accepted the
truth.

'The people want a saviour, but the Cinanac line is finished.
The Scion is dead.' Uran watched her carefully. 'It is an easy
dream for those who were dispossessed when the Empire fell,
but it is a false dream.'

He took her lightly by the shoulders, speaking to her, at least,
like an equal. 'Ellen, you do not have to follow fancies. Join with
me as wife. You will have Suul rank in Raynor and together we
could create a new line of Old Blood.'

Ellen turned away. It was clear to her now. His desire had
not been for her, but for the part she would play in his vision of
the future, in the rebirth of Raynor's power. But was it not *his*
power that had excited her?

'I shall consider it, Uran,' she said.

'That is all I ask, Ellen.'

They regarded each other through the cold dregs of the
night. Now they were two Suul contemplating a business deal.

'The night is ended, Uran,' said Ellen, trying desperately to
stifle her disappointment. She had hoped to use his influence to
support Osterac. That was clearly impossible. Estle had been
right.

Back within the warmer confines of Uran's apartments, Ellen

straightened her dress, embarrassed she had revealed herself to this total stranger. Uran withdrew and Ersta led her out of the apartments.

'You honour us,' said the Consort, as Ellen stood at the doorway to the apartment waiting impatiently for a servant to guide her back to her rooms.

'The honour was mine,' said Ellen unconvincingly.

Ersta could see something had gone wrong with the night and was eager to soothe Ellen. 'He is not a bad man, Lady Cintros. He can be cruel, but only through forgetfulness. In his heart, he is kind.'

Ellen felt a kinship with Ersta and sensed the two of them could become friends.

'I was his slave for years. He did not have to, but he gave me freedom. Now I have control of his household and I am proud to be his Consort,' she said, raising her chin with unconscious nobility. 'The mother of Suul.'

Ellen's anger and disappointment had eased. She was intrigued by Ersta. 'You were born a Suul. How did you become a slave?'

Ersta's face took on a wistful look. 'My family was from Althar, my father a Suul lord. He remained to fight while the rest of us fled to Athria. We were attacked by pirates on the Sea of Mists.' Her face grew hard as she remembered the distant horror. 'My mother and brothers were killed, my sisters and I enslaved and sold in Raynor. I don't know what became of my sisters.

'I had been a slave for ten years when Uran saw me in the slave market in Raynor. He is intrigued by his heritage, you know. We are all Cioan in this house, rebuilding what was lost.'

Ellen kissed Ersta on the cheek. It was time to leave. 'Farewell, sister.'

Ersta was overjoyed she had lightened Ellen's mood. She drew an embroidered handkerchief from her waistband and gave it to Ellen in a spontaneous gesture. 'Here,' she said. 'To mark our meeting.'

'Thank you.'

As the young servant led her through the corridors, Ellen

examined the handkerchief. It was finely done, the hand, neat and precise, showed a crest. Three golden towers on a background of yellow and blue. She did not recognise the crest, but would treasure the gift.

As they passed the guards, Ellen recognised the silent robed men for what they were, Uran's Druidin. She was wary of them, uncomfortable with Druids since the events in Athria and, as she walked by, she could not help but wonder what Matrices she would use to defeat them. They, in turn, watched as she passed, clearly aware of whom and what she was, prepared to deal with her. What was Uran hiding in the Eastern Tower besides glowmetal?

Once within her own apartments, she eagerly stripped off the formal gown and dressed in a soft robe of silk, picking up the scythe and swinging it absently.

Her defiance rose like a slow-building fire. She cared nothing for Uran, or the Warlord. Raynor had to be strong. It could be strong under a restored Cinanac Emperor as easily as under Daran. If Osterac was indeed the Scion, she intended to see that happen. Yet there was more to her quest than that.

The Scion must stand in the Temple of the Iris. The command resounded painfully in her head. Ellen staggered with the sudden intensity of it. She realised she had to follow that voice. What did it mean? Now she had discovered there were not two, but five Temples. Which Temple had her father meant?

Ellen sank to her bed, weary. She would never abandon her father's quest. When their minds and souls had touched at that last moment, a part of him had become hers forever. There had been something else as well, something that had passed from Myan to her, but her mind could not grasp it.

She sent a quick prayer to Larus that she would find the Scion, the true Scion, before life, power and opportunity passed her by. Finally, exhausted, she let her tired brain relax.

As she drifted to sleep, her last thoughts were on the tall calvanni, Cedrin, and the brief light of promise she had seen in his eyes when she had offered him a place with her.

Chapter Twenty-One

Ellen leapt and turned, her scythe cutting down.

Mendor hastily blocked, gritting his teeth as the impact jarred his arm. He swung again, his left greatscythe blade striking towards Ellen's right.

She spun, stepping inside the blow, closing on him fast. He tried to bring up his greatscythe, but she struck down with her elbow on the haft, knocking the weapon out of his hands.

Ellen stamped down on his foot.

With a yelp, he lifted it. Immediately she dropped, sweeping his leg out from under him. He hit the floor with a grunt. Instantly her blade was at his throat.

'You need to be faster, Suulqua,' she said, lifting her scythe blade and helping him to his feet.

'Yes, my Lady,' he said, rubbing the back of his head.

She looked at him critically. He and Valdas were competent, nothing more. Ellen and her brothers had been trained by weapon masters from an early age. Bored, she had offered to teach them. Their bemusement had quickly turned to anxiety as they faced her over the training mat.

'Do you need to see a healer, Valdas?'

'No, that will not be necessary, my Lady,' he said, dabbing a scythe cut across his right hand with a bloody rag. 'It's nothing a few lessons from Belin Kaidell would not fix.'

'What did you say?' she asked, Valdas backing away before her sudden intensity.

'Nothing, my Lady. Just that a weaponmaster like the famous Belin Kaidell might be able to prepare me better. . .'

That was it! It had been teasing at the edges of her mind all morning. *Belin Kaidell escaped through the Iris with the child!*

Mendor and Valdas watched her anxiously.

'You are both dismissed. I will see you tomorrow – at the same time.'

Why had she not realised before? Her father had always believed Belin had rescued the child so she had taken the words for granted, yet no one had actually *known*. Uran had betrayed himself in his attempt to sway her.

In the Last Days, when the family of Riin was slaughtered by the shapechanger, one man had fought his way to the side of Riin's wife, Evylin, seeking to save her and the newborn child. The legends called him the Hero of the Last Days, an unknown warrior who came, then vanished.

Belin!

Belin had rescued the child and escaped through the Iris. After all her setbacks, at last she was a step closer to solving the puzzle. What other clues lay hiding in the Eastern Tower?

Osterac may be a usurper, but if so, the real Scion was only waiting for his moment. She believed now. The Scion did exist and restoration of the Cinanac line was the only way to ensure cohesion in any emerging power in Kelas.

'Sister! You may want to see this.' It was Estle, calling from the balcony.

Quickly donning a cloak, she emerged onto a private balcony, one of the few that faced the palardos, the great street that encircled the palastrada district.

Outside, Storm Season had turned. From now until its end, it would earn its name with cold fury.

'Look!' said Estle.

Driven by hunger and desperation, the refugees from Hianer, having broken through the barricades, now massed at the palace gates and a riot was in progress. Swept up by the mood and incensed by the news of the Scion's declaration, they had seized one of the statues from the Forum, a depiction of the poet-Emperor Linyss, and were trying to batter the mought-bound gates open.

The crowd numbered in the thousands and, despite the

weather, was growing rapidly. Even from where she stood, Ellen could hear them cry out for the Scion. Uran had been right about one thing, the Scion was an easy banner to hold for those in desperation.

As much as the provincial governors and the people had hated the Emperors, they had been, throughout history, a rallying point, the single focus of a great nation. If Daran raised his own banner, the other nations of Kelas would see him as a threat, an aggressor, not the torch-bearer of peace and civilisation. Ellen believed the Scion meant more than the restoration of privilege, it meant peaceful reintegration.

The gates rolled open, but instead of surging forward the crowd fell back, the mought statue cracking as they dropped it. They tried to run, but in their panic the mob had packed the exits solid and was trapped. It was a few moments before Ellen saw what they had run from. Mounted troops on war-harena.

The beasts were massive, lumbering and naturally armoured with thick hide and plates. The more docile harena used for drawing wagons were kept with their single horn trimmed or capped, but these war-harena displayed sharpened horns, massive and curved. Each had a single, armoured rider, who directed the beast through reins attached by rings in the animal's soft inner lip.

The harena waded into the crowd as though nothing lay in their path, pushing people before them with sheer power, tossing others aside with their horns, like broken sacks of bloody clothing, impaled. Following in the harena's wake were press gangs and club-men, beating and seizing the rioters and placing them in chains.

Ellen had seen enough. Many of those below had been free men and women in Hend, some perhaps even Suul. The injustice of it struck her, yet what choice did the Warlord have?

She returned to the tower's main apartments, her brother close behind her.

They stripped off heavy coats.

'What will Daran do?' asked Ellen.

'Daran is a humanitarian. He will enslave them I would say, even though we can scarcely afford to feed them. The only alternative is to slay them out of hand. Either way, we can't afford riots when the city is soon to be under siege.'

Ellen shivered, even though the chill had been quickly cast off in the heated interior. 'He is enslaving a whole people, just because they want to be fed.'

'They are refugees, with no home, no wealth or means to support themselves. Remember, many of the refugees have already found themselves places here or moved further north.

'Daran is fair. Their slave-price will be low in many cases and I dare say he plans to give many of the men a chance to serve against the Eathal.'

Ellen knew he was right. At least they would not starve. It was one of the Emperors, Hunil, who introduced the concept of fixed slave-price. No matter how valuable a slave became, once their price was fixed it could not be raised, giving them a chance to buy their way out of bondage.

A slave entered the room, one of Estle's young girls. She bowed and looked at Ellen anxiously. 'There is a Druid of the Sisters here to see you, Lady Cintros.'

Ellen straightened immediately. A Druid of the Sisters? 'Did he identify himself?'

The girl grew uncomfortable under their scrutiny. She rubbed her hands together with discomfort. 'No, mistress, but I think he was one of 'em from Olcis. In the del'gation.'

Estle rose, but Ellen stopped him with a raised hand.

'No, Estle, I will see to this,' she said, straightening.

Estle was momentarily taken aback by her fierce determination. For a moment it seemed he would hit back with an angry retort, but instead his face lit up in wonder. 'It seems I will have to stop underestimating you, sister.'

'Send him in, girl,' said Ellen.

The slave-girl bowed and hurried towards the entrance chambers. Ellen was not going to rush to meet a Druid of Olcis. There was a time she would have given them a measure of respect, but that was before her flight from Athria. No, let him wait on her. She sat back.

The girl ushered in a brown-robed Druid. Mostly bald, what remained of his snow-white hair was cropped close to his skull.

Ellen vaguely recognised him from the entourage of Manel, the High Moon-Druid from Olcis. She stared at his rounded, kindly face for long moments before something triggered a distant memory.

'Raphal?' Ellen's severity melted away as the old Druid came forward. It was Crephis' brother!

'Have the ravages of time changed me so much?'

Estle gripped the old man's wrists. 'By Ur. . .Ah, it's good to see you.'

Ellen surged to her feet and embraced the old Druid and Priest of Larus warmly.

Her letter to Raphal, telling of Crephis' death on the Spire, had only been sent on to Olcis yesterday. There was no way he would have received it.

'Have you heard that Crephis . . . ' Ellen trailed off, unable to finish the question.

'Yes,' he said, nodding gravely. 'News reached me through the Temple.'

'He was a good man. His last words were of you.'

Raphal was Crephis' older brother and as physically different from his sibling as the Suns to the Moons, yet they were alike in heart; kindly, intelligent and extremely skilled. He was as thin as she remembered, almost emaciated, but when he gripped Ellen, he did so with a vital strength that surprised her.

Raphal held Ellen at arm's length and surveyed her like a proud grandfather. 'You've grown into quite a young woman.'

Ellen would have rebuffed a comment like that from anyone else, but his presence softened her heart.

A young Athrian Razor entered the room, to stand formally, swelled with his own importance. 'The Court summons you, Lord Cintros.'

Estle sighed heavily and waved the young man away.

'I must go,' he said to Raphal. 'But I would like to see you again before you leave Raynor.'

'Yes, my son. I see we have much to talk about,' said Raphal, glancing meaningfully at the slave-girl.

At Estle's pained look, Ellen perceived he was suddenly not so sorry to be leaving on urgent business.

When Estle had gone, Ellen and Raphal took tea together, sitting on cushions placed either side of a low table.

'I am surprised to see you here in Raynor,' said Ellen. 'And with the Hesguit's delegation no less.'

Raphal cleared his throat. 'Believe me, I would rather be in Olcis with my books, but Ranlan needed an expert on the prophecies.'

Ellen's heart leapt. *The prophecies of the Scion.*

As he lay dying, Crephis had bade her seek out Raphal. At the time she had dismissed it as the natural plea of a dying man to see his only brother, yet now she realised it had been much more. Crephis was telling her to seek out Raphal because he knew his brother would be a steadfast ally in her quest for the Scion!

Her head was filled with questions and here was a man who knew the answers, a Druid close to Osterac.

She remembered him as a kindly old man. Now as she regarded him over the steaming cup of tea, she saw intelligence and power beneath the gentle exterior. As well as being a talented Larus-Druid, Raphal was one of the rare men who could touch the Earth-Essence. A Priest dedicated to Larus, he was a holy man. True devoutness was rare among the Druids of Olcis.

They talked of Raynor and Athria, and those left behind in Regent's Hill.

Raphal took Ellen's hand. 'I was grieved to hear of Myan's death and the conspiracy he fell victim to. He was a great man in a time of petty men.'

Ellen felt the touch on her hand grow warm with Earth-Essence. The flow was like golden sunshine, flowing from a burgeoning heart. It washed through her, seeking pain, whispering secrets of fertility and new life. Ellen's gaze was fixed to Raphal's face.

She was afraid. The pain had lain buried for so long, rising as a bitter shard only to be buried again. She feared what it may bring. The part of her that put on the brave face wanted her to pull her hand away, but the spirit below was crying out for the touch of this life-giving flow. She could not move.

Raphal's eyes were full of love, a father's love.

The mystery filled her, exposing the wound, driving the tears of loss before it like a hot flood. The room blurred amid the torrent, the grief within her as poignant as the day her father died, leaving her alone. But her own spirit rose, like a spreading blossom, reaching outwards to every corner of her being with healing energy.

Ellen lost track of time.

When she roused, the tea before her was cold and Raphal's head was bowed in prayer. She felt spent yet renewed. A tight constriction had been taken from her chest, a crushing fist that had been with her all the long days since her father's death. The loss remained, dull and profound, but the wound had healed.

Raphal raised his head. He looked at Ellen kindly and signalled the slave for more tea as though nothing had happened.

'Myan hid your talents well, Ellen. I had no idea the Fire burnt within you.'

Ellen was unsure, and for a brief moment she doubted Raphal, wondering if he had tricked her. But no sooner had she thought it, then she was ashamed of herself.

'You have nothing to fear from me, it is the High Druids and their Templemen who play the games of power. I am just a simple scholar,' he said.

Ellen relaxed. Raphal was anything but a simple scholar, yet she believed him. The spell of healing was gone and she was eager to press Raphal about the Scion.

'Raphal. . .' She wondered if there was a more discrete way of asking. 'Is Osterac . . . ' Ellen trailed off, conscious of the enormity of the question and yet driven on by her need to know. 'Is he the Scion?'

The words rang heavy in the silence.

Raphal's face grew grave and, for an instant, Ellen caught a glimpse of the fierceness that Raphal reserved for his opponents. 'I am bound not to tell you, Ellen.'

Her heart fell. She knew Raphal would not lie, yet his words were damning nonetheless. Osterac was an impostor. They found an echo in what Uran had asserted.

'So, it is all a game, a play for power.'

'Ellen. . .' Raphal reached to take her hand, but she was not to be pacified.

'He is the Hesguit's pawn, isn't he?' she asked sternly.

Raphal took a breath to speak, but Ellen cut him off. 'No, you don't have to answer.'

A silence grew between them.

'The prophecies . . . the prophecies mean nothing,' she said.

Raphal's face glowed with the light of revelation. 'No, Ellen. The prophecies speak truly. The Scion will rise.' Raphal took on the attitude of a teacher giving a lecture. 'For example, the Arkon prophecy is centuries old:

'From the line of Carris,
shall the old order be raised again,
the empty throne of Raynor shall cry out,
a score years, calling for the Scion.
Until he rises in the smashed depths,
rises like a sun.
The One.'

Ellen saw the belief in Raphal's eyes, absolute conviction the prophecies would be fulfilled. After all those so eager to point out her father's dream as a lost cause, Raphal's faith was a balm. She listened enthralled as he continued, and wondered if, perhaps, it was this man who first gave her father his dream of the Empire's rebirth.

'The hand of Carris shall seize,
the two in a dance.
Within the Iris they shall,
meet Jykor's curse,
and dance between destruction and rebirth.'

At the mention of the Iris, Ellen broke from the thrall.

'The Iris, Raphal, what do you know of it?'

Raphal was in his element. With a sigh of pleasure, he sifted through the dusty scrolls in his mind to find the fragments. 'Ah yes. Many of the prophecies connect the Iris with the Scion and the Usurper.'

'The Usurper?'

Raphal answered with another chant.

'Tween the battle of the two,
and the Blood of the Three,
Carris' curse shall be set free.'

He continued to talk on. Quoting prophecies and dry excerpts from scholarly works that were ancient when the Empire was born, each more tenuous and obscure than the last. Like a guiding arm to a stumbling man, the words gave her strength and direction. She realised there was a clue she had been ignoring since she had reached the Yasser States. Her father had believed Cedrin had the key to the Scion. In her doubt, she had discounted his importance, but now, more than ever, she had to find him, to follow him. She had been drawn in by the familiar comforts, the bright illusions of Raynor. Now, in her heart, she knew Cedrin would somehow lead her to the Scion.

And the Scion was the only hope for Kelas.

* * *

Cedrin pulled the cloak closer about himself. The streets were cold, and the chill was deepening, the wind savage, its edge like blades of ice slicing into his unprotected flesh. He began to shake, and he felt the changes stirring within him. The Heat was beginning to rise, and he was powerless to stop it.

The two calvanni had trod the street for hours, moving between overcrowded taverns and boarding houses, turned away at every door. The price of a simple place by the fire would have rented them five rooms in Athria, and they could not afford to pay. The streets were filled with the poor and dying, silent and sombre as they watched the twilight fade and waited for the deep chill that would follow.

The dusk found them in a crowded dead-end alley. A Hend trading clan had taken control of an old building, its walls partly collapsed. Hundreds of once-wealthy refugees from Hianer sheltered with them. They were miserable, and yet the clan leaders had managed to instil some sort of organisation. Even though there were too many to shelter in the ruined building, clan men had spent the day dragging out sections of the massive hardwood supports from the ruins to build a bonfire for the others.

The two calvanni were sheltered in an alley doorway nearby. Around them a score of people waited together, each eyeing the others anxiously, wondering who the Heat would claim first.

A group of men were trying to set the heavy timbers alight with shaking hands, cursing as the lit brands from smaller hearths within the building guttered and went out one after the other, failing to ignite the heavy dark wood.

'They will never get that alight,' said Marken. 'It's rebin wood. From Armon. It would take a kiln-fire to even char it.'

'A pity,' said Cedrin. They had constructed a huge pile of the material along the centre of the alley. Once alight it would have heated the entire lane, warming hundreds.

Earlier they had tried to pay their way into the ruined building, but without success.

Cedrin filled the bowl of his pipe with shaking hands, staring at it for long moments before realising there was no way to light it. Anything that could burn had long since disappeared from the streets, used to fuel the fires of desperate people. Now nothing remained except stone, broken tile and rotting debris.

Cedrin put away his pipe and turned to Marken. 'The Heat,' he said, meeting his friend's eyes. Marken merely nodded. He too was beginning to feel it.

Madness and death were walking the streets of Raynor, as they had every night since Storm Season began.

'Now would be a good time for that bakta,' said Marken, pushing his body further into the shallow doorway to escape the bitter wind.

Cedrin took the flask from his coat. He stared at it reverently for long moments before he removed the stopper and passed it to Marken. 'After you, my friend. It may be the only thing that keeps us sane tonight.' Marken took a measured sip of the spirit, letting the warmth spread through him. Like Cedrin, he knew it could never be enough, not tonight. Cedrin took the flask and savoured the taste of the clear spirit, his mind fevered as the Heat rose within him.

The Heat was unstoppable, and Cedrin drew more heavily on the potent spirit as it came, suddenly possessed with a heady optimism. Warmth spread across his limbs like fire, and he burnt, his mind surging with images. Barely over a week ago, all of this had begun. He saw the soft lights of his rooms in Lookout Hill before him like a beaconing dream. He heard laughter, it was the courtesan he had hired for Storm Season, there right beside him, tossing her long hair as her delicate fingers caressed the lute's strings. By Uros, what a beauty she was!

Cedrin felt pressure on his shoulder and turned to see Marken's concerned face. The dream was gone, instead he saw the cold filth of the alleyway.

'Are you all right, ami?'

The Heat was sweeping through Cedrin in waves now, and with it came irrepressible energy. He swept back his cloak and stood, his chest bare against the freezing night. Around him in the alleyway the refugees cowered in fear.

'Calvanni!' said one.

'Sweet, Larus. A killer. And the Heat has him!' said another. They glared at him and Marken, too frightened to move.

'Look at the calvs!' said another in a hushed whisper.

Cedrin gave the flask to Marken and drew both his weapons, delighting in their feel. The moonlight gleamed and shimmered on the blades.

A young girl began to cry in the arms of her mother.

'Do you see the six degrees?' said one man.

'Quiet, you fool!' said another. 'Can't you see he has been taken?'

Marken drained the last of the spirit. 'Sheath them, ami. They are frightened.'

Cedrin looked around at the crowd and saw it was true. They cowered from him, many praying desperately under their breath. Hastily he sheathed his weapons. Another wave of Heat was coming.

A beggar could resist the Heat much better than they, he knew, they could strike a bargain with it. It had been many years since Cedrin had been forced to succumb, and Marken had known it only as a child, a time when its effect was much reduced. He could see Marken still resisted its will, yet it was taking all his effort.

Cedrin laughed, and began to pace across the broken pavement.

'Why do we sit in this squalid heap?' he asked. 'Enough!'

Marken's eyes flared with rage. 'You're right! Why should we cower beneath the cold? Why should we bend to its will?' Marken too, threw back his cloak, his eyes alive with passions long held in check.

'Cedrin,' called a woman's voice. He turned, calvs back in his hands quicker than thought. Somewhere nearby he could hear frightened whimpering.

Before him stood Ellen Cintros, lightly clad in the same silks his courtesan had worn the night Mat betrayed them.

'Cedrin,' she called, walking towards him. 'You are a fool to stand here on this cold stone.' The apparition looked meaningfully towards the wall of the palanac, rising like a monolith in the distance. 'I am warm, Cedrin,' she said with dusky sensuality. 'Feel me.'

The ghostly Ellen neared him, almost close enough to touch, and he was spellbound. 'Feel me!' she said, pleading, proffering herself to him like a lover, a promise of warmth and acceptance. A mere hand's breadth away the image dissolved, whipped away by a cold gust.

'No!' screamed Cedrin, turning with wild eyes to find Marken beside him. 'She was here!'

Marken paid little heed to Cedrin's words. He had been pacing, his body shaking. Now he ran from the alley.

After only the briefest of hesitations, Cedrin ran with him. His whole body alive, delighting in the action.

Time had little meaning. Sweat froze on them, unheeded. A voice whispered to Cedrin that he had been running too long, that soon they would drop from exhaustion, and yet he could not stop. Stone buildings passed them in a blur.

Cedrin knew he had run all his life, from the truth of his birth, and from Tarral. Together he and Marken had run from the Brotherhood. Now he ran from the Suul Ellen Cintros, fleeing in fear from a life he could not understand.

They did not see the attackers when they came. One minute they sped on, giving vent to an impossible torrent of energy, next they were surrounded by desperate men. Without a thought they were fighting, the two calvanni back-to-back as they wielded their bloody calvs with ferocity, without mercy. Then it was over, and only dead bodies remained around them, pathetic and emaciated, lying slickly in their own blood. The men had realised too late who they faced.

The wave of energy now left them, and brief clarity flooded their senses.

They were far into the city, surrounded by shabby buildings of rough stone, tight groups of men and women eyeing them warily, fearfully, from the encircling darkness.

Cedrin fell forward and retched, nausea gripping him in the wake of the Heat's savage touch. Marken hauled him to his feet. Their eyes met and Cedrin could see the tormented spirit within the golden depths. Visions of horror had passed there.

'We have to stop this, Cedrin,' said Marken. 'We have to stop the Heat from taking us again while we still have the chance.'

'Yes. Yes,' he said. He began to shiver in the intense cold. Cedrin looked around, desperate for somewhere to shelter. There! He saw a tiny flicker of flame in one of the alleyways.

'A fire! If we can reach it, we have a chance,' said Cedrin.

Warily they made their way towards it. It was hidden behind a rough barricade, sheltered from the wind. Five women, three children and an old man shared the fire. They eyed the two calvanni with hatred as they approached, and with sudden insight Cedrin knew they had just killed their men. Yet not a word was spoken as they approached, the group merely made room for them and the circle closed.

Once more they began to fight the Heat.

Cedrin squatted beside the fire, pulling his cloak tight around his chest, and the bloodied calvs sheathed there. Two of the women left the fire and returned with the clothes of the dead men, casting them in measured strips upon the fire. He understood. Those men attacked them not for coin, but for the mere cloth on their backs.

Cedrin looked at the women, searching for some sign they would act against them. Their eyes were like stone, so far gone into desperation and grief emotion had failed them. He looked away, feeling only pity.

Anger flooded him. How could the rulers of Raynor let things get so desperate? Surely they could have opened up some disused buildings on the outskirts and heated them until the end of Storm Season? The truth was bitter. The more desperate the people, the more likely it was they would take the chain. Traders and Suul alike were increasing their wealth at the expense of others. It only confirmed his opinion of the Suul. Content in their warmth, they cared nothing for their people.

A man could put trust only in his own will, his own skills.

Another hour passed, and the two calvanni successfully stopped the Heat from taking them a second time. Carefully Cedrin filled the bowl of his pipe once more and lit the tobacco from the fire, drawing on the heavy smoke. It filled his head and calmed him, soothing the memories of both blood and insanity.

He offered the pipe to Marken and they shared it.

As Cedrin looked at the desperate people before him, and knew how close death had been that night, he vowed he would never fall that low again.

He remembered the vision of the Suul Cintros with shame, knowing in his deepest heart he wanted her with a passion that terrified him. She represented everything he was not. She had power and beauty, and lay close to the heart of Kelas. The harsh truth was that he had always been an outsider, wanting desperately to belong.

Cedrin turned away from the fire. The tall, forbidding walls of the palanac, the palace of the Cinanac Emperors, rose there in darkness. There she lay, in a warm bed, within the embrace of the Suul. He wanted her. He could deny it no longer, even more, he wanted all she possessed; the power, the acceptance of the ruling class. It burnt within him.

In the icy cold of Storm Season, the past ten years were focussed before him in painful clarity. All those years ago he had stood on streets like this one, his heart full of bitterness for those who had betrayed him, clutching only the emerald signet ring of Kaidell. Tarral. Belin, the great Suul general who had discarded him to shame. How he cursed them, night after night, vowing he would rise high without them or their kindness. Driven on, he sought prestige in the dark alleys of Athria.

Cedrin had risen to fifth-degree. He had found power within the Brotherhood, and position. More than a score of men had lain under his command. All the battles, all the deceit, all the blood he had spilt, he remembered them all. Then the sixth-degree, and it had all come to nothing. The frustrated ambition burnt within him like a hidden cancer, shadowing and driving him onward into danger. Never before had he taken this thing out into the light to examine it. Now he could not avoid it.

It was all gone. Rage filled him as he remembered the events of Storm Season. 'Uros!' he cursed, unable to contain the fury. The Heat within him surged, rising dangerously, and those around him looked on with fear.

'What is it, ami?'

Cedrin looked up to see the face of the Trader's son before him. No, he thought, Marken was the son of the Suul. He looked deeply into the golden features, probing the eyes. All facade was gone now; revealed was the passion, the same flame that burnt in him. No wonder they seemed brothers.

'This Season has been cursed!' said Cedrin, his voice filled with fury, his chest heaving.

Marken watched Cedrin carefully, his eyes full of concern.

'It's the edge of the Heat. Come back towards the fire,' said Marken. His friend drew him closer to the flames, passing the pipe back to him. Cedrin took it with relief and drew heavily on the tobacco.

Then he began to talk.

'We have lost everything, Marken. Over ten years' work. My wealth, so carefully hidden away, is now useless to me.' He looked at Marken, his eyes grey like ashes in the dark. 'Are ten years to be made nothing? What am I now?'

Marken extended his hands to the fire. 'Ten years ago Macil lived. I was his chosen son in all but name and the Sarlord's court seemed so close. All I had to do was earn enough wealth to buy a Suulqua title. I had always believed power would come to me, called by my blood.' Marken shook his head. 'I was wrong.'

The silence grew long, Cedrin's anger fading, and the people around the fire relaxed once more, steeling themselves for the coldest hours still to come; and the morning light that would reveal the stripped corpses of those they had once loved.

'Let's walk together, my friend. I want to see this night with clear eyes,' said Cedrin.

'Leave the fire? What of the Heat?' asked Marken, fearful.

'I think it will be slower to take us again,' said Cedrin.

Marken shook his head, but said nothing as Cedrin led the way back onto the streets.

Cedrin began to get his bearings once more. Their Heat-driven flight had taken them around the palastrada. Everywhere there were sheltering, miserable groups, and the dark shapes of the Heat-possessed like palgur stalking the night, running insanely, blindly as they had done. Others had fallen to the stone, the life freezing out of them as the Hunger took its last meal.

Soon they had come full circle.

They arrived back at the ruined building and the massive bonfire of unlit rebin wood. Hundreds huddled here, sharing only the warmth of packed bodies. The need for survival was strong in the group, overpowering all. There was no room for talk.

As they stood in the cold, Cedrin's spirit rallied against fate, as it had countless times in the past. He stood close to himself that night, close enough to see the hidden strength that lay on his darker side, the need born of bitterness that had driven him through the years. He wanted Ellen Cintros, the Suul, yet this he would drive from his mind, for she was unobtainable. He would rise as before, and he would be calvanni no longer.

He touched the shape of the signet ring through his cloak. He had said Belin gave him nothing, yet this was untrue.

Belin had given him the Old Blood.

'Stand back!' he shouted. 'Stand back from the stacked wood!'

Marken looked at him in alarm, looking for signs of the Heat, becoming puzzled when he failed to find any.

The people did not move. 'They are too far gone, Cedrin,' said Marken.

'Stand back!' he bellowed.

Those near him cowered back, and this gave him the space he needed. He now had a clear view of the massive beams of rebin.

They needed heat, and the one thing that could never be taken from him, the one thing that the Old Blood had cursed him with, was the Fire. Ever since that night on the Spire it had seeped through him, breaking into his daytime thoughts, possessing his dreams. It would never leave him, as part of him as the scars on his skin.

He imagined it now. A molten lake of Fire, falling to descend on the wood. Instantly the Window entered his mind, and he sensed the Fire behind it.

As he had twice before, he reached for the Window, letting it surge open. The Fire filled him. He gasped with the intensity of it, and let it go immediately, feeling it flow through him, a sensation as natural as breathing.

For the first time, he consciously channelled the Fire.

It poured from him in a single wave of yellow-gold, sweeping through the rebin. The ancient, dark wood hissed then exploded into instant flame.

Hundreds of people screamed and ran back as the massive bonfire leapt into life, flooding the alley with precious heat.

Those near him staggered back in fear.

One man pointed at Cedrin, his hand shaking. 'Sorcerer,' he said, his voice lost in the roar of the flames as they rose higher and higher.

Cedrin's senses flared with alarm. Should the mob turn on him, he had nowhere to run. He looked at Marken to see his friend's mind working quickly behind his golden eyes.

Marken leapt up onto a pile of rubble and shouted above the

roar. 'It's a miracle! Larus has sent a miracle! Uros has been defeated!'

The cry was taken up, and soon hundreds were chanting the name of Larus. Spontaneous celebrations broke out through the alley. People poured from the building to stand before the bonfire, and hundreds more ran towards it from the cold streets around them, all sharing the precious warmth.

Cedrin and Marken pulled their hoods down and edged to the corners of the crowd.

'You have saved us, my friend,' said Marken.

'I might have condemned us if you had not thought so quickly.'

'How did you . . .'

'I'm not exactly sure. But you were right. For good or ill, it seems I do have the curse of Sorcery,' said Cedrin.

'Curse? You did a good thing here, ami. You have probably saved hundreds with this bonfire. How can that be a curse?' said Marken.

It was true. On his own, using a forbidden power he did not even want to recognise, he had done more than all the Suul of Raynor combined, or the Temple.

The last bitter hours passed in comfort, the scene around the fire turning festive. The rebin, now that it was alight, burned with intense heat, and many of those closest to the fire cast off their heavy cloaks.

Cedrin threw back his head, breathing deeply. This night had brought him low, but he had won through.

He unslung the heavy mought greatscythe from his back. Those around him watched him warily. He felt it beneath his hand, solid and sure. He would rise once more, he vowed to himself, without help or aid from the Suul.

'Scytheman,' he said, savouring the feel of the title on his lips. Yes, he thought, it was time to lay aside the calvs, the treachery of the Brotherhood, and take up a new path. He would rise far, command his own company, and once more he would be a leader of men. He would have power, his own power, given to him by no one, garnered only by his strength of arm and purpose.

As a calvanni, he would always owe allegiance to a Brotherhood, be it of Athria or the sewers of Raynor. As a scytheman, bound by the strict honour code of that warrior class, he could walk tall in any city. There would be no need to hide in the shadows, or to run.

As the light shades of first dawn began to tint the eastern sky, Cedrin turned to his friend. 'Take up your scythe, Marken.'

Marken took the finely crafted scythe from his shoulder, reverently, and held it before him, his eyes falling sadly to the crest of Kye; three golden towers on a background of yellow and blue. He raised his golden eyes, meeting Cedrin's with renewed purpose.

'I will find a free-company,' said Cedrin, ignoring those around him, his voice strong, 'and move north. Henceforth, I will follow the Way of the Scytheman. By Larus and Uros and the thousand gods, I swear it!'

'I swear it,' said Marken, his face alive with passion as he raised his scythe, 'by Uros and all the cursed gods who hold our fate!'

They swung their scythes high. As the hafts met, the first rays of Larus flooded the alleyway. The night was over.

They were scythemen.

* * *

Ellen threw aside the covers. She sat up on the side of the bed and glared into the dark.

'Why can't I *sleep?*'

Her temples pounded as though she had drunk a bottle of Leygen red, her neck and back stiff from hours of wakeful rest in the hard and unfamiliar bed.

She reached across to her bedside table and turned up the spigot on her lamp to lengthen to the wick. Light flooded the bedchamber, falling across the big bed with its tangled covers and her desk, now scattered with heavy Cioan texts, glowmetals, quills and parchment.

Ellen eased the tension from her neck, massaging her muscles with strong, callused hands.

'This is hopeless.'

Dawn must be close. It was hardly worth returning to her bed. Dressed in her light shift, she walked across the heated room and sat at her desk.

Releasing the hidden panel on the front, she reached inside and drew out the Seeker.

She laid the glass sphere on the desk in front of her and stared at it. This was the seventh time tonight.

Her heart thumping, her body alive with thoughts of all she should do, sleep had completely eluded her. The room was stuffy, overheated, while outside she knew the coldest night of Storm Season passed, thousands struggling with the demon of the Heat.

And meanwhile, everything – her meeting with Raphal, the prophecies of the Scion, the knowledge that Belin had rescued the Scion and escaped through the Iris, her father's dying plea – crashed around inside her weary, overtaxed mind.

Beneath it all was a fire of new determination, and anger at herself that she had ever doubted her father.

The Scion must stand in the Temple of the Iris.

She looked across the room to her gear. Three hours ago, in the dead of night, she had begun to assemble it. A few essentials, a sturdy pack, her scythe. A few glowmetals. Some currency in the form of gems and coin, a portion set aside to be sewn into her clothes. It was all she would really need.

It was clear to her now that Cedrin did not intend to come to her in Raynor. She had learnt enough from the glowmetal to know he was passing the night on the streets. If he was determined enough to do that, she knew he would never change his mind and present himself to her as Suulqua. Although angered by this, she found she also respected his determination. He insisted on independence. She could understand that. Reluctantly she decided that her own pride would need to take second place to her quest.

She had a vow to fulfil. A vow given to a man who had loved her all his life, striving to give her what was best, to prepare her to take his place as one of the few who stood between the Eathal and the final destruction of mankind.

She had let the promise of Raynor, the lure of new status, deflect her up until now; but no more. She was more convinced than ever that Cedrin was the key.

Fate had sealed her from the throne of Athria, and now it showed her a new path, away from Raynor.

Almost everything her father had told her in those dying moments – as unlikely as they seemed at the time – had been borne out. Now she had decided to trust the rest; to trust that her father, this great man who among a handful had saved Kelas from the Eathal, a man praised by all who knew him for his integrity and foresight, truly knew what was best for Athria, for Kelas.

Her mind was made up. She was going to follow Cedrin.

Ellen turned back to the globe in her hands, looking through the clear glass to the glowmetal within.

She was more desperate than ever to get a clear idea of exactly where he was heading. She knew he was still in Raynor – less than five leagues from the palace – yet the darkness of the Storm Season night had defeated her. Over the long, sleepless night – her mind wound tight with thoughts of her quest – she had tried six times to get clear images from the device, yet she had received nothing but fragments. At first complete blackness, the ring no doubt hidden beneath his cloak, then a confusing mixture of images rushing past her. Then darkness again.

The last time she had been blinded in the dark of her room by an image of flame. As her eyes adjusted she saw a raging inferno of burning wood, and a crowded alley of refugees laughing and talking excitedly as though attending a festival. Infuriating. And nothing she could use.

Ellen walked across to the covered windows, the Seeker balanced in her left palm. She threw back the curtains and peered out over the palastrada. Daylight filled the room.

Finally!

Her hands shook as she lifted the globe. She swiftly drew the Matrix that converted the glowmetal's subtle emissions into light, channelling Fire into it to finish the spell.

Images flooded her.

A street. She could see the Cioan, walking beside him.

Cedrin was carrying Tarral's greatscythe. They paused at a tavern. The door was reluctantly opened to them, then closed again. It was obviously full. They continued on, stopping at another, then another, finding no entry.

Finally they found one that would admit them.

Ellen's heart surged with triumph. She could see the tavern's name, painted in flaking paint on the sign. *The Scytheman.*

Now she could find him.

And together they would find the true Scion.

About the Author

Being able to escape into the realm of the imagination was handy growing up as the youngest in a family of eleven. Chris continues his fantasy and SF writing habit from his home town of Brisbane, where he lives with his lovely wife Sandra and three children, Aedan, Declan and Brigit. He has a third-dan black belt in Moon Lee Tae Kwon Do and also enjoys movies and exploring narrow alleyways. Chris is very passionate about music, if a little inconsistent, and loves singing and playing classical guitar.

Website: www.chrismcmahon.net.

Preview Of Book Two – Scytheman

Eighth day of Storm Season
Torren Cintros sits on the Athrian throne

Kalyth laid his hands on the cracked battlement of Blackthorne Tower. The furious wind numbed his face, bearing all the chill of the waning Storm Season. He blinked against it, his eyes watering.

'Damn you, Belin.' His voice was harsh. Raw from disuse.

He kept his gaze on the wide valley below the tower, determined to look anywhere but the stairs that led to the Temple of the Iris. His callused hands curled into fists, squeezing against the pain. Every day it was the same. He would fight the magical Compulsion that drew him to the ruined temple, and the pain would grow until he could no longer resist it. His legs and back were on fire with it, the muscles in his neck twisted with the desire to turn towards the stairs. He fixed his eyes on the overgrown graves of his wife Mari and his children on the slope below, fighting pain with pain. It would take only a single step, a single twitch and the Compulsion would have him.

At first he had been unable to resist it. The spell would take hold and he would run to the Iris like a crazed fool. After twenty-five years, he could fight it for almost an hour.

His legs began to tremble. His eyes drifted away from the view. He squeezed them shut.

Would Belin make an appearance today? The man who commanded him to leave his family to die to save the Emperor's squalling babe? *Damn them all.* The Empire had fallen. The Eathal were stronger than ever, and his wife and children were still cold and in the ground. If the Emperor's boy still lived, he would change nothing now.

'The Scion.' Bitter bile filled the back of his throat.

If he dared to move, he would spit on the Scion. Spit on all the Suul nobility. Traitors. *Self-serving bastards.*

His head jerked to the side, and his eyes opened. *Stairs.* A tiny particle of relief flowered in the muscles of his neck. The pain in his legs became unbearable. His right leg spasmed forward and before he knew it he was in motion, tears flooding down his face in relief as the pain vanished. There was no stopping it now.

He hissed air through his teeth in fury as he rushed down the stairs, past the small guardroom in the ruined tower that he had made his home, down and down into a maze of narrow tunnels. In this dank labyrinth, he knew every cracked tile, every fallen block of masonry, every sharp curve and jutting piece of head-cracking stone. He pushed against a concealed panel and raced up the stairs behind it, taking the stone flags two at a time until he reached the Temple rooms above. It was bright here. The roof had given way five years ago.

The corridor beyond emptied into a domed chamber, shafts of light stabbing down through cracks in the roof onto the wide floor mosaic. The design was comprised of five identical panels of flame and smoke, linked together by the great Iris at the centre.

As soon as his feet touched the coloured tiles, Kalyth staggered to a halt. He sucked in a lungful of the dusty air, the skin beneath his ragged beard prickling with sweat. He glared at the Iris.

Kalyth carefully circled the floor. After an hour or so, blue lights would flicker at the corners of his vision and he would be free to leave the tiles. Sometimes he would visit the Kaidell estate to teach the warriors, but his visits were becoming less frequent. The newer troops mocked him behind his back. The crazy hermit of Tower Blackthorne, they called him.

As if he had a choice.

Kalyth knelt at the small fireplace he had built at the edge of the tiles. He took a small lead glowmetal from his pocket and rubbed it briskly on the stone. It remained cool in his fist, but he kept a careful eye on the bands of greyish light in the glowmetal as they thinned. Just before the bands became fully metal, he tossed it into the fire pit. Immediately it released the stored heat. The tinder curled with smoke then popped into flame. He flicked the little glowmetal out of the fire with a stick and carefully nursed the small fire into life. Satisfied, he scooped up the glowmetal, already cool to the touch, and slipped it into his pouch.

If only he had never returned to the Kaidell estates. After the defeat of the Eathal, it had seemed natural to take work as weaponmaster to Belin's nephew and heir, Linnas Kaidell. The man was no warrior, and a far cry from Belin – or at least the Belin he had known – but Kalyth had been young and eager to start again. Then the whispering began, night after night. By day, he would find himself staring at the sight of the ruined tower on the horizon. He should have left then. Instead, he had searched through the ruins and found the Temple.

And the Iris had come alive.

Belin Kaidell – a man he had known as a simple warrior – had stepped from the Iris, his eyes alive with blue light, his face drawn into a mask he barely recognised, an archaic spear strapped to his back. Kalyth shivered at the memory. Two lines of glowing blue had lashed out from Belin like hungry snakes, holding him fast, biting deep, binding him with a magic that compelled him to return to the Iris each day. He had been forced to make his home amid the ruins of Blackthorne, as though standing vigil on the memory of his life, forced to endure the taunts of his men, and the ridicule of that worm Linnas.

He sat at the edge of the mosaic and watched the Iris.

He would never forget Belin's eyes. They had fixed on him as though considering a new mount. 'I may have a use for you.'

A use for you.

Belin had ignored his pleading questions.

'I trusted you, Belin. More than life,' muttered Kalyth, stabbing the fire with the stick.

He had given up trying to understand the change in Belin, or his old general's inexplicable command of magic. No. After a time, it was not Belin that he feared. He quickly learned that Belin was not alone in the Iris.

The other mind within the Iris took the form of a horned beast in his dreams, bringing with it a madness of bloodlust and desire. Kalyth would wake in fear, heart hammering, his clothes damp with sour sweat.

Since that first time, the Iris had only come to life twice. Each time, Belin had sent the snakes into his mind and left in silence. Inspecting him without a hint of acknowledgement.

Light flickered off the tile near his feet.

His head snapped up.

'*No.*'

Sweat rolled off his forehead, chilling immediately in the cold air beneath the dome.

The Iris was stirring.

Kalyth dropped the burning brand back into the fire, his gaze fixed to the Iris as the glowing light rose and expanded. A distant song grew at the edge of his hearing. He covered his ears against it and became aware of his breath, coming now in ragged gasps. Soon the whole Temple was swathed in light, a turning whirlpool that scattered his tiny fire and flung the burning brands at the wall.

Belin stepped from the Iris. Like the other times he had manifested, he seemed no older than the day he first appeared with the babe almost thirty years before.

'What do you want?' asked Kalyth, edging to the very limit of the mosaic.

Belin raised his hand and blue lightning leapt at Kalyth, who grunted in fear as the twin streamers struck his head. His vision was lost in glowing blue, but it was over quickly. He trembled as he watched the glowing lines flow back into Belin like ghastly appendages.

Belin turned to go, then suddenly paused. The passive, drawn expression fled and a new tension overtook the old general.

'Kalyth,' said Belin.

His heart leapt. This was not the high, thin voice he had come to dread. It was a voice of command and deep solidity, more like the Belin of old. The lights had also vanished from his eyes. For the first time since this nightmare had begun, Kalyth looked into the familiar grey eyes of his old commander.

Kalyth stepped towards him, drawn by instinct.

'Kalyth. I have only a moment before the Ward takes me again. The boy is in danger. You must protect him. The Ward seeks him. It has breached the Athrian Iris…'

Belin jerked. The grey eyes filled once more with blue light, the face becoming slack and cold. As though nothing had happened, Belin turned back to the Iris.

A heartbeat later the Temple was cold and empty.

Released, Kalyth fled the Iris. He paused on the slopes outside to look down at the tiny shapes of the Kaidell estate buildings in the distance. Belin had broken through some sort of forced control.

The hairs at the base of Kalyth's neck stood on end. All these years … had Belin been as bound as he was? Overtaken by this *Ward* he had spoken of? Could it be that Belin had not betrayed him? Not abandoned him as he thought?

Kalyth's eyes fell on the graves of Mari and his children.

He gritted his teeth and started the climb back to his small room in the tower above. What difference did it make? He was still trapped.

And his family was still dead.